ts

of

Somersby Hall

The Sunrise Coast Series

New Beginnings at the Harbour Inn

The Secret of the Summerhouse

The Cottage by the Sea

The Guest House at Shingle Cove

The Houseboat by the Quay

Return to Willow Tree Cottage

The Bookshop of Memories

The Beach House

A Summer to Remember

Sunrise Over Seashell Bay

The Secrets of Somersby Hall

AUTHOR'S NOTE

The Secrets of Somersby Hall is best enjoyed following on from Sunrise Over Seashell Bay.

The Secrets of Somersby Hall

A Novel

ELISE DARCY

Penny Lane Press

ISBN 978-1-913147-43-3

"Every moment is a fresh beginning." – T.S. Eliot

1

'Who do you think you are, demanding to see my grandmother?'

'I'm not *demanding* to see her!' Hannah grimaced. And to think Saturday morning had started off so well. They'd had a lovely night's sleep in their new home and a hearty breakfast in the dining room, and Maisie had even done a bit of painting, starting a watercolour of the overgrown garden of Gatekeeper's Cottage in the grounds of Somersby Hall.

Unfortunately, this was just what she was expecting – Rupert standing in her way when all she'd decided to do was call in at the hall and ask to speak to her new landlady.

'I'm your new ...' Hannah hastily rephrased, 'I'm your grandmother's new tenant.'

'Tenant? What are you talking about? We're not renting out the house.'

Hannah looked at him, surprised. 'Wait – you don't know about Gatekeeper's Cottage?'

'What about Gatekeeper's Cottage?'

'Your last tenant moved out.'

'You mean the gardener? Yes, I know that. We couldn't afford to keep him on, and besides, he said he wanted to retire anyway and move nearer his grandchildren. My grandmother was very sad to see him go. He'd been here forever.'

'Was his name Owen?'

'Owen? What a strange question. No, his name was Bill.'

'Oh, right.' Hannah added, 'Anyway, I've moved in.'

'Moved in where?'

Hannah felt the conversation was going round in circles. And wasting her time. She'd called at the house as soon as she'd returned from dropping Maisie off at Nate and Lili's. After a quick chat, with Lili asking how the house move had gone and Nate frowning – Hannah suspected because his daughter had gone through another move – Hannah had left, eager to get back to Somersby Hall and speak with Lady Jemima before the auction started and before Ray arrived.

'I told you.' Hannah was getting irritated. 'I've moved into Gatekeeper's Cottage.'

'You're the new gardener? Nobody consulted me on this! I didn't think we could afford one.'

'No, I'm not the new gardener.'

'Then who the hell are you?'

'Don't swear at me!'

Rupert surprised her by dropping his eyes, scuffling his foot on the carpet, and apologising. 'Sorry.'

Hannah had a sudden impulse to reach out and touch his cheek, brushing his hair away from his eyes. He was so cute when he wasn't being rude and obnoxious.

The moment didn't last long. 'Just tell me who you are, will you? I'm too busy for games.'

'Games?' Hannah frowned at him. 'If you'd just listen, I told you I'm the new tenant. I moved in yesterday. Signed the rental agreement, handed over the deposit, paid my first month's rent and everything.'

Rupert gaped at her. 'Are you serious?'

She was just about to answer when Rupert turned on his heel and stormed off, slamming the door in her face. He slammed it so hard that the old door didn't catch.

Hannah stared at the door. Reaching out, she pushed it open and took a tentative step inside the house. 'Hello?' She heard footsteps and glanced up to see Rupert storming up the wide staircase that rose straight ahead of her. He hadn't heard her calling.

'Grandmother!' he shouted out angrily as he took the stairs two at a time.

Hannah pursed her lips and muttered, 'Oh dear.' She got the distinct impression that his grandmother had gone behind his back in renting out Gatekeeper's Cottage. A smile spread on Hannah's lips. Good for her. It was her house. Why shouldn't she?

Hannah had a feeling she was going to like Lady Jemima, although she wasn't sure how she would get to meet her with Rupert barring her way.

Hannah looked around the impressive oak-panelled hallway. The floor was tiled with small red tiles with a motif, and there were several doors leading off the hall.

Well, he's not barring my way now, thought Hannah. *Do I dare climb those stairs and follow him? I'm trespassing.* She'd assumed that Lady Jemima would be at the auction the next day, but it occurred to her that she might not be able to get down the stairs and attend. That was why Hannah had decided to visit. It would be nice to have a moment or two alone with her.

Hannah had no idea if Lady Jemima was so old that she didn't venture downstairs at all. Hannah looked up the stairs. This might be her only opportunity to meet her. She stepped forward and put a foot on the stairs, expecting someone to walk out of one of the rooms off the hall and ask who she was and what she was doing there.

Hannah was halfway up the stairs, and nobody had appeared to question her presence there. A little voice in her head said, *Don't do this. Leave now, in case you get into trouble with your landlady.* She didn't know Lady Jemima. She might just tell her to leave – and not just the house.

By the time she'd thought this, she was at the top of the stairs and a floorboard had creaked loudly. Rupert put his head around the door. 'What the hell are you doing up here?'

'Rupert – what's going on?'

Hannah decided she'd come this far, so she might as well go the whole hog. Instead of running back down the stairs, she headed straight for Rupert.

He looked surprised. 'What are you doing?'

'I've come to see your grandmother.' Hannah looked at him as if to say, *just try and stop me.*

'Who are you?' the old lady asked, eyeing her coldly as she stepped into the room, followed by Rupert, who said, 'Grandmother, I didn't let her into the house, I swear.'

'You're the young lady who waved at me when I was at the window the other day,' Lady Jemima said, cutting across Rupert.

Hannah nodded and said in a small voice, 'I'm also your new tenant.'

'You are?' Her face broke out in a grin. 'How wonderful. What a coincidence. Rupert, go and fetch that chair over there, and make us some tea.'

'Are you joking? I didn't even know you'd rented out Gatekeeper's Cottage for fu—'

'Don't be rude. And do as I ask.'

Rupert shut up and grimaced at Hannah.

Hannah threw him a self-satisfied smirk.

Rupert stormed out of the room.

2

'You must excuse my grandson,' Lady Jemima began.

Why? Hannah felt like saying, but held her tongue, waiting to see just what excuses the old lady came up with for her grandson's behaviour.

'He means well. He's just very protective over his grandmother.'

You mean his inheritance. Hannah also kept that thought to herself, along with her first impressions of Lady Jemima. She was old; in her nineties, Hannah guessed, but she didn't look as frail as Hannah had imagined. She was sitting in a comfortable chair by the window, but she didn't have a throw over her legs, and she wasn't wearing the multiple layers that she imagined very old people often did, as they could be prone to feeling the cold. She wore a dress, and jewellery, and her surprisingly thick grey hair was cut short, in a style that rather reminded Hannah of the way young women wore their hair in the 1940s – short and neat. Hannah felt a little guilty for thinking in generalisations, but apart from Ray and Sarah, who were young enough to be Lady Jemima's children, she hadn't met any *really* old people before.

Lady Jemima's soft grey eyes stared back at her, making her

feel uncomfortable. She wondered how long Rupert would be with the tea, suddenly thinking she'd welcome the interruption, even if it was from the rude grandson.

At that moment, Rupert walked into the room with another chair, but he quickly departed again.

'I must look very old to you,' Lady Jemima said as she motioned for Hannah to take a seat.

Hannah looked at her as she sat down. It was as though she'd read her mind. 'Oh, no – not at all.' Now she was there, all her bravado had deserted her. She felt quite tongue-tied and a little overwhelmed in Lady Jemima's presence. Hannah had never met a real Lady before.

'You know, one thing I can't abide is people telling fibs.'

Hannah stared at her, wide-eyed. *Oh god – now things have got off on the wrong foot.*

'Unless, of course, it's to save someone's feelings.'

Hannah breathed a sigh of relief.

'But even then, I think honesty is the best policy.'

Hannah said, 'Yes, you do look very old … to me.'

'Well, of course I do. I am ninety-five! And you are …?'

'I'm twenty-seven.'

'Twenty-seven! My goodness. I remember being that young like it was yesterday. I still get rather a shock when I look in the mirror. Let me give you a piece of advice.'

'Use face cream?'

Jemima suddenly let out a little scream, startling Hannah, until she realised that Jemima was laughing. Hannah didn't see what was so funny.

Neither did Rupert. He walked into the room at that moment, carrying a tea tray, and nearly dropped it. He quickly put it down and rushed over, apparently thinking for a second that his grandmother, writhing in her chair, was having some sort of medical episode.

Jemima slapped his hand away. 'What are you doing?'

'Are you all right?'

'Of course I am.' She wiped a tear from her eye.

'Has she made you cry?'

'Of course – tears of laughter, if you must know, which is more than I can say for you. Now, pour some tea for our guest.'

Rupert grudgingly did as he was told. Hannah could tell because when he handed her the tea, he slopped it over the saucer on purpose.

'I hope you put a biscuit on her saucer too.'

Hannah looked down at the soggy biscuit, and then up at Rupert as she took the cup and saucer. Their eyes locked for a moment, Rupert looking pleased with himself over the slopped tea and soggy biscuit. Hannah rolled her eyes at him for being such a child and a spoilsport.

Rupert left a cup of tea for his grandmother on the little coffee table by her chair and went to take a seat on the sofa across the room.

Jemima was just reaching for her cup when she noticed Rupert lowering himself on to the sofa. 'What do you think you're doing?'

'Having tea with you and … and … what is your name?'

Hannah was just lifting the cup to her lips. 'It's Hannah.'

'Pretty name,' Jemima said, casting a glance at her grandson. 'Now, if you don't mind, Rupert …'

'Mind what?'

'Leaving us in peace.'

'You mean I can't stay and have tea with you? I want to talk about you renting out Gatekeeper's Cottage. I didn't know anything about that.'

'Do you tell me everything that's going on in your life back in London?'

'No, but that's not the point.'

'I rather think it is, Rupert. You see, I live here. This is *my* house. And may I remind you that I'm still undecided what is going to happen to it on my demise.'

'But I thought—'

'Now what did I say about leaving us in peace? It's ladies only.'

Hannah heard him comment as he left the room, 'There's only one lady in this room, and it's not Hannah.'

'Apologise immediately, Rupert!'

Rupert was almost at the door. He swung round, looking at his grandmother in shock.

Hannah was looking at her too. Surely, she hadn't heard him. Hannah had barely heard the comment herself.

'Yes. Surprising, isn't it, Rupert? I may be old, but my hearing is as sharp as a pin.'

'I'll say,' blurted Hannah.

Rupert threw her one of his now infamous grimaces and mumbled an apology.

'Haven't you got an auction to be organising downstairs?'

Rupert left the room.

'Close the door please, Rupert.'

He must have still been just outside the door, as he reached almost immediately for the door and closed it none too gently. Hannah heard him storm off down the hall with heavy footsteps, taking the stairs two at a time.

Hannah turned around in her seat and said, 'You've got hearing like a hawk.'

'Yes, thanks to modern tech.' Jemima reached in her ear, and held up an earpiece. 'Cost a small fortune. Don't tell Rupert, but it's definitely worth it. I don't want to lose one of my faculties, and when you get to my age, or often earlier, your hearing can be the first thing to go, and that does leave you at quite a disadvantage.'

Thinking of age, Hannah steered the conversation back to Jemima almost falling about laughing when she'd mentioned face cream. Hannah observed, 'Your complexion is quite smooth, if you don't mind me saying.'

'Not at all. I have always been told I have aged well. Must be in the genes.'

Hannah scratched her head. 'If you weren't going to tell me to use face cream, what was your piece of advice about ageing?'

'Don't do it,' said Jemima with a sly grin.

Hannah frowned. 'Do what?'

'Get old.'

Hannah stared at her. Was she joking? Hannah didn't know her well enough to tell, until Jemima burst out laughing again. 'Ignore me, I'm just having a little joke. My piece of advice to bright young things like you and Rupert is to fall in love.'

Hannah hadn't expected her to say that.

'Love keeps you young at heart as the years go by. You look into your lover's eyes and are immediately transported to your youth, and all those years just fall away.'

Hannah stared at her. She was about to be very forward and ask who her love was, or had been, when Lady Jemima asked her an unexpected question. 'So, what do you think of my grandson?'

'Honestly?'

'Of course, honestly.'

Hannah chose her words carefully, deciding not to include any swear words, but it wasn't easy. 'He's … he's a bit of an arse. Sorry.'

'No need to apologise. I know my grandson can be a bit … prickly at times. He's got a lot on his shoulders at the moment.'

'The auction?'

'Among other things.'

Hannah expected Jemima to enlighten her regarding those *other things*. Then again, she was a stranger; why should Jemima tell her what else was going on in Rupert's life, especially when she had called him a bit of an arse?

'Well,' said Jemima, 'let's see if we can't change your opinion of him.'

'Yeah – that'll be the day,' scoffed Hannah.

'You might change your mind if you get to know him.'

'Nah, I don't think so.'

'We'll see about that.' Jemima leaned back in her chair and picked up her cup. 'Rupert does make a lovely cup of tea.'

Hannah smiled. 'Still not convinced.' She tried to change the subject. 'You said earlier that who inherits the hall is undecided. I assumed that it would be your grandson.'

'Would that make him less of an arse in your eyes?'

Hannah smiled, although she was surprised by the question. 'Um, no. I'd have to love someone and want to spend the rest of my life with them. I wouldn't be marrying their house.'

'Well said.'

Hannah looked away, embarrassed. She couldn't believe she'd said that. She wondered where it had come from. After all, Lady Jemima hadn't asked her whether she'd marry Rupert. She wasn't sure why she'd brought up the idea of marrying someone. That was the furthest thing from her mind. Then again, she did have weddings on her mind generally, and had been thinking of how good it would be to have a stepfather for Maisie in her life. Hannah didn't want to think of all her past relationships and how they would all have made lousy fathers. All they had ever wanted was Maisie out of the way.

But getting on to that subject reminded her that she had a question for Lady Jemima. 'Look, the reason I wanted to see you …' She took a breath. Of course, she wanted to ask her about Owen and Kitty, and the painting, but Thea's warning came to mind. What if she opened up old secrets – a love triangle that Jemima didn't know about involving Owen? What if he was her first love and she knew nothing about the love letters Owen had sent Kitty during the war? Jemima was ninety-five years old, for god's sake. Did Hannah want her to go to her grave knowing she'd been betrayed?

Of course, Ray was right – it was all conjecture, assumptions. She needed to ask her to find out more. Or perhaps she didn't. Maybe if they talked more, as Lady Jemima got to know her, she would reveal her past. Or maybe one of the staff would. Maybe the house would offer up its secrets.

3

'The reason you wanted to see me …' Jemima prompted.

Hannah was just looking about the room, trying to find the right words to present Lady Jemima with her idea for saving the house, when her eyes settled on a painting over her fireplace.

'Oh, my god!' Hannah jumped out of her seat.

'What is it? What's wrong?' Lady Jemima asked, looking about her. 'Is something on fire?'

'No, no.' Hannah cursed herself for overreacting. But she couldn't help herself. She forced herself to slowly walk over to the fireplace. 'I just spotted this painting. It's rather wonderful.'

'Well, Hannah, I must say, you rather put the wind up me.'

'Sorry about that.' Hannah stood staring at the painting. '*Sunset Over Seashell Bay*,' she murmured.

I knew it, she thought. *I just knew there was another painting.* There was no VW campervan in this painting, although it was very similar in tone, with the same beautiful orange, gold and yellow hues, the expert brush strokes vividly evoking the wild enclosed bay, just like its companion, *Sunrise Over Seashell Bay*. But this painting was different; there was a woman walking away from the sea, seashells falling from her open hand, as though she was discarding them. The sunset, unseen behind the dunes, as opposed to the sunrise over the water, still invoked the same stunning orange, gold sky above the beach.

'Hannah?'

Studying the painting some more, Hannah decided the woman wasn't walking away but running. Unlike *Sunrise Over Seashell Bay*, which filled Hannah with joy, this made her feel inexplicably sad.

'Hannah!'

She whirled around at the sound of Lady Jemima's voice.

'Oh, sorry. I was just mesmerised by the painting.' Hannah wasted no time asking about the painter, whether Seashell Bay actually existed, when it was painted, and most importantly of all, who the young woman in the painting was. She was very, very careful not to accidentally drop any names.

Lady Jemima regarded her for a long moment, her eyes shifting to the painting. 'I'm pretty sure you did not come here to ask after a painting or a painter that you knew nothing about before you stepped into this room …'

Hannah held Lady Jemima's gaze for what seemed like an eternity, although she imagined it was only a few brief seconds while she debated whether to come right out with it and tell her what she'd discovered in the charity shop.

Hannah thought of Maisie's reaction to her new home – *I love it here* – and immediately lost her nerve.

Hannah was desperate to ask Jemima about the airgraph and Owen. Instead, she shared the other reason she was there. 'It's about your house. Look, I've just moved into Gatekeeper's Cottage today and we love, absolutely adore it, so—'

'We?' Jemima raised her eyebrows.

'Oh, my daughter. She's nine. I hope … I hope that's not a problem, having a child living in Gatekeeper's Cottage.' Stupidly, when she'd signed the paperwork for the rental, she'd ticked 'single' as in single parent, not thinking that there might be a rule against renting out to families.

'She's very good, I swear. She spends most of her time painting.' *Why did I say that?* she immediately thought.

'A painter.' Jemima sat forward in her chair, eyebrows raised. 'I'd like to meet her. She can show me one of her paintings.'

'Look, not a lot of people know this, only close family and friends – I want her to have a normal childhood. She's a prodigy. I'm not just saying that because I'm her mother. I wouldn't know one end of a paintbrush from the other, but Maisie, well, she can copy the Old Masters. If I'm honest, I'm a little afraid of her talent. I want her to go to university, have a normal life. I don't want anyone to take advantage of her.' Hannah suddenly realised she'd said too much – pouring out her fears, hopes and dreams for Maisie's future to a stranger.

Lady Jemima eyed her. 'You know, some people in your shoes would have used her talent, if she's as talented as you say, and sold the paintings of a nine-year-old and made a lot of money. Perhaps put her on social media – what's that platform where families parade around, and children don't have their privacy, filmed just to make the parents money? But you wouldn't do that.'

Hannah shook her head vehemently no. 'Not in a million years.'

'Hmm.'

Hannah wondered what she was thinking. 'Is it still all right, Maisie and I living in Gatekeeper's Cottage in the grounds of your house? She won't be out playing in your grounds and being a nuisance, I swear.'

'I should hope so.'

Hannah frowned at her. 'Don't you mean, I should hope *not*?'

'No, I meant what I said. It's been too long since there was the sound of children's voices here at Somersby Hall. I want grandchildren before it's too late. I fear it might already be too late. But let's not dwell on the Grim Reaper. I'm determined to keep him at arm's length for as long as possible.'

Hannah didn't doubt it.

'So, I positively encourage Maisie to play in the grounds, or in the house, wherever she wants. Bring her friends, have tea parties on the lawn. It will bring a smile to my lips, remembering my childhood here.'

Hannah thanked her, surprised. She'd just assumed the old lady would want peace and quiet – not the sound of screaming children running around her lawn or in her house. *Just shows what I know about old people,* thought Hannah. But hearing that, Hannah saw an open door to ask Lady Jemima about her past there, specifically the wars years. She did just that. 'What was it like here growing up? Can you tell me what it was like during the war?'

'No.'

Or not. 'Oh.' Hannah was taken aback by the abrupt no.

'We don't talk about the past in this house.'

Hannah stared at her.

'You will let Maisie come and play, and show me her paintings – won't you?'

'Of course. She'll be excited to visit the big house.'

'Is that what she calls the hall?'

Hannah nodded.

Lady Jemima smiled. Perhaps she'll paint the big house for me one day.'

'I'm sure she will,' Hannah said. 'Then you can leave the painting of the big house in your will to Rupert, if you choose not to leave him the actual house,' she joked.

'Oh, he's getting the house. Of course he is.'

Hannah frowned. Had she misheard? 'I thought you weren't leaving him the house, or at least that it was undecided.'

'Oh, he should lighten up. I don't mean it. I'm just keeping him on his toes.'

'Oh, I see.'

Jemima looked at her curiously. 'You don't think my grandson should inherit the house?'

'Well, I'm just afraid of what will happen to the house when you …' Hannah immediately stalled. 'Sorry, I didn't mean …'

'Yes, you did. And it's a fair question. That's why I'm leaving it to my grandson. He loves this house as much as I do, you know. I don't want the house sold.'

'Neither do I.' Hannah looked at her hands.

'There's something on your mind. Come on, out with it. At my age, there's no time like the present, you know.'

Hannah looked up. She'd rather not tell her, but … 'I think Rupert has got designs on selling it soon, perhaps as soon as you—'

'Pop my clogs.'

'Yeah – that. Sorry. Look, I really don't want to alarm you. I know it's none of my business, although I rather think it is, now I've moved into Gatekeeper's Cottage. I don't want to leave, but if the house is sold, I expect Gatekeeper's Cottage will go too. I've heard there are financial problems …' Hannah immediately shut her mouth. She could tell by Lady Jemima's expression that she should not have brought that up.

'What financial problems are you referring to?'

'Er, the leaky roof. I guess the house needs repairs and you might not have the money.'

'Spent it on my hearing aids.'

'Pardon me?'

Jemima laughed out loud again.

Hannah joined in when she realised what she'd said. 'Oh, yes. So you said.'

'Do you have an idea, then, of how to save the house from being sold from under me?'

Hannah looked at her in surprise. 'Can Rupert really do that?'

'Yes, if I suddenly fall ill. He has power of attorney. He can then do what he likes with the estate. I know he will struggle with the upkeep of the house.'

Hannah thought of the airgraphs. She could hand them over right away and they could go in the auction. She'd heard an auctioneer was coming from a prestigious auction house in London. Now would be the time to hand them over.

But I can't. I want the money for Maisie. She thought of Lili and Nate saving for Maisie and William's university education. She wanted to do her part too.

Hannah leaned forward in her seat. 'I've got an idea. You might not like it. In fact, I'm sure you won't. It would involve opening the house to the general public.'

Lady Jemima's eyebrows shot up. 'You what?'

Hannah was surprised. She'd been chatting to her ladyship for nearly fifteen minutes and all she'd heard was the King's

English and suddenly Lady Jemima sounded quite … *common.* Hannah almost laughed.

'What I meant to say,' Jemima continued, coughing delicately into her hand, 'was pray do tell what this idea may be so I may consider it.'

'All right. So, I was thinking … the hall would make a fantastic wedding venue.'

Jemima's mouth dropped open.

Hannah sighed. She knew that even suggesting it was a bad idea. There was no way Jemima would think it was a—

'Rupert!' Jemima bellowed, taking Hannah by surprise that such a slight old lady could have such a set of lungs on her.

'Rupert!'

Wherever Rupert was in the large house, he came running. He flung open the door, breathless. 'Grandmother, what on earth is the matter? Do you want me to get rid of … I mean escort Hannah out of the house?'

'Not at all. My new tenant has just told me her marvellous idea.'

Hannah looked at Lady Jemima in shock. 'You think my idea is marvellous?' They'd hardly discussed it.

'Oh, yes.'

Hannah turned in her chair and eyed Rupert. Lady Jemima might think her idea was marvellous, but Rupert was never going to let it get off the ground.

Rupert looked from Hannah to his grandmother. 'What's going on?'

'Rupert, come and join us for tea,' Jemima said sweetly.

4

Hannah closed the door to Lady Jemima's bedroom and hissed at Rupert, 'This isn't going to work.'

'Oh, you think?' he said sarcastically before storming down the stairs.

Hannah followed. She was almost at the bottom of the stairs when he did an abrupt about-turn and said in her face, 'And where do you get off, walking into Somersby Hall and persuading my grandmother to turn her home into a wedding venue?'

'Well at least I'm not trying to sell her home from under her!' Hannah shot back.

Rupert turned on his heel and walked off.

'Hey! Don't turn your back on me when I'm talking to you!'

Rupert stopped abruptly and turned around. 'I know your game. You're trying to ingratiate yourself with my grandmother. After the house, are we?'

Hannah was taken aback that he would think such a thing. 'I just want to help her save the hall.'

'Why are you so interested in this place?'

'Because I live here too now, and I don't want to move any time soon, and neither does my daughter.'

'You have a daughter?' he said in surprise. His voice softened. 'I didn't know. How old is she?'

'She's nine.'

'You don't look old enough to have a nine-year-old.'

'Not that it's any of your business, but I had her young.'

'I'll say.'

Hannah narrowed her eyes. 'Not *that* young. I'm twenty-seven.'

'Just the two of you?'

'Yes, I'm a single parent.'

'Hmm.'

'What's that supposed to mean – hmm?'

Rupert strode off down the hall.

'Hey, will you just stop a moment. We need to discuss—'

'In case you hadn't noticed, I'm busy.'

Hannah had to dodge two men who were walking into the house carrying chairs.

'Ah, they've arrived,' said Rupert.

'Who's arrived?'

'The company setting up the dining hall for the auction tomorrow.' He stopped and turned around. 'What are you still doing here? You heard my grandmother – she stipulated that we have to work together on your stupid idea. Now, since I've got no intention of working with you, your idea is dead in the water.'

Hannah grimaced. 'I wouldn't work with you if you paid me.'

'And I wouldn't work with *you* if *you* paid *me*. There, we finally agree on something!' He walked off – yet again. 'You can see yourself out.'

Hannah turned around and nearly fell over a chair someone had left in the hall. She picked up the chair and followed Rupert into the room where they were holding the auction. She stopped in the doorway, taking in the lovely room with its ornate wallpaper from a bygone era, its ceiling with decorative plasterwork, and two floor-to-ceiling Georgian windows that overlooked the grounds at the front of the house. She discovered it was a double-aspect room with French doors that led out into the back garden.

'Excuse me, miss.'

Hannah turned to see a young man carrying two chairs. 'Oh, sorry.' Hannah walked into the room to allow him to get by, ignoring Rupert, who was at the far end of the room, shuffling through some paperwork at a small podium that didn't look as though it belonged there. Hannah guessed that it had been brought in for the auction.

This must be the dining room, she thought. There was an oak table that normally stood in the centre of the room – Hannah could see the indentations in the carpet where it normally stood – which had been shifted against one wall, along with the dining chairs. She wondered if they were in the auction.

Although the room wasn't large, there was space for rows of six chairs. She estimated they'd manage eight rows. If there were more people than seats, she guessed they'd have to stand at the back of the room.

Hannah walked over to one of the Georgian windows, brushing the thick, lined blue velvet curtains as she peered outside. She could see part of the walled back garden with a long wooden greenhouse at the far end. Surprisingly, this garden wasn't as overgrown as the front. Someone was obviously mowing the lawn.

There were wide flower borders surrounding the garden on

all sides, full of established flowers and shrubs. She thought the borders could do with a prune and a tidy up. She could see weeds from the window.

Behind her, Hannah could hear the young men moving in and out of the room, chatting as they carried in chairs.

'Why are you still here?'

Hannah didn't even bother acknowledging Rupert's remark. She stared at the garden, feeling deflated. The back garden, with its flower borders, neat lawn and backdrop of the small but elegant Georgian house would have made a lovely wedding venue. It wouldn't host a huge wedding party with hundreds of guests, but it would make a lovely intimate wedding venue for smaller parties.

She could just imagine the wedding guests enjoying their sit-down meal in the room and then spilling out through the French doors on to the patio to have their wedding photos taken. Perhaps there would be a small gazebo in the garden for a garden party afterwards. She was staring at the garden, imagining the scene – Lili in a simple yet stunning wedding dress, Nate looking very handsome in a top hat and tails, William, the page boy, looking very sweet in a little suit matching his father's, and Maisie, the flower girl, making her cry at how grown up she'd look in a white dress and strappy sandals.

She could just imagine all their family and friends, and all the shop owners from Cobblers Yard, gathering on the lawn. It would be wonderful; a much grander setting than Nate's house. There was nothing wrong with his house – it was just that it wouldn't be the same having wedding photos in their garden. She knew that as soon as Lili saw this place, she'd fall in love with it, just as she had.

'I said, why are you still here?'

Hannah turned around at the sound of Rupert's irritating voice and glared at him. Unfortunately, he was right: there was no way they could work together. Hannah thought, *life is just too short to put up with him.*

She didn't know why Lady Jemima had stipulated that she'd only go ahead with hosting a wedding there as a trial to see if it worked if they *both* worked together on it. What was her game? She knew Hannah's thoughts on her grandson – he was an arse. Hannah couldn't imagine her opinion of him would change any time soon.

She took one last look at the garden, thinking she probably wouldn't set foot in the house again – she didn't want to speak to Lady Jemima again either. And as for Maisie going to play there and painting the house – well, she could forget it.

Hannah had been so excited at the prospect of showing Lili around Somersby Hall, and planning Lili's wedding there, if Lili and Nate agreed – and she couldn't see why they wouldn't. And then Lady Jemima had ruined it. She'd tried to get her to change her mind – wasn't Rupert returning to London after the auction? Didn't he have a job to do?

It had turned out that Rupert didn't have to return to London immediately because he could do his job working from home. Not just his home in London, but his grandmother's home too, as he'd had super-fast broadband installed the previous week.

Hannah didn't care to know what he did for a living, but she didn't understand why he'd chosen to stay behind. She thought he had a fiancée. Was she heading down to stay too? And why exactly was he staying on after the auction?

All these questions had been on her mind, but she'd had no chance to broach them with Lady Jemima because Rupert had been in the room. And then it had all become rather a moot point when Jemima had stipulated that they had to work together.

5

Hannah was just turning from the French doors when something caught her eye – a glint of sunlight on something shiny and metallic. She craned her neck and could just see off to the side of the house a yellow gravel driveway and a garage. There was a car she thought she recognised. Her breath caught in her throat. 'No way!' she said as she tried to undo the French doors. They were locked. She bolted out of the room.

'Oh, good – you're finally leaving,' Rupert commented in her wake.

Hannah didn't even bother dignifying the snide remark as she raced out of the front door and ran past the dining room windows in front of the house. She happened to glance in one of the windows as she scooted by and caught Rupert looking her way, perplexed.

A moment later, she skidded to a halt on the gravel drive around the side of the house and stood staring at the car parked in front of a double garage. It was the car Percy had got into when she'd followed him out of Cobblers Yard.

She looked about her but the old gentleman with the long coat was nowhere to be seen.

Hannah raced back past the dining room windows and straight into the house, rudely barging past one of the young men, who was about to step inside.

'Sorry,' Hannah said breathlessly.

'Oh, my god. You're back.' Rupert sighed heavily. 'You know, this is getting tiresome.'

'What is?' Hannah said breathlessly.

'You are.'

Hannah was getting used to his insults. She felt like hurling one back, but her question was far more important. 'That car …'

'What car?' Rupert said offhandedly. He was walking along the first row of chairs, making sure they were evenly spaced.

'The car – the old, shiny blue car outside the garage. Is it in the auction?'

Rupert paused. 'You mean the Jaguar?'

Hannah just nodded. She didn't know the make of the car, but she presumed that was what he was referring to.

'No way,' he scoffed.

'Is it yours?'

He shook his head. 'No, it belongs to my grandmother, but she'd never sell it, otherwise Percy might up and leave.'

'Percy – is that your grandfather?'

Rupert shook his head. 'My grandmother's driver ... chauffeur.'

'Does Percy take it out without your grandmother?'

'Well, yeah – it's his car, really. He runs errands in it, buys her things.'

'Books?' Hannah was double-checking they were talking about the same person, remembering Ray's words of wisdom – you couldn't make assumptions. You had to know the facts.

Rupert was moving the chairs around again. He looked at her and narrowed his eyes. 'Why all the questions?'

'I've seen the car in town, in Aldeburgh, I mean, and it is a lovely car,' she said genuinely.

'Percy used to take me out when I was a little kid visiting my grandmother. He was very naughty and let me sit up front, sometimes riding on his lap and steering the car …'

Hannah saw Rupert's face soften; a smile creased his lips as he stared off into space. Her heart skipped a beat. When she got past his condescending rudeness, and he actually smiled, he was a very attractive guy. *God, why does he have to be so hot?* she thought.

Hannah sighed, reminding herself that they hated each other – for some reason, they'd got off on the wrong foot. And secondly, he had a fiancée, probably some posh type who'd been to boarding school like he had and worked in something that needed a degree, or even a master's. Perhaps she was a lawyer. She had no idea. But what she did know was that he was out of her league.

'Well, as I said, it's not in the auction, although thinking about it, it should be. I'm sure it would be worth a lot of money.'

'Oh, don't sell Percy's car.'

'What's it to you?'

'Nothing, it's just that he must love that car, and if you sell it then Percy won't be able to run errands for your grandmother or take her out.' *And I might not see Percy in Cobblers Yard again.*

'My grandmother does love her books from the old bookshop in Cobblers Yard.'

'You've heard of it – Cobblers Yard?'

'Yeah, The Bookshop of Memories. Percy used to take me there as a child before I was sent to boarding school. I must have been six or seven. He's a stickler for routine, is Percy.'

Hannah could hear the affection in Rupert's voice. It occurred to her that if Rupert had never known his paternal grandfather, perhaps Percy had filled that void when Rupert was a child.

Hannah knew all about grandparents filling voids – hers had. When she was a teenager, and her parents couldn't cope with her behaviour, Hannah's maternal grandparents had stepped in. They had paid for her to go to boarding school when her parents had just wanted to put her in care. Hannah remembered fondly the school holidays she had spent with her grandparents.

But Hannah had felt betrayed by her parents. She'd thought she'd never forgive them, but at Lili's urging, she'd built bridges and now they were in her and Maisie's lives, albeit at a distance. She supposed she and Rupert did have things in common after all – grandparents who had paid for their education, and parents who lived abroad.

Hannah's parents now lived in Spain, running a seaside beach bar and living in a small villa they'd bought outright. Although they didn't have the time to return to England, Maisie skyped them every week, enabling them to catch up with their daughter and granddaughter.

Hannah smiled. If they ever wanted a holiday in a Spanish villa, she knew where to go.

'I keep telling them both they could buy books online, but no …' said Rupert, interrupting Hannah's thoughts. 'Percy still insists on getting them from that bookshop, says we must support local businesses otherwise they'll just disappear, and then where will that leave us – with no shops in the high street in Aldeburgh, or in Cobblers Yard.'

Hannah hadn't mentioned that she ran a business in Cobblers Yard.

'Does Percy live here at Somersby Hall?'

'Yes, he's been here forever. Why do you ask?'

Hannah stared at Rupert, thinking about what Ray had said during his police investigations – *in my experience, nothing is ever quite what it seems.*

Hannah was thinking about Lady Jemima and Percy the driver. Was it possible there was something more to their relationship than merely a chauffeur and his employer?

Whatever their personal relationship, as Rupert had said, Percy had been at Somersby Hall forever. He had seen the painting in her shop window before, and she expected he knew the painter, Owen Hartley, too.

It was terribly nosy of her, and she was dying to tell someone about the airgraphs, about Owen and Kitty. She'd love to know what had happened to them. But not for the first time, she was thinking of Thea's observation. Lady Jemima might not take kindly to her prying into the history of the hall, into *her* history. She might be told to leave Gatekeeper's Cottage.

There was only one way to find out more about Somersby Hall – by spending more time there.

'Look, I'm busy, so would you mind making yourself scarce? Either that, or if you're going to hang around, and you've got nothing better to do, you could pitch in and help.'

Hannah was about to tell him to sod off – why should she help? He hadn't even asked her nicely; just implied that she was being a nuisance. Then she had a thought. She was going to help all right. 'I've changed my mind.'

'About what?' Rupert was moving up the rows of chairs,

adjusting their position so each chair was not directly behind the other and everyone would have a view to the front of the room.

'About the wedding idea.'

Rupert looked up abruptly. 'What? I thought we had an understanding?'

Not anymore. Not now she knew Percy lived there. 'I think your grandmother is right: we'd make a good team.' Hannah slapped a smile on her face. That was a lie: it was going to be hard work trying to convince Rupert that hosting weddings at the hall was a good idea. He'd want her to fail because he had his sights on selling up. It would be the easier option. He'd drag his heels every step of the way. Unless Lady Jemima told him he had to help, otherwise she'd cut him off.

Hannah pursed her lips. Time for another chat with Lady Jemima. She walked to the door.

'Where are you going?'

Hannah ran up the stairs before he had a chance to object to another visit upstairs to see his grandmother.

'Hey! Don't you go upstairs …'

'Too late!' Hannah shouted down the stairs as she belted up.

'Hannah!' Rupert called after her, heading up the stairs too.

Hannah quickly rapped on Lady Jemima's door before diving inside and slamming it shut behind her. She kept her hand on the door handle and leaned her weight on the door. Bizarrely, Hannah was actually enjoying herself – at Rupert's expense, of course.

'Good grief, you two are like a pair of children,' Lady Jemima observed, staring at her. But she didn't look cross. A wisp of a smile crossed her face. 'I remember when I was young and I used to be chased around this house by—' she stopped abruptly.

Hannah was about to ask who when she felt the doorknob twist back and forth in her hand. She held on tightly.

'Hannah – I know you're in there. Open this door at once!'

'Go away, Rupert,' Hannah and Lady Jemima said in unison, exchanging a smile.

Hannah immediately felt the door handle go loose. Rupert did as he was told. He was gone.

'Now, what is it that's so urgent that you burst into my room and disturbed me?'

'Sorry. I decided I want to go ahead with the wedding idea here at the hall.'

'You and Rupert are going to work together?'

Hannah still didn't know why Lady Jemima was insisting they work together. 'Honestly, I think Rupert is going to be a problem.'

'Rupert!' Lady Jemima called out. She lowered her voice, 'Step away from the door, please, Hannah.'

Hannah reluctantly released the doorknob and took a seat. She heard footsteps. Rupert burst into the room.

'Rupert, we're going ahead with the wedding idea here at the hall.'

'I'm not working with—'

'Yes, you are. If you're staying here under my roof, then you are going to do as I ask. Unless you're going back to London after the auction.'

Hannah eyed Rupert, wishing he would, wondering why he was staying on.

Rupert looked at his shoes.

'I thought not.' She turned to Hannah. 'Now, what's the plan?'

6

Rupert butted in before Hannah had even opened her mouth to explain the plan. 'I don't see the point of this. We're not going to make any money. Her friend is going to get a wedding here for free.'

'No, she's not!' exclaimed Hannah. 'I explained already. She's a landscape gardener. You're not going to get anybody to have their wedding here with the gardens at the front of the house all overgrown. If she landscaped your garden, then in return she could have her wedding here. Obviously, my friends would have to pay for the catering and flowers.'

Hannah had thought it through. They'd have to provide that sort of thing for their wedding if they were having it at home.

'I still don't see how this can develop into a business that earns money.'

Hannah explained that they could set up a website and use the photos from their first wedding there as free advertising to draw people in; perhaps have a small billboard made at the entrance to the house advertising that it was a wedding venue.

'Sounds wonderful – doesn't it, Rupert? I think it's definitely worth a shot.'

The only problem she could foresee was if Lili was too booked up to work on their garden. Or she didn't think it was a worthwhile exchange because she didn't like the house and didn't want her wedding there.

Hannah couldn't imagine that. She was convinced Lili would fall in love with the place.

Rupert eyed Hannah. 'Have you asked your friend?'

Hannah laughed nervously. 'Of course I have.' She didn't like to lie, but she knew Rupert would just love to hear that she hadn't even asked her friend yet.

That was the problem; her whole plan rested on Lili's agreement. Hannah still wanted to save the hall, but her idea was also to spend more time in the house, and with Lady Jemima. However, it occurred to her that this business, if it took off, might have the potential to provide a second income or even her main income.

Hannah had never thought of becoming a wedding planner. But wouldn't this be the perfect opportunity to find out if she could do it? And what a perfect setting, a beautiful place to live and work. And she could turn her shop into a wedding boutique selling bridal gowns. Ray was right: it was worth a shot.

But what happens when Jemima passes on? she wondered. *Do I think Rupert is really going to let me carry on the business?*

'And if your friend can't fit in the landscaping job?' Rupert asked, clearly trying to find every which way to disparage the wedding idea.

Lady Jemima answered that question. 'Then you and your fiancée can marry here in their place, Rupert.'

Hannah frowned. 'But the front garden wouldn't be landscaped.' It wasn't that, really, although they could really do with the grounds in front of the house appearing looked-after to give a good first impression. It was the thought of watching Rupert getting married. *What is my problem?* thought Hannah. *I don't even like him.*

'Then they can have their photos taken in the back garden.'

'I was thinking of the wedding photos in the back garden anyway,' Hannah explained.

'Well, there you go,' said Lady Jemima. 'Problem solved. You'll still plan a wedding here, whichever one it turns out to be, won't you, dear?'

'Hold on one minute.' Rupert stepped forward.

'You've been engaged long enough. Have you even planned your wedding yet?'

Hannah turned to look at Rupert.

'No, but—'

'Well, isn't it about time? No buts, Rupert. We have a Plan B. Now off you both trot and get wedding planning!'

Hannah followed Rupert out of the room and shut the door to Lady Jemima's smiling face. She still didn't get why they had to work together.

'Oh, Rupert!' Lady Jemima called out.

Rupert had been striding down the hall without a backward glance. He turned on his heel and frowned. 'What now?' Hannah heard him say under his breath as he walked past her.

Rupert opened his grandmother's door. 'Yes?'

Hannah had just been heading for the stairs, thinking about how to talk to Lili about having her wedding there. It was now even more important that she agreed – Hannah didn't want to plan Rupert's wedding. A little voice in her head said, *You're jealous of the young woman who's engaged to Rupert.*

What a daft thought, she said to herself. Then she overheard Lady Jemima ask Rupert, 'Did you find the painting?'

Hannah stopped dead at the top of the stairs.

'No. I told you before – I've looked everywhere. If I do find it, shall I add it to the list of items up for auction this afternoon?'

'No! Absolutely not!'

'Then why do you want me to find it?'

'To make sure it *doesn't* go in the auction.'

Rupert sighed. 'Well, there's no fear of that if I can't find it, is there?'

'I'll have none of your sarcasm, young man.'

Rupert fell silent.

Hannah stayed standing at the top of the stairs, staring at Rupert's wiry frame leaning into the room. 'Look, I don't know what happened to your painting, all right? Can you remember the last time you saw it?'

'Years ago. Did you look in the old servants' quarters in the attic?'

Hannah raised her eyes to the ceiling.

'No, of course not. I imagine all that's up there is ancient furniture and a lot of dust and cobwebs. Why would it be up there anyway?'

That was what Hannah was wondering too.

'Just go up there and look – will you?'

'All right,' he said tightly. He turned from the door, saying under his breath, 'I haven't got time for this.'

'Jolly well make time!' Lady Jemima shot back, clearly surprising Rupert again.

'How does someone that old have ears like a hawk?' he whispered to Hannah as he joined her at the top of the stairs.

Hannah whispered back, 'She's quite formidable, your grandmother, isn't she?'

'Yeah, she is that.'

Hannah was surprised that they actually agreed on something. She was about to walk down the stairs, assuming that Rupert would follow, when she heard the sound of a latch door being opened.

Hannah turned around to see Rupert opening a wooden door. Hannah saw a steep, narrow flight of stairs behind the door. She joined him.

Rupert noticed. 'What are you doing?'

'Coming with you.'

'Why?'

Hannah shrugged.

Rupert took one step up. He turned around. 'I'm still not happy with this wedding idea. Don't think that I am.'

Hannah nodded. 'I know.'

He took another step. Hannah followed suit. He stopped and glanced at her over his shoulder. 'You don't need to come up here. It's not going to be very nice, I imagine, with the dust and cobwebs. No one's probably ventured up here for years, ever since the last of the live-in staff left.'

'When was that?'

'No clue. Before my time. Well, I say that. When I was a child and lived here before I was sent to school, there were some still here – like the housekeeper but she hasn't lived in for years now.'

Hannah was about to ask if he remembered their names, when he said, 'I only have vague memories. You'd have to ask my grandmother.'

Hannah looked up the stairs. 'I'd still like to come up.'

'Suit yourself.'

Hannah held on to the handrail on the right as she climbed the steep, narrow stairs. At the top, the stairs arched around, and the stair treads narrowed. She was surprised when Rupert reached the top and turned around holding out his hand. 'Here, take my hand.'

The handrail had disappeared, so there was nothing to hold on to. She grasped his hand as she carefully took the last two stairs and had just reached the top when her foot slipped on the worn carpet.

'Careful!' Rupert exclaimed, pulling her towards him so forcefully that she ended up in his arms, their noses almost touching.

For a moment, they stood there together, his hands tightly around her waist, her arms around his neck, those slate-grey eyes staring down at her. 'Are you all right?' he asked, the concern in his voice surprising Hannah.

She glanced behind her down the steep flight of stairs, knowing she was safely in his arms. 'Yes, but I have no idea how the staff got on using those stairs day in, day out.'

'Me neither.'

She turned back to look at him. They'd agreed on another thing too.

'You just saved me from a tumble, Rupert. Thank you.'

'Don't thank me!'

For a moment, Hannah thought they were back to their usual bickering, until Rupert added, 'It's my fault. I shouldn't have let you follow me. An accident on these stairs could so easily happen. Sorry.' He dropped his arms from her waist and his eyes from her gaze.

Hannah reluctantly released her grip from around his neck. 'Don't be. It's not your fault. I can be stubborn, you know.'

'Yes, I've noticed. Little wonder you and my grandmother get on. You're alike.'

'I can see why you don't like me.'

'That's not true …'

Hannah smiled until she realised that he was talking about his grandmother, when he added, 'I love my grandmother, although she can be prickly at times. It's just I think over the years my grandmother's distrust of strangers in this house has rubbed off, I'm afraid.'

'I can understand why she's distrustful of strangers in her home. I think most people are.'

'Oh, it goes far beyond that. I'm afraid she's a bit paranoid. Even if it's just a local plumber coming in to fix something, she wants me to give them the third degree, find out as much about them as I can before they can come and do a plumbing job.'

'That's odd. Why do you think that is?'

'Honestly, I have no idea. I don't like to bring up the age thing, but you know, it's the only thing I can think of. But you can imagine the bloody arguments we had when she found out the auction would be here at the hall and involve lots of strangers coming here tomorrow. I did point out that it will be mainly local people. You would have thought that would make her feel better about it. But I swear, if anything, it just made things worse.'

'Strange.'

'Yes. It didn't help that she assumed the auction would be taking place in London. I was like, all this stuff is not going to be good enough for Sotheby's unless by some miracle there is something really valuable amongst all her stuff that people wanted to pay a lot of money for.'

Hannah looked at her shoes. She was thinking of the airgraphs. One of them belonged to Lady Jemima. She could give it back. But would it be worth the heartache when she found out that it had never been delivered – that was, if Hannah and Ray's assumption had been correct, and Kitty, one of the staff, who had quite possibly lived on this floor, had failed to send the letter.

Rupert continued, 'I'm just so surprised, actually shocked, that she had no problem with you walking into the hall, and agreed virtually on the spot to open up the hall to strangers' weddings. It's just not like her at all.'

'She likes me,' said Hannah, smiling. 'You said so yourself that we're alike.'

'Nah, I think she's just getting senile.'

'Hey!' Hannah slapped his arm.

'That was a joke. She must have seen something in you.'

That's more like it, thought Hannah. *A good businesswoman with a very good idea for the hall.*

'God knows what, though!'

Hannah looked at him crossly, thinking that it was a mean thing to say, although the slight curl on one side of his mouth suggested that he was having some fun at her expense.

'Hey!' Hannah said again, folding her arms. 'Are you joking with me right now?'

'Maybe.'

Hannah stared at him. *Is he flirting with me?* she wondered. Their eyes locked. His grey eyes stared back at her for a long moment. She wondered what he was thinking. She was going to ask, when he suddenly looked at his watch. 'Christ, the auctioneer will be well on her way, and I have to make sure the guys have brought all the sale items downstairs. I haven't got time to look around for a painting she hasn't see for years. She probably got rid of it ages ago and forgot. I'm not going to bother looking up here.' He made a move to the stairs.

'I'll look.'

Rupert turned around. 'What?'

'I'll look for it – what is it anyway?'

'A painting.'

'Any particular painting?'

'Yeah, she mentioned a beach, no, a bay, and a sunrise.'

Hannah's breath caught in her throat. '*Sunrise Over Seashell Bay*?' she blurted before she had a chance to censor what came out of her mouth.

He narrowed his eyes. 'How did you know that?'

Hannah thought she ought to tell him that the painting was in her shop. Instead, she said, 'The painting hanging in your grandmother's bedroom – it's called *Sunset Over Seashell Bay*.'

'Oh yeah – of course.' Rupert looked at his watch again, distracted.

'Look, about the painting …'

'I don't know why she still wants to find it. I told her that I haven't seen it, so it can hardly go in the auction, can it? But the auction has clearly brought it to mind, and now after decades she wants to know where it is. She's got one already, as you pointed out, so why does she want to find the other one now?'

'Maybe she just wants to make sure that it doesn't end up in someone else's hands.' Hannah said, thinking, *There's no maybe about it.* She was gearing up to tell him it already had.

'Well, I doubt very much it would be up here. Why would it be in the servants' quarters?'

It was where Hannah imagined Kitty had lived, and the painting had, she presumed, been painted for Kitty. She realised that if she were to tell Rupert about the painting, then she should really tell him about the letters too.

'You'll be careful coming down those stairs – won't you?'

Hannah had been staring off into space and hadn't noticed that Rupert was already making his way down the stairs.

'Rupert!' she called out. For a moment, she thought he'd gone, then his head popped around the door. 'What is it? Do you want me to hang around, help you down?'

'No … I—'

'Good. Let me know when you *haven't* found it. Then I can report back to Grandmother, and hopefully that will be the end of it.'

And with that, he was gone.

Hannah stared down the stairs. She knew it wasn't going to be the end of it. The attic search was just the beginning. There was a reason that Lady Jemima wanted to find the painting. Perhaps she'd been searching for it for a long time; it was just that this was the first her grandson had heard of it.

Perhaps she knew about the letters and wanted them back. Or perhaps it was something else entirely. But what Hannah knew for sure was that whatever had happened in Jemima's past, it was all connected to that painting – and the painter, Owen Hartley. If only he had become a famous painter, then perhaps she'd be able to track him down.

Hannah knew she didn't need to do that. The person who

had all the answers was right there in the hall – Lady Jemima. She should just come clean and tell Jemima she had the painting and the letters. Then maybe the old lady would confide in her about what had happened. That could work. They'd already hit it off. Like Rupert said – they were very much alike.

And there was something else that Rupert had said that made her think it was a good idea; Lady Jemima had so readily agreed to her plans to turn Somersby Hall into a wedding venue. According to Rupert, that was quite unprecedented – letting a stranger, even if she was her tenant, have access to the hall and plan for her friend's wedding there. Unless Lady Jemima's age was catching up with her and she was starting to forget that she didn't let strangers into her house. But in the little time that Hannah had known Rupert's grandmother, there hadn't seemed to be anything wrong with her faculties. Hannah thought she was quite remarkable to have aged so well, both physically and mentally, into her nineties.

Hannah's mind was made up. Lady Jemima was searching for the painting – and she deserved to know the truth.

7

Hannah was carefully making her way down the staircase from the attic, the stairs creaking beneath her feet, when she heard someone coming up the main house stairs from the ground floor. She was about to call out to Rupert that she was fine, and that she didn't need a hand going down, and that there was nothing up there apart from some old worn furniture that wouldn't be worth including in the auction, together with lots of cobwebs, when a male voice she didn't recognise called out, 'Rupert – what are you doing up there?'

Hannah stepped into the hallway and recognised the speaker. It was Percy.

'Oh, pardon me,' he said. 'Are you the auctioneer?'

'No, I'm Hannah, the wedding planner.' Hannah frowned. *Why did I say that?* she wondered.

Before she had a chance to tell him that she was also Lady Jemima's new tenant at Gatekeeper's Cottage, Percy said, 'Well, I'll be damned! Rupert is finally getting married to that fiancée of his. I thought I'd never see the day.' He cast his gaze up the stairs to the attic. 'What were you doing up there?'

'Percy – is that you?'

Percy rolled his eyes. 'Her Ladyship calls …' He held out his hand. 'Lovely to meet you, Hannah.'

'Oh, er … likewise,' said Hannah, taking his hand.

'I'm Percy. Lady Jemima's … chauffeur.'

Hannah stood in the hall, staring after him. He didn't know she ran the art and craft shop in Cobblers Yard. He hadn't seen her in the shop window when he'd paused in front of the painting.

She followed him down the hall to Lady Jemima's bedroom, intending to tell him that she was the new tenant of Gatekeeper's Cottage, and that she wasn't really a wedding planner. She wanted to see Lady Jemima anyway and tell her about the painting that Percy had seen in her shop window – the one Jemima was looking for.

Percy hadn't noticed her following. He closed the bedroom door behind him.

Hannah was about to knock on the door when she heard Percy say, 'I just bumped into a young woman by the name of Hannah – says she's a wedding planner. What do you think she was doing in the attic?'

'She was in the attic? I sent Rupert upstairs to look in the attic. Perhaps she followed him up there. I don't really know how they're going to work together on the wedding. They do squabble so.'

Hannah smiled. That was true.

'Remind you of someone?'

'Oh, do stop, Percy. We don't squabble anymore.' There was a pause. 'Well, all right, maybe we still do – at times. But that's what people do who love each other.'

Love each other – Lady Jemima and her driver? Hannah shook her head. She realised she could easily have misconstrued the situation. Lady Jemima probably meant that they had a great fondness for each other, born out of Percy working for her for decades. They loved each other, like very good old friends would.

'How long has Hannah known Rupert?'

'Five minutes. Not literally, but it's not long since they met. The arguments, though! That's the way you and I began – don't you remember?'

'How can I forget?' Percy said, chuckling.

If they were in a relationship, Hannah wondered if perhaps they'd kept it to themselves. She was Lady Jemina, after all, and he would have been seen as below her station in the past. They didn't need to hide their relationship though – not now. Nobody would care. But maybe they were still living in the past. Of course, Hannah realised that everyone but her might know that they were in a relationship – that was what came of eavesdropping. She didn't know these people really. All she knew was that she liked Lady Jemima very much and was pleased by the fact that at her age she was open-minded enough to let a stranger into her home and try out Hannah's wedding idea in the house. Rupert had said that was unprecedented.

I must have made quite an impression on her. She must like me very much, thought Hannah, smiling at the door. It made her feel more than ever that she had found her home right there at Somersby Hall, and that moving to Gatekeeper's Cottage had been the right decision. *Who knows*, thought Hannah, *this move might lead to a new, and more profitable business.* She was still thinking of Ray's idea to turn her art and craft shop into a bridal shop.

'Why did you send Rupert up to the attic anyway?'

'Well, I know you can't get up those steep stairs now,

otherwise I wouldn't have got Rupert involved.'

Hannah was about to knock. She slowly dropped her hand, wondering what Lady Jemima meant about getting Rupert involved. Involved in what?

'What are you talking about?'

'The painting of course. It didn't occur to me that it might be found and end up in the auction.'

'Why would you do that? Tell him about the painting?'

'He knows nothing of the significance, so it doesn't matter.'

Hannah stood outside the door feeling terribly guilty for eavesdropping on their conversation, but she just couldn't help it. So, the painting *was* significant.

'He's looked everywhere else, so I sent him to look for it in the attic.'

'It's not in the attic.'

'Oh, Rupert told you he's been up there and couldn't find it?'

'No.'

'Then how do you know it's not in the attic?'

'I saw it.'

'You came across it? Rupert clearly didn't do a good job of finding it. Well go and fetch it right now. I want it in this room.'

Hannah raised her eyebrows, wondering where she was going to hide if Percy walked out of the room that minute. Then she remembered to breathe. Percy wasn't going to fetch the painting, and any moment he was going to tell Lady Jemima why.

'I can't go and fetch it because it isn't in the house.'

'Then where is it – in the garages?'

'No.'

'Oh, for pity's sake, Percy, this isn't a game of twenty questions!'

'It's in a shop window.'

'I beg your pardon?' Jemima said haughtily. 'What's it doing in a shop window?'

'Presumably it's for sale.'

'For sale? But how … where …'

'How and where did the shop owner come by it?' Percy asked. 'That's rather a conundrum, isn't it?'

'A conundrum?' Lady Jemima's voice was rising several octaves. 'It's a bloody big problem – that's what it is, mate.'

'You sounded rather common just then.'

'Don't mock me, Percy. This is serious.'

'Is it?

'Of course it is! Have you forgotten?'

'You don't have to spell it out. How could I forget?'

A long silence followed – so long, in fact, that Hannah started to wonder if their conversation was over and Percy might suddenly open the door in her face.

'When did you spot the painting?'

'A fortnight ago.'

'A fortnight ago?' Lady Jemima said, sounding shocked. 'Why didn't you tell me?'

'I thought … I thought we'd left all that behind. It's not like you asked *me* to look for it, otherwise I would have told you I'd seen it. Besides, it was decades ago. Nobody is going to find out now.'

'I knew you'd have that flippant attitude. That's why I thought you wouldn't make an effort to look if I asked you.'

Hannah heard Percy mutter something, but she didn't catch it.

'You stupid fool. Go straight back there and buy it.'

'I did call into Cobblers Yard yesterday afternoon to visit the bookshop and put in that order for that book you wanted. I stopped by the art and craft shop window, just to be sure I hadn't imagined the painting.'

'You didn't imagine it – did you?'

'No. I told you. It's hanging in the window. There was no mistaking Owen's painting.'

Owen's painting. Hannah stared at the door. So, Percy had known Owen.

'Did you go inside, make enquiries as to how the shop owner came to be in possession of the painting?'

'The shop was closed.'

'On a Friday afternoon?'

'I'm afraid so. Today too. I was out this morning collecting your book order. I must say, it came through very quickly.'

'Never mind that. What about the painting? Was it still in the shop window this morning?'

'Yes, but as I said, the shop was closed today too.'

'Well, I suppose that's something. At least no one can buy it while the shop is closed.'

Hannah thought how, of all the times Percy could have chosen to return to Cobblers Yard, it had to have been the previous day, when she'd been moving house, *and* that very day, when she'd decided to close the shop until Monday so that she could spend the weekend getting organised in her new home while Maisie was spending the weekend at Lili and Nate's.

'Who runs the place?'

'I don't know. Used to be Joseph's antique shop.'

'Percy, you must go there first thing Monday morning.'

'I really don't think there's any urgency – if you're worried about someone buying the painting in the window. I don't expect whoever is running it is exactly going to be overrun with customers.'

'What do you mean?'

'When Joseph passed on, someone obviously took it over and turned it into an art and craft shop. Bit daft, if you ask me. The last one didn't fare too well, run by a fellow – what was his name? Oh, yes – Ray. Rumour has it that he only took it on because his wife was running The Potting Shed across the way. Then she retired, and he moved on too. I heard his art and craft shop was haemorrhaging money, and he was on the verge of closing it down anyway.'

'I do not need a potted history of the shops in Cobblers Yard, thank you very much, Percy. So, do you know who runs the new art and craft shop or not?'

'No, I do not.'

Hannah frowned at the door, thinking of what Percy had said about Ray's shop haemorrhaging money.

'So, when can you go and fetch the painting?'

'You mean buy it?'

'Well, yes. I wasn't asking you to steal it, was I?'

'I don't know – were you?'

Hannah's breath caught in her throat at the mention of stealing her painting, even though she was pretty sure an elderly man was not going to break into her shop and take it. But they might know a man who could.

She shook her head. She was pretty sure Rupert would not do that, even if it was his grandmother who asked.

'What if we haven't got enough money to buy it?' Percy asked.

'We will cross that bridge, so to speak.'

But what would happen when Percy discovered it wasn't for sale?

8

Hannah was just turning from the door when she heard Lady Jemima comment, 'Do you know that Rupert and his fiancée never argue?'

Hannah put her ear closer to the door, admonishing herself for being so nosy.

'How could you possibly know that?'

'Remember when I met her last year on a rare visit when they came here together. I took her to one side, not that it was difficult – Rupert always seemed to find something to do.'

'Are you saying he was avoiding her?'

'She is … let's just say high maintenance.'

Percy guffawed. 'Takes one to know one.'

'I take great offence at that, Percy.'

'You never used to be like that, with all your fancy clothes, and jewellery and highfalutin things.'

'We don't talk about my past – it's always been the golden rule, remember? Not even in private.'

There was a silence during which Hannah took shallow breaths, worried they might hear her standing just the other side of the door. Why didn't they talk about Lady Jemima's past?

Hannah stood stock still, afraid a floorboard might creak beneath her feet.

'So …' Percy began. 'How do you know they never argue?'

'Because I asked her. I wanted to know if they ever row, like normal couples. Like us.'

'Like us?'

'Yes. It turns out they haven't rowed, quarrelled, had a falling-out – not a bad word has passed between them.'

'Surely that's a good thing. What's that saying – *who plays together stays together*?'

'I'm of a mind that it's pretty normal to have a falling out once in a while, and that it makes for a stronger relationship, weathering the ups and downs.'

'They've never had any sort of lovers' tiff at all, then?'

'That's what she said, and why she thinks Rupert is the one. I, on the other hand, firmly believe he is not the one for her, or rather, she is not the one for him.'

'Did you tell her about us then?'

'Of course not. Are you stupid?'

Hannah thought that was rather a mean thing to say.

'Get off your high horse. You don't have to act all hoity-toity when you're around me, you know,' Percy said, sighing.

'I didn't tell her because it wouldn't be seemly,' Hannah heard Lady Jemima say.

'You mean if everyone knew about you and me?'

'Yes.'

'It's not like that anymore, you know. Times change. A lady and a chauffeur can—'

'I'm not talking about that! I'm aware times have changed since I was widowed and we fell in love. But you're still ten years my junior – that hasn't changed. I've got a toyboy, for god's sake.'

'You didn't mind when we were young and I—'

'Percy!'

He chuckled again. 'Those were the days – eh? I wouldn't recommend getting old to anyone.'

'Yes, it is rather tiresome, is it not?'

'I'll say,' Percy replied. 'Everything seems to give up the ghost. Whatever it is you want in life, do it while you're young, because the years roll by so quick, and before you know it, you're an old fart like me who struggles to get upstairs. That's the advice I'd give the young-uns. I'm glad Rupert is getting married.'

'Yeah – I'll see it when I believe it,' scoffed Jemima.

'Well, you will soon, won't you?'

Hannah raised her eyebrows. So, he *was* getting married sooner rather than later. She hadn't realised.

There was a pause. Hannah heard Lady Jemima. 'What do you mean *soon*? They haven't even set a date yet – as far as I'm aware. Unless you know something I don't?'

Hannah listened intently.

'But he's got Hannah – the wedding planner.'

'So?'

'To plan his wedding,' said Percy.

'Is that what she said when you bumped into her?'

Another pause.

'Um, no she didn't, but I assumed …'

'Well, you assumed wrong. She's planning her friend's wedding.'

'Here at Somersby Hall?'

'Yes.'

'I don't understand. When did this place become a wedding

venue?'

'Since today, when a young woman walked into my bedroom and took an interest in that painting on my wall.'

'*Sunset Over Seashell Bay*?'

'Yes.'

'Hold your horses. You said this young woman walked into your bedroom? What was she doing in the house in the first place?'

'She's the new tenant at Gatekeeper's Cottage.'

'I'm still sad that Bill left after retiring. He was the last of us.'

'No, he wasn't. There's still you and me, and Hazel the housekeeper.'

'Yes, I know. It just there used to be so many of us. What happens when Hazel leaves? I know she's as old as me. She shouldn't still be working… but we don't want strangers in this house. You said so yourself.'

There was a long pause until Percy said, 'That was quick, finding a tenant.'

'Wasn't it? The estate agent said she instantly fell in love with the place and wanted to move in as soon as possible. She'd rented before, so they quickly chased the reference – glowing, I might add – from the previous landlord.'

'Sounds good. Who is the new tenant?'

Hannah heard Lady Jemima sigh before she said, 'Oh, do keep up, Percy. That's what I was explaining to you. You asked what Hannah was doing in my bedroom. She's the new tenant. She came here wanting to meet her new landlady.'

'That's all well and good, but why on earth did you agree to let her plan her friend's wedding here? Do you know her friend?'

'No.'

'Hold your horses,' said Percy, 'now I'm really confused. You never let outsiders here. Do you know the risk you're taking?'

'It was decades ago. Nothing is going to resurface.'

'The painting has. Who knows what else—'

Lady Jemima interrupted, 'Well aren't you the pot calling the kettle black?'

'I don't follow,' Percy said slowly.

Neither did Hannah. She frowned at the door.

'A moment ago,' said Lady Jemima, 'You were on at me about us putting the past behind us, and not bothering with the painting and what it might dredge up.'

'I'm worried, that's all. I think I can see why you're doing it, to save the hall from being sold if holding weddings here takes off. You know Rupert is right – he couldn't keep this place going. It would have to be sold. So turning Somersby Hall into a wedding venue is actually a brilliant idea. Brilliant.'

Hannah grinned. She thought so too.

Percy said, 'But what worries me …'

Hannah had known there was a *but* coming. Wasn't that the story of her life? Just as things seemed to be working out for her, a *but* would come along and throw things off course and ruin everything.

'What worries you …' Lady Jemima prompted.

'Social media. Have you heard of it?'

'Don't patronise me, Percy. I may be old, but I don't live in the past. I know what social media is – Facebook, TokTok and the like.'

'TikTok,' Percy corrected her.

'Oh TikTik, TokTik – you know what I'm talking about, Percy,' she said, sounding irritated. 'What is your point?'

'Although I do think this wedding business makes sense financially, there's going to be a huge downside. You're going to be opening up Somersby Hall to the public and putting it on the map. What if someone takes an interest in the history of the hall, the history of the people who live here?'

'I get the feeling somebody already has.'

'Who?'

'Hannah, of course.'

'Just because she took an interest in that painting?'

'It wasn't just an interest, Percy.'

'How do you mean?'

'She didn't just comment, *that's a lovely painting*, and leave it at that. She asked too many questions. It made me suspicious. There's something more to her than meets the eye – I'm sure of it.'

'So, you invited her into your home to plan her friend's wedding?'

Hannah could hear the incredulity in his voice.

'Yes. You know the saying – keep your friends close, but your enemies closer.'

'Is that what you think she is – an enemy?'

'Quite possibly.'

Hannah gaped at the door. She'd thought she'd managed to dampen her surprise and excitement when she'd seen the painting, and not let on, but Lady Jemima was right: she'd focused on it too much, asked too many questions. Hannah just hadn't realised that it had not gone unnoticed.

'But you still let her go ahead with planning her friend's wedding here.'

Hannah smiled. *She may not trust me completely*, she thought, *but she does trust me to turn the hall's fortunes around if my wedding business takes off.*

'It's never going to take off, Percy.'

Hannah stopped smiling instantly. Why was she saying that? She'd thought Lady Jemima was behind it one hundred per cent and that she believed in her.

'*That's* why I'm letting her go ahead with this silly idea. It's only her friend having her wedding here. And by the sounds of it, it's going to be a simple affair, no frills and not many gucsts.'

'So, why go to the bother of it?'

'Because it's the only way I could think of to keep her coming back, find out if she knows anything. I insisted Rupert and Hannah work together so that Rupert can keep an eye on her.'

'You mean spy on her.'

'Hannah stared at the door angrily.

'Does he know why you asked him to work with her?'

'Of course not. You know Rupert. He wouldn't do something like that. He just thinks I'm being overly protective of the hall, and I want his involvement in the wedding planning to help Hannah out so that things go smoothly. And report back to me, of course.'

'He's spying, then.'

'No, he's reporting back to me about the wedding details. I just might drop in a question or two regarding what's he's gleaned about my new tenant.'

'I see. You hadn't thought to just ask Hannah why she appeared to have such an interest in the painting?'

Hannah rolled her eyes. *Yes, why didn't you just ask me?*

'Of course I thought of asking her, but I just had a feeling she wouldn't tell. Do you think I'm stupid?'

'I think I do, Kitty.'

Kitty? Hannah shook her head, thinking she must have misheard, surely.

'Don't call me Kitty!' she hissed. 'How many times have I told you!'

'I don't think I've called you that since I walked into the room.'

'Yes, but it isn't the first time – is it?'

'But it's just you and me, darling.'

'The walls have ears.'

Hannah, eyebrows raised, eyes wide, clamped a hand over her mouth lest she inadvertently exclaim what she was thinking out loud – if Lady Jemima was really Kitty, what had happened to the *real* Lady Jemima? She took a step back from the door without thinking. A floorboard creaked underfoot.

'What was that? Quick, Percy, see who's outside the door.'

'Nobody is outside the door,' he said flatly. 'You're just being paranoid.'

'Do as I ask. Please go to the door and check.'

A moment later, Hannah heard Percy say, 'See – there's no one here.'

9

Hannah stood in the bathroom next door, hoping to goodness neither of them needed the loo. Fortunately, she heard the bedroom door close again and muted voices next door. The walls were so thick that she couldn't distinctly hear their conversation.

Hannah crept out of the bathroom and down the stairs. Lady Jemima, or whoever she really was, was using both her and Rupert. She'd felt angry and upset when she'd discovered Jemima wasn't her friend and thought her wedding idea was stupid. *But it could work. It could save the hall,* she thought. She realised that Lady Jemima, or whoever she really was, wasn't interested in saving the hall. She was more concerned about protecting her secret.

Hannah wiped away a tear from her cheek. Then another. She turned around and grabbed a fistful of loo roll and sat on the toilet lid, silently crying, feeling utterly betrayed. *But she was so nice to me. I thought she believed in me, and my idea*, she thought. *Whoever she is, she's not a nice person.*

But Owen had loved her. What had happened to him? More to the point, what had happened to the real Lady Jemima?

For a split second, Hannah thought of barging into her bedroom and demanding answers. But she knew Lady Jemima –

or Kitty, as Percy called her – would not give up her secrets easily.

Maybe she would ask Jemima's grandson. Surely, he knew.

Hannah suddenly heard the creak of a floorboard. Was that Percy next door, about to leave Jemima's bedroom? Perhaps he'd stop in the bathroom and spend a penny before he went downstairs.

Hannah was still sitting on the toilet lid. And she'd forgotten to lock the bathroom door.

Hannah leapt for the door. But instead of locking it, she stepped outside, not caring who saw her.

Nobody was there.

Hannah thundered down the stairs, feeling the tears welling up again. 'I've been so stupid,' she muttered. She didn't know why her grandparents came to mind at that moment – perhaps because she'd thought Lady Jemima was like them. They had believed in her, but Hannah realised that since they'd passed away, she'd lost her anchor in life and had foundered. If it hadn't been for Lili, she'd have lost Maisie too.

Even though Lili had given her the shop, she knew she was still foundering, still hadn't found her place in the world, her home. Bizarrely, though, her finding the painting and it coinciding with Gatekeeper's Cottage coming up for rent had meant everything had just seemed to fall into place so neatly. Suddenly, she'd seen her future.

Not anymore.

Hannah reached the bottom of the stairs, still wiping tears from her eyes. She saw Rupert walking across the hall, carrying a clipboard. She imagined he was checking the auction inventory. Whatever he was doing, she didn't care.

Rupert was entering the room containing the furniture and

paintings for the auction when he stopped. She realised that he must have heard her on the stairs.

He turned around and looked up. 'Hannah – what took you so long? I take it you didn't find the painting?'

Hannah wiped her eyes again, avoiding his gaze. All she wanted to do was get out of the house, but when she reached the bottom of the stairs, Rupert was standing there, barring her way.

'Hannah, what's the matter?' He stepped forward, the concern in his voice evident. He reached out a hand and touched her shoulder.

Hannah brushed him off. 'Leave me alone. Let me pass.'

'Of course.' Rupert raised his eyebrows and stepped to one side.

She stopped in the hallway and whirled around. She sniffed, fighting back tears. 'Do you know your grandmother thinks my idea of setting up a wedding venue here is stupid and it won't work?'

'Why do you say that? She was the one that gave you the go-ahead and told me I had to help.'

'I came down the stairs from the attic and overheard her in her bedroom talking to her chauffeur, Percy,' Hannah blurted, realising too late that there was no way she could have overheard them from the hallway unless she'd walked right up to the door.

She stopped short of mentioning what other shocking thing she'd overheard – Percy calling Lady Jemima Kitty. She stared at Rupert. Did he know that his grandmother wasn't who she claimed to be?

Hannah turned to go, wondering how she could stay living at Gatekeeper's Cottage while knowing that Rupert's grandmother wasn't the sweet old lady she'd thought she was. She wished she hadn't signed the tenancy agreement.

'Then let's prove her wrong.'

Hannah was about to step outside. She stopped and slowly turned around. 'What did you just say?'

'I said let's prove her wrong. Let's plan your friend's wedding and make it amazing, truly stunning. I've got a friend in London who works in IT. He can set up a website for the hall, get the wedding photos uploaded, make the place look really something. There'll be some admin – insurance and things like that. But I like your idea, Hannah. This could be a niche market, you know. I bet a lot of country houses and hotels are big, but this could be for small, intimate weddings, like you said. There are plenty of spare bedrooms – we could do this properly, open up the house to the wedding guests to stay here too.'

Hannah's mouth dropped open. 'But I thought you didn't want to help me or save Somersby Hall? I thought you hated the wedding idea?'

'At first, yes. It's not that I don't want to save Somersby Hall. Why would I want to sell my childhood home? I was happy here after my mother died. I have the fondest memories of this place.'

'Oh, I'm so sorry,' Hannah said, trying to act surprised, like she didn't know already. It was a bit awkward revealing that she'd been talking about him with her best friend.

'It's all right. It was a long time ago. I wanted to stay here living with my father and grandmother, but unfortunately my father left for France, and I was sent to boarding school. I've always wanted to come back here, but …' he trailed off.

Your father stopped you from visiting the hall, thought Hannah, recalling what Lili had told her she'd heard from Mabel and Marjorie when she'd chatted to them about the flyer they'd put up in their shop for the auction. Lili had said it sounded as though his father and grandmother were estranged.

Hannah wanted to ask Rupert why his father had left and never returned. Rupert hadn't shared that information. Question suddenly arose in her mind – did his father know about Lady Jemima? Had he found out his mother wasn't the person he'd thought she was? Was that why they were estranged?

Hannah remained tight-lipped.

'I've got to be honest, Hannah. I was a bit miffed that you'd actually come up with a really good idea.'

'You think my idea is good now?'

'Of course. I've always thought your idea was good – no, brilliant.'

Hannah looked taken aback. 'So, why didn't you just say so?'

'I was annoyed that I hadn't thought of it myself.' Rupert averted his gaze. 'Then I was even more miffed when my grandmother agreed to it. I couldn't believe it. She wouldn't have agreed to it if it had been my idea, I'm sure of it. I was thinking, *what makes you so special?* Apart from the fact that you're much prettier, and so self-assured, and have all this business acumen.'

Did he just say I was pretty? Hannah thought, feeling her cheeks growing hot under his gaze.

'Well, you're not so bad yourself.' Hannah couldn't believe she was flirting with him, but he had started it.

An awkward silence followed until she met his gaze and he smiled his disarming smile.

Hannah scoffed at what else he'd said. 'Self-assured, business acumen – me?'

'Yes, you.'

'Is that what made you change your tune about my idea?' *The fact that you think I'm pretty*, thought Hannah, *and you want to spend time with me?* Oh, how she wanted to ask him that question, but she already knew the answer – it was her so-called business acumen. She tried not to frown.

'Well, I've been mulling it over while I was down here organising the auction. I did have it all planned, what I was going to do – once the auction was done, I intended to get an estate agent in, have the place valued and put it on the market, if I could persuade my grandmother that it was the only way to get hold of some more cash to pay off my father's—' he stopped short.

Hannah stared at him. She had thought Rupert wanted to sell because they couldn't afford to run the house and do the much-needed repairs. That was what his grandmother had implied.

Rupert coughed awkwardly, avoiding her gaze. 'The house needs repairs, and there just isn't the money to pay the bills …'

Hannah noticed he'd changed tack.

'And when I inherit the place, I won't be able to afford to run it, let alone find the money to repair the roof, replace the rotting windows, install a new boiler – the list goes on.'

'Isn't your father going to inherit Somersby Hall?'

Rupert shook his head, casting his gaze around the hallway. 'He doesn't want anything to do with the house. Hasn't been back here in years, not since—'

Two men whom Hannah recognised, the ones who'd delivered the chairs for the auction, walked out of the room opposite the dining room, interrupting their conversation. 'We've moved the furniture like you said.'

'Thanks, guys.'

Hannah frowned at them. She'd wanted to hear what Rupert

had been going to say about his father, and why he hadn't been back in years. According to The Gossip Girls, they'd had a blazing row, but how could they possibly know that? They didn't. It was just gossip because he hadn't been back.

'Anything else?' one of the young men asked.

Rupert glanced at his clipboard. There's a piano upstairs in the third bedroom along the hall. That needs to come down too.'

As the guys walked upstairs, he turned to speak to Hannah. 'Look, my grandmother is stubborn. She's going to dig her heels in with me selling this place. I don't know why she's told Percy your idea won't work. Perhaps she's afraid it won't work, and she's just saying that, preparing herself, in case she's in for a big disappointment.'

Hannah knew that wasn't it, but she kept her mouth shut – for the time being.

'You've come along at the right time, Hannah.'

Have I? She was thinking of what Rupert's grandmother had said about keep your friends close, but your enemies closer, all because of the interest she'd taken in the painting. Now she knew her painting was important – and she knew why: the airgraphs.

She didn't know whether Percy was aware of what was hidden in the painting, but Lady Jemima was. Perhaps she'd hidden them in the painting herself. Was it she who had hidden the real Lady Jemima's letter in with her own? Hannah could only surmise. But what she did know was that they were worried about social media, and Somersby Hall getting 'out there'.

What were they so afraid of – that the real Lady Jemima or her descendants would return to claim what was rightfully theirs?

'So, what are you thinking?' Rupert asked.

You really don't want to know, thought Hannah.

'What do you say? Shall we help my grandmother save her house?'

After what she'd overheard, Hannah didn't want to help her save anything. She wasn't a nice person. Hannah had the impulse to throw in the towel. She didn't want to help her or give her the satisfaction of thinking that she had Hannah just where she wanted her to be – in the house so she could keep an eye on her.

On the other hand, what if she proved her wrong and the wedding idea wasn't stupid after all? If it really took off, with Rupert's help, they could put Somersby Hall on the map.

Hannah said, 'Your friend would set up a website?'

'That's right.'

'We could advertise on Facebook, TikTok, Instagram and X as well,' mused Hannah.

'Yeah – good plan. Let's get it really out there.'

Hannah cast her gaze up the stairs, thinking about Percy's warning. She smiled. 'Yes, let's.'

'You're still up for it then?'

'Oh, yes,' said Hannah, thinking of sweet revenge. She knew what they were afraid of; once again she thought of the real Lady Jemima's descendants, hoping that someone would crawl out of the woodwork and expose this person masquerading as Lady Jemima. Or perhaps she could do that herself – but who would believe her?

Her eyes dropped to Rupert. She had to ignore the guilty feeling that if that were to happen, his inheritance might be forfeit. But did he know?

10

'Rupert, has your grandmother ever gone by …' Hannah didn't know quite how to put it … 'another name?'

'How do you mean?'

'I guess like a nickname, instead of Jemima.'

'You mean like Jem – or something?'

'Or something …'

'No, and if you're thinking of calling her anything other than Lady Jemima, don't. Percy once called her something – I don't know what it was because I'd just walked into her bedroom, and she was telling Percy off for using *that name*. God knows what it was, but she told him off for it, and reiterated that he was only to call her Lady Jemima, or Lady J.'

Hannah nodded her head knowingly.

'I wasn't surprised that Percy called her by a pet name though. Lady Jemima is a bit of a mouthful. He's been working for the family for years, decades. They go way back to when they were very young, I think.'

Oh god. He doesn't know that Percy and his grandmother are in a relationship. But then it wasn't surprising he didn't know – Rupert had hardly visited the hall. Hannah pursed her lips.

A shrill noise interrupted their conversation. It sounded as though someone had played a couple of keys on a piano. This was followed by the sound of something heavy being dragged across a carpeted floor above them.

'What's that noise?' Lady Jemima called out.

They both looked up at the sound of her shrill voice, Hannah frowning.

Rupert turned around and put one foot on the stairs, calling up, 'It's all right, Grandmother, it's just the piano being brought downstairs for the auction tomorrow – remember?'

Hannah watched Rupert hovering there, looking up the stairs, listening for his grandmother's reply.

'All right, dear,' she called out.

Rupert turned around, smiling. 'Won't she be surprised when she finds out we're working amicably on the wedding?'

And pleased, thought Hannah, imagining that Rupert's grandmother could then quiz him about what he'd learned about her new tenant and wedding planner. Hannah smiled tightly.

She heard the piano's notes again as the two guys trundled it along the hallway upstairs. She didn't want to know how they were going to get it safely down the stairs.

Rupert must have heard it too. 'Look, I'm probably going to have to give them a hand. We can discuss the wedding plans later. Can you come to my study this evening after the auction? We can … oh, hold on, it will be late, and you can't leave your daughter alone at Gatekeeper's Cottage.'

'She's with her father this weekend.'

He raised his eyebrows. 'Your ex?'

'He's not exactly my ex. We never married. Just a one-night stand, at a house party when we were teenagers.' She didn't know why she was telling him all this. Even so, she thought she should explain. 'He doesn't get to see her much during the week. Nate works shifts at Aldeburgh Hospital, and he has a son from his previous marriage. So, we have an arrangement – Maisie stays with him, his partner Lili, and Maisie's half-brother, William, every fortnight for a whole weekend.'

'I bet you miss her.'

Hannah looked at him. 'Yes, very much.'

'Well, at least all this can keep your mind off her absence.'

And feeling lonely, thought Hannah, staring at Rupert, now wishing she didn't have to return to Gatekeeper's Cottage on her own. Then again, she didn't fancy hanging around in case his grandmother came downstairs. Hannah had changed her mind about attending the auction, especially as Lady Jemima would doubtless be there. She'd have to phone Ray and say she didn't want him to accompany her to the auction the next day after all, as she wasn't going.

However, there was something she wanted to discuss with Ray – something had happened to Lady Jemima, the real Lady Jemima, many years earlier. She didn't know what to do about it.

'So, you can come this evening?'

'Yes.'

'Great.' He looked at his watch. 'I made an appointment to see the auctioneer this afternoon. I think it's going to take some time for her to value all the items – that's why it's best we meet up this evening when I know she'll be finished.'

'Sounds good to me,' Hannah said, smiling at the thought of not having to spend the evening on her own. She knew it wasn't a social call; they'd be starting work on her business idea. But she couldn't think of anyone she'd rather spend the evening working with. Hannah lowered her gaze as though he could read her mind. She looked about her.

Rupert noticed. 'What is it?'

'I haven't seen your dog again.' Hannah remembered her first visit there, when Rupert had answered the door and been quite rude. A large dog had come to the door, whining, and it had licked her hand. She recalled Rupert's surprise, and his comment that he'd thought the dog was a good guard dog, and that he growled at everyone else, even growled at him – but not at Hannah, apparently.

'Oh, that's not my dog.'

'Then who does the greyhound belong to?'

'Greyhound? You don't know your dog breeds, do you?'

Hannah shook her head. 'No, never had a pet.'

'Me neither. I don't know one dog breed from another really, but I know what my grandmother's dog is.'

'Your grandmother's dog?'

'Yeah – she's always had Irish wolfhounds. Says they're really soppy creatures, but their size will put off any strangers coming here.'

Hannah nodded knowingly.

'Funny the dog likes you, though, just like my grandmother has taken to you.'

Hannah wanted to say, *no, she hasn't taken to me.*

'I was quite impressed that you didn't jump back in fright, and you let her approach you instead.'

'It's a girl?'

'Yeah – but just like my grandmother she can be a—'

Hannah raised her eyebrows wondering what he was going to say.

'A grumpy guts, and quite intimidating, like you don't really know what she's thinking.'

Hannah couldn't agree more.

'Claudia, my, um … girlfriend is really frightened of her.'

'Your grandmother?'

'No – the dog. Although …'

'Although …?

'Oh, never mind.'

Hannah wondered what he had been going to say, although she'd rather not be reminded that he had a fiancée. If Lili didn't agree with the plan to get married there, then that left Rupert and Claudia.

'Personally, I don't find Lulu soppy at all.'

'That's her name?' The name sounded very soppy to Hannah. She imagined that if she was taken to the park and she was called, no one would imagine a great big shaggy grey wolfhound would come bounding along.

'You're a little afraid of her,' Hannah said. *And of your grandmother*, she thought.

'Try a lot.'

'Where is she?'

'Ah, with people coming in and out, we left her in her doghouse in the back garden.'

'Does she have toys or a bone to keep her occupied?'

Rupert did a double-take. 'No – should she have?'

'I don't know.' Hannah had only thought to ask because when Maisie talked of getting a puppy, she'd once written a list of all the things they'd need to get. 'Perhaps Lulu is grumpy because she's bored.' *Or old*, thought Hannah, *like her owner*. 'How old is she?'

'She's two.'

'Really? She seems much older.' Hannah felt a little sad for her, imagining Lulu wandering around the hall with nothing to do and nobody to pay attention to her. She wasn't old; she was bored and unhappy. It was little wonder she growled at everyone.

She needed someone to play with her – a playmate. Hannah would be the last person to suggest buying another dog to keep Lulu company. She certainly didn't like the idea of getting one herself – it would be too much hard work, and hassle. She did make a mental note, though, not to let Maisie play by herself in the grounds of Somersby Hall. She didn't want Lulu growling at Maisie and frightening her. *Although she was friendly to me*, she thought.

If for any reason, Maisie came with her to the big house, as she called it, she'd have to introduce her to Lulu. *At least I'll be there, and she'll be supervised.*

'So, we're still on for this evening?' Rupert asked, double-checking. 'I'll try and make sure Lulu is kept out of the way.'

'Oh, no – don't do that on my account. I'd like to say hello again.'

'Well, maybe that's just as well. My grandmother does insist that Lulu has the run of the hall at night, in case of prowlers.'

'Prowlers?' Hannah frowned.

'I know, it's stupid. Nobody is going to come along and steal anything from Somersby Hall. We're in the middle of nowhere here, really. It's not like an opportunist is going turn up outside the house. We'd hear them first, coming up the drive. In any case, by the time the auction finishes tomorrow, there will be nothing much to steal – if all goes well and we sell a lot. But nevertheless, we've got Lulu to scare people, just in case. If they're not scared off by her appearance, you should hear her howl.'

Hannah smiled. Then she thought of Gatekeeper's Cottage. It was something she hadn't considered – living in the countryside with no nearby neighbours apart from Somersby Hall up the drive. Someone could drive by along the country lane, an opportunist, like Rupert had said, and with nobody nearby, burgle her home while she was out. Or while she was in.

Hannah shuddered at the thought. She had half a mind to ask if she could borrow Lulu for night duty at Gatekeeper's Cottage. Not that she had room for a dog.

'I have an idea,' said Rupert.

'Yes?' Was he going to offer her Lulu for the night?

'Rather than knocking at the house this evening, disturbing my grandmother – you know what her hearing is like – why don't you come straight around the back to the dining room patio door? I'll leave it open. The study is off that room.' He smiled. 'I rather fancy doing all this in secret, then surprising my grandmother.'

Hannah's gaze shifted upstairs again. 'Yes, I rather fancy that too.'

Rupert stepped closer, casting an eye up the stairs, before he whispered, 'Why don't we pretend like we still don't get on? When we're around her, anyway. It will really throw her when she discovers we've been working together just fine, and your idea is really going places.'

Hannah was about to say that it was a good idea, until she recalled what Lady Jemima – Hannah couldn't think of her as Kitty, not until she really knew the facts – had said to Percy about Rupert and Claudia who, by the sounds of it, had never had a lovers' tiff.

Hannah had wondered herself how that was possible in a normal relationship. Although, thinking back, she could say that about all her past relationships – they had never argued because she had always, always given in. Whatever they wanted, whatever was good for them, they came first. And every time she had started a new relationship, she realised, she had lost a little bit more of herself – the real Hannah, who wanted something different out of her life. She wanted to be a good mother and to run her own business. It was just that nobody had believed in her other than her late grandparents and her best friend, Lili. Nobody until Rupert.

He was standing very close now, smiling his disarming smile. She really wanted to stand on her tiptoes and kiss him. Instead, she backed away and said, 'I don't think that's a good idea.'

'Oh, really?' He seemed genuinely surprised.

He had not overheard the conversation between Percy and Lady Jemima that she had. Lady Jemima believed normal couples rowed, quarrelled, fell out. If they continued to do that, his grandmother might start to wonder if there was something more going on between them. And she knew for a fact now that Lady Jemima, or whoever she was, would not want her grandson falling for the enemy.

Enemies-to-friends. She remembered the romance trope with a smile. Was there more going on between them than a little flirtatious banter after they'd got off on completely the wrong foot?

'You're smiling,' Rupert observed.

'Oh, I was just remembering something someone said to me recently. Look, your grandmother isn't stupid. Let's just forget about her and get on with the job at hand.'

He grinned. 'I like your style.'

'I like yours.' Hannah pursed her lips. She wasn't actually talking about business just then, but those casual chinos he looked so good in, and that tight polo shirt showing off his lean physique.

'Great! We're in agreement,' said Rupert.

Hannah stared at him as he smiled at her. Once she had set this train in motion, she knew there was no going back. Assuming the wedding was a success. But if it was … Thea came to mind and all her talk of opening Pandora's Box. She stared at Rupert, his beautiful smile, those slate-grey eyes, disarming her. She was suddenly undecided whether she could go through with it. He was doing it to save the Somersby Hall from financial ruin or from being sold, but ultimately so that he could save his inheritance, his legacy – which might not be his at all.

'Now, where's that auctioneer?' she heard Rupert say as she left the house, suddenly undecided over whether to meet him that evening in his study. Starting her business and putting Somersby Hall in the public eye wouldn't blow up in her face if her business was successful, but it could very well blow up in his if what she'd overheard was true – that the woman living in Somersby Hall was not Lady Jemima – and somebody out there discovered the truth.

She paused outside the house and looked up. There she was, sitting in the window, waving just like the first time Hannah had seen her. Hannah had the impulse to turn on her heel and ignore her. Instead, she forced a smile onto her face and waved, pretending nothing had changed.

But everything had changed.

Hannah stared up at her, thinking of the painting in her

shop window. She didn't trust Jemima not to ask Percy to steal her painting if she wouldn't sell it.

'I've got to remove it from the window,' Hannah muttered under her breath, 'as soon as possible.' It might be her lucky charm, sitting there in the shop window, but it was no use to her if someone took it. Better to keep it safe than risk losing it, Hannah decided.

She dropped her gaze from the window and saw Rupert standing in the doorway, looking at his watch and frowning. She heard him comment, 'Not a good start – she's late.'

11

Hetty looked at her watch. 'This isn't a good start – I'm late.'

She'd just packed her bag with the catalogues and books she needed to value the items in the auction and go over the inventory, along with her laptop, had checked she looked pristine in her trouser suit, and had brushed her chestnut hair, which fell in waves to her shoulders. She'd debated whether it would look more professional to have her hair up, while staring at her reflection, her own wide brown eyes staring back at her, but had decided she didn't have time to redo her hair.

Then the phone rang.

She'd just been walking out of the door. It wasn't her mobile phone. It was the house phone that stopped her in her tracks. There was only one person in her life who still called her on the landline – Grandad. He wouldn't normally phone her first thing in the morning. He was getting on in years and was not an early riser. Something was up.

Reluctantly, she left her bag by the door, slipped off her heels, and padded along the carpeted hallway.

'Everything all right, Het?'

She passed one of her flatmates (and good friends) in the

hallway, who was putting on his helmet and reaching for the handlebars of his bike. He biked to work through the London rush hour every morning. He was doing weekend shifts to earn more money.

She knew why he'd asked that question. He knew that the only person who rang the house phone was her grandfather. She said, 'I hope so,' throwing him an anxious look. She could do without more bad news.

Hetty answered the phone. 'Hi, Grandad. Is everything all right?'

'Yes, perfect.'

Then why are you phoning me so early, today of all days? She'd told him she had a work thing on. In fact, it had turned out she'd made a mistake in telling him exactly what and where the work commitment was. She breathed a heavy sigh. She expected that was what he was phoning about.

Hetty decided not to share her other piece of news just yet. Her landlord had given her and her two flatmates notice to quit their three-bedroomed ground-floor flat. He wanted to sell.

Normally there would be friendly chatter at the breakfast table, especially at the weekend, but that morning there had been a sombre mood in the communal kitchen. It wasn't surprising.

Hetty had looked into a flat-share again, as it was still the most economical way of renting, but even a bedroom in an apartment with communal living spaces was getting ludicrously expensive; demand was driving up rents in London. Hetty was a self-employed valuer working for various auction houses, which meant that although she could earn a good commission, her income wasn't always guaranteed. As well as the rising rental costs, she was worried another landlord might not want to take on a self-employed tenant.

Hetty watched Daniel wheel the bike out of the hallway, praying, like she did every day, that nothing bad happened on his way to and from work. She couldn't imagine starting the day without seeing her two flatmates or ending the day without seeing them either – Daniel especially.

She watched his tall, lithe figure as he put his helmet over his thick mop of curly black hair, now peppered with grey.

Over the time they'd been sharing the ground-floor flat, Daniel – who had split up from his wife – had gone through divorce proceedings. His wife had had an affair and left him, although he was the one who'd moved out of the house they'd rented together. Her boyfriend had moved in. Hetty and Daniel had each been in a couple of short-lived relationships during that time.

Hetty didn't know why he hadn't found someone else. He looked much younger than his forty-six years – at least he did to her – and he was very handsome in a world-weary kind of way.

She knew why her relationships weren't working; her last boyfriend had told her.

'I see the way you look at him,' he'd said on the doorstep on a rare occasion she'd invited him round to the flat for dinner. She'd had no clue what he was talking about until he'd spelled it out. 'Now I know why when you're with me you seem distracted, unavailable even.' He'd ended it that night with the words, 'This relationship isn't going to lead anywhere because you're in love with someone else.'

'I don't know what you mean,' Hetty had said. She'd been beside herself about the fact that another relationship had failed, wondering what was wrong with her – until she'd got up the following morning and had spoken with Daniel. Now she could pinpoint what the fluttery sensation was in her tummy every time she saw him. *I'm in love with Dan, and I didn't even know it.*

Daniel could never reciprocate her feelings, even if he wanted to – could he? He was nearly twenty years her senior and he had children in their early twenties – not that much younger than her. It wasn't the age gap. That shouldn't matter if you loved someone. The problem was that he treated her like a daughter, cared for her, worried about her – loved her as a friend. *But could he love me, the way I love him?* she wondered. *The way Rosie's boyfriend loves her?*

Rosie, the other single housemate, wasn't single anymore. She'd just met the love of her life – another teacher. For her, the landlord giving them notice to quit couldn't have come at a better time. They'd already been applying for jobs outside London, where renting a house would be affordable. They might even be able to save a deposit to buy their own home.

Hetty had been quite envious when she'd heard their plans. She didn't know what she was going to do. She had a sinking feeling in the pit of her stomach; a feeling that everything she loved about her life was about to change – and not for the better. The only bright spot on the horizon was where she was going that day – Somersby Hall. It would be her first time running an auction herself. And yet even that, which she should have been looking forward to immensely, now had a damper put on it – all because of her grandad.

'Are you still there?'

She wished she wasn't. She wished she'd left already and missed his call. 'Yes, I'm still here.'

'Ah, good. I thought we'd been cut off, Henrietta.'

Only her grandad called her by her given name. To everyone else, it was a bit of a mouthful. Her good friends shortened it to Het.

'You did do as I asked, didn't you?'

Hetty sighed. She knew what this was about, but she couldn't turn the assignment down. It was tantamount to a promotion, being given the responsibility of running an auction herself. And not just any auction, but one at a *real* stately home. She was *so* excited. She just wished he shared her enthusiasm and that she wasn't running late; the last-minute phone call wasn't helpful.

Are you okay? Dan mimed, pausing at the front door and turning around, waving to catch her attention.

Hetty took her hand away from the phone. She nodded. 'Just my grandad,' she said unnecessarily. Her two flatmates knew who it was when the phone rang, always joking that her grandfather must have something against mobile phones.

He didn't. But he was in his late eighties and just found it easier to hear her on a landline in their quiet hallway than if he'd phoned her mobile when she was out.

But it wasn't just her grandad, still trying to dissuade her from attending the auction, that was holding her up that morning – it was the news about the flat.

'Everything all right, sweetheart?' her grandad said.

No, thought Hetty. *Not at all.* The sleepless night she'd had, tossing and turning, upset about the flat and what she would do next, not to mention the thought of leaving her flatmates, had meant she'd missed her alarm. When she'd finally woken, she'd been relieved it was Saturday, until she'd suddenly remembered that she had somewhere to be.

And her grandad not explaining why he didn't want her

going to Somersby Hall wasn't helping. Hetty slapped a smiled on her face, trying to sound cheerful. She didn't want to burden him with her own news just then and get into another conversation over what she was going to do on the housing front. It was enough that he'd called again about the auction.

'Look, I'm still going, unless you can give me a specific reason why I should avoid Somersby Hall.' It was only the previous weekend that she'd visited her grandad down in Devon. It was her parents who had bought the cottage that her grandparents had rented for years when the owners had decided to cash in their investment. Her parents weren't made of money. They were teachers and had rented in London for years while Hetty went to school. The small two-bedroomed cottage was where her parents would permanently retire to in the future, and they would leave it to their only child.

Since Hetty had started work and moved into the flat-share, her parents had decided to leave their jobs and teach abroad. They were only in their early fifties and had called their plan of semi-retiring to travel their *adventure*. She'd been so happy for them. It had been their dream for years. She knew, though, that they'd left on their adventure because she had somewhere else to live in London.

And now she didn't. Hetty was not going to phone them up and tell them. Knowing them, they'd be on the first plane back. But they had their own lives to lead. She didn't want them to give up their dream to support her again. She was an adult. She'd just have to figure things out for herself.

If it really came to it, her grandad had a spare bedroom, so she wouldn't be homeless. It would be difficult, but not impossible, to work from there. She travelled all round the country with her job anyway. Now that her parents were abroad, she made the trip to Devon as often as she could, keeping an eye on him since her grandmother's recent passing. Fortunately, he was in good health, and surprisingly agile for one in his ninth decade. He told her to always just keeping moving. Walking, he said, was the secret of his longevity. He could shop, cook, and take care of himself.

Her parents had shown him how to shop online, so he had his shopping delivered by the local supermarket. Contrary to assumptions about his generation, her grandad was computer-savvy. Her parents paid for a cleaner once a week, who also did extra odds and ends of grocery shopping or errands like picking up prescriptions for him if needed. She'd heard her parents discussing selling the cottage if he ever needed full-time care. It wasn't something they wanted to do. Their plan had been to keep the cottage as Hetty's inheritance, but there was nowhere else the money could come from, although it hadn't proved necessary so far.

Hetty thought her grandad was amazing. He reminded her a lot of the actor who played the chimney sweep in her favourite childhood movie, Mary Poppins; he was always smiling, always looking on bright side of life. He had always been a glass-half-full guy, her grandad; that was, until she'd told him about the auction at Somersby Hall during her visit the previous weekend when she'd travelled to the little cottage in Dartmoor to tell him the news.

Although she was nervous about the first auction she was conducting all by herself, she'd thought he'd congratulate her and share her enthusiasm. Certainly, he'd be supportive. He normally was. But this time he was no such thing – far from it. And worse still, he was getting angry with her over the phone.

It just wasn't like him. What was he getting all worked up about? She was about to ask him. Then she stopped. There was a solution to the problem – she would just lie; tell him that she'd changed her mind and wouldn't go. He'd never know.

'Look, Henrietta, I'm aware that your grandmother filled your head with stories about a grand house where she once lived, and you wanted to know where that place was.'

'Yes, I did. Why wouldn't she tell me?' said Hetty. *Why won't you?* she thought.

'Because she left that life behind when we married; *far* behind.'

Hetty remembered that her grandfather had been angry when he'd heard the stories Hetty had been told by her grandmother, just before she died, about her past. He'd never talk about where they'd met. She had no idea why.

'I'm surprised she talked to you about it, but please bear in mind, Henrietta, that this was towards the very end of her life and I expect most of what came out of her mouth was nonsense.'

Hetty went quiet. Why was he saying that? Her grandmother had sounded perfectly coherent to her. She knew that her paternal grandparents had met at a stately home deep in the English countryside before the outbreak of World War Two. She knew this because her grandmother had told her.

They had been so young – just teenagers – when they'd met before he was conscripted and sent to Cairo. Their history, the beginnings of their love story at some fancy house, had proved a life-long fascination for her, which was why she had ended up studying history at university.

She adored stately homes, and enjoyed her work as a valuer, visiting grand houses – some private, others managed by entities like The National Trust – to value pieces of furniture and artwork that had either been bequeathed to them or had come up for auction.

She had always been frustrated that her grandparents had refused to talk about their past, as though it was some big secret. She would have loved them both to have sat down with her and told her about it – especially the war years, when they'd met.

But her grandmother had revealed something to her before she died, something Hetty hadn't told her grandad – not until that day, when she decided she'd share what had been said to her on her grandmother's death bed.

'She told me something …' She'd been so sincere, it didn't sound to Hetty like the ramblings of someone who was losing their faculties.

'What did she say?'

Hetty could tell by her grandfather's tone that he was worried for some reason.

'What did she say?' he asked again, breathing heavily down the phone.

Hetty hesitated. 'That she had regrets.'

'Regrets? What kind of regrets?' he asked slowly.

'Just that she wished she could leave me, her only grandchild, what is rightfully mine. I didn't understand what she was getting at – do you, Grandad?'

There was a long silence on the end of the phone, which was so unlike her grandad. Something was definitely up.

Hetty glanced at her mobile phone to check the time. At this rate, she'd be *really* late. Fortunately, the actual auction wasn't until the next day. Today, she'd made arrangements to arrive at the house to value the items, check the inventory, and generally make sure everything was prepared. And that *she* was prepared. Just then, though, she wasn't – not at all.

She regretted specifying a time. As long as she arrived some time that day to get the preparations done, and as long as it wasn't late in the evening, there was no reason why she couldn't turn up later in the afternoon instead. She'd have to at this rate.

She decided to text the grandson, whose contact number she'd been given, and rearrange the time. She had little choice now. She just hoped he was amenable. She couldn't just put the phone down on her grandfather.

When he still said nothing, Hetty added, 'I did reassure Grandma that she didn't have to feel bad about not leaving me anything in her will, if that's what she meant. I don't need anything more. I have you, and my parents. A job I love.' *Someone I'm in love with.* Hetty put that thought aside for now. Thinking of Daniel, she said, 'And the most wonderful friends.' Her two flatmates would still be her best friends even if they weren't all living together. Hetty added, 'I asked Grandma: *what more could a girl want?*'

'What did she say to that?'

'A legacy.'

12

Rupert retreated into the house. No amount of waiting by the door was going to conjure up the auctioneer any quicker. The young men had finished shifting the piano by themselves, cleverly hoisting it out of the landing window; they'd had to take out the sash and put it back when they were done.

Rupert stood to one side of the front door as they put down a makeshift ramp and carefully trundled the piano on wheels back into the house and through to the storage room opposite the dining room.

He was just waving them off, thinking that at least the local removal firm he'd hired to deliver the chairs and move the items for the auction was reliable. He made a mental note to use the firm again if he moved into the hall permanently at any point. Just then, he was there temporarily; he still had his personal stuff at the rental flat in London that he shared with his fiancée.

Rupert frowned at the thought of Claudia, wondering why it wasn't her, rather than his personal possessions, that had come straight to mind when he'd thought of his inheritance and the possibility of moving to the hall – assuming things worked out financially with the auction and Hannah's plan to save the hall.

He'd met Claudia at university – she was an international student from Denmark – and they'd had an on-off relationship, mainly because of his issues with commitment.

He didn't need therapy to understand that his issues stemmed from his childhood and the upheaval he'd experienced in his young life – losing his mother, and then his home at Somersby Hall.

He still remembered that awful night vividly; being woken up by raised voices, hearing the shouting and slamming of doors, being bundled into the car in his pyjamas in the dead of night, and the terrifying feeling of the car speeding down the driveway. *Who does that to a child?* thought Rupert.

In a short window, he'd lost his mother, his grandmother and Percy, and all he'd had left was a good-for-nothing father who had no job and no money, and could barely take care of himself, let alone a child. Luckily for Rupert, he had been sent to boarding school. It had been his escape. He'd been happy there. The old-fashioned school in a former stately home had reminded him of his own home at Somersby Hall.

But all that was behind him, and his relationship with Claudia was now very much on. They'd just moved out of a house-share and into a spacious rental apartment in a brand-new purpose-built block of flats in what, according to Claudia, was an up-and-coming area of London. Then he'd got the call to return to Somersby Hall.

Rupert knew it was little wonder Claudia hadn't wanted him to visit Somersby Hall in case he didn't return, given their on-off relationship in the past. She'd said, *you promised you were here to stay this time and were committed to building a future together.* Rupert had assured her that was still the case. *Don't forget about us*, she'd said before he left. Rupert stepped outside and looked up at the house. His initial intention had been to see an estate agent once the auction was over, have *the talk* with his grandmother he'd been dreading – raising the subject of her leaving the hall and going into a care home – and then sell the hall. It hadn't been his intention at first, but the house had appeared even more run down than on his last visit with Claudia.

The front gardens didn't help. Now the gardener had packed up and left, it just made the house look worse.

But the house, which should have been his inheritance, had brought to mind his happy childhood memories from back when the house was a home filled with warmth, laughter and a happy extended family – the staff had been part of that family, Rupert recalled. There had been a lot more of them when he was a child, and their numbers had dwindled over the years as they grew old and retired. Rupert's fond smile faded.

Rupert knew his grandmother had paid for his expensive boarding school. His father had never really worked, living off money he'd inherited from his father, who Rupert had never really known. He'd passed away when Rupert was still a child, leaving his grandmother in charge of the hall.

He suspected that his grandmother had paid for his education at the expense of maintaining her beloved house. What sort of grandson would he be if, after everything she'd done for him, he forced her into a home and sold the house from under her? Not that he could force her, but even coming up with the idea and asking her to leave the house she'd lived in all her life, especially at her age, might be considered cruel and unfair.

He was glad she'd forced him and Hannah together to work

on the wedding idea. He hoped Hannah didn't change her mind and that she did turn up that evening to start going over the plans.

Not only did Claudia not want him to return to the house; she didn't ever want to return herself. He recalled what she'd said: *your grandmother – I think she's hiding something.*

Claudia had met his grandmother once. Rupert still didn't understand why she'd reached that conclusion. How could she possibly glean that his grandmother was hiding something – and what exactly?

Rupert stepped outside the house. When he turned around to go back inside, he happened to look up. 'Speak of the devil,' he said under his breath, smiling. She was at her bedroom window, beckoning him to go upstairs and see her.

Rupert dropped his gaze to the driveway. He'd wanted to be around to greet the auctioneer when she arrived. On the other hand, he did have some last-minute things to check with his grandmother about the auction.

He was just thinking, *oh, sod it, the auctioneer can turn up and wait at the door until I'm finished – she's made me wait long enough*, when he got a text message. He read it as he walked back into the house. He raised his eyebrows. She was going to be two hours late! She wanted to rearrange the time.

'Well, that's a great start.' The one consolation was that the auctioneer was booked into a local hotel, so she couldn't possibly be late for the auction the next day.

Rupert was about to shut the front door when he glanced down the driveway, catching a glimpse of Gatekeeper's Cottage. He was reminded of what Hannah had said earlier when she'd been upset about thinking she'd overheard his grandmother say that her idea wouldn't work. He was still convinced that his grandmother hadn't meant it and was just preparing for the disappointment if it turned out to be the case. Even so, he thought he might mention what Hannah had overheard and hear his grandmother's thoughts for himself. He hoped she wasn't going to change her mind and call off the idea of planning Hannah's friend's wedding there at the hall.

13

Rupert hastened up the stairs and took a seat opposite his grandmother in the easy chair by the window. He cast his gaze around her large, airy bedroom with its old-fashioned oak furniture, delicate floral printed wallpaper, and large double bed with a patchwork throw. His eyes settle on Lulu, who was lying on the floor by the bed, large head on equally large paws, eyeing him. She growled.

He stared at the dog. 'Does Lulu have to be in here?'

'Yes.'

Rupert rolled his eyes and fixed his gaze on his grandmother. She didn't normally spend all day in her bedroom, but she'd said that she didn't want to get in the way of the preparations downstairs for the auction.

He smiled at Percy, who was sitting on the chaise longue on the other side of the room, reading a newspaper. It was good of him to keep Jemima company.

'The lady from the auction house will be here later to appraise the items for the auction.'

'I thought she would be here already?'

'Change of plan.' Rupert decided not to mention that she

was going to be late. It wouldn't fill his grandmother with confidence about the auction. It didn't fill *him* with confidence. She sounded quite young. It made him wonder what experience she had.

Lady Jemima just nodded, a shadow passing over her face. 'I know it's necessary, to raise some cash, but it still feels like losing a part of our history, selling some of the things that have been in this house for generations.'

Rupert reached across the small round table where she'd put down the novel she was reading, and her cup of tea, and squeezed her hand gently. 'I promise I'll do everything I can to save Somersby Hall.'

She raised her eyebrows. 'You've changed your tune. I got the feeling, when you first returned, that you'd rather washed your hands of the place. I expected that you might ask me to move out and sell up.'

Rupert looked away, admitting, 'It had crossed my mind.' That had indeed been the plan. Then along Hannah had come – she'd barely been there five minutes but had clearly fallen in love with the house along with her new cottage. Her enthusiasm was catching, as was her spirit. She was so determined to save the place. Because of her, he'd seen the house with fresh eyes, along with his future. He realised that Somersby Hall was more than just a house for him; it was his heritage, his identity, and his home. Losing it would feel like losing a part of himself.

He told his grandmother this too. 'I'll do everything I can so that we don't have to give up the house.'

Jemima smiled, though it didn't quite reach her eyes. 'I know you will, dear. I suppose sometimes we have to let go of the past to make way for the future.'

Rupert nodded, relieved that she wasn't going to suddenly back out of holding the auction – or the wedding they were planning there.

'Talking of which,' said Rupert, 'you wouldn't consider putting that painting in the auction – would you?' His eyes had drifted to the painting over the old fireplace. He knew it well. It had hung there ever since he could remember. The beautiful red-gold sunset over a beach always made him smile. Seashell Bay. He always wondered if the beach existed or whether it was a figment of the artist's imagination. Rupert supposed he would never know.

He looked at his grandmother, who had turned in her chair to look at her painting. He knew he was wasting his time asking; he imagined she'd never part with it. But he thought a beautiful painting like that might fetch a good price, even though it was by an unknown artist.

She had never told him where she had acquired the painting. He'd asked once, but she'd claimed it had been so many years earlier that she'd forgotten. Rupert knew his grandmother. Despite her advancing years, she did not forget a thing. Claudia suddenly came to mind along with what she'd said about his grandmother – *I think she's hiding something.* When Rupert had pressed her over what she'd meant by that comment, he'd gleaned that Claudia had been talking about a secret – perhaps from Jemima's past.

Rupert didn't want to think about that. Claudia was into astrology, and reading the stars, and Zen, and meditation, and her intuition. Their whole apartment had been organised around feng shui. There had been nothing wrong with all that, thought Rupert, until she'd started to say things about his family and the house. That wasn't right.

Rupert put Claudia from his mind. Instead, he turned his thoughts to Hannah who, like himself, was into just rolling up her sleeves and getting on with things; none of this meditating on a problem, or relying on her intuition, or consulting her horoscope. He didn't actually know if Hannah read her horoscope before she made any decisions, like Claudia, but he very much doubted it.

He turned his attention from the painting, taking his grandmother's silence as a no, and said, 'There's just one more thing, Grandmother. You weren't thinking of calling off the wedding idea – were you?'

'Of course I'm not calling it off – whatever gave you that idea?'

'Are you sure?' he asked her.

'Yes, I'm sure. Why are you asking all of a sudden?'

'It's just that Hannah thought she overheard you say it wasn't going to work.'

Rupert heard the rustle of a newspaper. He glanced at Percy, who a moment earlier had been avidly reading. He'd lowered his newspaper, looking their way.

'What do you mean, *overheard*?' Jemima asked slowly.

'She'd been upstairs in the attic, and must have overheard you talking to Percy when she came down the attic stairs into the hallway.'

'How could she have overheard unless she was standing right outside my door?'

'Perhaps she was going to knock and let you know that she hadn't found the painting.'

'What painting?'

'The one you asked me to find …' he glanced at *Sunset Over Seashell Bay*. 'I was busy, so I told her what I was looking for and left her have to have a nose around up there – see if she could find it.'

'You told her *my* business.' Jemima half rose from her chair.

Rupert looked at her, taken aback, wondering what she was getting all het up about. It was only a painting.

'It's all right, Rupert,' Percy said, folding his newspaper. 'I found the—'

'Percy! Don't interrupt!'

'Fine.' Percy closed his mouth.

Rupert looked from Jemima to Percy. 'What's going on?'

'Nothing,' Jemima snapped. 'Don't worry about the painting. Just get on with the wedding planning.'

'All right.' He was relieved the wedding idea was still on.

Jemima leaned forward in her chair. 'Did Hannah mention anything else she'd overheard?'

'No. She probably thought you were going to call off her plans for a wedding here.'

'Not at all.'

'Well, that's great then.' Rupert couldn't wait to tell Hannah that she'd misconstrued the situation and that his grandmother was still happy for it to go ahead, although he did see her exchange a look with Percy across the room. Rupert caught Percy frowning at her as he unfolded his newspaper and resumed reading.

'You do still want it to be a success – the wedding, don't you?'

'Yes, I want it to be a success, Rupert. Why wouldn't I?'

Rupert tried to ignore the waver in her voice. He imagined

she was just apprehensive at the thought of all those people who would be attending the wedding. It would mean a huge change at Somersby Hall, inviting so many strangers into her home. He knew how much she valued her privacy; he was still so surprised, and quite in awe of his grandmother, that she'd agreed.

At least there wouldn't be a large wedding party – just close family and friends, by the sound of it. But even so, it would undoubtedly feel like an invasion.

He smiled. 'I bet it will bring back some memories, Grandmother, from when the men returned here after the war and there was a huge celebration.'

Rupert had no idea whether there had been a party to celebrate those who had returned. Rupert knew how rare it was nowadays to have a living relative who was a link to that time. He just wished she'd talk about it.

He waited in anticipation.

'Hmm.' That was all that passed her lips, along with, 'I'm tired now, Rupert.'

Rupert frowned at her. He knew how old she was, so he really shouldn't get annoyed with her. It was just that whenever he asked a question that he got the feeling she didn't want to answer, he just knew she was using the age thing. She was faking it.

Rupert sighed heavily, realising she wasn't going to talk to him about that time in her life, there in the house in the forties – not that day or any day. She obviously had her reasons.

Jemima said, 'Haven't you got things to do?'

He did. But he'd much rather sit there and listen to her tell him all about the grandfather he'd never known because he'd died before Rupert was born, and all the people who used to live there back in the forties, in the hall's heyday, when her grandmother was in her teens and the house would have been bustling with people.

He glanced at Percy, who had resumed reading his newspaper, holding it up high, also hiding from Rupert's questions. Rupert had asked Percy, when they'd been alone, if he could tell him about the hall all those years earlier. Percy had clammed up.

Rupert sighed heavily. He stood staring down at his grandmother. She'd picked up her novel and opened it at the bookmarked page.

'I guess,' said Rupert, 'that you don't want to revisit the past.'

Jemima put on the reading glasses that were on the table. She looked over the rim at her grandson. 'The past is best left where it should be. In the past.' She licked her finger and turned the page, starting to read.

Percy, who had lowered his newspaper, quickly held it up again when Rupert glanced his way.

'I'll go now, then.'

He didn't get a response as he walked to the door. He opened it, cast one glance back over his shoulder before he stepped out in the hall, and closed the door behind him.

Rupert stood for a moment outside the door, wishing he hadn't recalled Claudia's words, yet again – *she's hiding something.*

Rupert was just turning to go when he heard the rustle of a newspaper. Percy commented, 'Shame you don't take your own advice.'

'What about?'

'You know, the past is best left in the past.'

'Well, it is.'

Percy guffawed. 'Well, you could have fooled me after our chat about the painting. I'll have you know I will not steal anything.'

Rupert's eyebrows shot up. Had his grandmother asked Percy to steal something?

'Even if, by so doing,' Percy continued, 'it means protecting your secret.'

'*Our* secret.'

There was a silence during which Rupert stood there feeling uncomfortable at listening in on their conversation. He was afraid of what else he might hear that couldn't then be unheard – such as if his grandmother and Percy were in a relationship. Was that their secret? He wouldn't care. Everybody deserved happiness, especially at their age. It would be the fact that they'd felt they had to keep it a secret that would bother him.

Rupert hated secrets. They never did anyone any good; he believed they could do more harm than good. His father was a case in point. Whatever had happened at the hall that night when his father had bundled him into the back of the car and had sworn never to return, he wouldn't divulge. He'd kept it a secret, and it had caused a rift between them. If he wouldn't tell Rupert the reason he wanted his son to steer clear of the hall, then Rupert had decided he wasn't speaking to him. It was infantile and stupid. But Rupert wanted to know.

So, far he still hadn't broached it with his grandmother either – or Percy. He imagined they wouldn't tell him anyway. Besides, the moment wasn't right: one thing at a time, Rupert decided. First, get his father out of his debt-ridden misery, save the hall, and figure out what wasn't working in his relationship with Claudia – because something wasn't.

Rupert raised his eyebrows at that last thought. Why did Claudia keep coming to mind? It was because it was another thing he had to sort out. He'd confided in his best friend, Olly, about how he felt. Olly was Percy's nephew, and he was a painter and decorator, and sometimes a chauffeur; he'd run errands for Percy when he wasn't feeling up to it.

Olly was the brother Rupert had never had, the boy he'd played with when he'd lived there as a child, and the friend he'd even been to school with for a brief time until he'd been sent away to boarding school. Somehow, through the years, and their diverging lives, they'd remained firm friends because of their connection to the house.

He was about to go – his grandmother was right, he had things to do – when he overheard her again. 'How long do you think Hannah was listening outside my door?'

'How do I know?' Percy replied.

'Do you think she overheard you call me Kitty?'

Kitty?

'Wouldn't she have said something to Rupert if she had?'

Rupert had never heard Percy call her Kitty before. Was that her middle name? He hadn't known she had one. Or was it some sort of nickname?

'Nickname,' he said under his breath, recalling Hannah asking him a rather odd question: *Rupert, has your grandmother ever gone by another name? … I guess like a nickname, instead of Jemima.* Why would she ask him that unless she'd heard that name too? She must have overheard the name Kitty, so why hadn't she mentioned that name?

'Do you think she knows?' Jemima hissed.

Knows what? Rupert thought, staring at the door.

'Well, that's a big leap, isn't it?' said Percy.

'She *was* in the attic.'

'Of for goodness' sake. She was looking for the painting. She has no idea what happened up there.'

Rupert raised his eyes, wondering what on earth they were talking about.

'And besides,' said Percy. 'without the letters, nobody is any the wiser. You did say you'd hidden them, didn't you?'

'Of course.'

'Like I said before, don't tell me where. As long as they're safe, that's all that matters.'

Rupert stood there a while in the silence that followed, thinking he couldn't move now. They might hear a creaking floorboard. Is this what had happened to Hannah? She'd stopped outside the door and hadn't known how to retreat in case she was heard.

Then he heard footsteps on the rug in the bedroom. He prayed nobody came to the door. Neither did. What he heard next gave him the opportunity to move – the sound of someone opening drawers and cupboards in the old oak furniture near the bed.

Rupert sighed in relief, wondering why he'd hung around. He turned on his heel just as another drawer slammed shut and overheard his grandmother say, 'Ah, I found them.'

Rupert had the sudden impulse to stay and find out what she'd been looking for.

'I found the box of tissues.'

Rupert shook his head and smiled. Luckily, he'd reached the bottom of the stairs when another text came through on his phone. It was Hannah asking him if the auctioneer had arrived.

She hadn't noticed a car pass by Gatekeeper's Cottage.

Rupert replied that the auctioneer was on her way, adding that he hoped he'd still see Hannah that night in the study as planned.

He stopped on the bottom stair to check his phone. Disappointingly, she hadn't replied. He hoped she wasn't thinking of backing out of the whole idea. He couldn't imagine that. The only thing he could think of that would throw their plans into disarray was if her best friend didn't agree to tend to the gardens in exchange for holding her wedding there. That would be a huge setback.

14

'A box of tissues!' exclaimed Percy. 'That does not look like a box of tissues.'

'Shush! Keep your voice down, for goodness' sake. Go and check there's no one outside.'

Percy rolled his eyes. 'Oh, not this again.'

'Yes, this again,' she hissed back at him. 'Go, do it now. Be quick about it. Move yourself.'

Percy strolled to the door, making no effort to be quick about it and move himself. Even if he had made the effort, Percy's days of being quick were long gone. He opened the door, and said, 'There, *nada*.'

'What?'

'Nothing. I said nothing.'

'But you did, you said—'

Percy shook his head. 'Never mind. Look, you can see for yourself, nobody is here.' He closed the door. 'So, the box of tissues was a subterfuge.'

'Of course.'

'Thank goodness. For a moment there, you had me worried.' He put a hand to his chest and breathed deeply as though he'd just had a shock.

'I am not going senile, if that's what you were thinking. I know a box of tissues when I see one.'

'And I know a letter when I see one,' said Percy, pointing at her hand.

Jemima retreated to her chair by the window, indicating for Percy to join her.

'Is that one of *the* letters?'

She nodded.

'You hid them in your desk drawer? I'm sorry, but I wouldn't call that a suitable hiding place.'

'No, you're right. That's why I didn't hide the majority of the letters here. It's just I couldn't fit this last one in with the others – there just wasn't room.'

'Either that, or you kept one back,' Percy said under his breath.

Jemima gave him a sideways glance. She didn't respond. She'd tied the letter in a red ribbon, just to be sure it didn't get caught up in any other paperwork in her old bureau and get torn up and thrown away. She'd be heartbroken if that happened.

The old ribbon had become rather threadbare and had faded to a crimson pink, but it still did its job – the letter had sat in the bureau for decades. As she removed the ribbon, her eyes scanned the familiar handwriting. She carefully took the letter out of the envelope.

'What's that unusual postmark on the front of the envelope?' Percy asked.

'This is an airgraph – remember?'

'Oh, yes. Is that what Owen sent from Cairo?'

'It is.'

'Would you like me to leave you in peace to read the letter?'

'No, stay with me. I've read it many times.' She looked at him. 'Would you like me to read it out loud? He wrote the most exquisite love letters.'

Percy frowned. 'If you want to.'

She looked at him sharply. 'Why the frown?'

'Because I couldn't write you love letters like Owen.'

'That doesn't matter now. You've been by my side through thick and thin, my constant, unlike Owen. It doesn't matter now.'

'But it mattered then.'

They both looked at the letter.

'Read it,' said Percy.

'All right.' Jemima took a deep breath. She knew this letter off by heart. It was the last one he had written, but she still loved to read it and see his hand.

'*Dearest Kitty*, she began, '*I think of you every day as I watch the sun set over the desert. It reminds me of our secret cove, our Seashell Bay. I cannot wait to return to you, to hold you in my arms and never let you go.*'

Tears welled up in her eyes as she read. Owen's words were a balm to her soul, but they also reopened wounds she had tried to keep closed. The letters were a tangible connection to a past that, at times, felt more real to her than the life she was living now – not that she'd ever admit that to anybody, especially Percy. Nor would she admit that the more she had written to Owen, and the more he'd replied, the more she'd fallen head over heels in love with him. Although she thought Percy had suspected, he'd never said. It was heartbreaking that Owen didn't love her back. Even so, she knew she had to protect these memories, just as she had to protect her secret. Perhaps she was foolish keeping one letter back – to remember.

They both stared at the open letter in her hand for a full minute before she carefully placed it back in the envelope, retied the ribbon around the letter and stood, walking across the room to put it back where she'd found it in the drawer of her bureau.

She returned to her chair but didn't sit. Instead, she stood in front of the window, looking out at the gardens of Somersby Hall. The estate needed saving, but more than that, she needed to keep her past hidden. The auction was a necessary evil, but she would not let it expose the secrets of the house. She knew that her grandson would love to talk about what it had been like there in the forties, but she could never tell. Not now, not ever, if she wanted to pass the house down to him and keep his legacy intact.

With a heavy sigh, she turned away from the window. The next day, she would go downstairs and face the auctioneer along with all those people who were going to turn up and buy her possessions. She prayed she didn't see a face from her past.

But that night, she would let herself remember. She would let herself be Kitty, if only for now.

'Jemima?'

She turned around and looked down at Percy. There was concern in his voice. She reached out and touched his cheek. 'Call me by my name, just for tonight.'

'But I thought you said …' He put a gentle hand over hers. 'Are you sure?'

She nodded.

'I'm sorry, Percy.'

'What for?'

He followed her gaze to the bureau where she'd placed the letter from Owen.

'Don't be, my love. We can't help who we fall in love with.

It's … it's just biology, I suppose.'

'I suppose so.' She raised her eyes to the ceiling.

'Do you want to go upstairs?'

She laughed.

'Did I say something funny, Kitty?'

'It sounded like a proposition – you know, shall we go upstairs …'

'Oh, my goodness. So it did.' He laughed too. Then the laughter subsided. 'I meant, shall we go up to the attic rooms and take a trip down memory lane?'

She shook her head. 'For one thing, I think you're forgetting that neither of us could manage those stairs like we did in our youth.'

Percy nodded. He raised an eyebrow. 'And the other thing?'

'Reading that letter again and using my real name is as far as I dare go because …' she trailed off, dropping her hand from his cheek and turning to the window. 'I have regrets.'

'As do we all, Kitty, especially at our age, when people start looking back on their lives. You are certainly not alone. It's human nature.'

'But I have regrets about all this.'

'About Lady Jemima?'

She turned to him. 'How could I not?'

'Indeed,' Percy said, sighing heavily as he stood, joining her in front of the window. He took her hands in his. 'Kitty, it's a little late to have regrets over that – don't you think? It won't do you any good looking in the past. You can't turn back the clock and change your mind, no matter how much you yearn to do so.'

'Sometimes, as I travel ever closer to meeting my maker, I just want to be me again.'

'But you like all her nice things, always have done. You wanted to be her, remember?'

She frowned at Percy. 'Isn't hindsight a wonderful thing?' She sighed heavily. 'If only I hadn't agreed to—'

She was interrupted by the sound of a car turning up outside the house. They exchanged a glance and leaned forward in their chairs. 'I imagine that's the auctioneer finally turning up, Kitty,' commented Percy. 'Sorry, I mean Lady Jemima.'

She smiled at him. Kitty was no more – for the time being.

They stood watching the young woman lock her car before crossing the gravel drive towards the house. She paused and looked up, catching them both in the window.

'Is she waving at us?' said Percy.

Lady Jemima lifted her hand and waved back. 'I think so. Reminds me of Hannah when she first turned up.'

'Yeah – and you thought that was a good omen, and it turned out to be quite the reverse.'

She stopped waving and grimaced. 'Thank you for reminding me of that fact,' she said sarcastically.

They faintly heard the doorbell downstairs. 'Shall we go down and meet the auctioneer?' Percy asked.

She shook her head. 'I'm not in the mood. There will be plenty of time for that tomorrow morning when she auctions off all my stuff.'

'Sorry about that.'

'It's not your fault, Percy, that my son squandered the inheritance my late husband left him and then got himself into another mountain of debt. I just hope there's some money left over to do some repairs on the house.'

'You know what my attitude is. Don't bail him out, otherwise it's going to happen all over again, the gambling debts. Spend the money on repairing the house, because you said yourself that the wedding idea isn't going to take off. Not that you want it to, either.'

'It's true – I don't. God knows who will crawl out of the woodwork if this place becomes a wedding venue.'

'The same could be said of this auction – it is open to the public, after all.'

'Don't remind me,' she said with a huge sigh.

'I hope it's worth the risk,' Percy commented, shaking his head. 'I just feel so bad that I haven't been able to help you out financially.'

'If you want to help, then fetch the painting, first thing in the morning.'

'Oh, not that again!' Percy got out a white handkerchief from his breast pocket and wiped the beads of perspiration that had broken out on his forehead.

'Yes, that again. It's important.'

'Why?'

'Because that's where the airgraphs are hidden.'

'You mean …' Percy looked at her wide-eyed. 'How can that be?'

'In the backing.'

'In the backing of the painting?'

'Yes.'

'All of them – from Owen too?'

'Yes. Well almost.'

They both turned in their chairs to look at the bureau.

Percy had a question. 'So, how on earth did that painting end up in the shop?'

'How do I know?'

'But … but … I don't understand. If the airgraphs fell into the wrong hands, and it was someone local who found them, they could very well expose your secret. And then poor Rupert … why on earth would you let the painting out of your sight?'

He was just shifting his gaze from the bureau when he saw the twin painting, *Sunset Over Seashell Bay*, hanging over her mantel shelf. He stared at it for some time, his eyes narrowing. When he turned to her, she was gazing at the painting too.

'Oh no!' said Percy, staring at her. 'You kept the wrong painting.'

She bit her lip and didn't deny it.

'How?' Percy asked staring at her intently. 'How did that happen?'

She knew Percy's concern wasn't just for her – it was also for her grandson. 'I asked Owen if I could have one of his paintings when he left, as a keepsake. I knew he didn't want to destroy the letters, so when he framed the paintings, he told me he'd hidden the letters in one of them.'

'Did he tell you which one?'

'Of course. And I said that's the one I wanted over the mantel shelf. I was relieved when he hung this one. It doesn't remind me so much of her every time I look at it.'

'But she's in that one too, although not quite front and centre like *Sunrise Over Seashell Bay*,' Percy noticed.

'I know. It was always all about her. But anyway, that's beside the point. He hung the wrong one.'

'He hung the wrong painting?'

'Yes, apparently so.'

'So, how did you find out they weren't in the backing of that painting after all these years?'

'Hazel.'

'Hazel? The housekeeper, Hazel?'

She rolled her eyes at Percy. 'Of course. Who else would I be talking about?'

'What did she do?'

'Go and see for yourself.'

Percy slowly rose from his seat, rubbing his knee. His arthritis was playing up again. He hobbled over to the painting. 'I don't see what the problem is.'

'Take it down. That's what Hazel did, to dust it.'

Percy reached up, taking hold of either side of the frame, and carefully lifted it from the picture hook, slowly lowering it, hoping his back didn't give out. 'Oh dear. The frame has come away from the backing.'

'You don't notice it when it's flush with the wall.'

'That's when you discovered the letters weren't there?'

'Exactly.'

'When was this?'

'The other day when Rupert arrived and started organising the auction. I thought, *bloody hell* – pardon my French – *what if Owen left the other painting upstairs when he left decades ago, and I never knew?*'

'That's why you sent Rupert up there to look for it.'

'Yes, I can't afford for it to fall into the wrong hands.'

'But it already has.' Percy resumed his seat. 'So, what now?'

'Who owns that shop – do you know?'

Percy shook his head. 'I do not. But I can make enquiries. I'm sure Thea in the bookshop would know who her shop neighbour is in Cobblers Yard.'

'Don't bother. Just go there first thing on Monday and get that painting.'

'You mean *buy* the painting.'

'Whatever it takes.' She reached out her hand. 'Promise me, Percy. We need it back before someone discovers there's a lot more to that painting than meets the eye.'

Percy sighed heavily. 'All right, I promise. First thing Monday morning.'

15

Hannah finally put her feet up. She'd unpacked the boxes Ray had helped her move into her new home the previous day. The lounge looked quite lovely in a cluttered kind of way. Since moving back into the flat from the cottage in Aldeburgh, Hannah had left a lot of her personal things taped up in boxes. Not envisaging that the move back to the flat would be permanent, there hadn't seemed any point unpacking everything. So the boxes that didn't contain their clothes and cooking utensils had remained taped up and sealed.

The only problem was that Gatekeeper's Cottage was smaller than the cottage they'd been renting. Although two-bedroomed, the rooms were small. 'But cosy,' Hannah said out loud as she relaxed on the sofa, which was piled with cushions and throws, her feet resting on the wooden trunk that sat on the rug on the light oak wooden floor and doubled up as a coffee table.

She hadn't intended to go shopping that day, but Hannah had spent a bit of money in one of the shops in Aldeburgh, bringing back some throws, along with two cosy blankets that she and Maisie could sit under on the seats on the little patio outside the back door. They'd be able to watch the sun go down in their little garden, enjoying the views across the lawn to the house. Hannah glanced at the empty cardboard boxes she'd left stacked up in the corner of the lounge. She'd have to flatten them later, for storage and possible future use. She debated whether to just dump the packing boxes. She liked it there. She wanted to stay there, for it to be permanent. Of course, that wasn't possible – it was a rental. She had no idea where she'd get the money to buy it if Lady Jemima did choose to sell Gatekeeper's Cottage. If Hannah won the lottery, she'd quite happily buy Somersby Hall.

Or would she? Hannah was having a rather lovely daydream about owning Gatekeeper's Cottage and thought it would be preferable to owning the hall. Her thoughts of staying there permanently were a far cry from her attitude in the wake of overhearing Lady Jemima disparaging her idea to save the hall. Hannah had intended not to bother even finishing her unpacking. Instead, she had nearly called Ray and asked him to help her move back to the flat.

It was Rupert who had inadvertently persuaded her to stay. And now there she was, in the little cottage, looking as though she'd lived there for years. The bedrooms, along with throws, books, and cushions, were filled with lots of her little ornaments, which she'd bought from bric-a-brac shops and Camden Market near where she'd lived in London. Being surrounded by her things made her feel so at home.

The small kitchen with shelving above the kitchen units was now full of the cookbooks her grandmother had bought her. But the lounge was her favourite place of all. She'd covered the old sofa that had been left behind with multicoloured throws and cushions to hide the threadbare sofa cushions. Similarly, the two match armchairs were draped with throws, one of which displayed Maisie's favourite cushions – they had cartoonish drawings of a hare on one and the head of a highland cow on the other. Hannah smiled to herself, recalling asking Maisie why she hadn't chosen cushions with cute kittens or puppies on them. She'd just shrugged and said, *I like these.*

Hannah was going to enjoy living there – she just knew it. She just had to make the wedding idea a success, otherwise she imagined the house would have to be sold, along with Gatekeeper's Cottage – unless Rupert came up with a better idea. Or the items in the auction were far more valuable than Rupert had thought. That would be down to the reserve price the auctioneer suggested, and what people were willing to pay on the day.

She had just unpacked the last box and had enjoyed finding a home around the cottage for all her little ornaments. She heard a car turn into the driveway of Somersby Hall and jumped off the sofa. She just caught a glimpse through the window of a young, pretty woman as she drove passed the cottage on the way to the house. She guessed that it was the auctioneer, come to value the items in the auction and make any final preparations before the big day. She raised an eyebrow. The auctioneer was running very late. She remembered Rupert mentioning she was a young woman – not the person Hannah had been expecting. Not the person Rupert had been expecting either, by the sound of it.

Hannah was sticking to her plan not to attend the auction after all. She wasn't interested in bumping into Lady Jemima at the auction and engaging in small talk. She didn't know how she would be able to stop herself from saying something about what she'd overheard – Lady Jemima dismissing her wedding idea. And she didn't know how to look her in the eye, knowing what else she'd overheard – Percy calling her Kitty, and Kitty demanding that he buy Hannah's painting from the shop. Even suggesting he steal it.

'Well, that's not going to happen,' Hannah said to the empty room as she turned her attention to the painting she'd hung on the wall above the fireplace in front of her.

Earlier, when she'd been busy unpacking, she'd become worried about what she'd heard and had made a decision. She'd got straight in her car and driven into Aldeburgh, parking her car haphazardly at the kerb, rushing down to Cobblers Yard, afraid the painting in her shop window was already gone.

She'd breathed a huge sigh of relief when she'd discovered that her shop door was still locked and her front window was still intact – there was no sign of a forced entry, and her painting was still there, on the easel in the shop window.

Well, it isn't anymore, she thought, smiling up at *Sunrise Over Seashell Bay*. The vibrant yellow and burnt orange hues complemented the colours in her throws. Lili had been right: the beautiful painting deserved a home. And here it was.

At first, Hannah hadn't known what to do with the painting once she'd run inside the shop, taken it off the easel, and put a blanket over it. She couldn't risk leaving it in the shop, even if it wasn't on display. She'd had no choice but to take it home with her. Once back at Gatekeeper's Cottage, she'd been careful to keep it covered up as she carried it into the house; not that anybody could see her from Somersby Hall, but even so, she didn't want to take any chances. What if Percy suddenly came down the drive in his car and spotted her?

Once the painting was safely inside, and she'd shut the door, she'd felt rather foolish over her mad dash to Cobblers Yard.

There really was no reason for it. Percy had been in the house all along; she hadn't heard his car. Unless he'd teleported over to Cobblers Yard, there was no way he could have gone out without her knowing about it. Of course, there was another possibility, she belatedly realised, which should have occurred to her. They could have asked someone else to pay her shop a visit.

Hannah shuddered at the thought. Would it have been the same person involved in the real Lady Jemima's disappearance? Something had happened to her. Hannah was convinced of it – she had disappeared, obviously, never to be heard from again.

But who could it be? They were all elderly, other than Rupert, and there were only a few people there: Percy, Lady Jemina, and the housekeeper, Hazel, whom she'd bumped into on her way out of the house that day and who had eyed her suspiciously, making her feel uncomfortable. She'd heard there was a handyman too, who came to do odd jobs around the house, but he sounded just as ancient as the others.

She took her hat off to them for sticking by Lady Jemima and still working at Somersby Hall. She wondered what kept them there well past retirement – they clearly loved Somersby Hall, but were they all in on it too? Did they know her secret – that she wasn't who she claimed to be? Percy certainly did.

Thinking of someone stealing her painting, she couldn't imagine that Percy, Hazel or the old handyman could force a door or smash a window without hurting themselves.

There was also Percy's nephew, Olly. He was young, like Rupert, and would have been the most likely contender. But he seemed really nice. He'd been driving up the drive when she'd been walking down it to Gatekeeper's Cottage and had stopped his car, winding down his window to introduce himself. It sounded as though Rupert had mentioned their new tenant to him. Olly had seemed too nice to go and commit a burglary, but then again Hannah thought she was a nice person, but *she* had found herself committing a burglary. He'd told her that Percy had called him to the house to run an errand. After she'd heard that, she hadn't been able to get into her car fast enough.

Hannah stared at her painting. She imagined some people would think she was mad, hanging it in full view where anybody could see it when the people in the big house just a few hundred yards away were looking for it.

She glanced at the window with the heavy net curtains. She hadn't liked them at first, although the leaf design in the net curtains was pretty. She had been planning to take them down to let in more light, but now she was glad of them. Without the net curtains, anybody walking up the front path could see into the lounge; they might spot the painting hanging over the fireplace.

Hannah wasn't worried about Jemima, Percy or Rupert calling round. They could if they wanted to, she supposed, but as a tenant she knew her rights: unless it was an inspection, and the appointment was prearranged through the letting agency, they couldn't just come into her home unless she invited them in. Hannah had no intention of doing that.

She hadn't left the airgraphs in the shop either. They were already in the cottage, in an airtight container – she'd found a suitable storage box while she was out shopping. She'd put them away in a locked cupboard of the dresser in the dining room. The old G-Plan furniture had been left there by the gardener and there were locks on some of the doors and drawers.

She had wondered if the furniture might have made some money at the auction. It was in very good condition, and there might have been interest for nostalgic reasons. Hannah hadn't mentioned it to Rupert because she liked the old-fashioned furniture; it suited Gatekeeper's Cottage. There was even an old-fashioned plastic dial phone in vintage green.

'I love this place,' Hannah said, patting a cushion beside her. Now she just had to make sure that Rupert and his grandmother didn't sell up. To that end, she rose from the sofa. She had a phone call to make.

16

'Lili, it's Hannah.'

'How's the move? All settled in?'

'Yes. It's amazing. I love it here.'

'Oh, I'm so happy for you, Hannah.'

Hannah bit her lip. But would she be happy to do her a huge favour and have her wedding there? She remembered what Lili had said to her when she'd called into her shop – *You will tell me if you need anything, won't you?*

Well, I need something now, thought Hannah. She asked conversationally, 'How's Maisie? Is she enjoying herself?' It was a silly question. Maisie always had a great time with her little brother, her dad, and Lili at their house. She'd only spent Friday night at their new home before going to Nate's for the weekend. She had said she loved it, surprising Hannah when she said she didn't want to go to her dad's that weekend.

Hannah thought Maisie would love Gatekeeper's Cottage even more now. It hadn't looked as good on Friday evening, with all the unopened boxes, and none of their things around, apart from in Maisie's bedroom.

'Yes, um … I think so.'

Hannah heard the waver in Lili's reply. 'Is anything the matter?'

'I think it's just the move. She's found it unsettling. First you were in the flat, then you rented that lovely cottage in Aldeburgh, then you moved back to the flat …'

Hannah frowned. She didn't need to be reminded of all the moves while Lili and Nate had been in the same house all along, getting on with their lives.

'And now you've moved out of Aldeburgh,' Lili continued. 'I think she's worried about getting to school on Monday.'

'Nothing's going to change. I told her she can still meet her friend at the entrance to Cobblers Yard and walk with her and her friend's mum to school as normal.'

Lili fell silent.

Hannah sighed. 'What else has she said?'

Hannah noticed that Lili lowered her voice as she spoke. 'She's worried that she'll get all settled in and then you'll be moving again, like the last time with the cottage.'

Hannah sat up. 'That's not going to happen. I told you, I love it here.'

'But you loved the cottage …' Lili trailed off.

Hannah had not expected the third degree about her living arrangements. 'Look, the shop is doing well …'

Sort of, she thought.

'Is it?'

Hannah knew why Lili was questioning that. It had been dead quiet when Lili had popped into the shop, although there had been some customers eventually.

Hannah raised her eyes to look at the painting. *The good-luck charm isn't in the window anymore.* She didn't want to think about that. At least she still had the airgraphs. Thinking of which, she said, 'Look, I've come into a bit of money.' At least she would if she sold them to the highest bidder.

'Really?'

'Yes. I'll tell you all about it when you drop Maisie home tomorrow.'

'You're not collecting her and having Sunday dinner with us?'

'No – I thought it would be nice if you, Nate and William joined me and Maisie here in our new home for Sunday lunch instead.' Hannah thought it might help Maisie settle in, having everyone round. 'We could make a little occasion of it.'

'Ah, we've invited Sarah and Ray to Sunday dinner with us tomorrow.'

'Oh.'

Lili asked, 'Have you got enough room around the dinner table for two more? I know Ray helped you with the move, but I'm sure Sarah would love to see her granddaughter's new home. I think she's a bit disappointed that you've moved out of Aldeburgh, to be honest.'

Hannah knew why – Sarah loved Maisie popping round to her house once a week after school for tea.

'Nothing is going to change. She can still go round to Sarah's after school once a week.'

'She'll love to hear that, Hannah. So, have you got room for two more?'

Hannah just needed to get hold of some more chairs. 'Yes.'

'Great. I'll let them know. As we're all getting together, it could be like a housewarming party.'

'Oh, I love the sound of that,' Hannah said excitedly. 'You're so full of good ideas.'

Thinking of good ideas, Hannah remembered her ulterior motive for inviting them over to hers. 'If you get here a bit early, I could show you round Somersby House. They're having an auction later in the afternoon – of course, you could attend if you wanted to, but I thought you'd like to see the house and grounds before everyone arrived for the auction.'

'A private tour? Amazing. I've passed by Somersby Hall a couple of times, on my way to a gardening job, and glanced up the long drive at the magnificent house, thinking I'd love an excuse to visit.'

Hannah smiled when Lili called it a magnificent house. 'Well, now you have that excuse.'

'I never thought I'd get a chance to look inside the hall. You must have a lovely landlord if they let you take your friends round their home.'

'Landlady,' Hannah corrected her. She frowned when she thought of Lady Jemima. She wouldn't call her lovely. Not after the conversation she'd overheard.

Hannah wasn't going to ask Lady Jemima if she could show her friend around the house. When she saw Rupert that evening as planned, she'd ask him. Of course, he'd agree to Hannah giving the bride-to-be a tour of the house. She needed to talk to Lili about the idea of holding her wedding there and then let Lili talk to Nate. She had a feeling it had been Nate's idea to hold their wedding at his house, and she didn't want to discuss it over the phone.

Hannah thought it best to show Lili the house first. When Lili fell in love with the place, Hannah was sure she wouldn't resist the idea, especially as there would be no cost to them using the hall. As long as Lili was happy with the trade-off – working her gardening magic on the grounds.

'I'm excited to hear all about this money you've come into,' said Lili. 'How much is it?'

The money from selling the airgraphs wouldn't save them from being turfed out of Gatekeeper's Cottage if the wedding idea didn't work. *Lili has to say yes to holding her wedding here*, thought Hannah, biting her lip. She desperately wanted to ask her now, but she knew she had to stick to the plan.

'Hannah?'

'I'm not sure how much yet. I'll tell you all about it tomorrow.'

It was silly really – the thought that someone might be listening in on their conversation. She rarely used a landline. Hannah thought it was rather childish, perhaps, but she'd phoned Lili using the old seventies phone, which she'd discovered actually worked – it had a ring tone and was still connected. She liked the feel of the chunky phone receiver in her hand.

'Ooh, can't you just give me a little hint?'

'I don't want to talk about it over the phone.'

'Sounds mysterious.'

Hannah thought of the old woman calling herself Lady Jemima. She was back to thinking – *what happened to the real Lady Jemima?*

Hannah heard Maisie's voice in the background, and Lili say, 'Of course you can speak to your mum. Hold on …'

'Mum?'

'Hello, sweetheart!' Hannah said, hiding her surprise. Maisie never normally wanted to speak to her when she was staying over at Nate's house. She was only ever gone one night, and normally she was too busy to think of her mum.

'Everything okay?'

'Yes.'

Hannah guessed she just wanted some reassurance. After all, she had just moved house the night before her sleepover. Hannah told her what she'd been up to, unpacking, and how lovely and cosy Gatekeeper's Cottage was now she'd unpacked all the boxes.

'Grandma Sarah said she's got a surprise for me. A moving-in present. She won't tell me what it is, though. She said she's bringing it over this morning. I wanted to find out if she'd delivered it yet.'

'Ah – so that's why you wanted to speak to me.' Hannah grinned, relieved that Maisie hadn't wanted to talk to her because she was unhappy about the prospect of going home to Gatekeeper's Cottage. It hadn't occurred to her until then that that might have been the case, and that she might ask to stay on at Nate's instead.

She thought, *I must thank Sarah for the idea of a moving-in present to get Maisie settled.* 'I'm going to give your grandmother a big hug when she comes round.'

'Will you phone me and tell me what it is?'

'Absolutely not!' Hannah said, grinning. 'It's a surprise, remember? Besides, I don't want to get into trouble with Grandma Sarah if I tell you what it is.'

'All right, Mum.'

'Good girl. Now you go and enjoy yourself and have a good night tonight. I'm going to be busy this evening, so I'm sending you hugs and kisses now, and a goodnight kiss down the phone.' Hannah blew her a kiss down the phone that sounded like a rather rude raspberry instead.

Maisie laughed and then blew her one back. She fell silent for a moment afterwards, before she asked, 'Are you going on a date?'

'No! Why do you ask?'

'Because you said you're busy this evening.'

Hannah thought of seeing Rupert in his study that evening to talk over the wedding plans. It was a bit presumptuous to do so before she'd even asked Lili, but this way round, at least if Lili agreed, she could present her with the plan and they could get the ball rolling quickly.

Hannah said, 'I'll see you tomorrow, sweetheart. You're all coming here for Sunday lunch. How's about that?'

'Yippee! I can show William my surprise.'

'Love you!'

'Bye, love you too.'

The next thing Hannah heard was Lili's voice. 'I didn't know Sarah was popping round to yours with a moving-in present for Maisie.'

'Neither did I.'

At that moment, Hannah heard her phone buzz with a text message. 'Ah, I've got a text.' Hannah reached for her mobile. She'd left it on the dresser. Sure enough, it was Sarah.

'Is it from Sarah?'

'Yes. She's on her way. I can't wait to see her. I told Maisie I'm going to give Sarah a big hug for being so thoughtful and getting her a moving-in present.'

17

Hannah did not want to hug Sarah when she walked in carrying Maisie's moving-in present.

'What is *that*?'

'Oh.' Sarah looked at her in surprise. 'I thought you discussed this with Maisie. She told me she'd be getting a pet when you moved into your next house.'

'Yes, but—'

'She said you promised.'

'I did. We've only just moved in, though, so I didn't have time to—'

'I thought not. It's enough going through a move without trying to look for a pet too. I do understand …'

But you don't, thought Hannah. *I was going to get her a budgie or a hamster.*

'I imagine you were feeling ever so guilty that you haven't fulfilled that promise yet. I imagine she was badgering you the first night you moved in.'

'Yes, she did remind me about my promise. I've got to be honest, I thought she'd forgotten about it.'

Sarah smiled. 'That's my grandchild for you – she never

forgets a promise. So, anyway, I thought I'd lend a helping hand.'

'But I wanted to choose the pet myself with Maisie.'

'I thought you'd say that. When I found out you were moving, I kind of covertly started asking Maisie questions about what sort of pet she wanted.'

Hannah frowned. 'Anything with four paws, a waggy tail, and a woof.'

'Yes, so I gathered. And here we are.'

She sighed, looking at the black puppy in Sarah's arms. What on earth was she going to do with it? She didn't have time for a puppy. And the cottage was small. Did they have the room?

'My friend's beautiful pet had a litter.'

'What sort of puppy is it?' Hannah asked as Sarah put the puppy down in the lounge. She hoped the puppy didn't do a diddle on the rug.

'A Labrador.'

Oh, my god, Hannah thought.

'Sarah, this place is far too small for a—'

'Nonsense! They are very adaptable. And besides, you have a large garden.'

'No, I do not.'

'But I saw it when I pulled into the parking space next to your car at the side of the cottage.'

'That's the front lawn of Somersby Hall.'

'Ah. Well, I'm sure they wouldn't mind if you walked the dog there on occasion.'

'You don't know Lady Jemima.'

'Who?'

'My landlady.' Thinking of whom, Hannah said, 'I don't even know if I'm allowed pets here.'

'You are – I checked.'

'You did?'

'Yes, of course, with the letting agent. I wouldn't be that irresponsible, would I?'

What do you call this, landing me with a puppy without checking with me first? Hannah thought.

'Now, I'll just go fetch his things.'

'His things?'

'Yes, I bought a basket, and blanket, toys, food bowls, food, comfort blanket …'

Hannah listened to the endless list before Sarah walked out of Gatekeeper's Cottage, leaving her in the lounge with the puppy, who was sniffing the rug. 'Please, do *not* go on the rug.'

'His name is Marlowe, by the way,' Sarah called out from the door.

The dog's sniffy nose made its way to her shoe. He whined.

'Oh, don't cry.' Hannah's heart melted in an instant. She sat on the floor beside the puppy, giving him a tentative stroke. 'You're missing your mummy and litter mates, aren't you?'

He climbed in her lap, or tried to. Hannah picked him up. He settled on her lap and stood up on his hind legs, front paws on her chest, sniffing her blouse, then biting her buttons. 'Hey.'

'Ah, good, you're making friends,' said Sarah, depositing a soft dog bed in the corner by the fireplace. 'Here all right?'

'I guess so,' Hannah replied, looking at the dog bed in bemusement. She didn't know what she had been expecting when Sarah turned up with Maisie's moving-in present, but it was certainly not a conversation over the best spot in the lounge for a dog bed.

A few minutes later, Sarah had brought in the rest of the

puppy's things, along with a chew toy. Sarah dangled it in front of Marlowe. His jaws closed around it. He sat happily on Hannah's lap with his chew toy while Hannah listened to Sarah opening cupboards in the kitchen until she found an empty one. She could hear her emptying the contents of a plastic bag full of puppy food tins into the cupboard. Then she heard Sarah put the kettle on.

When Sarah walked into the lounge, Hannah had to be honest. She looked at the puppy and said, 'Sarah, this is really lovely of you. So kind. But I just don't think I can accept such a—'

'I thought you'd say that. I wanted to do this for Maisie.'

'I realise that.' Hannah also realised that Sarah didn't understand what she was getting at. She couldn't afford a dog, and she didn't have the time for a puppy. She was going to say she couldn't accept such a responsibility.

'And I wanted to do it for you,' Sarah added.

'For *me*?'

'This puppy is as much for you as he is for Maisie.'

'But I don't need a dog.'

'You will.'

'What do you mean?'

'I imagine it feels lonely on those weekends when she's staying over at Nate's house.'

Hannah nodded, admitting that it did.

'Well, it's only set to get worse – trust me.'

'She's talked about staying at Nate's house more often?' Hannah said in alarm.

'No, I don't mean that. Maisie is getting older. It won't be long before she'll want to go out with her friends, and go for sleepovers with them instead. Very soon you'll find her more out than in.'

Hannah stared at her. Of course, it had crossed her mind that her daughter was growing up, more times than she cared to admit.

'I know you're thinking of the practicalities, the time, and the expense of owning a dog.'

'I am, Sarah.'

'I just know he's the perfect fit for you, Hannah. Labradors are people-pleasers. So easy to train. All they want to do is please their owners. You can take him to work with you. He'll be no bother. After a walk, they like nothing more than having a nice nap, lounging around. I'll help you out with the cost.'

Hannah thought of all the things she'd already bought, along with the puppy. She'd already spent far too much. 'I couldn't possibly take your money.'

'I knew you'd say that, so I'm going to increase Maisie's allowance on the proviso that she spends it on taking care of her dog.'

'You seem to have thought of everything.'

'I have. Ray doesn't mind popping round, dog-sitting if required, and I'm sure he wouldn't mind some puppy training thrown in. Now, how about it? I will obviously take him home with me now, so that Maisie will be none the wiser, if it's still a no.'

Hannah looked down at the puppy, who had flopped down on her lap, little head resting on her arm, eyes closed. She looked up at Sarah. She could have brought the puppy round the next day when everyone was there or gone straight to Nate's house and given him to Maisie. But she hadn't. She'd brought him over to Hannah for her to fall in love with him first.

'Oh, my god,' she breathed. 'I'm a puppy parent.' She eyed Sarah. 'You knew this would happen – didn't you?'

Sarah grinned. 'He's adorable, isn't he? You can change his name, if you want.'

Hannah shook her head as she soft stroked him. 'No, Marlowe suits him.'

'Well, that's just as well.' Sarah handed her a soft dog collar. Hanging from it was a round silver disc. Hannah read the inscription. It had his name, her name, and her mobile phone number. 'There, you're all set for your next adventure. It won't be long, and as my friend said, you won't be able to imagine your home without him.'

Hannah felt a tear roll down her cheek. 'You know, Maisie is going to be beside herself when she sees him. She's been asking me for a dog for so long and I know she thinks it's never going to happen.'

'I think there are going to be tears tomorrow.'

Hannah smiled. 'I think you're right. By the way, talking about tomorrow, you're all coming to Sunday lunch here instead of Nate's. Lili said it could be like a little housewarming party.'

'What a wonderful idea.'

'I just wish …' Hannah looked around her cosy lounge.

Sarah followed her gaze. 'You wish this house was yours.'

'Yes.' Hannah met her gaze.

'Well, it's yours for now,' said Sarah. 'And who knows where things might lead in the future. Perhaps they'd consider selling Gatekeeper's Cottage.'

Hannah hadn't thought of that. Of course, they could release some cash by selling some of the estate. It wasn't large, but Gatekeeper's Cottage would be the obvious choice. She wasn't sure that made her feel any better. Would she be able to afford it?

'I've heard that the owner of the hall is in a bit of financial trouble,' said Sarah, perching on the arm of the sofa.

'Where did you hear that?' Hannah immediately knew that it was a silly question.

'The Gossip Girls,' Sarah replied, smiling.

'Do you know her – Lady Jemima, the owner?'

'No, she keeps herself to herself, doesn't she? Funny place, Somersby Hall. None of the occupants, staff included, ever mixed with the local community. Very insular, I think. At least that's what I've heard. It's quite strange,' she added, staring off into space. 'It's almost as though …'

'Almost as though …?' Hannah prompted.

'Oh, never mind – it will sound daft.'

'No, please do go on. What were you going to say?'

'Mabel and Marjorie obviously heard snippets about the hall over the years. From some of the things they've said it's almost as though the people who lived there, including the staff, closed ranks to protect a secret.'

Hannah stared at her. Now would be the time to tell Sarah what she'd overheard Percy call Lady Jemima. But she hesitated. She knew why – Rupert.

'There, I told you it would sound daft.' Sarah shrugged. 'But you know The Gossip Girls. Best to take anything they say with a pinch of salt.' She picked up her handbag and stood.

Hannah looked up at her. 'Oh, you're leaving already? I thought you were staying for a cup of tea?'

'No, but that reminds me, I was just going to make you one

before I popped off. I've got an art class starting in half an hour.'

Hannah stared at the puppy. She hadn't felt this scared since she'd brought Maisie home as a newborn baby from the hospital.

Sarah read her mind. 'You'll be fine, Hannah. Feed, poop, play, sleep. That's about it for now.'

Sarah walked into the kitchen and returned with a cup of tea. 'I've made it sweet, as I think you'll need to sit there for a bit and get over the shock of the sudden new addition to your family. Sorry about that.' Sarah grinned, not sorry at all.

A new addition to *my* family. Hannah liked the sound of that. She smiled up at Sarah as she carefully took the mug of tea, and said, 'You're right, you know, about Maisie. I think this is just what I need.' She caught sight of the painting hanging over her fireplace. She hadn't just hung that painting. She had put up some of Maisie's artwork on the walls. The gardener who'd lived there before hadn't removed the picture hooks. They'd come in handy. But it had made her think. 'I haven't done wrong by Maisie, have I, keeping her talent under wraps? Sometimes I think I'm being selfish wanting to keep her to myself.'

Sarah patted her on the shoulder. 'Not at all. I'd do the same thing if I were in your shoes. It's a mother's instinct to protect your children for as long as possible from the outside world. Maisie, with her talent, will need protecting more than most. Ray and I, we're just so happy that you're her mother. Some would exploit her for financial gain.'

'I'd never do that.'

'We know.'

Sarah was just on her way out, when she suddenly stopped and turned around. She pointed at the fireplace. 'Lovely painting you have there, by the way.'

'It's the one from the shop window that I was going to show you.'

'I'm glad you didn't sell it, and you brought it home instead.'

'So am I,' Hannah replied, thinking about Lady Jemima wanting to get her hands on it. Hannah kept that thought to herself. 'It's called *Sunrise Over Seashell Bay*. Do you recognise the beach, by any chance?'

Sarah shook her head. 'Might just be a figment of the artist's imagination.'

Hannah frowned. Sarah wasn't the first person to say that.

As she turned to go, Hannah called after her, 'Sarah – about the painting …'

She backtracked to the lounge, popping her head around the doorway. Hannah saw her glancing at her wristwatch as she said, 'Yes?'

'Never mind. It can wait.'

'I don't recognise the artist – if that's what you were going to ask me.'

It wasn't. Hannah had been going to show her the airgraphs and tell her about the strange conversation she'd overheard between Lady Jemima and Percy, when Percy had called her Kitty. But Sarah was in a hurry, and the puppy was fast asleep in Hannah's lap. Clearly, it was not the time.

'Well, I'm off now.' She quickly walked into the lounge and patted the puppy on the head. 'Now, you be a good puppy, Marlowe.'

Marlowe stirred, his little tail wagged, but he didn't wake up.

Sarah marched to the door and then did an about-turn. 'Oh, by the way, Hannah, the puppy's name was Ray's idea. He's named after the famous detective.'

Hannah looked at her blankly.

'Philip Marlowe – Raymond Chandler's famous fictional hard-boiled detective in his novels?'

'Sorry, doesn't ring any bells.'

Sarah smiled. 'Before your time. Are you sure you don't want to rename him? I don't mind ordering another name disc online if you do.'

Hannah shook her head. 'No, not at all. Like I said, it suits him.'

'Good. Now, I'd really love to hang around and chat more, but I must go. See you tomorrow.'

Sarah heard the front door close and the clunk of Sarah's car door, and then her engine revving as she backed off the driveway.

Hannah gazed at Marlowe. 'Now what am I going to do?' She was sitting on a cushion on the floor, legs crossed, with a sleeping puppy in her lap that she didn't want to disturb. Despite all her misgivings about getting Maisie a dog, she couldn't wait to see her face when she found out her dream had come true. She smiled at the thought of lots of paintings of a black Labrador puppy hanging on her walls very soon – that was, if Maisie could tear herself away from her puppy for long enough to paint him.

Hannah sat, gently stroking the sleeping puppy, thinking of Rupert. She was wondering how things were going with the auctioneer and the valuation of the items to be included in the auction.

18

Rupert eyed her as she walked around the room, stopping at each item to be valued. He followed in her wake. She was a lot younger than he'd expected, which didn't fill him with a lot of confidence, especially as she was late. Although it wasn't as though she was late for the auction itself, they'd still agreed a time for her to arrive to value the items. She hadn't even apologised.

'Look,' she turned around to face him. 'I'm sorry I was late for our appointment.'

A little late for an apology, thought Rupert, *she's been here half an hour already*. He shrugged. 'Well, you're here now.' He looked at her, perfectly turned out in a trouser suit and makeup, her chestnut hair falling below her shoulders in perfect waves. He reckoned she'd probably made herself late because she was doing her hair. She reminded him of Claudia, who spent an age every morning on her makeup routine – and that was without the time it took to perfect those waves.

Rupert anticipated the excuse – traffic. He thought he'd save her the trouble. 'Traffic bad?'

'Not at all.'

He looked at her in surprise. She could at least lie and come up with something by way of an excuse.

'This house is amazing. Can I be terribly forward and ask for a tour of the house when I'm done? I've always loved grand houses such as this. I'm a National Trust member, you know.'

Rupert didn't know what to say to the abrupt change of subject.

'You're so lucky having this house in the family. I expect you'll inherit it one day.'

Rupert frowned. 'It's a responsibility, a house this size, and a money pit, so no, I wouldn't call myself lucky.'

'Is that why you're having the auction?'

'No, we love to sell off our personal possessions, and have every Tom, Dick and Harry come to gawp at our stuff and our house.' Rupert immediately felt embarrassed at his outburst. It wasn't her fault that they were in a financial predicament, even though he did think she was being rather forward in asking about it. All the same, he said, 'Sorry. That was uncalled for.'

'Don't be. I'll get the best prices I can, I promise. I'm going to set the highest reserve prices I think I can get away with.'

'Thank you, Henrietta.' It occurred to him, a bit belatedly, that he shouldn't bite the hand that was feeding him. He needed her on his side to get the best possible prices and earn the most he could from the auction.

'Call me Hetty, please.'

'All right, Hetty.' Rupert smiled in relief that she hadn't taken offence. 'Look, I think we got off on the wrong foot.' Rupert knew he hadn't exactly been welcoming when she'd first arrived. She must have sensed the atmosphere.

He was aware that he seemed to be making a habit of that –

first with Hannah, now with Hetty.

'It was my fault for turning up so late.'

'Oh, I wasn't blaming you.'

'Like I said, I'm so sorry I missed our appointment time. This is my very first auction and I can't afford to screw it up. I work freelance, you see, so getting another assignment depends on the success of this one.'

Then why turn up late? thought Rupert.

'We had some bad news, my flatmates and me. We've been given notice to quit our rental apartment.'

'Oh, I'm so sorry.'

I had a sleepless night, last night, and I missed the alarm. I can't apologise enough. I should have said something when I first arrived, but I was just afraid you might change your mind and turn me away.'

Rupert shook his head, about to say he wouldn't do that.

'I've been so happy living there. I don't know what I'm going to do now. We've heard from other friends what it's like at the moment – rentals are in short supply, and there's more demand than there are the properties to rent. We've heard they often go for more than advertised.'

'I'm really sorry to hear that. I know what you mean about the rental market in London,' said Rupert, commiserating. 'I rent there too. I'm not made of money either – I work freelance too as an art dealer, and to be honest if it wasn't for my fiancée and her salary, and her bonuses as a banker, I couldn't afford to rent in London. I don't know where I'd live.'

'If I was in your shoes, I'd live here. It's not a bad commute into London.'

'That's not going to happen. My fiancée doesn't like it here.'

'You are joking.'

'No, I'm afraid not.' Rupert would rather not repeat what she'd said about the house, or rather its owner. He had a feeling that even if his grandmother was out of the picture, Claudia still wouldn't live there. The countryside and the Suffolk Coast just weren't for her. She liked the city.

He retreated to the door, watching Hetty finish making notes on the items. When she'd finished, she walked over to join him. 'So, when I get back to my hotel room, I've just got a bit of research to do online before I confirm the reserve prices of some of the items.'

'Okay. Where are you staying?'

'Um, it's not a hotel actually. I've got a room at a pub in Aldeburgh. The hotels round here are really expensive, but I didn't want there to be any chance I'd get held up tomorrow if I returned home this evening. It would be just my luck if there was an accident on the motorway and I got stuck in a huge traffic jam. I just didn't want to risk missing the auction.'

Rupert smiled at her. She was freelance, so staying overnight was at her own expense. After his initial misgivings that she wasn't up to the job, he now felt a lot more confident. In fact, he was so confident that the auction would go smoothly that he was rather looking forward to it. Thanks to Hetty, that was one less thing to worry about.

'When I've completed my bit of research online this evening, I'll email you the reserve prices for all the items, along with my projection for what they should ideally fetch at auction. Obviously, that will very much depend on the day, and your buyers.'

'Thank you, Hetty.' They walked out into the hallway. 'Would you like that tour of the house you mentioned now, before you go?'

'Really? Are you sure?'

'Of course – why not?'

Hetty hastily put her notebook back in her large handbag and said excitedly, 'Lead the way!'

❖

'It's just gorgeous – why wouldn't anyone want to live here?' said Hetty, part-way through the tour and clearly enjoying it immensely, mentioning in passing that her grandmother had once lived in a stately home before she was married. They were on the first floor, where Rupert had showed her around some of the bedrooms, excluding his grandmother's, of course. He'd asked if Hetty wouldn't mind creeping past her bedroom quietly so as not to disturb her.

He hadn't told her the real reason for avoiding his grandmother. He thought it best that she didn't know he was giving the auctioneer a tour of the house. She wouldn't like it. She didn't like strangers in her house. Then again, she had agreed to use the place as a wedding venue. He still thought it odd that she'd agreed.

They climbed the narrow back staircase to the unused west wing, dust blooming in the golden shaft of light from the landing window. The corridor was lined with ageing portraits and fading wallpaper.

Rupert said off-hand, 'Do you think this house would make a good wedding venue?' He brushed a cobweb from one of the paintings lining the hall. 'I realise it needs some work.' He didn't think they could have wedding guests actually staying at the house for the very first wedding there – they'd need to wait until they had the money to do up that wing. The guests would have to make their own arrangements in the meantime.

'A wedding venue? You mean like having guests to stay here, and a sit-down meal in the beautiful dining room overlooking the garden, and photos on the lawn with this gorgeous house at a backdrop?'

Rupert smiled. 'I take it you think it would?'

'Oh, yes,' she said enthusiastically. 'I'd have my wedding here.'

'Are you engaged?' Rupert was thinking that if Hannah's friend, Lili, backed out for any reason, even though Hannah was adamant her friend would have her wedding there, then he might just have an alternative couple.

'No, I'm not engaged, but if you go ahead with your plans, I'll get married here, no question. When I've found the right person.'

He was a little disappointed she wasn't engaged and so wouldn't be getting married any time soon. Even so, getting her take on the wedding venue idea was still invaluable.

'Of course, I'm biased because I adore this house,' said Hetty, 'but then who wouldn't?'

Rupert agreed, up to a point. He was thinking of Claudia. 'I spent my early years living here, so it's nice to get an outsider's perspective.'

'So, what's down here?' Hetty asked, skipping ahead and stopping to look down another rarely used hallway. Oak panelling adorned the lower half of the walls, and above were paintings of Rupert's forebears. 'Ah, more bedrooms. Not very exciting, I'm afraid.'

'Oh, but it is. Fancy having life-sized portraits of your ancestors – so posh,' she said.

Rupert smiled. He supposed it was.

'I'm not jealous really,' she said with a grin.

She skipped by, glancing at each one. 'You've got enough bedrooms here to accommodate wedding guests.'

Rupert realised they could have accommodated Hetty. He felt a little guilty for not inviting her to stay at the house overnight. But he knew there was no use suggesting it; his grandmother would have the final say. It was her house, after all, and she'd say no. He had been surprised she'd rented out Gatekeeper's Cottage, but that was at the end of the drive.

Rupert said, 'It's not a huge house. We couldn't accommodate large weddings.'

'That's true,' Hetty agreed as she examined another painting. 'Immediate family and friends could stay here, then anyone else could just travel to the venue and stay for the meal and the wedding party afterwards.'

'Yes, that's an idea, but the dining room can only accommodate so many for a sit-down meal, so we were thinking of smaller, more intimate weddings.'

Hetty turned around to face him. 'You and your grandmother came up with the idea?'

'Actually, it was my tenant's idea.'

'Oh, you have a tenant living here?'

'No, at Gatekeeper's Cottage.'

'Is that the little cottage I saw at the end of the drive? I noticed it on my way in.'

'Yes.'

'Lucky them.'

Rupert caught the tone in her voice, verging on sarcasm. He imagined she was thinking of her own situation.

Rupert felt sorry for her. It was tough trying to hold down a job and pay rent. It sounded as though she was single too, with no partner's income so they could pool resources and share costs.

Rupert's mind drifted to Hannah. He hadn't considered how tough things must be for her. She was trying to make her way in the world, like Hetty, but she was a single parent too. He didn't know her personal circumstances, apart from the fact that her daughter's father lived locally, but he hoped the wedding idea worked out – for her as well as for Somersby Hall.

He had phoned the letting agency when he'd found out that his grandmother had let Gatekeeper's Cottage. He'd discovered the young lady who'd signed the rental agreement had a glowing recommendation from the previous landlord she'd rented from and that she ran her own business – a shop in Aldeburgh. That explained her entrepreneurial spirit, thought Rupert. She loved the hall too and clearly wanted to save it from being sold. Of course, he realised she had her own motive too – her home was Gatekeeper's Cottage. If they sold the house, her home might be sold too, but that meant she was motivated, as was he.

He just wished he hadn't been such an arse by initially refusing to work with her on her wedding idea. He'd looked a gift horse in the mouth without realising it.

Well, I realise it now, he thought, hoping she turned up that evening and that the wedding idea was on. He really didn't think he could pull it off without her. It wasn't just that, though. He thought it could be the start of a long working relationship. Rupert liked that idea a lot – and not just earning the money, and saving this house, but having an excuse to see Hannah every day.

'Hey, this lady looks like me.'

Rupert's thoughts were interrupted by Hetty, who had paused further along the hall. She was standing in front of a painting.

Rupert strolled down the hallway and stood beside her. He hadn't really taken a lot of notice of these paintings. In fact, he'd rarely ventured down this corridor since he was a child – apart from a few days earlier when he had been in search of his grandmother's elusive painting.

He looked at the painting. The subject did indeed bear a striking resemblance to Hetty. In fact, it could *be* her if it wasn't for the Victorian clothing that his ancestor wore.

He turned to look at Hetty.

She grinned. 'What's that saying – everybody has a doppelgänger? Guess I found mine!'

Rupert stared after her as she continued down the hallway. 'I guess so.' He turned back to the painting.

19

The sun was beginning to dip behind the trees as Hannah drove up to Somersby Hall, the letters tucked in her bag. She didn't know whether it was the right time to confront Rupert with what she'd overheard and show him the airgraphs. If Lady Jemima was really Kitty and had been masquerading as her all these decades – Hannah didn't know for how long – that meant Rupert might not be the true heir to Somersby Hall.

Everything he'd ever believed about himself and his family background was built on a lie if his grandmother wasn't Lady Jemima. Worse still, what had happened to the real Lady Jemima?

Hannah looked up at the house. It stood solemn against the fading light, ivy clinging to its timeworn stone like secrets refusing to be shaken loose. She left the letters in the car. Then she had a change of heart. What if he knew? Or what if Kitty was simply a nickname, nothing more, and her imagination had run away with her?

Ray was right when he'd said, *we really mustn't make assumptions, we need facts,* after they'd talked at length about the contents of the letters. Ray had told her that in his experience, nothing was ever quite what it seemed.

He had remarked that the letters gave away nothing about who Kitty was, nor Owen Hartley – apart from his wartime service, along with his talent for painting and for writing beautiful, heartfelt love letters.

Hannah knew she couldn't show the airgraphs to Lady Jemima – the one person who could answer all her questions – without risking her tenancy when she discovered her new tenant was indeed *the enemy*, as she called her, snooping around her home, her past. Hannah was heeding Thea's advice – up to a point.

Hannah decided instead that she would ask Lady Jemima's innocent grandson if he could remember a woman called Kitty at Somersby Hall, or if he'd heard the name. She wished she'd asked that question when she'd talked to him before about his grandmother's name without revealing her reasons. She knew why she hadn't mentioned what she'd overheard then – she'd had to find out whether he was in the know.

Clearly, he wasn't. Now she decided to ask him outright. She also intended to ask him whether he knew of someone called Owen Hartley. His grandmother had Owen's painting hanging in her bedroom, and she'd asked him to search the house for *Sunrise Over Seashell Bay*. Did he know of the painter? Had she mentioned his name to Rupert?

Rupert answered the front door, sleeves rolled up, a smudge of ink on his forearm. 'Hannah,' he said, surprised, glancing at her car. 'Everything alright?'

'Ah, I was just going to make my way round the side of the house and come in through the patio door into the dining room like you asked.'

'I heard a car, so I came to the front door.' He smiled. 'I'm so pleased you came.'

'How was your meeting with the auctioneer?' Hannah asked as she stepped into the hallway and followed him through the dining room and into his study, where an open fire crackled in the hearth and a mug of coffee steamed beside a thick folder of estate documents.

'Hope it's not too warm in here – it's just that this room can be a bit damp.'

'No, it's fine. It's very … cosy. Love a real fire.'

'So do I. Even with the warm autumn weather we're having, I still like to get a real fire going for the cool evenings. Adds a bit of atmosphere as well.'

'Yes, it does. I'm looking forward to using the wood burner in the cottage.' They exchanged a smile. Hannah was enjoying them agreeing over things. She felt it was a good omen that they'd get on well working together after all.

'Would you like a cup of tea or coffee?'

Hannah could smell Rupert's coffee. 'Coffee, please.'

He poured her a mug from a coffee machine on the sideboard. 'How do you like your coffee?'

From Mabel's coffee machine, thought Hannah, suppressing a smile. 'Black with two sugars, please,' she said instead.

He handed her a mug.

She took a tentative sip. 'Hey, this is really good,' she said in surprise.

'Yeah, it's a really old coffee-maker, belonged to my father. I think he would have taken it with him if we hadn't suddenly—'

Hannah lowered her coffee mug, wondering what he was going to say. Was it something to do with his father and grandmother's estrangement? In the awkward silence, she decided to ask after the meeting with the auctioneer again.

'The meeting went really well, actually.' She noticed he seemed relieved she'd changed the subject. 'She said she's going to give me the best possible valuation and email me the opening price along with a ballpark figure for what the items might fetch.'

'She sounds quite organised. That's good.'

'Yes, I thought so for someone so young. She's younger than I expected.'

He fell silent.

'You seem preoccupied.'

'It's nothing.'

'Well, it must be something.' Hannah frowned. 'You haven't changed your mind about the wedding idea, have you? If that's the case, please just tell me—'

'No, no – not at all.' Rupert turned to her and took her hands in his. 'On the contrary, I was worried you'd change your mind and wouldn't come this evening.'

Hannah looked down at his hands in hers. His touch sent shivers down her spine. She had the impulse to draw him close.

'Oh, sorry.' He let go of her hands.

Don't be, she wanted to say. *You can hold my hands any time, or take me in your arms, or kiss me.*

She looked away, embarrassed. He had a fiancée.

Rupert cleared his throat. 'Ahem. Well, let's get down to planning our new business – shall we? Oh, I mean your business. It was your idea, after all.'

'No, no. We're in this together.'

He smiled his disarming smile.

Hannah felt like cursing. Why did he have to have such a gorgeous smile? She was starting to wonder if maybe it wasn't a good idea; she wasn't thinking of the wedding idea, but of working with Rupert. Originally, she'd thought she'd hate working with him because he'd been such an arse and would do his best to sabotage it. Now, she wished he wasn't being so nice to her. She sighed. If only he was single. *Not that he'd be interested in me*, she thought Hannah, *even if things don't work out with Claudia.* I'm a single parent. My life is complicated.

'There *is* something on your mind, though,' Hannah probed.

Rupert sighed. 'It's the strangest thing. Henrietta …'

'Henrietta?'

'The auctioneer.'

'You're on first-name basis already?'

'Actually, she asked me to call her Hetty.'

'Right.' Hannah inwardly sighed.

'She said she loves the house.'

Hannah tried not to frown at the thought that an attractive young woman had met with Rupert that day, even though it was only on business. Hannah had seen her fleetingly as she passed in the car and had caught sight of her beautifully wavy chestnut hair. She'd looked to be a very pretty young woman.

I'm young too, thought Hannah. But she knew she wasn't young and carefree. She imagined she came across as older than her years – it was inevitable, with her being a mother and a single parent and having all that responsibility. And she didn't have time to take care of herself as much as she would have liked – having her nails done, styling her hair.

Sometimes she straightened her blonde bob, which only took minutes. She supposed that if she had time, she could style it into soft waves, accentuating her cheekbones.

Her make up-routine was almost non-existent, apart from a

little bit of blush on her cheeks, her go-to mascara, and some lippy. Gone were the days where she took time over her appearance, sporting a full face of makeup and spending all her spare cash on clothes for herself just to impress her boyfriends. She had never liked the person she had presented herself as, the way she had dressed or behaved. It just wasn't her.

If I can't meet someone who can love me for who I am, rather than what they want me to be, Hannah decided, *then I'd rather be on my own*. Remarkably, for someone who'd thought she was one of those people who just couldn't survive on her own, who had to be in a relationship, being single had turned out to be the best decision she'd ever made. Now she wasn't looking for a relationship just because she couldn't hack being on her own; she was looking for love. The kind of love Ray and Sarah had, and Owen and Kitty. Hannah was never going to settle for anything less ever again. And if she was single for the rest of her life as a result, then so be it.

20

Hannah had been drinking her coffee and thinking about remaining single for the rest of her life as she stared off into space when her gaze settled on Rupert.

He was sitting on the leather chair behind his desk across the room, smiling at her. For a split second, she wished she'd made more of an effort with her hair, makeup and outfit – she was still wearing the same dungarees, t-shirt and flannel shirt she'd been wearing to unpack dusty packing boxes. Then she reminded herself she wasn't going to doll herself up for any man ever again – unless of course they were already in a relationship and were having an evening out.

Besides, this wasn't a date; this was a work meeting. And Rupert was unavailable.

He sat back in his chair, still smiling at her.

Hannah lowered her mug. 'What?'

'Hetty says turning the house into a wedding venue is a fantastic idea.'

'You spoke to her about our idea?' Hannah felt irrationally betrayed that he'd spoken to her about it, as though he'd shared something intimate that was just between the two of them. She silently admonished herself for being so silly, realising with a start that she was being a little possessive of Rupert, jealous of him speaking with another young woman.

'Yes, it was interesting to get another perspective.'

'And what was that?' Hannah asked coolly.

'Just what I said – that she thought it was a fantastic idea. She said she'd get married here herself.'

'She did?' Hannah brightened. 'Well, we must book her and her partner in, then.'

'No can do, I'm afraid.'

'How come? Oh, she hasn't got the money?'

'Probably not, but money isn't the issue right now. She's not with anyone at the moment.'

Hannah rolled her eyes. Why was she not surprised? She guessed who this Hetty would like to get married to in the house, given half the chance.

Rupert caught her rolling her eyes. 'What?'

'Nothing.'

'It was strange, though …' said Rupert thoughtfully.

Hannah stared at him. Was he going to share what had been on his mind a moment earlier? She'd cut across that when they'd got on to the subject of Henrietta – Hetty – and Hannah had got all riled over the thought of Rupert meeting the pretty young lady.

'What's strange?' Hannah prompted.

'When I took her on a tour of the house—'

'You took her on a tour of the house – why?'

'Because she asked. It sounded as though she'd grown up listening to stories from her grandmother, who'd lived in a place such as this, a stately home, before she was married. At least that's what I gleaned. Sounds as though she was quite taken by her grandmother's past – so much so that she is a National Trust member and loves visiting these sorts of houses.'

'I see.' Hannah was doing her best to keep a smile on her face, wishing that Rupert and Hetty's meeting hadn't veered off from work into their personal lives – or hers, at any rate.

'Did you have time to take her on a tour?' Hannah asked unnecessarily. He had taken Hetty round the house already. She realised she was just cheesed off that he'd decided to do so and spend more time with her.

'Well, no I didn't, especially as she was bloody well late turning up to our appointment.'

Hannah's face broke into a grin. She'd forgotten about that. He obviously hadn't forgotten. Hannah's smile slipped when she thought that Hetty must have made quite an impression; she'd been really late and yet he'd still volunteered to take her on a tour.

'I just felt that if she was going to do a really good job at the auction tomorrow, I ought to stay in her good books.'

'Oh, right.' That explanation did make Hannah feel better, but she said, 'You haven't taken me on a tour of the house.' She stopped, realising she sounded quite childish.

Rupert didn't seem to notice. He smiled. 'I'll take you on the grand tour.'

'Good. That's a date then.' Hannah raised her eyebrows thinking, *why did I say that?* He hadn't even told her when.

'How about after the auction tomorrow?' Rupert said, not commenting on her turn of phrase, as though it was of no consequence.

She supposed it *was* of no consequence – just a turn of

phrase. Which was just as well because there wouldn't be just the two of them, alone, on the tour. *Shame*, thought Hannah, having second thoughts about inviting Lili along.

Once again, she silently scolded herself for being so silly. It was not a date. There never would be a date with Rupert – he was taken. And besides, she'd sworn off relationships unless she fell madly in love. The trouble was, Hannah had so many failed relationships behind her, and in all of them, she'd believed at the time that she'd fallen madly in love. She hadn't.

So, how will I ever recognise the real deal? she thought sadly.

'Hannah?' Rupert asked.

'Oh, yes, the tour after the auction tomorrow. Sounds good to me. There's just one thing … can we do the tour *before* the auction?'

Hannah told Rupert her plan to show Lili around Somersby Hall before everyone arrived for the auction. She'd intended to broach it with him anyway, so it was the right time to bring it up. She might have forgotten otherwise.

Hannah told him that some family and friends were coming round for Sunday dinner – a little get-together to celebrate her and Maisie moving into their new home. And as the bride-to-be was coming too, it would the perfect time to show her around the wedding venue.

'Bring Lili's fiancé as well. I'm sure the groom will be interested in seeing their wedding venue too.'

'Oh, er …' Hannah stared at Rupert. And therein was the flaw in her plan. Rupert didn't know that she hadn't broached the idea with Lili and Nate yet. Thinking of the subterfuge made her wonder how Rupert's grandmother had kept up a much bigger pretence for so many years if she wasn't really Lady Jemima.

Hannah's thoughts switched back to Rupert. She realised a bit belatedly that Rupert accompanying them was a bad idea. But it was his grandmother's house. He was bound to walk round with them. There was no way out of it now – unless she told Lili and Nate beforehand.

But I don't want to do that. I want her to see the fantastic house – Lili had called it magnificent, what she'd seen of it when she'd passed by on her way to a gardening job.

It had pleased Hannah no end when Lili had appeared very excited at the prospect of seeing inside the house, saying she would love an excuse to visit.

Hannah hadn't apprised her best friend of what exactly that excuse was yet. But if Lili just fell in love with her idea, then she'd convince Nate – Hannah was sure of it. Especially after what Ray had said when they'd talked about her idea of hosting weddings at Somersby Hall, and about the prospect of asking Lili and Nate if they'd be the first to get married there. After she'd told him what Lili had said – that they wanted a low-key wedding at their house – he'd said, *no woman wants a low-key wedding*. It was their special day, and their house didn't have the backdrop of Somersby Hall.

He'd encouraged her to talk to Lili, assuring her that she'd change her mind about having the wedding reception at home.

'I don't know if I will have time to show you around before the auction, I'm afraid, Hannah.'

'Of course. Sorry, I didn't think …'

'It's okay, but you're welcome to take Lili yourself and go and explore. I expect by the time the auction is finished, and I've spoken with Hetty and wrapped things up, it might be quite late anyway, thinking about it. So perhaps it's for the best that you go with the bride-to-be, and groom, if he can make it.'

Hannah smiled tightly at the mention of the bride and groom, who had no clue what she was planning.

'Just avoid my grandmother's bedroom.'

'Oh, I intend to, believe me,' Hannah exclaimed. She quickly added, 'I, um … wouldn't want to disturb her.'

'Yes, best to keep your voices down as you pass by. I know Lili is the bride-to-be, and my grandmother has agreed to holding weddings here, but even so, I know how prickly she can be about having strangers in her house.'

Her house, Hannah nearly scoffed. She kept her mouth shut.

'I don't want there to be any chance that she changes her mind about your idea.'

'Neither do I.' Hannah wanted a chance to prove her wrong about the wedding idea. She looked across the room at Rupert, disappointed she wouldn't be having that tour, just the two of them, after all.

'What is it?' Rupert asked.

'I'd still like to go on a tour of the house with you.'

He grinned. 'And you will. It will be an opportunity for us to assess the different rooms in the house and see which ones we think will be used for the wedding venue.'

Hannah wasn't thinking of the business – she just wanted an excuse to spend more time with Rupert, but disappointingly Rupert clearly had business on his mind. He was right, of course; this was all purely business.

'That's a good idea. Perhaps during Lili's tour, I can ask her for her thoughts regarding the rooms. Obviously, we can pop our heads into the downstairs rooms too, the ones off the hallway that have been set up for the auction.' Hannah intended to broach the idea with Lili on the tour. She had no intention of inviting Nate. Besides, he'd want to hang back in Gatekeeper's Cottage with Maisie and William.

'Look at us,' Rupert said, grinning, 'aren't we just full of good ideas, putting our heads together?'

Hannah returned his smile. 'Yes, perfect enemies-to-friends,' she concluded.

'I'm sorry – what?'

'Oh, it's silly. You don't want to hear it.' Hannah waved that comment away.

'I do, really. Tell me.'

Hannah sighed and repeated what Ray had said about reading all those romance novels in the course of trying to win his wife back, and what he'd discovered in the pages of a book about the romance trope – enemies-to-friends. She didn't mention the further trope *friends-to-lovers*, not wanting to embarrass either him or herself any further.

Rupert burst out laughing. When he had recovered from his fit of giggles, he said, 'Didn't anyone tell Ray that us guys are never going to figure you lot out? Not in a million years. And no romance book will have the answers.'

Hannah couldn't help laughing too. 'I didn't want to tell him.'

'So, where does it go from there, according to the romance tropes, for two people who go from enemies to friends?'

Hannah looked at him sheepishly. She rolled her eyes. He had to ask. She said in a small voice, 'Lovers.'

21

'So, um, what were you about to say a short time ago – something was strange on your tour with Hetty?'

'Oh, yes.'

Hannah noticed that they were both avoiding eye contact. He seemed relieved at the change of subject. She wished she'd never mentioned Ray and romance tropes. She imagined he felt the same. *So awkward*, thought Hannah.

'Well, we were walking down a hallway upstairs in another wing of the house where there's old paintings of my ancestors lining the walls. It was the strangest thing – Hetty looks just like one of my ancestors.'

Hannah laughed. 'I bet that was a surprise. Must be her doppelgänger.'

'That's exactly what she said.'

'Well, there you go. Great minds think alike.' Hannah glanced at her bag. She hesitated, then got up and placed the bundle of airgraphs on his desk. If she didn't do it straight away, she'd change her mind, again. 'Talking of strange things, I found these hidden behind a painting I bought in a charity shop.'

Hannah didn't want to mention the specifics of the painting

because she didn't want there to be any possibility that she'd have to give it up. 'I was wondering if I could ask a few questions … about the hall. And about the people who used to live here.'

His brows lifted slightly. 'I thought you'd be interested in the history of the hall.'

Hannah was not so much interested in its history as the inhabitants.

'All the letters, well they're actually called airgraphs …'

'Airgraphs?'

Hannah explained what Thea had told her about them, and how valuable they were.

'You could sell them in the auction, you know. Of course, I wouldn't ask for a cut just because they're in with stuff from the house.'

You might, thought Hannah, when you find out their connection to this house. 'They're from a man named Owen – sent during the war to someone called Kitty. Here. At Somersby Hall.'

Rupert picked up the top letter, frowning as he examined the envelope. 'This was sent here, alright. But … Kitty? I don't know anyone in the family called that. Or Owen, I'm afraid.'

Hannah stared at him. It was just as she'd suspected. Whatever had gone on there decades earlier, Rupert was not in on it. If, that was, there was something to be in on. Hannah sighed. She wondered if there was a perfectly innocent explanation for it all.

'She might have been a housemaid or nurse when the hall was used as a convalescent home,' Hannah suggested. 'The letters talk about love, and his time in the army stationed in Cairo, and … there's something intimate about them.'

'Owen was in love with her,' said Rupert.

'Yes.'

Rupert sat back slowly, rubbing a hand through his hair. 'This house has had a lot of people pass through it over the years. During the war, especially. The best person to show these to is my grandmother.'

'No!' Hannah quickly collected herself. 'I mean, I wouldn't want to disturb her over something so … trivial.' She hated telling a fib. It wasn't trivial.

Hannah had kept back the letter from Lady Jemima to Owen that had never been sent. She hadn't figured everything out yet, and because of that she did not want to bring his grandmother into the equation yet.

If he'd seen the letter from Lady Jemima, he was bound to insist on taking the letters up to her, and Hannah suspected that once his grandmother knew she was interfering, and was quite possibly about to blow the lid on a secret, it would be the end of the airgraphs being in her possession, and of her wedding venue plans, and even of her tenancy of Gatekeeper's Cottage. She suddenly regretted taking the letters to the house.

Hannah was about to reiterate that she was not showing them to his grandmother, when Rupert added, 'You'd be wasting your time, in any case. I remember when I lived here, and I went to the local primary school for a time. We were doing something on World War Two. Perhaps it coincided with VE day. I don't recall. We had to think about who was involved in the war and write about that person. It didn't have to be someone fighting in the war like Owen here; it could be anybody who lived through the war – an evacuee, or a land girl, a fire warden – anybody really.'

Hannah listened intently, nodding and smiling. This was the first time Rupert had opened up about his experiences living there as a child, even if it was only a snippet.

'I don't think the idea was that we actually found someone and spoke to them, although the teacher did mention that if we did have a very elderly relative who had experienced the war then perhaps we could speak to them and share their story in class. I did. I had my grandmother. She could tell me her story, her recollections of the war.'

'And did she?'

'Nope. She said there were things not worth digging up. Old wounds.'

'She said that to a child?'

'Yeah – weird, huh. I told my teacher.'

'What did she say?'

'I don't recall her words verbatim, obviously, but it was along the lines that some won't talk about the war; it's still very much alive in their memories, while for us it's just history, something we study at school.'

'Whereas they lived through it.'

'Precisely. It must have been a harrowing time, one we couldn't even fathom or imagine. Not something everyone would want to relive through retelling. Things happened that understandably people wouldn't want to dredge up.'

'People like your grandmother.'

'Yes, although I'll never know – will I?' There was an edge, a bitterness, to his voice.

Hannah hadn't really thought about what his grandmother might have gone through during the war, what sacrifices had needed to be made, how her generation had to grow up so quickly while facing the unimaginable. Hannah wondered what had happened to Lady Jemima's father. The upheaval of the men from the hall going to war – was he one of them? Apparently, it had become a convalescent home for the war-wounded for a time, according to Lili, who'd heard it from The Gossip Girls. That must have involved a lot of change for a teenage girl.

There was no point asking Rupert about his family history – he'd already said his grandmother wouldn't speak of it.

'Maybe your grandmother was just trying to protect someone,' she said, eyeing him keenly.

'You mean this Owen character who may have been having a clandestine relationship with someone who worked here? Someone by the name of Kitty.'

'Yes, maybe. But why do you think it was a clandestine affair?'

He shrugged. 'Perhaps the things that were unsaid in the letters rather than said.'

'Hannah glanced at the airgraphs. 'How do you mean?'

'Well, apart from professing their love for each other, there was nothing personal, hinting at who they were, you know.'

Hannah nodded. It was true.

The fire popped softly as Hannah sat back in her chair.

Rupert eyed her thoughtfully. 'Kitty. You know, that name does ring a bell.'

Hannah leaned forward in her seat. 'Does it?'

'There's just been so much going on at the moment, I'm trying to recall where I heard it.' He shook his head. 'Well, it couldn't have been important, but if it comes to me, I'll let you know.'

But it is important, thought Hannah. She was still torn. Should she tell Rupert where she'd heard that name – right there in the house, standing outside his grandmother's bedroom door? Why should she protect Jemima's secret? She realised, though, that she wasn't. She was protecting Rupert.

'It's intriguing, though, isn't it? The letters from Cairo. You're right: it's a real love story. I wonder what happened to the couple after the war.'

Hannah packed the airgraphs back into her bag, still thinking of Rupert's grandmother. 'I wondered that too.'

'Is that why you won't consider including them in the auction, earn yourself a bit of money?'

Hannah did want the money, but she had to admit, 'They're someone's forgotten love letters.' And besides, his grandmother would be at the auction.

'But if you find Owen, or Kitty, then you might feel obligated to hand them back with no financial recompense.'

If Lady Jemima was really Kitty, she didn't feel any obligation to hand them back to her.

She sighed and caught the time on the clock on the wall. It was getting late. 'Look, sorry, I've taken enough of your time up on the letters.' She wished she hadn't brought them up. The only thing she'd achieved by showing them to Rupert was to confirm that he had no clue that his grandmother might in fact be Kitty. 'Shall we get on with the wedding planning?'

'Before we do, I just had a question, Hannah.'

'Go on,' Hannah said nervously, wondering what was on his mind.

'Why did you drive here? You know the drive is well lit, and it's not exactly a long walk. I would have accompanied you walking back if you're afraid of the dark.'

A beat passed. Then Hannah suddenly shot out of her chair. ‘Oh, god.’

‘What is it?’

‘Just wait right there. I’ve forgotten something.’

22

Hannah returned by way of the back patio through the dining room. She tentatively stepped through the open doorway to the study, wondering what Rupert's reaction would be.

'What is that?' Rupert asked, rising from his chair.

Not good, thought Hannah. He could see what it was in her arms. And so could Lulu. On her way back into the house, Lulu had appeared out of nowhere, the large wolfhound following her and sniffing the bundle in her arms. At first, she'd given Hannah a fright, until Hannah realised that Lulu was just interested in meeting her puppy.

Thankfully, Marlowe had still been asleep in his crate on the back seat, the crate secured with a seatbelt and dog harness. Sarah had thought of everything. Hannah had not. She'd driven the car the short distance to the house because she hadn't wanted to leave her puppy alone in his new home – and then she'd promptly forgotten about him by the time she'd arrived.

How could I have done that? she asked herself. She knew how. She'd only just got him. 'I'll never leave you again,' she promised her puppy, who'd been sleeping the whole time and was none the wiser. She realised she could probably have left him safely in his crate back at home, but she'd panicked, afraid he would wake up, find himself all alone in strange circumstances and cry.

He's just a dog, Hannah reminded herself. But he wasn't; he was a puppy, and her new baby.

Marlowe was wide awake and chewing the buttons of her blouse again as she cradled him in her arms.

'I couldn't leave Marlowe alone on his first night in his new home.'

'I didn't know you had a pet.'

'I didn't until a couple of hours ago.'

'Huh?'

Hannah told Rupert about the promise she'd made her daughter, Maisie, that she'd get her a pet when they moved into their next home. 'She's always wanted a puppy,' Hannah remarked. 'I never actually said the *d* word. Just the word pet. I'd resolved to buy her a goldfish, hamster or budgie.'

'I see your resolve crumbled,' Rupert said, laughing.

Hannah loved to see Rupert laugh; properly throwing his head back and laughing out loud. His whole face lit up. It suited him. Hannah couldn't resist a smile too.

'That doesn't look like a goldfish, a hamster or a budgie,' he said, tongue-in-cheek.

'No, it's a black Labrador. Little did I know that Maisie had talked about the promise I'd made to her paternal grandparents. Although I did not say dog, or puppy, Maisie had made up her mind that was what she was getting.'

'So, they saved you the trouble and expense of going to choose a dog.'

'Yes. Rupert, meet Marlowe.'

Rupert was about to walk over when he hesitated.

Hannah followed his gaze to Lulu, who was still by her side, a wet nose sniffing the puppy all over. She licked the puppy's face.

'What shall I do about Lulu?' Rupert asked. 'I don't like her in the study.'

'Why?'

'Because she growls at me.'

'I don't hear her growling now. She's too busy making friends.'

'Well, it's a shame she won't make friends with me,' Rupert commented.

Hannah stroked Lulu, then stroked her puppy. She beckoned Rupert over.

'I don't get it. Why is Lulu like that round you?'

Hannah walked over, Lulu still by her side. As she suspected, Rupert couldn't resist petting Marlowe, although he still had an eye on Lulu as he stroked the puppy. 'Wow, he's adorable.'

'I know.' Hannah glanced at Lulu. 'Her turn.'

'What?'

'Rupert, give Lulu a pet too.'

Tentatively, he held out his hand and stroked her. 'Oh, wow. Where's that growly dog I used to know?' he said to Lulu.

'There – you two have broken the ice,' Hannah said, satisfied.

'You're so good with dogs.'

Hannah laughed. 'I can assure you that I have no clue.'

'But—' Rupert looked at Lulu.

Hannah shrugged. 'Don't ask.'

Rupert smiled at Marlowe. 'You know, I've always wanted a dog, but it just wasn't possible when I was sent away to boarding school.'

'I'm so sorry. What's stopping you now?'

'Claudia.'

'Who? Oh, your fiancée.'

'Yes.'

'What's she got against dogs?'

'She says they're unhygienic.'

'Unhygienic?' Hannah didn't even know what to say to that. She burst out laughing. 'Sorry, sorry – didn't mean to laugh at your fiancée.'

Rupert smiled. 'Don't apologise. It's the dumbest thing I've heard too. I'm sure she'd change her tune if she met a cutey like Marlowe.'

Hannah didn't want her puppy to bring Rupert and Claudia together. She caught herself. She was being childish again. The fact was that Rupert *was* with Claudia. All couples had ups and downs. That was a fact of life. Although she remembered what she'd overheard Jemima and Percy talking about regarding her grandson's relationship with Claudia – that from what Claudia had told Jemima, she and Rupert had never once argued, which his grandmother thought wasn't normal.

Hannah said, 'I bet you had a bit of a falling-out about the pet thing, when she found out you wanted one.'

'Not at all. We haven't got the space for a dog in our flat in London, or the time with our work commitments.'

'Is that what Claudia said?'

'Well … yes.'

'I don't know if I've got the space at Gatekeeper's Cottage for a Labrador, and I'm worried about having the time to spend with him too, but you know, when there's something in life you really, really want, you just have to make it work somehow.'

Rupert was staring at her, making her feel uncomfortable under his gaze.

'What?'

'I like your thinking.'

Hannah grinned. 'I like my thinking too, although to be honest, I did kind of almost flip out when I saw what Sarah – that's Maisie's grandmother – had brought over as Maisie's moving-in present. But you know what?' She stared lovingly at her adorable puppy, who was ruining the buttons on her blouse, and said, 'It was love at first sight. Know what I mean?' She raised her eyes and met Rupert's. Their eyes locked for a brief moment. He was nodding his head. Hannah wondered what he was thinking.

He quickly averted his gaze, looking at the puppy.

'Do you want to hold him?'

'Can I?'

'Of course. But don't get any ideas – he's mine.'

'I thought he was Maisie's,' Rupert said with a knowing smile.

'Of course, of course.' Hannah reluctantly handed him over. She'd better get used to this because when Maisie returned home the next day, she'd barely get a look in.

Rupert took Marlowe in his arms, suddenly looked worried. 'How shall I hold his head?'

Hannah rolled her eyes. 'He's not a baby, Rupert, he's a puppy.'

'Yes, of course! Silly me.'

Hannah watched him. At first, he wasn't quite sure how to hold him.

'Here, put your hand under his bum, like so …' Hannah took Rupert's hand. 'There.'

Rupert lifted the puppy up, over his shoulder, like he was going to burp a baby. He patted the puppy's back.

Hannah was about to say something but held her tongue. A thought came out of nowhere; Rupert would make a very caring, attentive dad.

Marlowe licked Rupert's ear, making him smile, and then burrowed his head into Rupert's neck, his tail furiously wagging. 'Hey, I think he likes me.'

Hannah frowned, absurdly jealous. She hoped Marlowe wasn't going to favour guys. Some dogs were like that. *Perhaps Sarah should have brought us a girl dog*, she thought. She flicked her hand. 'You can hand him back now.'

Marlowe whimpered when Rupert lifted him gently and handed him back. Marlowe wriggled so furiously she had to put him down.

'Oh, I'd better get Lulu out of the room. She's too big. She could hurt the puppy.'

Hannah was about to agree, when she saw Lulu crouch down on all fours, and slowly move around the floor, her nose following Marlowe. 'No, wait! I think …' Hannah smiled when she realised what Lulu was doing. Her mothering instincts had kicked in. 'She wouldn't hurt him. She's looking after him.'

Rupert stared at Lulu as she lay down, letting Marlowe come to her. She licked his muzzle. 'Well, would you look at that,' said Rupert in surprise. 'I get the impression Lulu thinks you've brought her a present.'

'You mean the puppy?' She looked down at Lulu. 'Oh, dear. She's going to be upset when he leaves.'

'Well, you'll just have to bring Marlowe with you when you come to the house.'

Hannah looked up sharply. She knew what he was doing – using Lulu as an excuse to see Marlowe himself.

Rupert skipped over and shut the study door in case Marlowe headed out of the room.

'Is he okay exploring?' Hannah asked. She had put him down when she got him out of the car, hanging around watching him to see if he needed to wee.

They both looked about them, checking for anything that needed puppy proofing. 'I think we're fine.'

We're fine. Hannah glanced at Rupert, smiling down at the puppy.

Rupert said, 'You know, if you need someone to look after him during the day while you're at work … you run a shop in Aldeburgh, don't you?'

Hannah shook her head. 'No, I'm fine. Although …'

'Yes?'

Hannah was looking out of the study window at the gardens. 'The cottage garden of Gatekeeper's Cottage is quite small. If he could have a little run around your grounds from time to time.'

'Perhaps you and I could meet up, and we could go for a walk together …'

Hannah said, 'I'd like that.'

'I could throw him a ball,' suggested Rupert, 'play with him.'

'Oh, yes, right.' Hannah eyed Rupert, wishing he was really angling to meet up with her after work rather than see her puppy.

Hannah had a thought. 'Ah, what about your grandmother? Wouldn't you have to ask her? It's her house, after all. I can have pets at Gatekeeper's Cottage, but I'm don't know if she'll appreciate my dog running around her lawn.'

'That's okay, I'll just tell her the dog is mine.'

'No! Marlowe is mine!'

'Hannah, it's only a little white lie. Of course he's yours.'

Marlowe chose the wrong moment to pad over to Rupert and jump up against his legs. 'Ooh, you want another cuddle, little man.'

Hannah decided that next time, Marlowe was staying safely in his crate at home. This wasn't doing her any good. Absurdly, it was bringing to mind Nate in his lovely big house. It was nowhere near the size of Somersby Hall, but every time Maisie went over for the weekend, she was afraid one day Maisie would ask to stay for good.

Hannah reached out. 'I'll have my puppy, if you don't mind.'

'Er, of course.' Rupert dutifully handed Marlowe over.

She could do without the same feeling arising over her puppy, which actually wasn't hers, but Maisie's. Even so, it was dredging up her fears of being abandoned; Maisie defecting to her father's house, Marlowe preferring Rupert.

'Are you okay, Hannah?'

'Of course. Why wouldn't I be?'

'I don't know – you tell me.'

Hannah frowned. She could feel this turning into an argument.

Rupert said, 'Let's get down to planning your friend's wedding, eh? I think we're both tired. It's been a long day.'

Hannah managed a smile. That was true.

Rupert saw her smile. 'Great! Now, first things first. Your friend, Lili, has agreed to have her wedding here, hasn't she?'

Hannah hadn't been prepared for the question. 'Yeah, yeah, of course.' *She will,* thought Hannah, *as soon as she sees what a beautiful place it is.*

Rupert had taken a seat behind his desk and opened a large notepad that looked new. He clicked the top of a biro.

'You know that tour you mentioned, of the house?' Hannah said.

'Yes.'

'So, I *can* bring a plus one?'

Rupert looked up sharply. 'Oh, I thought you were single.'

'Oh, no – not that sort of plus one.'

Hannah was a little surprised when Rupert let out an audible sigh of relief. What did it matter if she was single or not?

'Who did you have in mind?' Rupert asked.

'The bride-to-be, of course, like we discussed.'

'Oh, of course.' He rolled his eyes. 'As I said, it's been a long day. You do remember that you'll have to take her on the tour yourself? I'm going to be quite busy.'

'Yes, of course.'

He looked down at his notepad. 'Right, now that's all sorted, let's make a start.'

Hannah was about to take a seat opposite him, her puppy still in her arms, Lulu by her side again, when they both heard the door knocker on the front door.

'Or not,' said Rupert, putting his pen down and frowning.

'Were you expecting someone?' Hannah asked. She thought it was a bit late for callers.

'No.'

Rupert got up and rounded his desk when someone knocked again, insistently this time. 'I'd better answer that.'

23

Hannah's curiosity got the better of her. She left Marlowe under the watchful gaze of Lulu, making sure to close the study door, and followed Rupert through the dining room, dodging the chairs set up for the auction. Ahead of her, she heard him answer the front door.

'Oh – it's you again.'

Hannah drew closer, hearing a woman's voice reply, 'Yes – bet you didn't expect to see me back so soon.'

'Come in. Did you forget something?'

Hannah retreated to the dining room doorway as she watched a tall young woman wearing a business-like trouser suit step into the hall. She knew immediately who she was from her long, wavy chestnut hair.

Hetty said, 'Would you believe I turned up at the pub to get checked in, and they've had a burst pipe? They were trying to call out someone as an emergency to get it fixed, so I waited, but they can't get anybody until tomorrow. They've had to turn off the water supply, so I can't stay there tonight after all.'

'Oh dear,' said Rupert.

Hannah noticed Hetty wasn't just holding a handbag. She

had a large bag slung over her shoulder. Was she thinking of staying at the house? Hannah remembered that Rupert had taken her on a tour of the house. She must have clocked how many spare bedrooms there were.

Hannah frowned. 'There are other hotels in Aldeburgh, not just the pubs, you know.' She added, 'There's one on the seafront that's quite large …' She had momentarily forgotten the name. She should know it. The hotel was where Lili had taken Maisie on holiday when Hannah had left her daughter with her best friend. It had resulted in the breakdown of Lili's relationship with her then boyfriend. Hannah still couldn't believe how selfish she'd been. Her only consolation was that thankfully Lili had met her soulmate there in Suffolk and fallen in love.

Thinking of falling in love, Hannah's gaze shifted to Rupert. In the past, she had always seemed to get involved in relationships that just weren't right for her. Now she'd met a guy who was right for her, but he was with someone. He had a fiancée.

Hannah thought that it was just as well because after all those bad relationships, she'd made herself a promise that she wasn't getting involved with anybody else until Maisie left home. She recalled Lili telling her that it was ridiculous to do so; what if she met someone really lovely?

She remembered her response – every relationship she'd ever been in had gone wrong, and it wasn't just her that had suffered, but Maisie. *But that's because I hadn't met the right person*, Hannah suddenly thought, staring at Rupert.

Rupert turned around, meeting her gaze. 'Oh, Hetty – this is Hannah. She's my grandmother's tenant.'

'Hi, I'm the auctioneer, Hetty.'

'I know,' Hannah said flatly.

Hannah looked at the young woman standing with Rupert in the hallway and cursed herself for not recalling the name of the hotel. She said, 'There are a few hotels in town. I'm sure one of them will have vacancies.'

Hetty looked at Rupert helplessly.

Hannah walked over and took Rupert's arm. 'Excuse us just for a sec.'

Hetty stood there with her overnight bag, glancing up the stairs while Hannah had a word with Rupert, pulling him into the dining room, and closing the door. 'It's not your problem, you know. Why didn't she just go and find another hotel? There's plenty in town.' Hannah knew the moment she said it that it was a dumb question. Hetty had turned up to see if she could stay at the hall for free first.

'She's paying for the hotel out of her own pocket.'

'Oh, really? I thought the auction house was paying?'

'No, she's self-employed. That means she has to pay all her own expenses.'

'Ah.' Now Hannah realised why Hetty hadn't just simply checked herself into another hotel. It wasn't an excuse just to turn up and stay in Somersby Hall instead. The rooms above the pub were probably the cheapest in town. The hotels would be very expensive. 'What are you going to do?' Hannah asked. If it was up to her, she wouldn't have Hetty stay at Somersby Hall, under the same roof as Rupert. She was feeling absurdly jealous, and a little bit threatened, by such a beautifully turned out, professional young woman. Not that she had reason to feel that way – Rupert was already in a relationship, as she reminded herself for the umpteenth time.

Hannah put her feelings to one side. If the auction was going to go ahead the next day with this auctioneer, then she had to stay at the hall. Rupert really had no choice. And neither did Hannah.

Hannah sighed, wishing she hadn't dragged him away to talk to him. He couldn't turn Hetty away.

'She can't stay here,' Rupert said, eyeing the door.

'Really – why not?' Hannah said in surprise. 'You must have lots of spare bedrooms.'

Rupert raised his eyes to the ceiling. 'My grandmother. I can't disturb her, it's late.'

'So, tell her in the morning. I'm sure she'll understand.'

Rupert breathed a heavy sigh. 'You don't really know my grandmother. She doesn't abide strangers in her house. If she found out I'd gone behind her back and let Hetty stay here without her permission, she'd be likely to call off the auction.'

'Really?'

'Yes – really.'

Hannah was about to ask about the wedding idea. She'd assumed that wedding guests would join the bride and groom and stay at Somersby Hall overnight after the reception. That was what other wedding venues did. How did he think that would work if his grandmother wouldn't even allow the auctioneer to stop over for one night to conduct the auction?

Hannah didn't bother bringing that up with Rupert because of what she'd overheard; Rupert's grandmother didn't think the wedding idea would take off, so hadn't bothered to think ahead to future weddings after Lili's.

Hannah was still determined to prove her wrong about the wedding, and together with Rupert, she would make Jemima eat her words – and have no choice but to open up Somersby Hall. Unless she was then going to tell Rupert she'd lied about believing Hannah's idea was good. And then she'd have to explain her ulterior motive for inviting Hannah – and her idea – into her home; the secrets she'd been keeping from Rupert.

Still, Hannah realised that all that did not solve Rupert's immediate dilemma.

Rupert said, 'She might even go so far as to call off the whole wedding idea we're working on too.'

Hannah looked at him wide-eyed. That had never occurred to her. 'What are we going to do?' she asked frantically. She couldn't imagine not working with Rupert. That wasn't all; she couldn't imagine not *seeing* Rupert. She touched his arm. 'I don't want that.'

Rupert put a gentle hand on her shoulder. 'Me neither.'

Their eyes locked.

'Is everything alright?' Hetty called from the hallway.

Rupert dropped his hand from her shoulder and opened the door. 'Just one more sec.' He closed it and turned to Hannah, lowering his voice again. 'There is one solution.'

'Yes?'

'It's going to be a lot to ask of you.'

'Of me?'

'Your daughter is away tonight staying at her father's – right?'

'Yes,' Hannah said slowly.

Rupert raised his eyebrows.

Hannah's mouth dropped open. 'Oh, you're asking if she can stay with me at Gatekeeper's Cottage?'

'I told you it's a lot to ask. You've just moved in, and it would mean she'd have to sleep in your daughter's bedroom tonight.'

Hannah turned her head and stared at the door. She'd been looking forward to returning to her new home that evening after seeing Rupert up at the house and spending the rest of the evening with her feet up, glass of wine in hand, having some time to herself just kicking back and relaxing.

Hannah made up her mind. She turned to Rupert and said, 'I hope she likes dogs.'

Rupert unexpectedly threw his arms around her and gave her a hug. Tentatively, Hannah put her arms around him, her head resting on his chest, hearing his heart beating quite fast.

All too quickly, the hug was over. Hannah could have stood there in his warm, gentle embrace forever.

Rupert gently took her by the shoulders. 'Are you sure about this?'

She smiled. 'Yes, I'm sure.'

Rupert opened the door while Hannah nipped back to his study to collected Marlowe. When she appeared at the front door, Hetty had already been apprised of the situation – that she'd be staying in Gatekeeper's Cottage with Hannah. Hetty nearly passed out with fright at the sight of Lulu, the big Irish wolfhound, accompanying Hannah.

Hetty backed away, retreating to the front door.

At first Hannah wondered what was going on, surprised that Hetty wasn't endeared by the puppy in her arms, until she realised it wasn't Marlowe that had caught her attention.

Hannah said, 'Don't be scared of Lulu. She looks a bit intimidating but—'

'A bit?' Hetty exclaimed, still keeping her distance. 'What … what breed is she?'

'She's an Irish wolfhound – a gentle giant, believe me.'

'Well, I'll take your word for it.' Hetty bit her lip. 'Lulu isn't your dog – is she?'

'No, she belongs to my grandmother,' Rupert replied.

'Oh, thank god. I'm sorry, but I just couldn't stay in a house with that.'

Hannah grinned. She'd never been so pleased to hear anything in her life. 'Then it's just as well you're staying with me and Marlowe tonight.'

'Isn't it?' said Hetty, staring at Lulu. 'I wouldn't want it any other way. Um, who is Marlowe – your … husband?'

Hannah laughed. 'Oh, dear me no.' She looked at her puppy.

'Oh, this is Marlowe?' Hetty went to reach out to stroke him, but her gaze quickly shifted to Lulu, who was still glued to Hannah's side. 'Isn't he adorable!'

Hannah said, 'Why don't you come with me in my car down to Gatekeeper's Cottage? You could walk up to the house in the morning for the auction.'

'Good plan.' Hetty was just turning to go. 'Oh,' she turned back. 'Rupert. Just one question. Will the dog …'

'Lulu,' said Hannah, having an idea just what Hetty was about to ask.

'Yes, er … Lulu. Will she be kept out of the way during the auction?'

'Absolutely. You won't see hide nor hair of her.'

'Thank god.'

Hannah exchanged a glance with Rupert, who was smiling knowingly. Hannah recalled what he'd said about Claudia, who was also frightened of Lulu, clearly finding her size intimidating, and – given his own wariness of Lulu – how impressed he'd been that Hannah hadn't jumped in fright at the sight of her.

Hannah was feeling rather chuffed with herself. She patted Lulu on the head, said goodbye to Rupert, and headed to her car with the new addition to her family in her arms, feeling positive; feeling that she had things to look forward to. Hannah was thinking about Maisie returning home the next day, and the little housewarming party. To borrow her daughter's favourite word – it was going to be epic.

24

'You're very lucky, getting this rental,' said Hetty, sitting under one of the two blankets Hannah had bought so that she and Maisie could sit outside on the garden chairs in the evening.

'Yes, I know.' Hannah handed Hetty a large glass of wine and took a seat on the garden chair next to her on the small patio outside the kitchen door. She wrapped the blanket around her legs, picked up the wine glass from the small wooden oval garden table set between them, and thought of her good-luck painting. Had that luck extended from the shop to her life there, at Somersby Hall? It certainly appeared so. She was looking forward to cracking on with the wedding idea and seeing Rupert again. She thought of the new member of her family.

Marlowe was asleep in his dog bed, which Hannah had placed in the dog crate in the kitchen along with a water bowl, a scented blanket and a chew toy. He was safe, so she didn't have to worry what he might get up to if he woke up while she was outside enjoying the beautiful autumn evening.

She turned in her chair when she thought she heard a whimper. She remembered the feeling of being on high alert all the time when she'd first brought Maisie home as a baby –

anxious if she woke up, anxious if she didn't.

'Did you hear that?' Hannah asked.

Hetty shook her head, casting a glance behind her too. She must have known Hannah was keeping her ear out. 'I don't hear him. Do you want me to go check?'

Hannah said, 'No, I'll go. Thank you anyway.' She had been intending to spend the evening alone, enjoying her own company in her new home, but now, with a new puppy, she was actually glad of the company; it would have been a long night without someone to talk to and take her mind off constantly and unnecessarily checking on him. She still thought it would be a long night, though, just like when she'd brought Maisie home.

Hannah returned to her seat, leaving the back door open. 'He's still sleeping.'

Hetty smiled. 'He's a sweetie.' She'd had a cuddle and a little play with Marlowe while Hannah had carried her bags up to Maisie's bedroom, ignoring her protests and insisting she was her guest. They'd shared a supermarket pizza that Hannah had bought that morning in Aldeburgh.

Hannah returned her smile. 'I know.' She knew who else was going to think that, when she'd got over the shock of coming home tomorrow to find her very own puppy. Hannah couldn't wait to see Maisie's reaction.

Hannah picked up her glass of wine, adjusted the cushion behind her back, and looked down the little cobbled path of her new, rather overgrown, cottage garden. She commented, 'The garden needs some work.'

Hetty agreed. 'Yes. I love it, though. It reminds me a lot of the cottage garden where my grandfather lives – so different to the flat in London where I rent. Well, actually, where I won't be renting for much longer.'

Hannah listened as Hetty talked about the flat-share where she'd rented with two other people for quite some time. Now they'd all been given notice by the landlord to leave, but properties in London were in short supply, which was driving up the rents. Hetty didn't yet know what she was going to do.

Hannah commiserated, although she knew she was fortunate – she had the flat above the shop to live in if she lost her rental. In fact, she could sell the whole thing – the shop premises with the flat above – and buy a nice home there on the Suffolk Coast. But that would mean she'd have to give up her shop. Even though her current shop wasn't doing especially well, if the wedding planning were to take off at Somersby Hall, she rather liked Ray's idea of perhaps opening a bridal shop and having somewhere her clients could go to plan their weddings. Perhaps they'd pop across the yard to The Potting Shed and buy their wedding flowers.

Hetty was still talking about her situation. It sounded to Hannah as though things had been about to change anyway in Hetty's household before they'd received notice to vacate the flat-share. One of Hetty's friends and flatmates, Rosie, had met a teacher like herself, and they were planning to leave London, applying for teaching posts in a more affordable part of the country where they were hoping to eventually buy a house together. That left Hetty and her housemate, Daniel, scrambling to look for somewhere else to live.

'I'd love to get married at Somersby Hall,' commented Hetty.

She remembered Rupert saying that Hetty had said the same to him, but he'd said she was single. Had he misheard?

'There is someone …' said Hetty.

Hannah was about to pour herself another glass of wine from the bottle she'd fetched from the kitchen. She stopped and looked at Hetty. 'Is there?'

'Yes, but he doesn't know.'

Hannah poured herself a large glass of wine, frowning into her wine glass, really hoping she wasn't going to say Rupert.

Hetty sighed heavily and turned to Hannah. 'It's … difficult. He's one of my housemates, but he's a lot older than me. He treats me like one of his daughters – they're not much younger than me. He had kids young.'

'Age is just a number,' Hannah said, relieved it clearly wasn't Rupert she had her heart set on. 'You should tell him how you feel.'

Hetty shook her head.

They both sat staring into the garden. The sun was setting behind the trees, the light from the kitchen illuminating their spot on the patio.

Hannah was thinking of Rupert. She poured herself another glass of wine and pulled the blanket up to her chin. It was getting chilly. 'When did you know you were in love with Daniel?'

Hetty told her about the last guy she'd dated who had ended it when he'd come over to hers for dinner and had seen the way she looked at Daniel. 'That's when I realised that I'd been in love with Dan all along, ever since the first day I met him – I just didn't know it.' She finished her glass of wine and put it on the table. 'So, how long have you been in love with Rupert?'

Hannah nearly choked on her wine. 'Excuse me?'

'You and Rupert? How long have you two been together?'

'Oh, you've got it wrong.'

'Have I?'

'We're not together. He's with someone else. Like he said, I'm his grandmother's tenant.'

Hetty raised her eyebrows, 'Are you sure there's nothing going on between you?' she probed, throwing her a lop-sided grin.

'No. What makes you think there might be, anyway?'

'Um, the fact that you were there with him in the house in the evening.'

'Ah.' Hannah smiled. 'He didn't mention we are in business together. Well, actually it's all very new. We're working together on turning Somersby Hall into a potential wedding venue.' Of course, Hannah was aware that Hetty already knew this. She probably didn't know that Rupert was working on the idea with the tenant.

Hetty's expression said she still wasn't convinced. 'Have you seen the way he looks at you?'

'I don't know what you mean.'

'No, obviously not.' Hetty grinned. 'I hate to be the bearer of good news, but he's fallen for you.'

Hannah scratched her head. 'No, you are reading way too much into the fact that we were together this evening.'

'Am I?' She put her wine glass down and turned in her chair to face Hetty. 'I think what I saw, the way Rupert looks as you, is just what my ex-boyfriend saw with me and Dan. I know what I saw, Hannah.'

Hannah stared at her. Could it be true?

'The question is, do you feel the same way about him?'

Hannah sighed and put her wine glass down next to Hetty's. 'It's not as simple as that.'

'Love is never simple.'

Hannah smiled. 'That sounds quite wise coming from someone so young,' she commented.

'That's what my grandfather said to me whenever I broke up with a boyfriend. And I've had a lot of break-ups, believe me.'

'So have I,' Hannah admitted. 'I'm single for the first time in a very, very long time and it's given me a chance to think, really think about my personal life, and all those bad relationships. And I realise all along, the problem hasn't been me, but them. I've just careered from one relationship to another without realising that I need to find—'

'The one?'

'Yes – that. And you know what? I'd rather be single forever than with the wrong person again.'

'What if Rupert is the right person?'

'He's with someone – I told you.'

'But what if the person he's with isn't right for him?'

Hannah stared at her, suddenly recalling what she'd overheard his grandmother say to Percy when she'd got on to the subject of Rupert's relationship with Claudia – *I firmly believe he is not the one for her, or rather, she is not the one for him.*

'Ah,' said Hetty, 'you know something.'

Hannah shook her head. 'It's all incidental, anyway.'

'What do you mean?'

Hannah was thinking of Maisie when she said, 'I'm not looking for love.'

'But what if love found you?'

Hannah suddenly heard a yelp from the kitchen. 'Marlowe?' She sprung out of her chair.

Hetty picked up the blanket that had fallen on the floor and brought her own too as she followed Hannah into the kitchen.

'Is he alright?' Hetty asked.

'Yes. He's woken up and discovered he was all on his own.' Hannah crouched down and opened the crate door. Marlowe came waddling into her arms, wagging his tail furiously and licking her face as she picked him up. 'Let's go outside and see if you need the toilet.'

Hetty had folded the blankets by the time Hannah returned to the kitchen. 'You were quick.'

'Yes, he was such a good boy. Went straight away.'

Hetty gave him a fuss too. They retreated to the lounge where they both played with Marlowe while Hetty chatted about her upbringing in London and her holidays spent with her grandparents in the little cottage in the Dartmoor National Park.

Hannah shared a little of her past about her late grandparents, whom she had adored. She wasn't going to inherit a cottage like Hetty would in the future. Her maternal grandparents had left the cottage to their two children. They'd sold it, split the money, and her parents had moved to Spain and bought a villa with the proceeds.

'Hey, free holidays in Spain – amazing.'

Hannah smiled. 'Yes, it would be if I could find the time to go there.' *And the airfares*, she thought. She said, 'Your work sounds really interesting.'

'I love it. I love getting commissions to work in stately homes. They are just amazing properties, with such interesting pasts, aren't they?'

Hannah narrowed her eyes, thinking of Lady Jemima, or whoever she really was. 'I'll say.' Thinking of Hetty's profession, Hannah had a thought. 'I don't suppose I could be really, really cheeky and ask you to value something for me?'

Hetty grinned. 'Oh, I love to see old heirlooms.'

Hannah pursed her lips. They weren't heirlooms of hers, but she decided not to tell Hetty how she'd come by them.

'Do you think it's valuable?'

'They …' Hannah corrected her.

'Oh, more than one thing.' She clapped her hands. 'How exciting.'

'I'll go and fetch them.'

'I'll come too.'

Hannah looked at Marlowe. He'd fallen asleep on the carpet, his head resting on a soft toy. Before she left the room, she carefully picked him up and put him in his dog bed. He didn't stir. 'Such a good boy,' she commented. Sarah had been right – feed, poop, play, sleep. Mostly sleep. So far, puppyhood was a breeze, Hannah decided.

What she hadn't decided yet was where Marlowe was going to sleep that night – in his crate alone in the kitchen, or in his dog bed by the side of her bed. Hannah looked adoringly at her puppy and already knew the answer.

Hannah took the little key she kept in a dish on the mantel shelf. She didn't know why she bothered to lock the cabinet in the dining room where she stored the airgraphs. Nobody else would be coming into her house apart from family. Thinking of family reminded her there was something she'd been meaning to ask Hetty.

She turned to find Hetty standing beside her, staring at the painting above the mantel shelf.

'Hetty, I'm having some family and friends over tomorrow for Sunday lunch and a little get-together housewarming party. Would you like to join us?'

For a moment, she wasn't sure Hetty had heard her, although she was standing right next to her. 'Hetty?'

Hetty tore her eyes from the painting. 'Oh – what did you say?'

Hannah repeated her question.

'I'd love to,' Hetty said, still entranced by the painting, 'but the auction is tomorrow afternoon, and I really need to be up at the house earlier just to make sure everything is organised.'

Hannah understood. 'Of course.' She followed her gaze. 'It's by an unknown painter – do you like it?'

'I do, yes. I hadn't really taken much notice of it since I arrived …'

'Well, don't bother asking if you can buy it,' Hannah joked. 'I love it too much to part with it.'

Hetty stepped closer studying the painting. 'Did the artist sign it?'

'Um, yes. See there …' Hannah pointed. 'You can just make out the name, Owen Hartley. I think it's the same person who wrote the letters.'

Hetty turned her head to look at Hannah. 'What letters?'

Hannah grinned. 'The ones I'm going to show you to be valued.'

She thought, *how fortunate to have a professional to cast an eye over them right under my roof.* 'Now, before you warn me that I'm in for a disappointment because old personal letters won't be worth much if anything, apart from their sentimental value, perhaps I should call them by their proper name.' Hannah paused for effect. 'Airgraphs.' She looked at Hetty, and for a split second, she wondered if she knew what she was talking about.

Hetty raised her eyebrows. 'Airgraphs. Wow. I have heard of

them, but never actually come across any before. How many do you have?'

Hannah could see the excitement written all over Hetty's face. 'Follow me.'

Hetty followed her into the dining room, watching Hannah unlock the cupboard in the dresser and get out a box.

Hannah pocketed the key in her trouser pocket and turned around with the box in her hands. 'I have a friend who used to work in a museum as an archivist. She suggested I store them in an airtight container. Although she also suggested I could store them back where I found them.'

Hetty stared at the box as Hannah carefully opened it to reveal the airgraphs. Hetty asked, 'Where did you find them?'

Hannah said, 'You'll never guess …' before she told her.

25

Hannah finally had a moment alone with Lili in the kitchen, preparing the Sunday roast. Maisie was playing with her brother in her new bedroom, enjoying the old-fashioned toys that had been left behind. She was taking some time out from her puppy who was now sleeping in his bed, which was in his crate in the kitchen, having had far too much excitement from all the new people arriving and giving him lots and lots of fusses and attention – especially Maisie.

When she'd first been introduced to her moving-in present, expecting a toy, or some books, or something for her bedroom, Hannah had been surprised by her reaction – Maisie had taken one look at her puppy, burst into floods of tears and run away to hide behind the sofa. She'd been followed by an inquisitive puppy, perhaps wondering why he wasn't getting fusses from one of the new visitors. William had asked Nate what was wrong with his sister. Maisie had emerged from behind the sofa, tears still streaming down her face and walked straight up to her mum. Hannah had given her the biggest cuddle, wiping her tears with the palm of her hand, reassuring her that the puppy was there to stay and wasn't going anywhere.

And now Sarah and Ray were sitting around the G-Plan dining room table, chatting while they waited for dinner. Nate was trying to be useful. Hannah could see him outside with a spanner he'd found in the little outhouse in the back garden. He was trying to fix the outside garden tap, which kept dripping.

Lili glanced out of the kitchen window. She could see the top of Nate's head. He was bent over the tap with the spanner. Beyond the patio, which was floodlit by the outside light, the rest of the garden was disappearing in the fading light.

Hannah said, 'He really doesn't have to do that. That's the owner's responsibility.'

'I know. He just wants to help make everything run smoothly in Maisie's new home.'

Hannah smiled and turned from the window to look at Lili. 'I feel so lucky, so blessed to have such a wonderful family and friends.' She walked over to the oven, slipped on her oven gloves and checked the chicken and potatoes roasting in the oven.

'I don't know why you asked me to come and help in the kitchen. You seem to have everything in hand,' said Lili.

Hannah closed the oven door and took off the oven gloves. She chewed her bottom lip, eyeing her best friend.

'There's something on your mind, Hannah. Come on – out with it.'

'I wanted you to meet Hetty, the auctioneer. You know she stayed the night here in Maisie's room. But unfortunately, she had to be up at the house early, so she left before you all arrived while I was busy preparing the roast.'

Lili folded her arms. 'Is that it?'

Hannah was stalling and Lili knew it. Hannah had had a bit of a sleepless night, and it wasn't because of the puppy. Marlowe had slept in her room on his dog bed, and apart from one whimper in the night, which Hannah had taken as her cue to get up and take him outside in case he needed to go, surprisingly he'd slept through the night.

It was Hannah who hadn't slept. She'd been tossing and turning and then lying awake in the early hours wondering whether Lili really would agree to have her wedding at Somersby Hall even after she'd taken her on a tour to show her what she'd be missing if she didn't. So much rested on her agreeing.

Hannah didn't want to wait until the house tour to find out. 'I've brought you here under false pretences.'

Lili laughed until she caught Hannah's expression. 'Oh, you're being serious.'

'Yeah – kind of. Obviously, I wanted to show you all our new home, but there's something else …'

'Oh, right. What is it?'

'You know you said to me, *you will tell me if you need anything, won't you?* Well, I need something now.'

Lili smiled. She reached over and brushed Hannah's arm. 'Things are working out for you, I can tell. You're doing so well getting your life on track. And I don't mean to sound patronising. I'm aware that everyone else we know who has come to the Suffolk Coast for a new beginning, well, things have worked out for them. You, not so much. If you don't mind me saying. But no one else has had a child to think of.'

'You did.'

Lili shook her head. 'All right, yes, I had Maisie when I brought her here on holiday, but she wasn't my child. I didn't have to make all the difficult decisions like where to live and where to send her to school.'

Hannah dropped her gaze. 'It was so kind of you to offer to use some of your inheritance to pay for her to go to private school, one that caters for her artistic bent, but I just want her to have a normal childhood, go to school with her brother.'

Lili touched her arm. 'As I said, I'm not her parent. That is completely your call.' She continued, 'Remember, things have been easier for me. I met Nate after I moved here, and since then I haven't been on my own. You still are, and I really admire you, Hannah, for making a go of things with the shop. I really didn't think you'd be interested in going into business.'

Hannah saw her opening. 'Well, here's the thing. Another business idea has cropped up.'

'Really? How exciting.'

Hannah was encouraged by her enthusiasm. 'Yes, especially as it's right here at Somersby Hall. I'll be working with Rupert, my landlady's grandson.'

'Wow, this is a turn-up for the books, isn't it? And you like him.'

Hannah really didn't want to get into that.

'So, what's the business idea?'

'Using the hall as a wedding venue.'

'A wedding venue. Oh, from what I've seen of the house up the drive when we arrived here, it would make the perfect wedding venue.'

'You think so?'

'Oh, yes. Just perfect.'

Hannah took a deep breath. This conversation was going beyond well. She was about to ask the question she'd been dreading, when Lili said, 'I think the grounds would need some work, though, from what I've seen.'

'Would you … would you have any time in your work schedule to possibly fit in another landscaping job?'

'Here at Somersby Hall?'

Where else, thought Hannah. She nodded enthusiastically.

'Is that what you were going to ask me?'

First things first, thought Hannah. She nodded. 'Yes.' She watched with bated breath as Lili got out her mobile phone and started scrolling through her calendar. 'Now, I don't know what timescale your landlady was thinking, but I have had a cancellation next week so—'

'Oh, my god!' Hannah was nearly jumping up and down. 'Next week – that would be amazing!' Lili was right: her life was coming together. If this wasn't a good omen that the wedding idea was going to work, she didn't know what was.

'I'll have to speak to your landlady.'

'I can do that – no problem. I can talk to Rupert, and he'll speak to his grandmother.'

'Shall I pencil it in then, do you think, just awaiting confirmation?'

Hannah was about to say yes, when she realised that she was getting ahead of herself, especially after Lili added, 'I'd just have to do them a quote for the landscaping work and see if it is acceptable.'

'Actually, there is one more thing …' Hannah winced. 'You won't get paid to do the landscaping job.'

'I'm sorry – what?'

'Yeah. You see, they've run out of money, Lady Jemima and her grandson. Property rich, cash poor, so to speak.'

'Ah, so that's why they're holding the auction. To get hold of some cash.' Lili sighed. 'Look, Hannah …'

'Wait, before you say no, you wouldn't be doing the gardens for free.'

'But you just said—'

'A barter. I was thinking of a barter.'

'A barter – what does that mean?'

'You give them something, and you get something in return.'

'I don't see what they could possibly have that I—'

'Somersby Hall.'

'What?'

'Oh, I didn't mean they'd give you the house. They'd give you the house for a day to hold your wedding reception here.'

Lili blinked. 'Really?' She walked over to the kitchen window, staring outside. Not that she could see anything past Nate's head and the floodlit patio, but Hannah knew she was imagining the beautiful house and what she could do with the grounds.

Hannah held her breath. It wasn't an outright no. That word hadn't passed her lips.

Lili turned around. 'So, we'd have a sit-down meal there?'

'Oh, you should see the dining room – it's a lovely room. There's a large oak table and enough chairs I'm sure to seat you all. You'd have to pay for the catering, I'm afraid.'

'We were going to pay for the catering at Nate's house.'

That was what Hannah had thought.

'And we could have our wedding photos taken outside the house?'

'There's a lovely back garden that the dining room French doors lead out into. You could have some wedding photos there too, and a gazebo in the garden for the first dance, and the party afterwards.' Hannah paused, looking at her friend. 'It's a big ask – I know,' she said.

'Oh, Hannah, it sounds like something I've always wanted. I just didn't want to tell Nate that.'

Hannah grinned, thinking of what Ray had said – 'It will make it a truly special, memorable day – that's what you want – isn't it?' *Of course she does*, thought Hannah.

'Of course I do.'

'So … you'll ask Nate?'

'What about?'

'About holding the wedding at the house?'

'I'm not asking, I'm telling him I've changed my mind.'

Hannah could not believe her ears. 'And you don't mind holding your wedding here in exchange for landscaping the front gardens?'

'No, not at all. I'll also tidy up the back garden too. The team of gardeners I use are all free next week.'

Hannah frowned. That was something she hadn't thought of. If Lili wasn't being paid to do the job, how was she going to pay them? She had to ask.

'I will use some of the money we'd set aside for the wedding.'

'But I thought that was for Maisie and William's university fund?'

'I had set aside the money for Maisie to go through private school. I can use some of that.'

Hannah knew that Lili really didn't need to worry about money, but even so Hannah would not have asked her just to do the garden out of her own pocket without something in return. But there was just one more thing.

'What is it?' Lili asked jokingly. 'What more could you possibly want?'

'To use your wedding photos for publicity stills to advertise Somersby Hall.'

'Wow, you are quite the businesswoman,' said Lili admiringly, surprising Hannah.

Hannah grinned. 'I guess I am. Is it a deal then?'

'Is what a deal?' Nate asked. They'd left the kitchen window off the latch in case he needed something. Nate had just opened it. He was looking red in the face.

Lili turned to him and said, 'I'll tell you later. How's that tap going?'

'I can't for the life of me turn the nut, I'm afraid.'

Hannah smiled at him. 'Thank you for trying, Nate.'

'Sorry I couldn't fix it. When's dinner?'

'Not long now.'

'Are Maisie and William still playing upstairs?'

Lili and Hannah nodded.

'Good – is Marlowe awake?'

Hannah almost laughed. Nate wanted play time with the new puppy all to himself. She glanced at the sleeping puppy. 'I'm afraid not.'

Nate looked disappointed. 'Well, I'll go and put this spanner back in the outhouse.'

Lili shook her head. 'I'm not sure why he bothered. DIY really isn't his forte.'

Hannah stared at Lili, who was looking adoringly at her fiancé as he disappeared up the garden path, his phone torch lighting the way. She imagined what it would be like having a partner around to share everything, an adult to talk to about the day, share worries and woes – and the good times, of course. Despite Maisie being home, and having her new puppy for company, she knew she'd feel lonely when everyone else left later that evening.

Hannah closed the kitchen window.

'So, now you've shared what was on your mind …' said Lili, pausing for effect.

Hannah had an idea what was coming. She bet that Lili was going to tell her she was expecting.

Lili said, 'What about that money you said you'd come into? You were going to tell me all about it – remember?'

'Oh yes! Remember my good-luck charm in the window?'

'The painting. But I noticed it's not in the window anymore.'

'Yes, well …' Hannah didn't want to get into the reason why she'd suddenly taken it down. Although she did want to tell her what she'd found in the painting. 'Look, I was going to show Ray and Sarah what I found in the painting. Come on, I'll show you too. The dinner has still got a bit of time to go yet.'

'You found something valuable in the painting?'

'Oh, yes – airgraphs.'

'I'm sorry – what?'

Hannah grinned. 'You'll see. Thea says they're very valuable and I'd get a good price at auction.' Hannah led the way out of the kitchen, across the small hallway into the dining room opposite the lounge. Ray and Sarah were sitting at the table, Ray shuffling an old-fashioned set of playing cards, Sarah leafing through an equally ancient cookery book. They'd been in the G-Plan dresser having a nose. Hannah didn't mind, although there was one place they wouldn't be able to nose – the locked cupboard where she kept the airgraphs. Thinking of which, Hannah said, 'Oh, wait here everyone, I'll just go and fetch the key.'

'Key to what?' Lili asked.

'Is it the locked cupboard?' Ray asked, pointing at the dresser.

Hannah nodded. 'I've got something to show Sarah and Lili.'

Ray smiled. 'Is it the letters?'

Hannah nodded, returning Ray's smile. She hadn't shown Sarah and Lili all the letters yet. She went to the dresser and then returned without the key and with a frown on her face. 'I can't find the key. I always keep it in the little decorative bowl over the mantel shelf. Oh, stupid me.' Hannah reached into her pocket. 'Here it is! I almost forgot – I showed Hetty, the auctioneer …' she'd told them all that Hetty had stayed over last night. 'She was very kind and valued them for me.'

Ray said, 'Was it pretty good – the valuation?'

'Oh, Ray, you wouldn't believe what she thinks they're worth.'

'Did you show her the … the special one?' He raised his eyebrows.

She knew what he meant – the one to Owen from Lady Jemima that hadn't been sent. She shook her head. 'I got out the letters tied up in the faded pink ribbon, but not the one at the bottom of the box.'

'Why not?' Ray asked. Before she had a chance to reply, Ray said, 'Oh, yes of course – she's going to be up at the house today, conducting Lady Jemima's auction.'

'Exactly!' Hannah knew Ray would understand why she hadn't shown Hetty that letter. 'In fact, she's already there.'

'She must have slinked off,' said Lili. 'I didn't notice her leave. Bit rude, if you ask me, especially as you let her stay the night. You didn't have to.'

'Oh, she went while I was preparing the dinner.' Hetty hadn't popped her head round the kitchen door when she left, but then again, she had left her bags there. 'She said last night she'll be returning after the auction to collect her things, so I expect she'll say goodbye then.'

Hannah got out her key and discovered the cupboard door was already unlocked. 'Oh, silly me, I must have forgotten to lock it when I put them back after Hetty had valued them. No wonder I didn't put the key back in the dish.'

When Hannah opened the cupboard door, she exclaimed, 'They're gone!'

26

'Look, I'm sure there's a reasonable explanation,' said Sarah. They were all running up the stairs to Maisie's bedroom.

Sarah continued, 'She probably just wanted another look, check her valuation was correct, and left them up in her room.'

Four adults burst into Maisie's bedroom, surprising the two children, who were sitting cross-legged on her bed playing an old-fashioned snakes-and-ladders board game. They both looked up, wide-eyed.

William said, 'Is dinner ready? I'm hungry.'

Maisie asked, 'Has my puppy woken up yet?'

Hannah looked from one to the other, and said, 'No. And No. Now, have you two seen a stack of very old letters, wrapped in a faded pink ribbon?'

'Do you mean the airgraphs?' Maisie asked.

'Yes, those. Have they been left on your desk?'

'I haven't had them – I swear, Mum. I know I'm not allowed to touch them anymore.'

'Oh, sweetheart. I know you haven't had them. I thought perhaps Hetty, the auctioneer, might have brought them up to your room when she stayed over last night and accidentally forgot to put them back.'

A quick search proved fruitless.

'Oh, that's odd. Her bags are gone. I thought she was going to leave her stuff her and collect it after the auction to pop in and say goodbye.'

'Obviously a change of plan,' said Lili unhelpfully.

'Oh dear,' said Sarah.

Hannah whirled around. 'What is it?'

'Perhaps she had some paperwork lying around and picked them up by accident, putting them in her things while she was packing.'

Hannah thought that unlikely. The letters tied together with a ribbon were bulky.

'She valued them for you, didn't she?' Ray mused.

Hannah whirled around and looked at Ray. 'Yes – what of it?'

'Do you think there's a chance she misconstrued the situation and thought you wanted them included in the auction up at the house this afternoon?'

'Oh, no!'

Lili said, 'But I thought you wanted to sell them?'

'Oh, Lili, you don't understand. I don't want to sell them yet, until I've found out …' she stopped. 'You know what? There's no time to explain. I just need to get them back.'

Four adults, followed by two children, came rushing down the stairs. Nate had just walked into the hallway, coming through the kitchen from the back door. 'I just checked the … dinner.' He eyed them all. 'What on earth is going on?'

Sarah said breathlessly, 'No time to explain. Hannah needs to get up to the house before her airgraphs are sold in the auction.'

'What's an airgraph?' Nate asked as Hannah dived for the front door. She opened it and stepped back in surprise. 'Rupert? What are you doing here?'

'Hannah – is Hetty here?' he asked frantically.

'No.' Hannah looked at him, bemused. 'She left an hour ago.'

'Where?'

'What do you mean – where? I thought she was going up to the house to prepare for the auction. Are you saying she never arrived?'

'Yes,' Rupert looked at her askance as he stepped into the hallway. 'I thought you'd drive her back up to the house.'

'I was busy preparing the Sunday roast. She said she'd walk up the drive and come back and collect her things and say goodbye. She left her bag … here.' Hannah frowned.

'We didn't see any bags up there,' Lili pointed out.

'Hold on … I'll check again.' Hannah ran back upstairs.

Sarah and Ray stepped out of her way, Sarah holding open the lounge door for William and Maisie, who was carrying her puppy.

Hannah returned a moment later, her eyes wide. 'She's gone.'

Rupert looked at her aghast. 'I thought I heard a car in the driveway. It must have been her driving off. What the hell am I going to do?' Rupert looked at his watch. 'I've got an auction starting in exactly fifteen minutes, and no auctioneer!'

Hannah swallowed. 'The letters. She took the letters.'

Rupert said, 'Do you mean the letters you showed me yesterday evening?'

Hannah nodded, although she knew he wouldn't understand their significance or how valuable they were. She did, because she'd stupidly had them valued, not realising they'd be stolen from right under her nose by the very person she'd invited into her home. Hetty had financial problems – she'd admitted herself that she would like to buy the property in London if she could. The airgraphs would not buy her that property, but they would set her up for a very long time with a lovely rental.

Hannah slapped her forehead. 'I've been such a fool! But … but this doesn't make any sense. Why would she take … steal them, and risk being prosecuted for theft, and losing her job she adores … she seemed so genuinely nice.'

'It was her first job as an auctioneer, apparently,' Rupert added. He got out his mobile phone. 'I'm calling the police.'

'No – wait!' said Hannah.

Rupert already had his phone to hand. 'Look, I don't care how valuable, or not, those letters are. She stole from us. And she's reneged on her contract to conduct the auction.'

Ray said, 'I don't think reneging on a work contract is a police matter, actually.'

'Who are you?' Rupert asked rudely.

Sarah said, 'This is the person who could help you out of your fix.'

'Grandad's an art cop,'

'*Was* an art cop,' said Ray.

Rupert said, 'I don't see how that has any—'

Ray, calm and collected under pressure, said, 'I have attended dozens and dozens of auctions over the years. Admittedly they were all art auctions, but I know a thing or two about them,' he said modestly. 'I don't mind conducting your auction for you.'

Hannah had been wracking her brains; there was something Rupert had said in conversation the previous evening that she had a feeling was somehow significant. And then she remembered; Rupert had mentioned something strange occurring on his tour with Hetty. 'Doppelgänger.'

Rupert turned to Hannah. 'Pardon me?'

Hannah looked at Rupert with a start. 'What was Hetty's name, her *full* name.'

'Henrietta Hartley.'

'Hartley?' said Ray, turning to look at Hannah.

Rupert didn't see the exchange. 'Look, whatever her name is, she's stolen something. I'm calling the police.'

'No, you can't. Don't you see? She's a descendant of Owen Hartley, the one who wrote the letters, Rupert. She might even be his granddaughter.'

Hannah's mouth fell open when she thought of Lady Jemima, or whoever she really was, and Percy. Was her secret about to be revealed? Perhaps not. She remembered to breathe. Owen might well be dead, but if he wasn't, like Lady Jemima, perhaps he wouldn't tell anybody, including his own granddaughter, Hetty, his family background either. After all, when Hetty had confided in Hannah why she had been late the previous day, she'd said that it hadn't been helped by her grandfather phoning her and telling her not to go to Somersby Hall. She'd said, *It's bizarre. I'm beginning to wonder if he had some connection to the house.*

Rupert lowered his phone. 'Suit yourself. But I still need an auctioneer.'

Ray said, 'I'm right here.'

'All right, come on,' Rupert said, turning to the front door.

Sarah, standing in the lounge doorway, said, 'Oh, what happened to your lovely painting?'

Hannah glanced at Sarah. 'What painting?'

'You know, the one over your fireplace. Did you take it back to the shop?'

Hannah poked her head into the lounge. Her eyes went wide when she saw the empty space above the fireplace where her painting had been. She'd been in the kitchen, busy cooking, when Hetty had left. 'Oh. My. God.'

'What's wrong?' Rupert remarked.

Still standing in the lounge doorway, in shock at her missing painting, she glanced at Rupert and immediately realised she could do without him finding out she'd had the painting all along. 'Rupert, haven't you got an auction to go to?'

He was just leaving when Sarah raised her voice. 'Do you think she made off with *Sunrise Over Seashell Bay* too?'

Rupert suddenly did an about-turn. 'Did she just say, *Sunrise Over Seashell Bay*?'

27

'You took it!' exclaimed Rupert, still standing at the door even though he had the auction starting imminently.

'What are you talking about?' Hannah asked. Hetty, whom she'd thought was her friend, and who she'd innocently asked to value her airgraphs, had taken them – *and* her painting. If only she'd known Hetty's last name was Hartley. It couldn't be a coincidence. She must be a descendant of Owen Hartley.

The children were in the lounge, playing with Marlowe, but Nate, Lili and Sarah were still gathered in the hall, Ray standing behind Rupert by the front door, waiting to go up to Somersby Hall for the auction.

'I'm going to see my grandmother about the painting.'

'Please don't,' Hannah pleaded. Now Rupert knew she'd had the painting his grandmother had been searching for all along.

'Yeah, I bet you don't want me to tell her. Wait until she finds out you've got the painting she was searching for. *Her* painting.'

Maisie appeared at the lounge doorway. Hannah was about to find out she'd overheard everything. 'You promised me, Mum, that you wouldn't steal anything ever again.'

Rupert turned around and stared at Maisie.

Hannah stared at her too. 'Maisie, I didn't break my promise, I swear. I didn't steal anything.'

'But the man says you took the painting,' Maisie cried.

'No, that's not what he—'

'You're not going to prison again, are you?'

'Again?' Rupert looked wide-eyed at Hannah. Everyone fell silent. He stared around the room. 'Oh, my god, is it true? You've been in prison?'

'Yes, but that's all behind Hannah now,' said Lili. 'She's making a fresh start, running a shop and—'

'Did my grandmother know about this before she rented Gatekeeper's Cottage to you?'

'Well, no. It's not relevant.'

'Relevant – my arse,' said Rupert, rudely. 'She welcomes you into her home, lets you start a business using her house, and you pay her back by stealing her painting?'

'What do you mean – *stealing* her painting?' said Ray.

Rupert glanced over his shoulder at Ray. 'My grandmother asked me to look for her painting. Hannah volunteered to look for it herself, and I stupidly fell for that. You found it, didn't you, and took it.'

'I did not – I swear!'

'But it was hanging right here in the lounge over your fireplace – she …' he pointed rudely at Sarah, 'said so herself. I'm going to see my grandmother.'

'Please don't! I'm afraid she might ask me to leave.'

'Well, perhaps you should have thought of that before you started nosing around the house and stealing my grandmother's painting! You found it, didn't you, in the attic, and you *stole* it.'

'No, that's not true. I bought it.'

'Yeah, right,' Rupert scoffed.

Ray stepped in. 'Let's all calm down and sort out this little misunderstanding after the auction.'

'Little misunderstanding?' Rupert turned around and glared at Ray. He then fixed his angry gaze on Hannah. 'I'm going to see my grandmother, and you can't stop me!'

'Well, you do that – and while you're at it, ask her where the *real* Lady Jemima is!' Hannah slapped her hand over her mouth.

Rupert stared at her. 'I don't know what your game is …'

'I'm not playing games – your grandmother is. Ask her. Ask Percy.'

'What's Percy got to do with anything?'

'He's in on it too.'

'In on what?' Rupert said, 'Don't answer that. I don't know who you are, coming into our home, our lives … I thought …'

Hannah stared at him.

He shook his head and stormed out, brushing rudely past Ray as he got his phone out of his pocket.

Hannah stared after him, wide-eyed, wondering who he was calling. She saw him do an about-turn. 'What are you doing?' he said to Ray who'd been following him out of the door.

'I'm coming with you to help with the auction.'

'I don't want your help, thank you very much. I'll conduct the auction myself. I'm an art dealer. At least I have some experience.'

Hannah stood stock still in the hallway. She couldn't believe he'd accused her of stealing the painting. And in front of her guests.

Lili sidled up to Hannah and put an arm around her shoulders. 'He's an idiot.'

Ray said, 'Don't worry, Hannah – we'll clear all this up.'

'Yes,' Lili agreed, 'You bought the painting from the charity shop. No one can dispute that.'

'Rupert didn't give me a chance to explain,' Hannah said, wiping a tear from her eyes. 'I can't believe he accused me of stealing the painting. I thought he knew me better than that.'

Maisie put her arms around Hannah's waist. 'Sorry, Mum.'

Hannah looked down at her daughter. What she'd said hadn't helped. Now Rupert knew about her past. If he told his grandmother she'd been to prison for theft … but that wasn't Maisie's fault. 'It's all right, sweetheart.' Rupert was right: she was afraid she'd lose her new home. She looked at everyone milling around the hall. 'What am I going to do?'

Sarah stepped forward. 'What you are going to do, what we are all going to do, is sit down, enjoy our meal, and then after the auction calmly explain to Rupert just where you acquired the painting – all right?'

Hannah nodded and managed a wisp of a smile. 'All right.'

Hannah didn't have much of an appetite, but she joined everyone, squeezing around the dining room table to eat the Sunday meal.

Nate asked, 'What are you going to do about the airgraphs? Lili mentioned they were quite valuable. Sounds as though they would have fetched a lot of money if you'd sold them.'

They'd just put their knives and forks down, everyone congratulating Hannah on such a tasty Sunday roast, everyone's plates cleared apart from Hannah's when Nate asked the question.

Ray added, 'Are you sure you don't want to report the theft to the police?'

She turned to Ray and shook her head. 'She must be the descendant of Owen Hartley. I know I bought the painting, but there was always that conflict that if I did find Kitty or Owen's descendants, I'd feel duty-bound to hand the airgraphs over. I just wished she'd talked to me, told me who she was, instead of taking them. I'd have given her the letters. And I would have loved a conversation with her about what she knew of Owen and Kitty. But my painting …' she trailed off, still so upset that it was gone and she'd likely never set eyes on it again. She recalled what she'd jokingly said to Hetty the previous night about the painting – that even if Hetty had wanted to buy it, she'd never sell. 'Stupid me,' Hannah muttered under her breath, thinking it was no wonder that Hetty had made off with the letters and the painting.

Ray, sitting next to her, said, 'We know how much that painting meant to you.'

They were just clearing the table when Hannah heard a car turn up outside Gatekeeper's Cottage.

Everyone else paused. They'd heard the car too. 'That wouldn't be Hetty, would it?' Lili asked. 'Perhaps she felt guilty and came back to return the letters and painting?'

Hannah ran out of the dining room and headed for the door. Then someone knocked. Perhaps it was Rupert, quickly driving down from the house to apologise for jumping to conclusions about the painting and giving her a chance to explain.

Hannah flung open the door. She took a step back when she saw who it was.

William shouted out, 'There's a police car outside!'

Behind Hannah, everyone was gathered at the door. She turned to look at them. 'Did any of you call the police?'

They shook their heads.

'It must have been Rupert,' Hannah remarked. She looked at the officers. 'Henrietta Hartley isn't here. I can give you a statement about the theft of the letters and the painting, but I don't want her arrested.' Hannah wouldn't wish that on anyone, the humiliation of being arrested and put in handcuffs, the horrible police interview, not to mention the time she'd spent in prison. She shuddered at the thought. But she'd been guilty of theft and had deserved her punishment. Hetty, on the other hand – those letters and the painting really belonged to her; they were part of her family's history.

She noticed the police officers exchange a glance. They said, 'We're not here for Henrietta Hartley in connection with a theft. We are here for the tenant who lives here.'

Hannah looked at them, wide-eyed. 'Who – me?'

Suddenly everyone behind her was talking at once.

The police officers – a man and a woman – shook their heads. The woman police constable said, 'Will everyone please calm down and take a step back.'

Hannah was about to step back too.

'Not you,' said the officer.

'Are you arresting me?'

'We'd like to take you down to the station for questioning.'

'You're arresting her, then,' said Ray.

The woman police constable said, 'We are arresting you on the suspicion of theft. You do not have to say anything. But it may harm your defence if you do not mention when questioned something which you later rely on in court. Anything you do say may be given in evidence.'

Hannah stared at them, wide-eyed. 'Rupert phoned the police to have me arrested?'

The woman police constable said, 'We had a report from Somersby Hall of a theft at their property by their tenant. That's you.'

Hannah knew why he'd done it; because he'd found out she'd gone to prison for stealing.

'I swear I didn't do it.'

Everyone was talking at once again.

Ray said, 'This is all a big misunderstanding.'

'We will still have to take her down to the station for questioning.'

Hannah saw one of them put their hand on a pair of handcuffs. 'Please come with us.'

'But how long will this take? What about Maisie?'

Nate stepped forward. 'Maisie, go pack your things, please.'

Hannah looked at him. 'What are you doing? She doesn't have to leave. I'll be back soon …' she looked at the police officers. 'Won't I?'

'Mum?'

'It's all right, sweetheart. This is all a big misunderstanding. Maybe it would be best if you had another sleepover tonight with Dad while this is all sorted out. Go pack your bag. Everything is going to be just fine.'

Maisie looked at her doubtfully before charging up the stairs.

Nate turned to Hannah. 'You heard what Rupert said. He's going to speak to his grandmother, who is your landlady, and from what I gather she's been looking for her painting, which you had all along – and you knew it.'

The police officers exchanged a glance.

Nate quickly added, 'Now, we all know you didn't take it, but she's going to be pissed off, and I doubt, when this is all cleared up, she will ever trust her new tenant again. I'm sorry to say this, but I think she's probably going to ask you to leave.'

'No … no,' Hannah shook her head. 'I can't move out of Gatekeeper's Cottage and leave Somersby Hall.'

Lili said, 'I think you might have to prepare yourself for that eventuality.'

Nate continued, 'Look, Maisie has been through enough house moves of late. I'm sorry, but she's coming home with me and … and I'm applying to the court to take Maisie full time.'

'What? No! You can't do that!'

'I'm sorry, Hannah, truly I am, but I *can* do that. I've got to think of Maisie's best interests. Please understand …'

'But … but she's all I've got.' Hannah turned to her best friend. 'Lili?'

Lili was looking at the floor. She looked up but didn't meet Hannah's pleading gaze. 'I'm sorry, Hannah. I can't come between Nate and what he thinks is best for his child.'

'But I'm the best person for her, I'm her *mother*.'

Lili said in a small voice, 'Maybe you need to think about Maisie for a change?'

'But that's what I've been doing!'

'Have you?' Lili said.

Hannah stared at her. Was it true? Had she lost sight of the promise she'd made herself to put Maisie's needs above her own all because she'd become obsessed with the painting, and Owen and Kitty's love story – and Somersby Hall?

Ray stepped between the officer and Hannah. 'Look, you don't need to arrest her. She bought the painting fair and square – and we can prove it.'

'Have you got the receipt for …' the officer looked down at

his notepad, '*Sunrise Over Seashell Bay* by one Owen Hartley?'

Ray glanced over his shoulder at Hannah.

Hannah sighed. 'No. I bought it in a charity shop in Aldeburgh for cash, twenty pounds. I didn't get a receipt. Can't you just go and ask Mabel and Marjorie who run the charity shop? They can vouch for me.'

'Friends of yours, are they?'

'What's that supposed to mean?' Ray asked.

Sarah said, 'Can't you go to the shop where she bought it and—'

The officer said, 'It's Sunday. The shops are closed in Aldeburgh. Now, we're taking you down the station for questioning. Everyone else step back please.' The officers stood to one side, indicating for Hannah to step out of the house.

'I'm coming too,' said Ray. He turned to Hannah. 'We can clear this up down at the station, I promise.'

Hannah stood there helplessly, thinking *how*? Until they contacted Mabel and Marjorie, she had no way of proving she'd bought the painting. And then the police officers had asked if they were her friends. They were. But were they intimating her friends would cover for her, lie that they'd sold her *Sunrise Over Seashell Bay*? They couldn't even prove where the painting originated from. It had appeared outside the door to the charity shop when it was closed. Would the police believe them?

'I'm coming with you,' Sarah said to Ray.

The police officers barred their way. 'No.'

Sarah looked at Ray. 'Can they stop us?'

He sighed heavily. 'I'm afraid so.'

'What about Marlowe?' said William, appearing in the hallway, holding the puppy awkwardly in his arms. Is he coming home with us too?'

Maisie came thundering back down the stairs with her backpack on her back.

Nate took her hand. He looked over at William. 'Lili, can you take Marlowe please.'

Hannah was walking out of the door when she saw Lili taking her puppy, Nate taking her child. She stopped. 'No! This can't be happening!'

'Please, don't resist,' said the police officer reaching for her arm.

Hannah slapped the officer's hand away without thinking. Next thing she heard were the words, *resisting arrest.*

Hannah looked down at her hands. 'Please don't do this,' she pleaded as they put on the handcuffs. 'I don't want to go back to prison!'

28

Hannah sat on a stool in her shop, elbows on the counter, face resting in the palms of her hands, staring at the window display and the empty easel where her good-luck painting used to be. She hadn't had a single customer all morning. She breathed a heavy sigh, thinking bitterly, *Isn't hindsight a wonderful thing?*

If only she hadn't stood outside the bedroom door and overheard Lady Jemima telling Percy to go and fetch the painting from the shop in Cobblers Yard. She doubted very much that Percy would have stolen it.

'Oh, god – why did I take it home with me?' Her eyes filled with tears as she looked towards her empty easel, her gaze shifting to the window. She sat up with a start. Was that Percy staring back at her through the window?

Hannah blinked the tears from her eyes. Now she could see clearly, there was no one there.

I imagined it, thought Hannah. She frowned. Imagining Percy standing outside her shop brought to mind the last person she wanted to think about. It was all her fault – Lady Jemima, or whoever she really was. Now she was back living in the flat, with no customers, but worst of all – no Maisie.

'What have I done?' Hannah asked the empty shop. If only she hadn't found those stupid airgraphs, and Gatekeeper's Cottage hadn't happened to come up for rent. Little did she know that a perfect storm in her life had been brewing, the aftermath of which had led her back to where she had started – but worse.

'At least you've been released without charge,' Ray had said to her when he'd come and picked her up late Sunday night from the police station. Ray told her that Mabel and Marjorie had a computer and kept detailed accounts with dates and times of all transactions that had taken place in their shop – including the twenty pounds they'd received for a painting called *Sunrise Over Seashell Bay*. Within a few hours of arriving at the police station, she'd been released.

Ray had run her home to Gatekeeper's Cottage, where she'd arrived to find a hand-delivered letter on her doormat, from her landlady, no doubt put through her letterbox by Rupert. The letter told her to vacate Gatekeeper's Cottage – she had one week's grace to pack up her things and leave.

Hannah had promptly packed a suitcase full of her clothes and left for the flat above the shop. She hadn't been back to Gatekeeper's Cottage since she'd been released from police custody and had returned there to find the letter. It was now the following Friday. She didn't want to return to Somersby Hall and her rental ever again. But unless she was going to forfeit the rest of her possessions – those she hadn't yet packed up and taken away – she knew she had to return. The next day, Saturday, would be her last opportunity before she had to put the keys through the door on Sunday morning, as per the letter.

Ray had read the letter too and had told her that her landlady couldn't do that. She had a six-month tenancy agreement.

'But she didn't know I'd been to prison when I signed that. I'd withheld vital information that would have influenced her decision to rent to me,' Hannah had said, wishing she had told them. Then she'd never have rented it, and moved Maisie again, or got involved with Lady Jemima and Somersby Hall. And Rupert.

Rupert – she'd never see him again.

'And did your landlady or the estate agents ask you for a voluntary disclosure of any convictions?' Ray had asked.

They hadn't.

Hannah stared into space, recalling that conversation. Ray was only trying to be helpful. She imagined she wouldn't have to vacate Gatekeeper's Cottage. A landlord couldn't just evict a tenant with seven days' notice when they had a six-month tenancy agreement. Hannah was sure it was four weeks' notice. But four weeks or seven days – what was the difference? The outcome was the same; she still had to give up the new home that she'd loved.

Hannah had ripped up her tenancy agreement and thrown it in the bin. It was worthless. Even if she hadn't returned to that letter, it wouldn't be the same living there on her own – no Maisie, no Marlowe, and no Rupert or her wedding business idea. Not that she cared about work right now. She cared about her little family. That life, and all her hopes and dreams for a future there, had been dashed in one horrible evening. She knew she could probably go to the courts get Maisie back. But Nate and Lili were right: she hadn't been thinking about Maisie's needs. Her heart had sunk when she'd come to the conclusion that her daughter was better off with them.

She slammed her fist on the counter. 'I'm still a terrible mother. After everything I've done, nothing has changed!'

Embarrassingly, someone walked into the shop at that moment.

Ray said, 'Hello. Everything … all right?'

Hannah looked at him. How could he ask her that question? Even so, she looked at her hand, and said, 'Oh, there was a fly … on the counter … right there.' She made a show of swatting the imaginary fly on the counter again.

'Is that a fact?' said Ray.

Hannah avoided his gaze. Instead, she eyed the door, wondering why Ray had been her only visitor since her arrest the previous Sunday after dinner. She'd thought Lili might have popped in with some flowers to cheer her up. Then again, she imagined why people were avoiding her. It was all so embarrassing; her life had imploded, and she was back living above her shop on her own.

Thinking of living on her own, Hannah knew why Lili was avoiding her. It was because she'd sided with Nate over Maisie. Hannah just wanted to tell her that she didn't blame her. She would have done the same thing in Lili's shoes.

'Is Lili with you?' Hannah asked, hoping her friend was on her way. She was still staring at the counter, avoiding his gaze.

'No – were you expecting her?'

Hannah shook her head, examining the swirling patterns in the old laminate counter.

'I didn't think so. She's been quite busy, you know.'

Hannah wasn't surprised. That was nothing new. She had plenty of gardening jobs.

'Yes, this past week, she and her gardening team have been

working on a new project.'

Hannah sighed. She wasn't particularly interested, but she thought it was only polite to ask about it, as Ray had brought it up.

'I know this is probably going to come as a bit of a surprise, and the timing is not the best after what had happened at Somersby Hall, but … well, Lili is doing a landscaping job there.'

Hannah looked up sharply.

'I must admit, it's coming on in leaps and bounds.'

'She's landscaping the front of the house?' *But that was my idea*, thought Hannah. Another thought hit her with a jolt. Did that mean the wedding idea, *her* wedding idea, was still going ahead? Without her?

Hannah couldn't help but ask.

Ray shrugged. 'She must have thought it was such a good idea, she couldn't give it up. She told me all about it. She's even bought her wedding dress.'

Hannah couldn't believe what she was hearing.

'I told you she'd prefer to get married in a stately home rather than have her wedding reception in her back garden,' Ray said smugly.

How had that even come about – Lili landscaping the front garden? She must have spoken to Lady Jemima or Rupert, or both of them. 'But that was my idea, Lili landscaping the grounds and then having her wedding there.'

'Well, I suppose you'll have to take it up with Lady Jemima and Rupert then.'

Hannah stared at Ray. Why was he smiling? 'I'll do no such thing. I don't want to go back there.' Hannah felt worse than ever now she knew that despite what had happened – Rupert falsely accusing her of stealing his painting and getting her arrested for it – Lili had gone ahead with the wedding plans. Hannah felt so betrayed. It was the last thing she had expected after everything that had happened.

Ray obviously sensed he'd said the wrong thing. 'Well, look at it this way – things can only get better.'

Hannah shot him a look. 'How?' Her painting, her lucky charm – which she'd had to admit to herself hadn't proved that lucky at all; it had turned out to be her downfall – was gone. But on top of that, she was losing all confidence that her life would ever get on track. Was this it now, living in a small flat all on her own above a shop that wasn't even profitable?

'I've brought someone to see you.'

Hannah had spotted Marlowe in his arms the moment he'd stepped into the shop. She didn't want to see the puppy. It just reminded her of everything she'd lost. She'd thought Ray had come to tell her he'd found Hetty. He'd said he'd make some discreet inquiries, see if he could find her. Now, she'd changed her mind. What would she do if he had found her? Have her arrested?

Hannah was still of a mind that she didn't want to get Hetty into trouble, even though she could really do with those valuable airgraphs back – she needed the money now more than ever. But in her heart, she'd accepted that those love letters from Owen, and the painting, belonged with Owen's descendants. Hetty had her own problems. Hannah remembered that it was likely Hetty would have to leave her home in London – the rental she shared with her flatmates. And now she'd jeopardised her career by leaving without conducting the auction. Hetty had enough on her plate without being arrested. Hannah knew just what an impact that could have on a person's life.

And there was something else – the painting Rupert had seen in Somersby Hall, supposedly of one of his ancestors; one that looked remarkably like Hetty. Hannah didn't know what Hetty's connection was to the hall, other than the fact that she must be related to Owen Hartley, but what if she was the true heir to Somersby Hall?

Hannah realised that despite what Rupert had done, she still wanted to protect him from the fallout of what might happen if Hetty reappeared. She said, 'I'm glad you're here. I want to tell you to stop looking for Henrietta Hartley.'

'Why?'

'I just do. You haven't found her yet – have you?' Unfortunately, Hannah had told Ray everything that Hetty had mentioned about her life on the way back from the police station last Sunday, hoping he could find her. Now she'd changed her mind.

Ray shook his head.

Hannah breathed a sigh of relief. Hetty lived in London, which was a huge metropolitan city, and her grandfather lived in rural Dartmoor in a small cottage. Neither property would be easy to track down. Of course, Hetty had been living in her rental property in London for years, so Hannah wondered whether they could trace her address.

She didn't want to mention that, along with suggesting that Ray could ask Rupert for the name of the auction house who'd employed her services to conduct his auction.

Ray started to walk towards her with Marlowe.

Hannah sighed. 'Just take him back to Nate's, will you?'

'Ah, you don't mean that.'

'What are you doing here with him, anyway? Doesn't Maisie want her puppy?'

'She's feeling sad for you being alone and wants you to have Marlowe to keep your company.'

Hannah suddenly put her face in her hands. 'It's all gone wrong, like I knew it would. I was so happy, Ray, *so* happy. Nothing works out for me. And … and I think I was falling in love. Now, I'm back to where I started, but it's worse – so much worse. I haven't even got Maisie.'

'You can see Maisie any time, you know that.'

'I know, but Nate wants full custody, and … and perhaps it's for the best.'

'You don't mean that.'

'I seem to have this propensity to cock everything up. I just know I'm going to end up all alone.'

'Marlowe is here.'

'Oh, Ray, I can't possibly have him in the flat, you know that. He needs a garden, and some space and … and a family.' Hannah didn't know why she didn't cry.

'Give him a cuddle at least,' said Ray.

Hannah didn't want to. She didn't want to be reminded of everything she'd lost. But she could see him wagging his tail furiously as Ray approached, trying to wriggle out of his arms, head angling her way, whimpering.

'He still remembers me!' Hannah said in surprise, darting around the counter and taking the puppy in her arms. He was licking her face, her nose, her ear, wriggling excitedly in her arms, and then nibbling the buttons on her shirt.

'Oh, sweetheart, I've missed you so much.' Hannah smiled even though he was destroying the buttons on another shirt.

Ray turned around and walked to the door, putting the *Closed* sign in the window.

Hannan noticed. 'What's going on? It's not closing time. It's the middle of the afternoon.' Hannah stopped abruptly. 'Oh, you've come to chivvy me along and take me to Gatekeeper's Cottage to help me pack up my stuff.'

'Actually, no. We have an appointment. Or shall I say – *you* do.'

Ray opened the shop door. 'Come on.'

Hannah slowly walked to the door. 'What's this appointment about?'

'You'll see.'

He waited until she was out of the door, took the key out of the lock and locked up the shop. They turned to the left.

Hannah stopped. 'Oh, Ray, did you make me an appointment for me with Joss to have some legal advice over my tenancy? I told you I don't care that she's told me to get out, and legally she probably can't. I've left already, and I don't want to argue with her, or you, about it.'

She couldn't bring herself to set foot in the cottage, the place where she'd thought her life on the Suffolk Coast was just beginning.

Hannah had a thought. 'Could *you* go and collect my stuff? I know it's a big ask, but I just don't know how to go back and—'

'We're not going next door to Joss.'

'We're not?' Hannah looked at him perplexed. 'Then where are we going?'

'To the bookshop.'

'The bookshop? Ray, I'm not in the mood to buy a novel.'

'I didn't think you were. Just humour me.'

Hannah followed him, sighing. She had an idea what he was doing, taking her to have a coffee with Thea in the bookshop to cheer her up. Didn't he get it? She'd lost everything. There wasn't a single thing that would cheer her up. Hannah scratched that thought when she looked down at her puppy and smiled.

Her smile faded as they approached the bookshop. Thea had been avoiding her too. She knew Hannah was back living above the shop in the flat. Thea had warned her against getting involved with the occupants of Somersby Hall. She hadn't been best pleased when Hannah had told her she was renting Gatekeeper's Cottage. It was all so, so embarrassing. She should have heeded Thea's advice.

Hannah was not looking forward to Thea saying, *I told you so.* Meeting up with Thea after everything that had happened was going to be beyond awkward. She halted and looked down at Marlowe in her arms. He was a perfect excuse not to visit the bookshop. 'Oh, are dogs allowed in the bookshop? I'm sure they're not. Let's go back to my—'

'They've got a cat, so I don't see the problem.' Ray grabbed her sleeve, propelling her forward.

Hannah rolled her eyes. She didn't see what having a cat has got to do with it. If anything, it would make matters worse, a cat and dog who didn't know each other, in the same room.

'Don't worry,' said Ray, 'Everyone falls in love with Marlowe. It will be fine.'

'Even a cat?'

Ray appeared to ignore that comment. 'Now, if you had Lulu in tow, that might be a whole other ballgame.'

Lulu. She wished Ray hadn't brought up the Irish wolfhound. She missed her terribly too.

'Come on!'

Hannah was dragging her feet, but she guessed anything was better than sitting alone in her shop staring at the four walls and her empty easel. And she did miss Thea's amazing coffee – and Thea, of course.

She turned to Ray as he opened the shop door. There was something she'd been meaning to say. She'd been so relieved at her release without charge the previous Sunday night that when Ray had turned up to pick her up, she had been speechless. And she had been so tired that she could hardly gather her thoughts. Well, she could now. 'You know, I haven't thanked you for getting in touch with Mabel and Marjorie to vouch for me.'

As she walked into the shop with Ray following, he said, 'Oh, is that what you thought happened?'

'Well – yeah. You told me about the accounts they kept.'

'Yes, I did get in touch with them as soon as you'd left for the station.'

Hannah thought so. 'Well, thank you so much for getting me released. I wanted to thank you in person.'

'Oh, didn't they say why they were releasing you?'

'Yes, they said they're not pressing charges.'

'It wasn't me.'

Hannah turned around. 'Oh, well … thank Sarah for me.'

Ray shook his head and smiled. 'It wasn't her either, or Lili and Nate, before you ask.'

'I don't understand.'

'Mabel and Marjorie did dig out their records, but in the end they weren't required.'

'I still don't understand.'

'The charges were dropped.'

Hannah looked at him. 'You mean, as in withdrawn?' Her heart leapt, her spirit soared. 'Rupert withdrew the charges and got me out?'

'No – not Rupert.' Ray pointed.

Hannah turned and looked at who was seated on the sofa in the bookshop. She nearly dropped her puppy in shock. 'What is *she* doing here?'

29

Hannah said, 'I'll come back when they're gone.' She did an immediate about-turn.

Thea barred her way, putting the *Closed* sign in the window. She locked the door too, making a show of slipping the key into her pocket. She folded her arms. Unfortunately, Marlowe chose that moment to wriggle free, forcing Hannah to deposit him on the floor. He made a beeline for the sofa.

'Marlowe – no!' Hannah stared at the two people seated on the sofa, each with a mug of coffee. She glared at them, realising that she hadn't imagined fleetingly seeing Percy's face in her shop window when her eyes were filled with tears.

Percy stooped to give Marlowe a fuss. 'Well, aren't you a lovely pup. Don't you agree, Lady Jemima?'

'I do.' She smiled as the puppy jumped up at her legs and got lots of fusses from her too.

Hannah frowned at Marlowe, who was busy making friends with the enemy. She was not going to thank Lady Jemima, even though she had not pressed charges and had got her off the hook for stealing the painting, which she hadn't stolen in the first place.

'I do not want to speak to that woman.' She looked from Thea to Ray, standing in front of the door, stopping her from leaving the bookshop. 'I thought you were my friends?'

Thea exchanged a glance with Ray.

'We are,' they both said in unison.

Thea said, 'Now, how about a nice cup of coffee?'

'Not if I will have to sit with *them*.'

'You won't get one otherwise,' said Thea with a sly grin. She added, 'Ooh, just smell that coffee aroma.'

Hannah narrowed her eyes. 'What's going on?' she said slowly, wondering why she was there.

Lady Jemima said, 'I thought we'd meet up on neutral ground.'

This must have been the appointment Ray was talking about. She couldn't believe he'd gone behind her back and arranged it. The question was why? Hannah didn't care. She said, 'I don't want to speak to you.'

She smiled, surprising Hannah. 'I know – that's why you've not been answering my calls.'

'Why should I?' Hannah shot back. 'You're just calling to make sure I've packed up and left Gatekeeper's Cottage. I got the letter from the estate agents. Is that what this is about?'

'Not at all,' said Lady Jemima. 'Now please, come sit.'

She looked at Thea, who handed Hannah a coffee straight from Mabel's amazing coffee machine. Hannah took the coffee and perched on the chair opposite them. 'What do you want, then?'

'Just hear me out,' said Lady Jemima.

Hannah pursed her lips. 'I suppose I can do that,' she said grudgingly. 'Ray told me they weren't pressing charges after all. I suppose I owe you that at least.'

Her reply was not what Hannah was expecting. 'You don't owe me anything. It was Rupert who phoned the police before he even told me he'd found the painting … well, he'd found where it had been until someone took it. Stupid boy. He should have spoken to me first.'

'You knew I'd bought the painting from the charity shop?'

'No, not at all. But I know *you*. You can be trusted.'

'I can?'

'Yes, with a secret.'

'I don't know what you mean,' Hannah said slowly.

'Now, before we get into all that.' She turned to Percy sitting beside her. 'Percy … will you do the honours?'

Percy chuckled. 'Of course.' He slowly stood and brought over something wrapped in a blanket to give to Hannah.

Hannah shot Lady Jemima a look. 'I don't want some sort of gift to pay me off for the wrongful arrest. There's no way I'm going to accept—'

He unwrapped the painting.

She gasped. 'What's this?'

'Now, I'm sure you recognise *Sunset Over Seashell Bay*. Call it a peace offering?'

'But …' Hannah felt overcome. 'Why on earth would you come here and give me your painting?'

'Because I have been a very, very silly old fool.'

Percy opened his mouth to say something. She held up her finger, 'Don't you dare say *I told you so*.'

He clamped his mouth shut, but that didn't stop him grinning.

Hannah looked from Lady Jemima to Percy. 'I don't

understand.' She still couldn't believe Jemima was giving her the painting.

'Now, you can have it on one proviso …'

Hannah sighed. What was that saying – nothing in life is free. She knew there would be strings attached. 'What's the proviso?' she asked flatly.

'That you *don't* put it on the easel in your shop.'

'Why not? Where else do you expect me to put it?'

'I expect you to take it home with you and put it on the wall there.'

'Upstairs to the flat?'

'No, you daft brush, to Gatekeeper's Cottage, on the wall above the mantel shelf.'

Hannah stared at her. Had she lost her short-term memory all of a sudden? She frowned at her. 'Now, just wait one minute. You told me to vacate Gatekeeper's Cottage. I got the letter …'

'That was Rupert, I'm afraid. Sorry.'

'Rupert? Rupert wrote that letter? So, how did you find out about it?'

Her eyes rose to look across Hannah's shoulder. She turned around. 'Ray?'

'I told Lili about the letter you'd come home to when you'd been released.'

Lady Jemima added, 'Yes, and by goodness did she go off on one when she found out. Marched right up to us in her muddy boots and green garden gloves demanding to see me. Percy and I were having a rather relaxing time sitting together in the autumn sunshine in the back garden, sharing a rather nice pot of tea when the green goddess – that's what I call our amazing gardener – came storming up, demanding to know why I'd sent you that letter, of which I knew nothing. And believe me, Rupert got the third degree over it.'

Hannah's mouth fell open before she took a sip of coffee. She stared at Lady Jemima. She was very pleased to find out that Rupert had got the telling-off he deserved for putting her through being arrested and then arriving home to the letter telling her to get out and never darken their doors again. In fact, when she thought about the letter, it hadn't really been professional; it had sounded more like a rant.

Something else pleased Hannah no end. Lili might be doing the garden at Somersby Hall, but she still had her best friend's back. Hannah wished she could run straight across the yard, find Lili in The Potting Shed and hug her.

'Oh, and one more thing,' said Lady Jemima. 'When you've hung your painting over your fireplace, I expect you to carry on with the wedding planning at Somersby Hall.'

Hannah nearly spilled her coffee. 'Is this some kind of joke?'

'Not at all. Please hear me out. I think I have an apology to make.'

'Not *I think*,' Percy corrected her.

She shot him a look. 'Don't be pedantic, Percy.'

Hannah sighed. She knew she should be over the moon to find out she didn't have to pack up her stuff and leave Gatekeeper's Cottage after all, but they obviously didn't understand. 'I can't go back to Gatekeeper's Cottage. It's not my home without Maisie,' she said miserably.

Ray said, 'I brought Marlowe. That's where I'm taking you after this little meeting. Stay for the night, see how you feel.'

Hannah smiled at the pup. How could she resist? 'All right.'

Ray grinned at her.

She turned to Lady Jemima and Percy. 'Why didn't you go in and hang it up in the lounge, and just tell me, instead of carting the painting all the way here?'

'It's your home. We have no right to enter your house …'

'Ahem!' Percy coughed into his hand to get Lady Jemima's attention. 'Well, that's a bit after the fact,' said Percy.

Hannah caught Lady Jemima frowning at Percy. Hannah said, 'I don't care if you've been in Gatekeeper's Cottage. I've got nothing to hide.'

'Are you sure about that?' said Lady Jemima, putting her empty coffee mug on the coffee table in front of her.

30

Lady Jemima leaned back in her chair and regarded Hannah. 'You know who I am, don't you?'

Hannah looked from Ray to Thea, who had appeared with a couple of stools to join them. Marlowe had flopped down at Hannah's feet, taking a nap after all the excitement of making new friends.

Hannah raised her eyes from her sleeping puppy, and said, 'I don't know what you mean.'

Lady Jemima started shaking her head slowly from side to side. 'I can't believe, after everything Rupert has put you through, that you're still protecting my secret, Hannah.'

Percy nodded. 'Neither can I, *Kitty*.'

Hannah raised her eyebrows, waiting for her to admonish Percy for calling her that name. But she did no such thing.

Hannah shot Ray and Thea a look, wondering why they weren't commenting on the sudden name drop from Percy.

Kitty shifted her gaze to Thea and Ray. 'Don't worry – like you, they also know I'm not the *real* Lady Jemima.'

Hannah's mouth dropped open at the admission, in front a retired police officer, that she wasn't the real Lady Jemima.

Ray began, 'Lady Jem—'

'Call me Kitty. You all might as well.'

Hannah said, 'You *are* Kitty – not Lady Jemima.' It wasn't a question. The woman masquerading as Lady Jemima didn't deny it. So, finally Hannah had her answer, and in front of witnesses.

'I don't understand.' Hannah's head turned from Kitty to Ray. 'Why aren't you arresting her for stealing Lady Jemima's identity?'

Ray sighed. 'For one thing, Hannah, I'm on civvy street now.'

'But … but can't you make a citizen's arrest?'

'Hannah, I think one wrongful arrest among us is enough for one week – don't you?'

'What do you mean?'

Kitty glanced at Percy and said, 'There's been no crime committed here, if that's what you're thinking.'

'Unless you count that coffee-maker,' chuckled Percy. 'Blow me, I couldn't believe it when Thea told us Mabel had given her the coffee-maker. How could you give something away like that, that makes the perfect cup of coffee? It's a crime, if you ask me.'

Everyone turned to look at Percy. 'Oh … sorry,' he mumbled.

Ray turned to Hannah. 'Remember, I told you once that nothing is ever what it seems. Your arrest last Sunday was a case in point, wasn't it? Rupert jumping to conclusions without getting the facts first.'

Hannah turned to Kitty. 'So, what are the facts – in your case?'

Kitty smiled. 'All in good time.' She said, 'You recognised the painting in my bedroom, the artist, didn't you? You had the airgraphs, and the other painting I was desperately searching for

– *Sunrise Over Seashell Bay*.'

Hannah wondered where she was going. She guessed this was what Lady Jemima – Kitty – really wanted to discuss.

'When Rupert mentioned that you'd overheard what I'd said about the wedding idea to Percy behind closed doors, I suspected you may have heard Percy call me Kitty. I knew for sure when Rupert came storming up to my room last Sunday evening, saying that *you* stole the painting, although he also said that the auctioneer had made off with some valuable letters in your possession too – letters from Owen to Kitty. He told me you'd showed them to him last Saturday evening, asking all sorts of questions. That's when I discovered you knew my secret, or at least suspected I wasn't who I claimed to be.'

Hannah stared at her.

Kitty said, 'The thing that puzzled me was: why were you still protecting my secret if you suspected? You'd shown Rupert the airgraphs and had even asked whether I went by a nickname. Why didn't you just tell him what you suspected? Rupert said he believed all these questions had been just because you wanted to get yourself into my good books by finding out if I had a pet name. But what I gleaned was that you were trying to find out if Rupert knew my secret. Which you discovered he did not. So, why not tell him your suspicions? Why protect my secret?'

'I wasn't.'

'I know that now. You weren't protecting me – why should you after overhearing me rubbish your wedding planning idea, when I'd said to your face something completely different? Then I realised. It was so obvious. Only a fool could miss what was really going on.'

'Which is? Hannah asked.

'You are in love with my grandson.'

'I am not!'

'I think you are,' said Ray. 'In fact, I know so. You told me yourself you'd fallen in love.'

'Ray!' Hannah glared at him. 'I didn't tell you *who*.'

He shrugged. 'No, you didn't. No matter how many romance novels I read, I can never figure out women.'

'Then how did you know, Ray?' asked Thea.

'Oh, that's easy. Lili told me.'

Hannah rolled her eyes. Trust her best friend!

'And you, my dear girl,' Kitty said, pointing a finger at Hannah, 'you know a thing or two about keeping secrets – don't you?'

Hannah frowned. She'd known *that* would crop up. It was like a bad penny that would follow her around for the rest of her life. 'You're talking about my previous stint in prison.'

Hannah didn't wait for her to respond before she added, 'I wasn't surprised, after Rupert presumably told you about that, that you'd want me out of Gatekeeper's Cottage and out of your life. That's why I never guessed the letter telling me to pack up my stuff and leave wasn't from you.'

Kitty nodded. 'But why would I want you to pack up and leave Gatekeeper's Cottage and Somersby Hall? Listen, we're all guilty of something. I'm sure nobody is spotless and can put their hand on their heart and say they haven't done something they knew was wrong, that they regret, even if they weren't caught.'

Hannah stared at her, thinking about her assuming Lady Jemima's identity. She'd known it was wrong. Did she regret it too?

'So, you knew about my history of crime?'

She laughed. 'You make it sound like you were some sort of master criminal working the underworld rather than simply a girl who'd made a mistake. Believe me, I know all about making mistakes. It's just some people, like yourself, unfortunately get caught.'

But you didn't, thought Hannah.

'But I digress,' said Kitty. 'I'm not talking about your previous stint in prison when I said you know a thing or two about keeping secrets.'

Hannah looked at her warily. 'Then what *are* you talking about?'

'Your daughter, Maisie.'

Hannah shifted nervously in her seat. She glanced at Ray. 'I don't know what you mean.' Hannah noticed Ray was avoiding her gaze. She raised her eyebrows. 'Ray, what did you tell them?'

Percy said, 'Your secret, or should I say Maisie's, is safe with us.'

'Ray?' Hannah's voice held a warning note.

Ray breathed a sigh before he said, 'Hannah, look. After Rupert's outburst about you taking the painting, Kitty and Percy visited Gatekeeper's Cottage after you were arrested.'

Hannah wasn't surprised.

'Sorry,' Kitty and Percy said in unison.

Hannah narrowed her eyes. 'You were looking for the airgraphs, wondering if Hetty might not have taken them, checking whether they might still be at Gatekeeper's Cottage.'

Percy and Kitty exchanged a glance, nodding their heads. 'Yes.'

Ray continued, 'That's when they came across the works of

what they thought were Old Masters. They called Rupert to come immediately after the auction and look too. He assessed them, rightly, as fake.'

Kitty looked at Ray, and said, 'But then that begged the question – why were there fake paintings in your home, Hannah? Were you intending to run a criminal enterprise from our house – selling forgeries? Were you thinking of getting Rupert involved?'

Hannah looked at Kitty and Percy. 'What on earth do you mean?'

Ray said, 'Because Rupert is an art dealer, perhaps they thought you would try and persuade him to pass the paintings off as genuine.' He grinned and turned to Kitty. 'There, look at her expression. I told you she was thinking no such thing.'

Hannah frowned at Ray. 'That wasn't all you told them, was it?'

'I had to, Hannah. I had to tell them about Maisie. I couldn't get the police involved in what they'd found in Maisie's bedroom in Gatekeeper's Cottage, obviously.'

'I bet they didn't believe you,' said Hannah, 'when you told them it was just an innocent nine-year-old painting copies of old works for no reason other than that she wanted to.'

'I believed Ray,' said Kitty, surprising her. 'I knew you weren't just protecting Rupert from the truth because you were in love with him – you were protecting someone else you loved too. Of course, you wanted to stay in Gatekeeper's Cottage, so blowing my secret wide open threatened your home, but I sensed there was something more … someone else you were protecting too.'

Hannah's lip wobbled. She wondered what they wanted in return for protecting Maisie's secret.

'I won't tell anyone your secret, Kitty – I promise.'

'Tit for tat,' said Kitty.

'Yes – that. I won't tell Rupert, I swear. But you know that already,' said Hannah, eyeing her a long moment. 'So, what else do you want?'

'I told you. I want you to carry on working on Lili's wedding – with Rupert.'

'*With Rupert?*' Hannan nearly fell off her chair. 'Are you joking? You'd better be, because there is no way Rupert will agree to—'

'Rupert, like his father, is very proud. He made a mistake by jumping to conclusions and having you arrested. He doesn't want you to leave Gatekeeper's Cottage or Somersby Hall.'

'He said that?' Hannah was finding that very difficult to believe after he'd written that letter.

'Not in so many words. But I *know* him. I know my grandson, and he can be stubborn.'

'Just like you,' Percy said with a chuckle.

'Thank you for that observation, Percy,' Kitty said dryly.

'Not at all,' Percy added, throwing her a mischievous grin.

'Look, Lady Jemima – I mean Kitty – I can't just turn up and resume planning Lili's wedding at Somersby Hall like nothing has happened.'

'Yes, you can. I expect Rupert thinks you won't come back even if he asks.'

Hannah knew what her game was. If Kitty thought she and Rupert could pick up where they'd left off, she was mistaken. She breathed a heavy sigh. 'Rupert is not going to be asking me to come back, I can assure you. He won't want me back, not after he found out I had the painting you'd asked him to find all along, and I didn't tell him. That's without what Maisie revealed about my past. He'll be running back to Claudia.'

'I think not,' said Kitty. 'Rupert has split up with Claudia.'

Hannah sighed. She wasn't really surprised, but that didn't mean anything. 'He'll probably blame me, say it's my fault.'

'I rather think it is,' Kitty quipped.

Percy cocked his head to one side. 'What she means is …'

'Really, Percy, I don't think you have to spell it out. Hannah knows in her heart why Rupert could never marry Claudia.'

'Because they never argue?' Hannah said.

Kitty laughed. 'Goodness me, Hannah, how much of our conversation did you overhear standing outside my bedroom door?'

Hannah confessed in a small voice. 'All of it.'

Percy chuckled.

Kitty said, 'Well, then, now you know my thoughts on their relationship, I'll share something else – Rupert could never marry Claudia because he is in love with someone else.' Kitty eyed her keenly.

Hannah looked away, although she did ask, 'How could you possibly know that?'

'Because I know a love-sick puppy when I see one. Goodness knows, I had one following me around for long enough before we got together.' She turned to Percy and took his hand in hers.

Percy patted her hand and smiled. He said, 'I think you should tell Rupert the truth.'

Kitty raised her eyebrows.

Percy nodded. 'You know the time has come. Better he hears it from you than … than if Hetty were to return and … well, you remember what happened when Rupert's father discovered you weren't really Lady Jemima.'

Hannah leaned forward in her seat. Was that what had led to her estrangement from her son? Hannah had suspected he may have discovered his mother wasn't who he'd thought she was, but of course she had no way of knowing for sure – until now.

Kitty hung her head, sharing with everyone in the room what had happened when Rupert's father had discovered she'd been keeping a secret of that magnitude from her own son. 'He bundled Rupert in his pyjamas into the back of his car and left, never to return.'

Now it all made sense. Hannah realised that some of the gossip Lili had told her that she'd heard from Mabel and Marjorie was true – Kitty was estranged from her son. And it explained the reasons Rupert's father had frowned on him returning to Somersby Hall and why his father wouldn't set foot in the hall – because his mother wasn't Lady Jemima, he wouldn't stand to inherit the house, and neither would Rupert – not if it was ever revealed. Rupert's father, however, had never explained that fact to Rupert.

Percy squeezed her hand when she said, 'I've lost a son. I can't lose a grandson as well.'

Kitty turned to Hannah. 'Will you help me? He loves you. He'll listen to you. Perhaps you can convince him to forgive me when he finds out.'

Hannah stared at her pleading eyes. As much as she wanted to, she knew she couldn't go to the hall. 'Rupert won't want me there. Besides, it doesn't involve me. It's about *your* family, Kitty. You and Rupert.'

Kitty exchanged a smile with Percy. 'Family is not just blood, is it? It's who you choose to share your life with.' She smiled at Percy. 'Family is whatever you choose it to be. Now, I would like my new family member,' she eyed Hannah keenly, 'to return to Gatekeeper's Cottage, and for Rupert to stop being so pig-headed and make up with her … you.'

'You can't make him,' said Hannah. 'I know he likes to please you; you're his grandmother, but I think in this instance—'

'I think in this instance, when you two do make up, your bond with be stronger than ever.'

Hannah suddenly recalled what she'd overheard Kitty say to Percy when they'd been discussing relationships; Rupert's in particular. *I'm of a mind that it's pretty normal to have a falling-out once in a while, and makes for a stronger relationship, weathering the ups and downs.*

Hannah didn't want to get her hopes up. She just couldn't. She'd suffered too many disappointments in love, in every aspect of her life, it seemed.

'Why don't you bring Marlowe up to the house?' Kitty suggested. 'That will break the ice.'

Hannah looked at her sleeping puppy.

Kitty said, 'He's always wanted a pup.'

'I'm not giving him Marlowe, if that's what you're thinking,' Hannah said quickly.

'Not at all. I was rather thinking that you could both butter him up, so to speak, and anyway … if a certain two people were to get together, romantically, then Rupert wouldn't need a puppy of his own because …' she trailed off.

'Are you seriously trying to set me up with your grandson right now?'

'I don't need to set up two people who are already in love. I think things will sort themselves out – as long as you meet up again, of course.'

'What do you propose? I can't just turn up at the house.'

'Yes, you can. You are the wedding planner. And it's still my house, for now. So I can invite who I want.'

That was the Lady Jemima that Hannah knew so well. 'Do you mind if I still call you Lady Jemima? It's just, you don't seem like a Kitty.' Hannah couldn't reconcile that name with the formidable woman she saw before her.

Kitty regarded her a long moment. 'After decades in her shoes, I do feel like Lady Jemima. You know I left Kitty behind a *very* long time ago.'

Percy sat there nodding his head. 'Ay – you did.'

'Now, I want you and Rupert to come and see me, together, and I am going to tell you a story about Lady Jemima, Kitty, and Owen Hartley, and what happened at Somersby Hall on the eve of war.'

31

When Hannah pulled into the drive of Somersby Hall, she discovered there was nowhere to park her car outside Gatekeeper's Cottage. The two spaces on the small shingle parking area at the side of the cottage were already taken.

Hannah had no choice but to pull up on the grass verge. She saw Ray, who'd been following in his car, doing the same.

Hannah's car was quite small, and Ray had been right when he'd said that putting Marlowe's dog crate and Marlowe in her car, along with her new painting, was asking for trouble. The last thing she wanted was to damage the painting or the frame.

Hannah got out of the car and looked up the drive. She immediately saw what Lili and her gardening team had achieved in just under a week. She was so in awe of Lili's skills and how hard her team had worked. It looked as though the landscaping project in the grounds in front of Somersby Hall was nearing completion. She wouldn't be surprised if Lili finished planting the borders and the areas between the cobbled pathways winding around the manicured lawn in the next week.

Hannah opened the rear car door and reached inside. She carefully lifted her painting off the back seat. Ray was already out of his car, getting Marlowe out of his crate.

Hannah said, 'What's going on?' She was eyeing the two cars parked by Gatekeeper's Cottage. She knew who they belong to – one was Nate's car and the other belonged to Sarah.

Ray turned around with the puppy in his arms, looking at her sheepishly.

Hannah frowned. 'I wasn't expecting a welcoming committee.' As much as she wanted to see them all – she hadn't seen any of them all week, not since her arrest – she really wasn't in the mood to entertain. She had spoken with Maisie several times on the phone, trying to reassure her she was okay and that she wanted Maisie to enjoy herself at her dad's house. She needed some time to figure things out. Just then, all she wanted was a quiet night in with Marlowe. Hannah admitted what she was thinking.

'I know,' he said, smiling.

Hannah rolled her eyes. If he knew that, why were they all there? She sighed. She guessed the reason even before she opened the front door to a big banner reading *Welcome Home*. Hannah slapped a smile on her face when Nate, Lili, Sarah, William and Maisie, who'd clearly been standing in the hallway waiting for her return, shouted out, 'Surprise!'

It all just reminded her of the get-together the previous Sunday when she'd thought her life was finally coming together. Although she was back, and Lady Jemima hadn't kicked her out of Gatekeeper's Cottage, in terms of her future, nothing was certain.

She couldn't imagine she was going to get a very good reception from Rupert when she turned up at Somersby Hall the next morning to meet with Lady Jemima and find out about her past. And as for resuming working with Rupert on the wedding planning, she'd believe it when she saw it.

No matter what Lady Jemima had said about Rupert, and the reasons he'd split up from Claudia, Hannah wondered whether he could forgive her for not telling him the truth about her painting or her past. Somehow, she doubted it. It was little wonder that Lady Jemima was worried. She knew her grandson – she was worried he wasn't going to forgive Hannah either.

Hannah decided not to think about the next day or her future. Or Rupert, although he was never far from her mind. Whatever happened in Somersby Hall, just then her family were all there, and that, Hannah realised, was all that mattered.

Maisie ran up to her. 'Mum, I made the banner.'

'So, did I,' said William, running up to her too.

'Oh, sweethearts, what a lovely, lovely surprise.' Hannah pulled them both close for a big hug. When she let the children go, she hugged Lili next.

'I brought you some flowers. They're in the window.'

Hannah could have cried. 'Thank you, Lili.'

Nate said, 'Shall I take your new painting and hang it in the lounge?'

Hannah glanced at Ray. He must have alerted them that they were on their way and that Hannah had a new painting.

'Yes, please.'

Sarah got a hug next. 'I must dash back to the kitchen. I'm cooking the dinner.'

'Oh, you didn't have to cook a meal.' She knew what they were doing – having another housewarming party to make up for the previous Sunday.

Lili said, 'I'm helping too.'

They both walked into the kitchen.

Ray disappeared and returned with Marlowe's crate and all his belongings – even his dog food and bowls.

Hannah hovered in the hallway. 'Why are you bringing all Marlowe's stuff back from Nate's? It's only for one night.'

Hannah caught Ray and Nate exchanging a glance as Nate walked into the dining room. She heard Maisie call out from the dining room, 'Mum, come and play with us.'

Hannah glanced in the lounge to see William busy playing tug-of-war with Marlowe and one of his toys.

She walked into the dining room. Maisie was kneeling on a chair, elbows on the table, playing a board game with her father.

Maisie got down from her chair and came running up to Hannah, taking her hand. 'Look, we've been playing this old board game from the bookshelf in my bedroom.'

'Oh, I see.' Hannah felt a lump in her throat at the thought of them all going home after dinner and leaving her there on her own. She knew Ray thought he was being helpful suggesting Marlowe stayed the night, but she wasn't sure that was going to help when she'd have to hand the puppy back to Maisie the next day.

'I found the game in my room on the bookshelf when I was unpacking my bag.'

Hannah looked at her. 'What do you mean … unpacking your bag?'

'I wanted to put all my things away before dinner.'

Hannah caught Ray smiling as he walked out of the room. He reappeared briefly, popping his head round the door. 'Nate, I remember you've got something to say to Hannah.'

Nate nodded.

Maisie put another playing piece on the game board. 'That's yours, Mum.'

'All right, but you'll have to explain the rules.'

It didn't take long, and Hannah was throwing two dice for her turn, moving her counter along the squares on the board. She glanced at Nate, who had the dice in his hand. He blew on them for good luck before throwing them and said, 'My parents called a family meeting before we all came over …' he looked at Hannah sheepishly before shifting his counter.

'Sounds ominous,' Hannah joked as Maisie took the dice and blew on them too, copying her dad.

'It was,' Nate replied.

'What happened?'

'I'm not living with Dad anymore,' Maisie said matter-of-factly, as she threw the dice. 'I'm still going to stay every other weekend with Dad like normal.'

Hannah's mouth dropped open. She looked across at Nate. 'Really, truly? Is that what the family meeting was about – Maisie is here to stay?'

'Yeah, I didn't want to take her away from you.'

'After everything that happened, I wouldn't have blamed you, Nate.'

'But it wasn't your fault. I acted in the heat of the moment last Sunday, said some things I wish I hadn't. I'm sorry. You've made a lovely home for her here.'

The last thing Hannah wanted was to appear ungrateful for Nate's decision, or to cause him to change his mind, but she had to be honest. 'I don't know how long we're going to be here for. I've got a six-month tenancy, but I don't know what will happen after that, especially if Hetty comes back and—' Hannah stopped abruptly. Just what had Ray told Nate during this family meeting. Was it just about Maisie, or was it about her landlady too?

'Ray passed on some pearls of wisdom from Lady Jemima's chauffeur, Percy.'

Hannah stared at Nate. She didn't hear the name Kitty.

Nate said, 'When ... if … things change, then we will cross that bridge. Together, I might add – not with me going off on one and being a—'

Hannah raised her eyebrows, nodding in Maisie's direction.

Maisie shot her dad a look. Although she'd been busy moving her counter along the squares, counting as she went, she was still listening to her parents' conversation.

Nate rephrased. 'We can work it out together. Besides, I have a feeling this wedding idea is going to take off, the hall won't have to be sold, and there will be no reason for you and Maisie to leave your new home.'

Hannah bit her lip. The problem was that Nate didn't have the full picture when it came to Somersby Hall. What if Hetty came back? It was no use mentioning Hetty to Nate – he had no idea of the significance of the airgraphs or Hetty or just who Lady Jemima really was. Come to think of it, on that last point, Hannah didn't know who Lady Jemima really was either – apart from a name. She guessed she was going to find out the next day, though.

'So, as I said, in the event that the untoward does happen …'

Nate didn't realise that the untoward could be travelling back to Somersby Hall right now.

'… we will cross that bridge then, all right? All that matters right now is that Maisie, and you, are happy in your new home together. Oh, and of course, Marlowe too.'

Hannah jumped out of her seat, surprising him, and ran up and put her arms around Nate. He stood and hugged her too.

Maisie smiled at her parents, and said, 'It's your turn, Mum.'

Lili walked in on Hannah and Nate hugging. 'Hey – what's going on?' She was smiling, knowing exactly what was going on.

Hannah released Nate and ran over and hugged Lili too, telling her that she'd seen the front garden, and it was amazing.

'I'm doing it for you, I hope you know that. I didn't want you to think that I'd forgotten about you and was just going ahead, planning to have the wedding here without you.'

Hannah caught Lili exchanging a glance with Nate. She wasn't quite sure what had passed between them. Nate was obviously going along with the idea. Whether he was happy about Lili dropping their original wedding plans to help Hannah out, she wasn't sure.

Sarah walked in. 'Ah, good. Nate has told you about Maisie. Wonderful. Now, I need to lay the table, so if you can clear away that board game.'

'Oh, Grandma!' Maisie said, objecting. 'We're in the middle of a game!'

Sarah raised her eyebrows.

Maisie threw her a look before packing it away in the box. 'I'll put it over here, for after dinner.'

Nate got up from the table, and Hannah watched Sarah lay two place settings while Maisie sat at the table.

Lili and Nate disappeared out of the room. She called after them, 'We need more knives and forks.'

Hannah asked Sarah if she needed help dishing up.

'No need, it's all in hand.'

Hannah was just reaching for more placemats sitting on the

dresser, when Sarah walked in carrying two plates. 'Oh, no need for more placemats, Hannah. Take a seat.'

Hannah slowly sat down opposite Maisie, who had picked up her knife and fork. Sarah set the plates down in front of them and promptly disappeared. Hannah waited. She looked to the door and saw Nate and Lili in the hallway putting on their coats. 'What's going on? Aren't you joining us for dinner?'

She heard William complaining, 'But I wanted to stay and play with Marlowe some more.'

Nate said, 'We told you we were only stopping by to drop Maisie off and have a word with her mum.'

Sarah and Ray popped their heads in the doorway.

Hannah looked at her dinner. 'Aren't you all joining us?'

They shook their heads. 'This is your evening, Hannah, you and Maisie together in your new home.'

'And Marlowe,' Maisie said, digging into her dinner.

'Of course,' Ray replied. 'And Marlowe.'

'Let me see you out,' Hannah said, rising from her seat. 'I don't know how to thank you all …'

'No need to see us out, or thank us,' Sarah said.

There were nods of agreement and smiles all round as everyone popped their heads in the room and said goodbye, apart from William, who asked, 'When can I see Marlowe again? Can I have a sleepover at Auntie Hannah's house soon?'

Hannah grinned. 'Of course you can, sweetheart, if that's all right with your dad … and mum.' Hannah glanced at Lili.

'Can I? Can I?' William pestered.

'Of course you can,' said Nate.

Hannah heard the front door shut and three cars leaving as they ate their dinner.

32

Hannah looked across the table at Maisie. She still couldn't believe her daughter was back. This was her dream come true. Her thoughts turned to Somersby Hall and Rupert. It was *one* of her dreams come true, at any rate.

'Mum.'

She fixed her gaze on Maisie. 'Yes, sweetheart?'

'When we've finished our dinner, can we play the board game again before bedtime?'

Hannah couldn't think of anything she'd rather do and anywhere she'd rather be than sitting that evening in her new home, playing a boardgame with her daughter, with their puppy sleeping peacefully at their feet.

Marlowe had come bounding in, looking for them. He'd jumped up at Hannah's legs. She'd resisted picking him up while she was at the dinner table. Whining, he soon realised, was futile, so he found a spot under the table and curled up, falling asleep.

'We'll have to start the game again,' Maisie was saying. 'It might take a long time.'

Hannah didn't care one bit. 'How about we stay up late tonight and play our game, watch tv, and just do what we want.'

'Yippee!'

The next day was Saturday, and Hannah knew she was meant to open the shop. She looked at Maisie, 'We can have a sleep in.'

'What about the shop?'

'I'm not going to work this weekend. We can spend it together, you and me.'

'All weekend?'

Hannah bit her lip. 'Actually, Ray will be popping in tomorrow to help you start doing some little training lessons with Marlowe while I have some business up at the house.'

'Planning Lili's wedding? Ray says you're going to have a new job as a wedding planner, and maybe you'll turn our shop into a wedding shop too.'

'A bridal shop,' Hannah corrected her. She wished Ray hadn't said that. She didn't know whether the wedding venue at Somersby Hall was going to take off. Hannah knew she was getting ahead of herself. She didn't know how the meeting was going to go with Lady Jemima and Rupert. But that didn't stop her resuming planning Lili's wedding. After all, as Lady Jemima had said, *you are the wedding planner*.

❖

Maisie was tucked up in bed. Hannah was about to close the curtains when she paused, staring across the floodlit lawn to the house. She wondered what the next day would bring when she returned to Somersby Hall.

'Is everything all right, Mum?'

Hannah closed the curtains, and turned to Maisie, remembering Percy's pearl of wisdom. She wouldn't worry about tomorrow; she'd just cross that bridge when she came to it.

'Right now, sweetheart, everything is just perfect.'

'Can Marlowe sleep on my bed?'

'Nope, but he can snuggle up and listen to a story with us before I put him down for the night.'

'All right.' Maisie put an arm around Marlowe, who was lying next to her.

Hannah had just opened the story book when Maisie said, 'Can you tell me a story about the big house?'

'Somersby Hall?'

She nodded.

Hannah reached up and opened her curtain slightly, catching the lights on in some of the rooms up at the big house and wondering which room was Rupert's. She already knew which was Lady Jemima's.

'Well, once upon a time there was a …

'Lady?'

'Yes, a lady who lived in a very big house. Her dad wanted her to marry someone very rich, but she had fallen in love with someone else, someone below her station.'

'What does that mean?'

'Ah, a member of staff, rather than—'

'Someone with lots of money?'

'Yes.' Hannah continued with her made-up story of the lady who ran away with the butler, eloping to a little cottage in Dartmoor, never to be seen again, but where they lived happily ever after.

'But why couldn't they live happily ever after in the big house?'

'Because her dad didn't want her to marry the butler, so she had to leave.'

Hannah frowned. That didn't explain why Kitty had stepped into Lady Jemima's shoes and taken her identity. It didn't explain a lot of things.

'But why …?'

'I'll tell you what? I'll finish the story tomorrow at bedtime, I promise.' *When I know the answers and am not just making things up*, thought Hannah, flicking on the night light.

'Oh look – Marlowe is asleep,' said Maisie in a hushed voice. 'Please can he sleep on my bed tonight?'

'All right.'

It was a fib. As soon as Maisie was asleep, she was going to shift him. She knew that once he'd had one night sleeping in their beds, that would be it.

Hannah returned to her bedroom a short time later to find Marlowe's head resting on Maisie's shoulder, a paw on her chest almost protectively.

Hannah's heart swelled at the sight of them. 'My little family,' she whispered. She was just retreating with Marlowe in her arms when she thought she heard a faint tapping on the cottage door. She wondered if Ray, Sarah, Lili or Nate had returned. She took Marlowe downstairs, thinking she should take him outside in the back garden to go to the toilet before bedtime. She popped him in his crate in the kitchen for a moment while she answered the front door.

There was nobody there.

She was about to close the door when she saw something on the step. There was a single red rose wrapped in tissue paper.

She bent down and picked up the red rose. Underneath was a small envelope. She opened it to reveal a message. It said simply, *Can you forgive me?*

She rushed to the front gate, looking up the drive at the house. She couldn't see him in the gloom. Hannah held the rose carefully by the stem and raised it to her nose, closing her eyes and breathing in the sweet scent. She whispered, 'Thank you, Rupert.' Her heart soared. Now, she couldn't wait to return to Somersby Hall in the morning.

33

'What are *you* doing here?' Rupert asked rudely when he answered the door.

Hannah took a step back in surprise. 'What do you mean – what am I doing here? Didn't your grandmother tell you to expect me this morning?'

And why was he talking to her like that? She hadn't thought she'd be in for such a reception that morning after finding that rose and note on her doorstep last night. She thought he'd be welcoming her home and apologising profusely for getting her arrested.

Lulu, her Velcro dog, appeared. She was sniffing Hannah's arms. 'Oh, sweetie, I haven't brought Marlowe. He's sleeping in his crate at home.' After receiving the red rose, she hadn't thought she'd need Marlowe to break the ice after all. Clearly, she was wrong. This was just the reaction she had been expecting before that knock on her door last night. Had he forgotten about the red rose and note already?

She thought she'd remind him. 'I'm not going to forgive you if you're going to have that attitude.'

'What are you talking about?'

'The single red rose and the hand-delivered note last night – or have you forgotten?' She couldn't imagine they'd come from anyone else.

Rupert sighed. 'No, I have not forgotten. My grandmother insisted, gave me the rose and told me to write something on the card.'

Hannah's shoulders sagged. So it was Lady Jemima's doing. Then again, he had written that message.

'Yeah, I should apologise for having you wrongly arrested.'

Hannah was just smiling when he added, 'But then again, thinking about it last night after I dropped off that stupid note, I thought – why should I?'

She looked at him sharply.

'You didn't tell me about your past.'

'Would you tell me about your past if you'd been to prison for stealing when you were trying to put it all behind you and start over?'

'Well, that's as maybe, but you didn't tell me you had that painting my grandmother asked me to look for. Is it any wonder I jumped to conclusions when I heard Sarah mention that it had been hanging over your fireplace?'

Hannah didn't know what to say to that.

'Ah, there you are,' Percy said, approaching. 'Come in, Hannah. We've been waiting for you.'

Hannah couldn't go in because Rupert wouldn't move out of the doorway.

Percy said, 'Rupert, please let Hannah in. She's expected upstairs.'

Hannah knew what was going on; Lady Jemima had sent Percy to make sure Rupert didn't turn her away. Jemima must have sensed some resistance when she'd had to twist his arm to leave the red rose and note on her doorstep.

She saw Percy head for the stairs, walking slowly with his stick.

Rupert narrowed his eyes and glared at her. 'I don't see why she insisted you need to be here for this so-called family meeting. I didn't think you'd have the gall to show your face here again. Quite frankly, I was very surprised to learn she *hasn't* given you notice to quit Gatekeeper's Cottage after I told her you had her painting all along, and about your past. And now this – inviting you back into Somersby Hall! I don't know what to think.'

Hannah returned his glare. She wished he hadn't had his arm twisted to deliver the stupid red rose and that note. She'd even put the red rose in a little vase on the mantel shelf under her new painting.

It was all turning out to be a bad idea. Although she wanted to hear his grandmother's story, Rupert was right: she wasn't part of the family, no matter how much Lady Jemima insisted she was.

'I'm leaving!' She turned on her heel, expecting Rupert to say *good riddance!* and slam the door in her face. Instead, he said, 'You can't.'

She slowly turned back. 'What did you say?'

'You can't leave.'

For a split second, she thought he was going to apologise for being so rude and ask if they could start over. Her hopes were dashed when he added, 'My grandmother insists she wants to see you … us … together.' He stepped aside so that she could go in.

Hannah just wanted to leave, but she reminded herself that Lady Jemima was her landlady and quite formidable. Hannah did not want to cross her; Lady Jemima clearly wanted her there, so she had no choice.

'Do you know what this is about?' Rupert asked.

'Yes, I do.'

'You do?'

She was about to head for the stairs when he caught her arm. 'Then tell me!'

Hannah cursed herself for still having that tingling sensation at his touch. She slowly turned to face him and looked into his beautiful, slate-grey eyes, wishing he'd take her in his arms.

Rupert still had hold of her arm. He held it gently, his gaze meeting hers as he stepped closer. But whatever had been about to happen, it was interrupted by the shrill sound of his grandmother's impatient voice.

'Hannah, Rupert!' Lady Jemima called out. 'What's keeping you? I haven't got all day!'

'She *has* got all day,' Rupert said miserably, turning around. He started up the stairs.

Hannah was still standing there, her heart beating wildly in her chest, staring after him, wondering if he had been about to kiss her. She ran after him and grabbed his arm, pulling him to a stop. He turned in surprise.

'Rupert …' she looked up the stairs. Lady Jemima expected her to have broken the ice before this family meeting, clearly hoping her presence would soften the blow of what he was about to hear. Hannah knew what Lady Jemima was afraid of – that she would lose him like his father before him; that Rupert would storm out when he discovered the truth, never to return.

'What is it?'

She didn't know quite how to put it. She wasn't thinking of

Lady Jemima just then; she was thinking of Rupert and the shock he was in for when he found out his grandmother wasn't the real Lady Jemima.

'Rupert …' She wanted to forewarn him, but she didn't know how. The last thing she wanted was for the meeting to backfire and for him to go storming out of the house in anger without giving his grandmother a chance to tell her story. Hannah wanted to hear her story too.

'Will you trust me?' Hannah quickly changed tack. That was a stupid thing to say; of course he couldn't after she'd lied to him. 'Rupert, will you promise me something?'

She expected him to throw that question back in her face too.

Instead, he looked at her warily. 'You know something – don't you?'

Hannah took a deep breath. 'What you are about to hear …' she stalled. 'Look, your grandmother has called this meeting to talk about her past – here in this house during World War Two.'

'Really?' He looked surprised. He'd already told her that his grandmother wouldn't talk about her past, especially the war years. It sounded as though he'd broached the subject on several occasions and had been met with silence.

Rupert started up the stairs. 'Come on. I can't wait to hear this.'

Hannah held back. He noticed and halted on the stairs. 'Well, aren't you coming?'

Hannah took one stair and paused, staring up at him. 'Look, there's a reason she wouldn't talk about her past …'

Rupert put his hands on his hips. 'She told you already?' He looked taken aback and a little cross. 'I don't believe it. She told *you* first instead of her own grandson.' Rupert turned on his heel and stormed up the stairs.

'Well, that went well,' Hannah muttered under her breath. With a heavy sigh she walked up the stairs and caught up with him outside his grandmother's door. Although the door was slightly ajar, he hesitated before walking into the room. He turned to Hannah. He whispered, 'Why am I feeling anxious all of a sudden?'

Hannah pursed her lips. 'Just remember this: sometimes we have to tell little white lies to protect the ones we love.'

In his grandmother's case, it wasn't exactly a *little* lie.

'I can hear you both mumbling outside my door!' Lady Jemima called out.

Percy opened the bedroom door but didn't make a move to leave the room.

'Oh,' Rupert said in surprise. 'I didn't expect you to be staying.'

Hannah rolled her eyes. She'd forgotten there was something else that Rupert didn't know. She wondered at how blind he'd been not to have guessed. She smiled at Percy, who winked at her as she walked in. Rupert raised his eyebrows on catching the exchange.

'Finally!' said Lady Jemima.

34

Lady Jemima was seated on the chaise longue with a letter in her hands. Percy took a seat next to her.

'Rupert,' she said, 'bring over those two chairs from the window, will you?'

Rupert did as he was told. Hannah helped him carry the two old wingback chairs over.

'Why didn't we all sit in the lounge, or at the dining room table?' Rupert asked as they positioned the two chairs in front of the chaise longue.

Lady Jemima raised an eyebrow. 'Because I wanted this meeting here.'

Hannah glanced at Rupert before she took a seat.

Lady Jemima said to her, 'Thank you for coming, Hannah.' She looked at Rupert as he took a seat too.

Hannah smiled.

'Did you bring Marlowe?'

Hannah's smiled faltered. 'Um, no.'

'Ah, he was surplus to requirements.'

Hannah thought of the red rose and the note Lady Jemima had persuaded Rupert to write. She'd probably thought that gesture would do the trick and that Hannah and Rupert would make up, and so the puppy wouldn't be required to break the ice.

Rupert looked from Hannah to his grandmother. 'Why would she bring her puppy?'

'Ahem,' Percy coughed into his hand.

Lady Jemima said, 'Now, where's Hazel with that pot of tea?'

As if on cue there was a knock at the door.

Rupert answered it.

Hazel walked in and put the tea tray down on the sideboard by the chaise longue.

'Oh, you baked scones, Hazel. How thoughtful.'

Hazel cast her a nervous glance. 'I thought it might help to … to have a scone and butter. There's some home-made jam.'

Help? Help what? thought Hannah. She turned in her seat and stared at Hazel. Something dawned on her. She knew Lady Jemima's secret too. But how long had she known?

'Wonderful!' Percy exclaimed, slapping his thigh. 'I do love a scone.'

Hannah glanced at Rupert, but the strange exchange had gone over his head.

'I baked some blueberry scones. I remember you always liked blueberry scones when you were a little boy.'

Rupert's face was a picture. 'Oh, er, I'd forgotten. Thank you, Hazel.'

Hannah watched Hazel walk to the door. She hesitated for a moment before turning around at the door. 'Do you want me to pour the tea?'

'No, Hazel, we can take it from here.'

Hazel cast an anxious gaze at Rupert before leaving, closing the door behind her.

Hannah turned in her seat, wondering where Lady Jemima was going to begin. She was suddenly looking anxious as she cast her glance at the letter on her lap.

Percy reached over and squeezed her hand.

'Oh. I know what this is about,' Rupert announced, interrupting the heavy silence. 'You two – that's it, isn't it? You and Percy, you're … you're together, aren't you? How long has this been going on? Were you two … together even before Grandad passed away? Is that it? Is that why you wouldn't talk about the war years?'

Percy sighed. 'Your grandmother never had an affair, if that's what you mean. It was some years after he passed away that we got together.'

'Why did you keep it a secret?' Rupert asked. 'You didn't have to. You know times have changed. No one would frown on a lady and her chauffeur being in a relationship.' He shook his head. 'And there I was, thinking you were going to reveal some deep, dark family secret.' Rupert grinned and stood up. 'Well, I'm glad we've cleared that up. Anyone for a cuppa?'

'Sit down, Rupert.'

Rupert turned his gaze from his grandmother and Percy to Hannah.

Hannah looked at her hands.

'Oh, I see. That's not it, then.'

'Not all of it, no,' said Lady Jemima. 'What I'm about to tell you … well, it's going to come as a bit of a shock.'

Rupert slowly sat down. 'All right,' he said slowly. 'Something happened here at the hall, didn't it? In the war years.'

'Yes.'

'Does it have something to do with that letter?' Rupert had

noticed the old, yellowed letter on her lap.

She picked it up. 'Yes, it has everything to do with this letter. You see, although I married your grandfather, I loved another. But it was not to be.'

'I thought you loved Percy,' Hannah blurted. She didn't understand. They weren't there to talk about her past loves; they were there to talk about Kitty, and how she had come to be Lady Jemima.

Jemima squeezed Percy's hand. 'He has been my constant. He loved me the moment he first saw me.'

'Which was when?' Rupert asked.

'When he first came to work at the hall with his brother, Owen Hartley.'

Hannah's breath caught in her throat. She hadn't known that Percy was Owen's brother.

Rupert said, 'I didn't know your surname was Hartley.'

'You never asked. But then you had no reason to. I've been here forever and a day, haven't I?' He chuckled. 'I was just Percy, the old chauffeur.'

Lady Jemima took a deep breath and then exhaled slowly. 'Let me tell you about a young lady's maid called Kitty who found herself the go-between for two young teenagers in love – a love that at that time could never be.'

Kitty. Hannah shot a glance at Rupert.

'Could never be?' Rupert asked.

'They had to meet in secret. Her father would never have allowed the match. They both knew their only recourse was to elope together.'

'So, who exactly are we talking about here?' asked Rupert looking confused.

Hannah had already guessed – the real Lady Jemima and Owen. But why were the love letters from Cairo addressed to Kitty?

Rupert said, 'Ah, we're talking about you and Owen. Why didn't you just say so?'

Lady Jemima exchanged a glance with Percy, and continued, 'And then along came the war – not that it affected us to start with; we were all so young, in our early teens. But towards the end of the war, Owen was called up. He couldn't write directly to the lady of the house, so he addressed the letters to Kitty, who then passed those letters, when they arrived, to Lady Jemima.'

Hannah smiled. Now she understood. She wanted to ask her why she hadn't sent that letter from Lady Jemima to Owen, but now was not the time. What she really wanted to know was how Kitty had ended up going from simply being a go-between for the letters to *becoming* Lady Jemima?

Rupert said, 'So, you were in love with Percy's brother, but your father, my great-grandfather, wouldn't have approved of the match. But you didn't elope together. You married my grandfather instead. You said just before: *I loved another. But it was not to be.*'

'Yes, I loved Owen, but he never knew. You see, he was already in love with another.'

Rupert scratched his head. 'I'm sorry, I'm a bit lost. What do you mean he was in love with another? You just said …'

'I said he was in love with Lady Jemima.'

'Yeah …'

Hannah bit her lip and drew in a breath. She gave Rupert a sideways glance.

There was a long silence.

Rupert said, 'I'm sorry to hear your sad story, that you didn't get to be with the person you were in love with, and I did want to hear about your life here during the war, but you've moved on, obviously.' He glanced at Percy. 'It's all in the past now.'

'Not quite. You see, I've been keeping a secret.'

'What kind of secret?' Rupert said slowly.

'I haven't told you the whole story.' She took a deep breath before continuing. 'When Owen returned from the war, Lady Jemima's father had suddenly taken ill. He died.'

Hannah said, 'So, why didn't she and Owen marry, and live happily ever after in this house?'

'Because Lady Jemima was engaged to be married to someone her father had chosen, whom she'd only met briefly as a young teenager. The whole war went by before he saw her again.'

Rupert looked at his grandmother. 'Why do you keep referring to yourself in the third person?'

'Let me finish – please, Rupert. Now, there was no way she was going to go through with the marriage, so even though she would never have wished her father ill, his timely death did solve her problem – or so she thought. Unfortunately, the will stipulated that if she were not to marry someone of her station, then the hall would be passed to her distant cousin in Australia. But she wanted to elope with Owen. That suited him because he didn't want this life, did he, Percy?'

Percy shook his head. 'He wouldn't have been happy here, living as the lord of the manor, so to speak. It just wasn't him. I think it was a relief that one way or another, if they were to stay together, it meant leaving Somersby Hall. That was the price she would have to pay, to be with him. But she wanted to pay that price. In fact, I rather worried that she wasn't in love with Owen, but the idea of the adventure, and leaving everything she'd known, and the life she had mapped out for herself, to run away. I wondered if Owen was her escape route.'

Lady Jemima stared at Percy.

'Sorry, I'll shut up now,' said Percy.

Lady Jemima continued, 'The problem was that although she wanted to leave, she knew what it meant if her distant cousin were to inherit Somersby Hall. It might be sold and bulldozed to make way for a housing development. Who knew what would happen to the hall and its inhabitants?' She managed a smile. 'She loved us all, you know. We had stuck together during the war years, and she just couldn't stand the thought of abandoning her beloved home and its occupants to their fate if this distant relation inherited and all her friends had to leave what was their home too. She was torn.'

Percy nodded, clearly casting his mind back.

She continued, 'And that's where Kitty came in, the young lady's maid who had acted as the go-between for the letters that had passed between them towards the end of the war.'

'Not just a go-between,' commented Percy. 'Kitty wrote those letters to Owen.'

'You mean, posing as Lady Jemima?' Hannah said, shocked.

She nodded. 'Lady Jemima said she just couldn't put into words how she felt, so I wrote them for her.'

Despite what Percy had just said, Hannah still said, 'You wrote to Owen?' in case she'd misheard.

'Yes. It was most peculiar, really. The letters had to be signed as being from Kitty in case they were intercepted and fell into the wrong hands.'

'They were beautiful love letters,' said Percy. 'But then why wouldn't they be? They were written straight from the heart. She was in love with my brother, after all.'

'But there was a letter signed from Lady Jemima herself that was unsent,' Hannah said.

'Yes. You read it, didn't you?'

'I did,' Hannah admitted. 'It was in with the other letters, but very different to the letters from Kitty. When I first found all the letters, I thought there was some sort of love triangle, that Owen had been writing to Kitty, whom I presumed was one of the staff. But at the same time, he'd also been carrying on with Lady Jemima, and one or both – Kitty and Lady Jemima – were not aware of the other, until Jemima asked Kitty to send a letter. So, I thought Lady Jemima had given Kitty the letter to send, and when Kitty discovered it was to Owen, she didn't send it.'

'It's true I wouldn't send it, but not for the reasons you think. It was soon after her father had died, and she could stop hiding behind Kitty to send that last letter. She wrote it herself, and as you are aware, it was very, very different to what he normally received. I was afraid he'd find out about the deceit, that all those letters had been by my hand, not hers.'

Hannah had a thought. 'How did you feel when he wrote to Lady Jemima?'

Percy looked at her.

'I felt like I was falling more and more in love with him.'

'You read her letters?'

'I had to. She knew that. How could I respond if I didn't know what was in the letters?'

Hannah stared at her, wondering if it had ever crossed her mind that although Owen might have been beguiled by Lady

Jemima, and thought he was in love with her, it was the woman who had written him those beautiful love letters while he was in Cairo, and their discourse back and forth, whom he had really fallen in love with.

Hannah forgot about Rupert, who was sitting there quietly, and blurted, 'So, Kitty, how did it come about that Lady Jemima's lady's maid, *you*, became … well … her?'

'It was a chance conversation Lady Jemima overheard downstairs among the staff that changed the course of our lives.'

'What did she overhear?' Hannah asked.

'A rumour that there was more to the young lady's maid, Kitty, than met the eye. That Lord Somersby had had an affair with a member of staff, who'd borne him an illegitimate child. Although that member of the household had been dismissed when she fell pregnant, there were rumours the young woman had come into a sum of money. And later, that child, just a year younger than Lady Jemima, had been employed here at the hall, getting one of the coveted roles in the household despite her youth and lack of experience as a lady's maid.'

Hannah stared at her. 'Why would he do that, employ her … you … knowing your history?'

'My mother told me he'd promised he'd always look after me. I guess he thought giving me a job at Somersby Hall was his way of doing just that.'

Rupert's grandmother continued. 'Lady Jemima must have seen our likeness and confronted her father, finding out the rumours were true; she had an illegitimate half-sister, Kitty. She was angry with her father's double standards. He could have an affair and bear a child with someone from a lower class, and yet he would not give his blessing for his legitimate daughter to marry someone for love whom he considered to be beneath her. She'd always been rebellious, pushing the boundaries, but now she wanted sweet revenge for the fact that her father had stipulated in his will that if she went against his wishes, he would strip her of her inheritance – even though it was a lifestyle that she didn't want anyway – and give it to some distant cousin if she eloped. She wasn't having that.'

Hannah said, 'That's when Lady Jemima decided her half-sister, Kitty, was going to step into her shoes, and inherit Somersby Hall?'

'Precisely.'

35

Rupert shot out of his seat.

'Rupert! Please don't leave,' his grandmother implored.

Hannah was wondering when he'd react to the revelation that his grandmother wasn't the real Lady Jemima.

Rupert didn't leave. He walked to the window and stood with his back to them.

Hannah looked wide-eyed at Lady Jemima and Percy.

Rupert said, 'I remember that night …'

Lady Jemima asked, 'What night, Rupert?'

'The night I was woken by an argument. I heard raised voices – you and my father, and a man I didn't think I recognised, but the memory plays tricks. It was Percy, of course. I didn't know what the argument was about. My father would never speak of that night when he bundled me in my pyjamas into the back of his car and we sped down the driveway in the dead of night.'

Rupert turned around. 'He told me never to come back here. He knew – didn't he? My father had found out your secret – that you're not Lady Jemima. You're *Kitty*.'

She nodded. 'I remember that night too, Rupert. How could I forget? I was going up to bed, and I caught your father searching through my cupboards and drawers, looking for money to pay off another gambling debt, and that's when he found this letter, the one I'd kept, the last love letter Owen had sent, still addressed to Kitty, of course.'

Rupert asked, 'Why was that a big deal? It wasn't addressed to Lady Jemima. He had no way of knowing you were really Kitty.'

Percy heaved an audible sigh. 'Unfortunately, I chose the wrong moment to wish your grandmother goodnight, before I retired to my room, calling her by her given name – Kitty. And then the truth came out.'

Hannah stared at Percy, feeling sorry for him.

'It wasn't your fault, Percy,' said Jemima. 'It was mine for agreeing to step into her shoes and become Lady Jemima. I should have told your father the truth, Rupert, but I knew what his reaction would be, believing that a descendant of Lady Jemima would eventually crawl out of the woodwork and deprive him of his inheritance. Not that it's going to him anyway. But he knew that a descendant of hers may add a complication, even though I showed him the Deed of Gift from Lady Jemima, witnessed by a local law firm, gifting me the hall and all its contents, in case my real identity were ever to become public knowledge.'

Rupert said, 'Why did you do it? Oh, silly question – why wouldn't you want to be a lady, and live in this house, pretending to be his legitimate daughter?'

'Yes, it was my dream, of course it was. She was everything I wanted to be but thought I never could be – her fine clothes and refined manners and beautiful cut-glass accent, and of course her beautiful home. When she asked me to step into her shoes, become Lady Jemima to save the hall, to save its occupants from falling into the hands of her distant cousin, how could I possibly say no? She could have told everyone who I really was, and that she was giving her half-sister Somersby Hall, but it would open up the family to scrutiny, and although she wanted to pay her father back for trying to force her into an arranged marriage, she didn't want the scandal when it came to light who I was. And quite frankly, neither did I. So of course I was a willing participant in the ruse – as was everyone else in the household …'

'They were in on it too?'

'Of course. How could they not be? They all knew Lady Jemima and Kitty.'

'But what about other people, outside the hall, who knew the family, knew Lady Jemima?'

'Five years, Rupert, is a long time, especially when we are talking of the war years. War changed people. And I was so young when the war started, and then I blossomed into a young woman. She taught me to be a lady, a proper lady, but as with all things in life, it came at a price.'

'You didn't marry for love.'

She shifted her gaze to Hannah. 'No, Hannah, I did not. The young man to whom Lady Jemima's father had promised her hand in marriage had returned. He'd hardly met Lady Jemima and barely remembered her after the years he'd spent at war. Surprisingly, when we met, we got on well. He liked my sense of humour, my beauty. I liked his easy-going temperament, his happy disposition, his caring nature, and the fact that he treated me like a lady. We were happy together, Rupert. Your grandfather and I, we enjoyed each other's company.'

'But it wasn't love,' said Rupert.

She sighed. 'There are all kinds of love, Rupert, not just the head over heels, heart skipping a beat, bottom falling out of your world love.'

Hannah stole a glance at Rupert. She knew all about that sort of love.

'You can grow to love a person over time. I was content with him. Like I am with Percy – happy to share my life with the ones I love.'

Not in love, Hannah thought.

She imagined Rupert was thinking that too, although he didn't say. 'Did my grandfather ever know … about Kitty?'

She shook her head. 'There were many times I wanted to tell him, but I could not. He was …' she glanced at Percy, 'He was a good man, with high moral principles. I doubt that if he knew, he could have lived with the deceit. I'd done it for the love of my friends, and this house, and for Lady Jemima so that she could go off and lead the life she wanted without the guilt that her friends – her family, as she called us – could lose our home if her decision to gift her half-sister Somersby Hall was challenged. But it depended on me playing the role. And I played it well.'

But at what personal cost, thought Hannah. *She never got to be with the man she truly loved.*

'Sometimes I wonder … what would have happened if I hadn't volunteered to write those letters? If I hadn't stepped into her shoes so that she was free to leave with Owen?'

Everyone fell silent.

Hannah wondered whether Rupert now understood why his grandmother had never wanted to talk about her past. She had regrets.

'What do you think would have happened if my grandfather had found out who you really were?' Rupert asked.

'I think he would have wanted to hand over Somersby Hall to the rightful heir.'

Rupert said, 'The second cousin in Australia?'

'No, the rightful heir of Somersby Hall – the real Lady Jemima's descendants.'

Rupert said, 'You mean Lady Jemima and Owen's descendants?'

'Yes, or the name she took when she eloped with Owen.'

'Kitty,' Hannah breathed. 'She took your name.'

'So, speaking of which,' said Lady Jemima, 'we have a problem.'

Rupert said, 'Oh, apart from getting my head around the fact that you are not who I thought you were!'

Rupert walked from the window and resumed his seat. 'That explains why you never wanted strangers in the hall, were suspicious of outsiders, and hardly ventured out of this house. You were protecting your secrets.'

'Yes, and latterly I have been protecting you, Rupert, from the possibility of losing the hall if the real descendants ever appeared.'

'But you have the Deed of Gift.'

She sighed heavily. 'And that brings us to the matter in hand. I've always anticipated that one day a stranger, the real descendant of Lady Jemima, would walk through our door and make a claim on what was theirs. We just haven't got the money to pay for lawyers to fight a claim.'

Hannah turned towards the bedroom door as though Hetty would appear at any moment.

'I thought that day had come when you arrived, Hannah, taking such a keen interest in that painting. I thought you knew more than you let on.'

'I did.'

'I know. You had the airgraphs and suspected something was amiss, although you only suspected my secret when you overheard Percy calling me Kitty.'

'Why didn't you tell me you'd overheard that?' Rupert asked crossly.

'Because …' said Lady Jemima, 'Hannah was trying to protect you from the truth.'

'Why would she do that?'

'Because sometimes we have to lie to protect the ones we love.'

Hannah dropped her eyes from his gaze.

'So, the question now is what are we going to do *if* Henrietta Hartley returns?'

'Henrietta Hartley!' Rupert exclaimed. He slapped his forehead. 'Of course! The airgraphs from Owen to the real Lady Jemima.' Rupert turned to Hannah. 'I remember you showing me the love letters from Owen Hartley to Kitty. That's why Hetty stole them – because she's a descendant and thought they were rightfully hers.'

'The *are* rightfully hers,' commented Hannah. 'That's why I didn't want her arrested.'

'Oh, god! I've been so blind. Do you know there's a painting of an ancestor who looks just like her?'

'You weren't to know,' said Hannah.

His grandmother and Percy exchanged a glance. 'Where did you see the painting?'

'In the corridor of an unused wing. I took her on a tour of the house, and that's where we saw it.'

'What did she say when she saw the likeness?' Percy asked.

'Oh, just waved it away, joking that she'd found her doppelgänger.'

'It's my fault,' said Hannah, hanging her head. 'If I hadn't shown her the airgraphs from Owen to Kitty, asking her to value them, and hadn't also shown her *Sunrise Over Seashell Bay*, with Owen Hartley's signature, she wouldn't have known. I am *so* sorry. I just can't believe she took the painting too.'

Rupert grandmother said, 'You can't blame yourself, Hannah. You weren't to know. She might have taken the airgraphs just because they were very valuable, but the fact that she took a painting by an unknown artist too, and her surname is the same as Owen's, is just too much of a coincidence, is it not?'

'She's the true heir to this house!' Rupert exclaimed, saying aloud what they were all thinking. 'So, what are we going to do if she returns?'

Percy turned to Lady Jemima. 'I rather think we should cross that bridge when we come to it, don't you, darling?'

Lady Jemima considered, before she met Percy's gaze and placed her hand on his. 'You know, I think you have a point. At our age, why worry? It could all be for nought. We might not be here tomorrow.'

'I'm inclined to think those pearls of wisdom can apply at any age,' Percy said.

She nodded and smiled at him. 'Let's just say, what will be, will be – *que sera, sera*.'

'But … but what about the house?' Rupert said in bewilderment. 'We need a plan. What if she turns up and—'

Lady Jemima and Percy exchanged a glance. 'Nobody has turned up in all these years. Just as I have kept Lady Jemima's secret, it was always an unspoken agreement that she would keep mine. Henrietta Hartley may have the airgraphs, and may have seen her likeness to a painting, but don't forget, she has letters from Owen to *Kitty* who used to work here as a lady's maid. Unless she gets the truth out of Owen or Kitty, or either of *us* …'

Or Hazel, thought Hannah, although she knew Hazel would never tell, and by the sound of it, neither would Owen and Kitty – if they were even still alive.

'Then the truth will *not* out,' Rupert's grandmother decided.

Rupert stared at them, slowly nodding his head. 'And if she does return?'

'I doubt very much that she will, considering that the last time she was here, she stole something. Why would she risk it?' his grandmother asked.

Everyone was in agreement, apart from Hannah, who still wondered if Hetty might somehow find out Kitty's secret.

Percy said, 'Now, how about a nice cup of tea and a scone, and let's get down to the business of saving the hall.'

Lady Jemima said, 'The wedding?'

'Yes, the wedding.'

❖

Rupert stormed out of the bedroom, followed by Hannah. He slammed the door shut behind them. Hannah grimaced. Rupert was clearly still angry with her because she hadn't told him what she'd overheard – Percy calling his grandmother Kitty. Finding that out had rubbed salt into the wound.

When Lady Jemima had told them they had to work together again, on the wedding, Hannah knew it wasn't going to work.

She hissed at Rupert, 'This isn't going to work.'

'Oh, you think?' he shot back sarcastically.

Hannah grimaced. 'I wouldn't work with you if you paid me.'

'And I wouldn't work with *you* if *you* paid *me*. There, we finally agree on something!'

They stopped bickering and stared at each other.

Rupert said, 'Why does this feel like déjà vu?'

They both turned and looked at the door. 'Why,' said Rupert, 'do I get the distinct feeling we are being set up?' His lip started to curl in a smile.

Hannah looked at the door, smiling too. 'Because we are.' Lady Jemima, as usual, knew exactly what she was doing, throwing them together again.

Rupert suddenly took her hand. 'Come on, we've got work to do.'

'Really?'

'Oh, yes.'

They started for the stairs, Hannah feeling as though she was walking on air with his hand firmly in hers. She couldn't be happier. Nothing was going to spoil Lili's wedding. Unless Hetty turned up. But she didn't want to think about that. Nobody wanted to think about that. It was best to leave that bridge to be crossed in the future.

'Let's start by going over the wedding plans,' suggested Rupert as they reached the top of the stairs.

'Oh, how far have you got?'

'Absolutely nowhere, but do not tell Lili that. I've just been lost. It hasn't been the same without you by my side.'

Hannah's heart leapt as they started down the stairs.

Hannah looked back briefly and saw Percy poke his head out of the door. Behind him, in the room, Lady Jemima said, 'Did it work?'

Percy waved at her for her to shush, then quietly closed the door.

Downstairs, Rupert closed the door to his study, turned around and found Hannah standing right behind him. 'Oh.' That was the only word he managed before Hannah's lips were on his.

The wedding planning would have to wait.

36

Maisie walked down the stairs in her new dress and strappy sandals, her hair expertly styled into plaits that had been put up with clips. She was putting her new mobile phone away in a little shoulder purse she'd picked up from Mabel and Marjorie's charity shop.

Hannah nearly cried when she saw Maisie. 'Oh, sweetheart, you look so pretty in that dress and …' Hannah swallowed. '*So* grown up.'

Suddenly Hannah fast-forwarded a little over seven years and imagined Maisie walking down those stairs in another dress, sweet sixteen, going to her prom. She wondered who might call at their house to take her to the—

The doorbell rang, making Hannah jump. She was glad of the interruption. She didn't want to think of her baby growing up. She just wanted to enjoy the here and now.

Hannah took a quick glance in the hallway mirror before she turned to Maisie. 'How do I look?'

'Very pretty, Mum.'

The makeup artist and hair stylist had done a wonderful job. Hannah had hired the couple herself. There was a lot more to this wedding planning business than she'd thought. Luckily Rupert had already applied and received the necessary licences to enable them to use his grandmother's private home as a wedding venue and to hold civil wedding ceremonies in the grounds of Somersby Hall, if that was what couples chose.

But now everything had been done, and whatever she hadn't done, covered, or thought of, it was too late now. The big day had arrived.

Maisie answered the door. 'Hello, Rupert.'

'Where's Maisie?' Rupert made a show of looking about him.

Maisie giggled. 'I'm right here.'

'You are?' He fixed his gaze on her. 'Did you grow up overnight into a beautiful princess? I think you did.'

Hannah rolled her eyes at her reflection, wishing he hadn't used the words *grow up*.

'And where is my fellow wedding planner?' Rupert's eyes roved over to Hannah. He fell silent.

She'd just been applying some lipstick when she noticed he'd gone quiet. She turned around. 'Is something the matter? Did you just think of something we've forgotten?' She stared at him wide-eyed.

'No … yes.'

'Yes?'

'I'd forgotten how beautiful you are.'

'Oh, stop!' Hannah said, embarrassed. They'd been so busy over the past fortnight since resuming the wedding planning. They'd spent plenty of time together, but there had been little time to enjoy each other's company or any romantic evenings together.

When they'd got down to planning Lili's wedding, they'd

discovered there was more to prepare than they'd envisaged. Fortunately, Maisie had been at school, which had given Hannah some free time to work on the wedding – not that Maisie wanted to go to school now that she had a new puppy. Hannah took Marlowe to work with her in her shop in Cobblers Yard, closing the shop one day during the week so she could spend that time working on Lili's wedding.

In between planning and preparations at Somersby Hall – hiring a band, a marquee, more chairs, caterers – Hannah had decided to keep her shop open along with her options in case the wedding idea didn't work out. When they posted all the photos on social media, and on the website that Rupert's friend back in London had set up, they had no idea how many people would express an interest in having a wedding at Somersby Hall – or whether any would at all.

Hannah turned back to the mirror. She saw Rupert's reflection. He was looking at her, smiling. He rarely saw her in a dress. In fact, it was just possible, if she thought about it, that he hadn't ever seen her in one.

'I didn't choose this, by the way.' It was Lili's choice, how she dressed her bridesmaids.

'Well, I'm impressed.'

'Oh, yes – I was impressed with the dress too.'

'I meant you.' He sauntered over, and said, 'May I kiss the bridesmaid?'

Maisie giggled.

'No! You may not!' exclaimed Hannah.

He was already leaning towards her.

She put gentle fingers either side of his mouth, and puckered his lips, turning his face away. 'You might smudge my makeup.

Do you know how long it takes a makeup artist to get a natural dewy look? It's crazy.'

Rupert sighed, taking her in his arms. 'I can't wait for the dance.'

'Really? I didn't know you liked dancing.'

'Depends on who I'm dancing with.' Rupert started dancing her round the hallway, sending Maisie into another fit of giggles.

Rupert stopped in front of Maisie, let go of Hannah and took a deep bow in front of Hannah's daughter. 'May I have this dance?'

Maisie stood on Rupert's shoes as he guided her around the hallway.

'Come on, you two,' Hannah said. 'Stop larking around. We've got a wedding to go to – remember?'

Maisie stopped and turned to Hannah. 'Can Marlowe come too?'

Apart from the day off during each week when Hannah closed her shop, most of the wedding planning had taken place after tea, when Hannah, Maisie and Marlowe would walk up the drive to the big house. Rupert would be waiting in the study.

Maisie would sit with Lady Jemima and Percy on the old sofas in the lounge next door, first doing her homework, then beating them at boardgames. Sometimes Rupert and Hannah would be interrupted by whoops of laughter from Lady Jemima, Percy and Maisie.

Maisie loved her visits to the Lady, as she called her, especially enjoying the tales she would tell of the house and its occupants in its heyday, when the house bustled with friends, family and lots of staff. This normally followed Maisie exploring the house and returning with a 'find' – an old croquet mallet, a toy, a book or a doll that she'd discovered in a long-forgotten room.

Maisie would often take Marlowe and Lulu and go exploring the hall. That was the reason Hannah had given in and bought Maisie her first mobile phone; so she could find her before bedtime. There were corridors, wings, rooms, and rooms off rooms. Hannah explored too, looking for Maisie; there were rooms that she guessed no one had ventured into for a very long time. It made Hannah think that if the wedding venue idea really took off, perhaps they could afford to renovate another wing of the house and open it up to more guests and bigger wedding parties.

William had been for a sleepover at Gatekeeper's Cottage the previous weekend. He'd been pressuring Nate to let him. Hannah had guessed it was to see Marlowe, but of course he wanted to see his big sister too. They had all walked up to Somersby Hall. Maisie had loved showing William the house and the grounds and telling him all about the little girl who had lived there years earlier and who had grown up to be a lady.

Hannah and Rupert had not told Maisie who Rupert's grandmother really was – how could they? Hannah knew Maisie thought very highly of Lady Jemima. Just that morning, when Maisie had been getting ready, dressing in her very grown-up dress and shoes, she'd surprised Hannah when she'd said quite out of the blue, 'One day I'm going to be a lady just like Jemima.'

Hannah had corrected her. 'I'm sorry, sweetheart, but I don't think Lady Jemima can leave you her title, Lady.'

Maisie had asked if that was because they weren't related and had told said that it wouldn't be a problem when her mum and Rupert got married.

Hannah had spluttered into the tea she'd been drinking, nearly spilling it down the bridesmaid dress. 'Who says we're getting married?'

'I do!' Maisie said grinning. 'I like Rupert a lot. Then I can be a lady.'

Hannah sighed. She didn't have time to explain the ins and outs of hereditary titles – not that she knew a lot about them. What she was pretty sure of was that marrying into Lady Jemima's family, if that were to happen, would not make her or her daughter a lady. She imagined some titles just didn't get passed down – or if they did, then they just went to a direct heir.

In any case, it really wasn't Kitty's title to pass on. Not that Hannah was going to explain that fact to Maisie. As Percy had said when they'd got onto the subject of the real heirs to the hall making a reappearance, they'd just have to cross that bridge when they came to it.

Hannah turned her thoughts to Marlowe. Maisie had wanted her to take him to the wedding. Maisie was used to taking her puppy along to visit the big house. This time Hannah had had to say no. Apart from the fact that the sweetest of Labrador puppies might just upstage and get more attention than the bride and groom, there would lots of coming and going of guests and caterers in and out of the house, and she'd worry about keeping an eye on him.

Thinking of her puppy, Maisie looked at Rupert. 'Where's Lulu?'

He looked at her wide-eyed. 'Oh.' He ran over to the door and opened it. There, standing outside the door, was Lulu, her head hung low, her sad brown eyes peering up at him.

'Oh, Lulu,' Hannah said, rushing over to the door. 'Did

Rupert forget all about you?'

Lulu was such a good girl that she had stayed standing outside quietly as though she was waiting for an invitation to come in. She had visited them at Gatekeeper's Cottage before. They hadn't spent every evening over the past two weeks at Somersby Hall; on a few evenings, Rupert had come to them.

Hannah had enjoyed cooking a meal and sitting all together, just like any other family, eating and sharing details about their day. Maisie especially enjoyed telling Rupert about what she was doing at school and showing him her artwork at home.

Hannah loved that he was so attentive, listening to her, chatting with her, and as an art dealer, he took immense interest in her work. Hannah could tell he was quite in awe of her daughter's talent, and very protective of her.

She had been worried that when Rupert discovered Hannah had a prodigy on her hands, he might suggest introducing her to the art world and selling some of her work to make a tidy sum of money.

She knew he could do that – act as her agent and take a cut of the profits. There was no one else that Hannah would trust more to act on her daughter's behalf. But not straight away; later, if Maisie decided after university that she wanted to be a professional artist and sell her work.

She had worried that Rupert would disagree with her decision to keep Maisie's talent under wraps, hidden from the art world. To Hannah's utter relief, he completely understood Hannah's decision to give Maisie a normal childhood and the chance to go on to university, leaving it to her daughter to decide what she wanted to do with her art and career in the future. It was something that would have come between them, and affected their relationship, Hannah realised, if they hadn't been on the same page.

Hannah had read stories of children who'd been thrust into the limelight – mainly in the movie and music industry – only for some to reach adulthood and lead unhappy, even tragic lives as a consequence. She didn't want to be that pushy parent taking away Maisie's childhood for the sake of fame and fortune. Rupert understood that.

Maisie ran over to the front door too. She patted the wolfhound on the top of her head. 'Hello, Lulu. Come in and see Marlowe.'

Lulu followed Maisie into the kitchen. Hannah had left Marlowe's crate door ajar, his feeding bowls, water, toys and chew toy all ready to keep him occupied when she was gone.

Hannah glanced into the kitchen. Before she closed the door, Maisie said goodbye to Marlowe. The puppy had grown so much in just two weeks that Hannah had needed to buy the next size up in dog beds to put in the crate, where she knew he'd be safe for a couple of hours whenever Lulu wasn't there keeping a watchful eye on him.

Marlowe was playing with Lulu's tail. The gentle wolfhound didn't mind. She lay down, front paws outstretched, and turned her head, watching her little friend attentively as he played.

Hannah didn't bother putting Marlowe inside the crate and shutting the door. There was no need. Lulu would take care of him. And when he got tired, he'd just go in there himself and fall asleep on his bed.

'You'll look after him, won't you, Lulu?' she said unnecessarily.

Lulu glanced her way as if she understood.

Hannah gently closed the kitchen door. Rupert was waiting outside. She caught sight of her painting hanging in the lounge. She had accepted that she'd never know where the beach was. Despite that, looking at the painting normally made her smile, fondly recalling Percy handing it to her in Thea's bookshop. It had been such a wonderful surprise. But today, it made her feel anxious. She knew why – she was still wondering if one day Hetty would return to claim what was rightfully hers.

37

Hannah closed the front door and looked at Maisie as she took her hand. 'Are you ready?'

'Yes.' She stopped. 'Mum …'

'Yes, sweetheart.' Hannah could tell there was something on her mind.

'When Lili and Dad get married, do I have to call Lili Mum?'

Hannah hadn't even thought about it. 'You can if you want to.'

'But you're my mum. Can you ask her if I can still call her Lili?'

Hannah reached down and tucked a wisp of hair that had come loose from her braid. She tucked it behind her ear. 'I'm sure that will be absolutely fine.' It certainly was for Hannah.

Rupert was already at the front gate. He turned around. 'Everything all right?'

Hannah smiled at Maisie. 'Are you ready now?'

She smiled back and nodded.

'Good. Let's go to a wedding!'

Rupert took Hannah's hand as they started up the drive. Walking turned out not to be the best idea. They found themselves walking on the grass instead, as cars were arriving already. It wasn't going to be a big wedding party, but that was what Somersby Hall was aiming at – small, intimate weddings to start with. Even so, there were more wedding guests than the planners had anticipated when they were organising the sit-down meal. In the end, Rupert and Hannah had abandoned that idea and organised buffet-style catering in the large marquee in the back garden. Fortunately, the autumn weather had proved mild and dry, and although it was a little windy, they could still sit under the marquee and eat instead. Tables and chairs had been positioned to leave a generous space in the centre for the wedding dance.

Hannah recognised some of the faces in the cars as they passed them by. She waved at Marjorie and Mabel, travelling with Reggie from the music shop, and then Thea and her family passed them. She didn't notice Thea's father in the car, although she was not surprised that he wasn't with them. But they'd brought Joss and the lovely Emily, a vet who had turned her parents' guesthouse into a veterinary surgery and pet hotel.

Hannah recognised Lili's friend, Abigail, in the next car. She'd grown up living in the guesthouse with her parents and little sister, Emily, so she'd been no stranger to the beautiful Suffolk Coast when she'd returned to live there.

Hannah had heard Abigail's car first, coming up behind them, the unmistakable sound of an old VW Beetle making them all jump.

There were other friends of Lili's too – Lexi, with her partner, Scott, and his daughter, Charlie, who was a year older than Maisie. Hannah was reminded that she wasn't the only single parent who come to Suffolk seeking a fresh start. They lived on the houseboat by the quay, next door to Ray. Lexi, like her counterparts who'd arrived on the Suffolk Coast, had made a home for herself there, and friends – and had found who she'd been searching for at Willow Tree Cottage, solving a family mystery.

Another friend, Briony, had arrived in Suffolk in search of her grandmother and had settled into a lovely place by the coast, aptly named The Beach House.

And then there was the family: Ray and Sarah, of course, and Lili's family, who had flown in from abroad to be there on her big day.

It was all so exciting, and rather nerve-racking for the wedding planners.

Rupert put an arm around Hannah's shoulders, obviously sensing her nerves. 'Everything is going to be fine. The website is up and running, and as the digital photos are taken, we're going to share them and the videos in real time. Remember, my friend in London is on standby to disseminate to social media and the website.' He clocked her expression. 'Hey, don't look so worried.'

'But what if there are no views or visitors to the website, and no one wants to book a wedding here after all the work we've put into this?'

'That's why we're uploading the photos straight away. It's better that we start to get some feedback, or not, sooner rather than later so we know whether the idea is going to work.'

They both wanted it to work. Rupert wasn't going to give up his job as an art dealer completely, but his plan was to continue helping Hannah with her wedding business at Somersby Hall and carry on working from home, commuting to London once a week. He'd already packed up his belongings from the flat he'd shared with Claudia and had moved into the hall.

Meanwhile, Hannah had already been researching where to source wedding gowns. She was seriously thinking about turning her shop into a bridal shop, even though she didn't want to get ahead of herself. Neither of them knew what the outcome of the day would be.

'Everything is going to be just fine,' Rupert said again.

'But … but what if something untoward happens that we haven't accounted for?' They needed the day to go well without a hitch, but Hannah was still worried. If some unexpected problem were to crop up, it would on their shoulders to sort it out. And it wasn't any old day – it was Lili and Nate's wedding day!

'What could possibly go wrong?'

Hannah shot him a look, wishing he hadn't said that. It seemed like tempting fate.

'Look, we've done our best. Whatever happens now, it's in the lap of the gods.'

38

'Did you see them arrive?' Rupert whispered to Hannah. They were both standing in the back garden, the white chairs arranged in rows, leaving a central aisle leading to a temporary raised oval decking area where the local vicar would officiate the wedding. At that moment she was greeting the guests, who were starting to take their seats.

Hannah whispered back, 'Well, no – why would I? There's been so many people arriving, they must have slipped in unnoticed.' Since arriving, she'd been in the kitchen at the back of the house, checking the catering, and then out in the back garden, directing guests to their seats and glancing at the odd fluffy white cloud, thankful that the weather forecast was correct and there would be no autumn rain showers on Lili's wedding day. That was imperative, as they'd chosen to conduct the wedding ceremony in the garden.

Lili and Nate knew the plan. Lili had decided that she would change into her wedding dress when they arrived at Somersby Hall on the morning of the wedding; that way Nate wouldn't see her in her bridal gown before the nuptials. The dress was hanging in a spare bedroom in the house, where Lili could change. The makeup artist and hair stylist were waiting for her. Tea and coffee had been delivered to the room.

Rupert looked at his watch.

'They've still got plenty of time,' said Hannah. 'I'm sure she'll be down soon.' Hannah imagined the hair stylist and makeup artist would have just put on the finishing touches and that Lili was getting into her wedding dress right about now.

Even so, Hannah said, 'Do you want me to go check how she's getting on?

'Would you?'

Hannah smiled, 'Of course.'

Maisie appeared by her mum's side, drinking a glass of squash. 'Mum, where's William?'

Hannah looked at Maisie. 'Oh, I assumed you were playing with William.'

She shook her head. 'I've been playing a board game with Percy and Lady Jemima in the drawing room.'

Hannah caught Rupert raising his eyebrows. She said, 'Perhaps William is with Nate.'

'I haven't seen Dad either. Do you think he's late?' asked Maisie.

'For his own wedding? I don't think so, sweetheart.' Even so, she turned to Rupert. 'I'm going upstairs to check on Lili. Perhaps she knows where Nate and William are.'

Maisie said, 'Can I come too? I can't wait to see her wedding dress.'

'All right, but you must finish that juice first and wash your hands.' Of all the things that she'd imagined could go wrong on the day of the wedding, Maisie spilling orange juice down Lili's beautiful dress had not been one of them – until now.

She waited while Maisie gulped down her orange and ran to the downstairs cloakroom. She was back super-quick. Hannah hurried up the stairs, Maisie following, and knocked on the bedroom door.

'Enter!' she heard the stylist call out.

Hannah grinned at Maisie. Neither of them could wait to see Lili in her dress. Hannah opened the door to what she hadn't expected – the hair stylist and makeup artist were sitting at a small table in the corner of the room, drinking tea. The hairstylist was reading a newspaper and his partner was scrolling through her phone.

'What's going on? Where's Lili?' Hannah asked.

'We were going to ask *you* that. We were about to come down and find you.'

Hannah hurried out of the room and back down the stairs. Some guests passed them in the hallway, on their way through to the back garden. She stopped them to ask if they'd seen Lili or Nate.

Rupert stared at her. 'She's not upstairs?'

Hannah shook her head. 'I don't know what's going on. Perhaps their car got a flat, or they broke down on the way here.'

'Have either of them texted or phoned?' Rupert asked.

Hannah stared at Rupert, wide-eyed. She was wearing a dress with no pockets. She'd left her little shoulder bag containing her phone in Nate's study.

'I don't know!' Hannah said, explaining she didn't have her phone on her. 'What about you?'

'My phone's charging in the study.'

They both turned to Maisie. Hannah said, 'Maisie, has your dad phoned or texted you by any chance?'

'I don't know.'

'What do you mean, you don't know? Your phone is in your bag – isn't it?' She pointed at Maisie's little shoulder bag.

'You told me I could only bring it with me today if I keep it silent.'

Hannah rolled her eyes. Of course she had.

Hannah and Rupert were just about to run into the study when the house phone rang, the shrill sound of the old phone reverberating around the house.

They all froze, apart from Maisie, who was unmuting her phone.

Percy walked out of the drawing room, muttering, 'Isn't anyone going to answer that?' He answered the phone. 'Oh dear. Oh dear, oh dear. I shall relay the message at once.'

Percy put the phone down and was just about to say something when Maisie looked up from her phone, exclaiming, 'Oh, no. Stupid William has fallen off his bike and broken his arm. They asked me to tell you to phone them.'

Rupert and Hannah ran into the study, where they both discovered numerous texts and missed calls. Rupert phoned Nate and Hannah phoned Lili. A moment later, they got off their phones after hearing what happened; William had been waiting for his dad and Lili, but rather than do as he was told and sit in the lounge reading a book or playing one of his Nintendo games, he'd gone outside to have a ride around on his bike on their gravel drive in front of the house. Nate had heard him and shouted at him from the window – William, the page boy, was dressed in his smart little suit for the wedding and Nate didn't want him falling off the bike and ruining his new suit.

The sound of Nate's angry voice made William look up at

the wrong moment. He careered into a flowerpot by the front door, which sent him flying over the front of the handlebars, ruining more than his new suit. He'd ruined their wedding plans, which in any case had been the furthest thing from their minds when they'd rushed him to A&E. Nate already knew he'd broken his humerus and may need emergency surgery on his arm, which it turned out he did. They hadn't texted Maisie this fact because they didn't want to worry her, but they'd had to text her as no one else was picking up on their messages.

Hannah realised all the guests probably had their phones either switched off or muted too for the wedding ceremony.

All Rupert and Hannah could do was tell them they were in their thoughts and hoped William's surgery went well. There would be no wedding that day.

Rupert sat behind his desk. Hannah sat down too, opposite Rupert. Facing the window, she could see almost everyone had taken their seats. The vicar was making her way to the raised decking area in front of the seats, getting herself into position in front of the pergola festooned with flowers to start the ceremony.

Hannah and Rupert's eyes met across the desk. Hannah said, 'What on earth are we going to do now?'

Rupert sighed. 'Call off the wedding.'

'We can't do that!'

'What do you suggest – we see if anybody out there wants to get married instead?'

'Actually, that's not a bad idea.'

'You think so? I was actually joking.'

'Yeah – I guessed that. But I still think it's a good idea. Hold on … I've had a thought …'

Hannah texted a message to Lili as she said to Rupert, 'I hope she doesn't mind me asking this under the circumstances …'

'What are you doing?'

'Asking Lili if someone can borrow her dress.'

'Her wedding dress?'

Hannah nodded as she sent the text.

'Who?'

'Well, I don't know yet, Rupert, do I? We'll have to go out there and ask.'

Rupert was shaking his head from side to side, saying, 'This is crazy. You know, you can't just get married on the spur of the moment because you suddenly feel like it. You need a wedding licence. It takes time to go through the legal formalities and make sure the paperwork is in order. Do you know what the chances are of someone being out there who is engaged and who has a licence already to get married?'

'Have you got a better idea?' Hannah stopped. 'Actually, don't answer that. It *was* your idea! Oh, she's texting back.'

'What on earth did she say to your request?'

Hannah sat back in her chair and stared at the text message.

'What is it?'

'Well, turns out she had a crazier idea than yours! Let's roll with yours first.'

'So, is she letting someone use her dress?'

'Yes.'

'Well, er … good. I guess the only way we're going to know if someone seated in the garden can get married instead is to go and ask them.'

'Exactly!' Hannah rose from her seat but noticed that Rupert was still sitting there. 'What now?'

'You know this is such a long shot. I can't think of anyone on the wedding guest list, and if there is, they might not want to get married right now, in Somersby Hall.'

'Yes, that's true. And as we're on the subject of long shots, what are the chances that Lili's wedding dress will fit and that they'll even want to wear someone else's dress? That's what we're doing it for, after all, isn't it, Rupert? The promotional photos for our business.'

'Yes, Lili obviously realises that, otherwise she wouldn't let someone use her dress.'

Hannah nodded, still staring at the text.

Rupert got up from his desk and looked at her phone. 'Are you going to tell me what exactly she said when you asked her about the dress?'

Hannah shook her head. 'Let's go and see if we can find a couple first. I think we're wasting our time going out there and even asking the guests, but I suppose we've nothing to lose now.'

'All right.'

Hannah and Rupert stepped into the garden and marched towards the vicar, who was standing ready to officiate the wedding.

As they stepped onto the decking, the vicar exclaimed, 'Ah, the chief bridesmaid and best man.'

Those who were seated clapped.

Hannah and Rupert exchanged a glance. Rupert wasn't the best man, but they didn't correct the vicar. Instead, they turned their backs on the wedding party, speaking in hushed voices to the vicar about what had happened to the bride and groom that morning, informing her that Lili and Nate's wedding was off.

'Oh, dear, oh dear,' she whispered back. 'I shall say my prayers for William's speedy recovery. Such a shame, though. It would have been a splendid wedding, and in such a beautiful venue. I heard that you were hoping this wedding would mark the start of many more to come at Somersby Hall.'

Hannah sighed as Rupert said, 'We were going to upload the photos to social media.'

The vicar was about to depart when Hannah said, 'Would you wait a moment? We were wondering if you would be prepared to marry a different couple, if there is anyone seated here who is in a position to marry, and chooses to go ahead if asked?'

'Well, this is highly unusual, but then, excuse my language, shit happens.'

'Doesn't it just?' said Rupert.

Hannah grinned.

They both turned around and walked to the edge of the decking, surveying the waiting wedding party.

Rupert addressed the crowd. 'I'm afraid there's been a bit of bad news …' It didn't take long to explain what was going on and that Lili and Nate's wedding had to be called off, but that they had a huge favour to ask while they were all seated, and the caterers, small band, and the vicar were still there if anyone was interested in what they were about to suggest.

'Would anyone be in a position – and would like – to get married, right here, right now?' Hannah asked.

She felt Rupert's hand in hers as they stood waiting to see if anybody stood up to take them up on their generous offer. Of course, it came with strings attached – they'd have to agree to their wedding photos being uploaded and used for promotional purposes for Somersby Hall. And what of Lili's beautiful dress – would it fit, and would the bride be prepared to wear it? But they'd already decided they'd have to deal with those issues if anyone were to rise from their seats, which they both knew was highly unlikely.

There were murmurs from the guests, and people looking about them to see if anybody could and would volunteer to get married.

Hannah glanced at Rupert. 'I don't think we're in luck.'

He nodded. 'It really was a stupidly long shot.'

They had turned to face one another, resigned to the fact that there would be no wedding at Somersby Hall that day, when suddenly clapping and cheering went up amongst those seated.

The vicar was clapping too.

Hannah and Rupert looked at each other wide-eyed, and said in unison, 'No way!' before they slowly turned to see who had risen from their seat.

39

'Sit down, Percy, you silly old fool!' Lady Jemima hissed at him, wishing the ground could swallow her whole. Why was everyone clapping and cheering? Didn't they realise this was a mistake?

She heard the young vicar ask, 'And who is the lucky lady?'

The crowd went silent.

Percy held out his hand. He leaned over and whispered, 'Come on, Kitty. How about it? Let's get married. What do you say?'

'Shotgun wedding?' said Kitty grinning, despite how embarrassed she was at all the attention. After hiding herself away in Somersby Hall for decades, afraid someone would discover her secret, she surprised herself when she replied, 'I do so want to marry you, Percy, in front of all these lovely people.'

Someone near them must have overheard, for the clapping resumed.

'Stand up, stand up!' the vicar called out.

There were chants of *Stand up! Stand up!*

Lady Jemima slowly got to her feet, Percy chuckling in her ear, 'I wouldn't exactly call it a shotgun wedding – would you? We did apply for the necessary wedding licence and all that paraphernalia after I proposed, remember?'

'Of course I remember. And I remember your proposal. It was a long time coming.'

'That's because I didn't think we'd ever marry, but we discussed this. We're not getting any younger, and I just thought we would know when the time was right to finally tie the knot and make our long-term commitment to each other official.'

'And that time is now?' she whispered back.

'I think so – don't you?'

'Percy, how fortuitous that we applied for our wedding licence when Lili and Nate did.'

'Yes, when they applied, it prompted me to think of doing it.'

'You must have had a sixth sense that something would happen.'

'Not at all. But with all the wedding prep going on around us, I thought it rather fitting that we marry here in our home. I just didn't think we'd have the opportunity to do it today!'

'Yes, but aren't you forgetting something?'

'No,' he said slowly. 'I have the wedding licence, and we've done all the legal things which means we can marry, and we've got the rings …'

'Oh, Percy, I'm not talking about that. I'm talking about the photos.'

'The wedding photos?'

'Yes, remember they were going to be uploaded to a website, and TokTok.'

Percy smiled but did not correct her this time.

'Are people really going to be swayed to come have their wedding here by two wrinkly old—?'

'You're not that wrinkly,' said Percy, whispering in her ear while the clapping continued.

'And you're not so bad yourself,' she whispered back, 'but you do know what I mean.'

The looked at each other and slowly resumed their seats.

The clapping subsided. A murmur arose among the wedding guests wondering why they'd sat down.

The vicar waved at them. 'Well, if you're getting married, we need you up here, not down there.'

Light-hearted laughter rippled through the crowd.

Percy turned to his fiancée. 'I really want to do this.'

'So, how are we going to get round the promotional wedding photos?'

'We need some stand-ins for the photos,' said Percy.

'Stand-ins …' Lady Jemima mused. 'What a brilliant idea. You are clever, Percy. And I know just the couple.'

'Ah, of course,' said Percy.

They looked at each other, grinned, and turned their heads, focusing on the two people standing with the vicar.

'We're coming!' they called out as they slowly rose from their seats once more. 'We just have one condition before we proceed,' said Lady Jemima.

Percy said, 'We'd like a word with Rupert and Hannah.'

❖

Rupert and Hannah exchanged a glance as they stepped off the raised decking, about to find out what condition his grandmother and Percy wanted to discuss with them before they proceeded with their wedding.

Hannah said, 'I think it's wonderful they are getting married, just wonderful. Don't you?'

'I do. I think my grandmother is probably checking we're okay with this, and they'll marry on the condition that we're happy for them to proceed.'

'Why wouldn't we be? It's her house, and you know, they're not getting any younger. They obviously intended to marry and must have the marriage licence and all the paperwork in order. I think it's probably been a very, very long time coming.'

'I'm going to tell them we don't need to discuss it,' said Rupert as they walked towards the couple. 'I'm in total agreement that they should marry.'

'But would it be legal?' she said in a hushed voice.

'How do you mean?' Rupert asked, pausing mid-stride.

'Well, her name – she's not really Lady Jemima.'

'You'd have to ask her. I think there is such a thing as changing your name by informal usage. Although knowing my grandmother, I imagine she's covered that. You can change your name by deed poll, you know, if you want to legally change it. It's quick and cheap. I'm not sure that would be required, as she will be taking Percy's surname anyway.'

'But what about her title, Lady?'

'I imagine that you can give yourself that title too.'

'God, don't tell Maisie that,' Hannah joked.

'Not legally, of course. You can call yourself Joe Bloggs, Lord of the manor of … well whatever estate you've bought, but it wouldn't be a title of honour, which is one bestowed by the sovereign and passed down.'

Hannah nodded.

'Well, it's so lovely to have your blessing, Rupert,' Percy said as Rupert and Hannah stood with him and Lady Jemima in the garden to one side of the seated guests. They'd just told the couple how happy they were that they were getting married.

Lady Jemima said, 'However, there's something else we need to discuss …'

40

'This was Lili's crazy idea?' Rupert said, looking quite taken aback as he followed Hannah into the house, leaving the guests waiting for Percy and Lady Jemima's wedding to take place.

'Yeah, remember I texted her to ask her whether somebody could borrow her dress, and I said she had a crazier idea than yours. It was just what Percy and your grandmother proposed. That I wear the dress, and we pose for photos as if we were getting married.'

'You mean stand together in front of the vicar, pretending we are saying our wedding vows?'

'Yeah – your grandmother is going to lend me one of her rings so we can be photographed with you appearing to put the ring on my finger.'

'This is going to be *so* weird,' Rupert said.

'Isn't it just?'

They both looked at each other. Rupert said, 'I don't think I can go through with it.'

Hannah had just been about to take the stairs and go to try on the dress, hoping it fitted. She turned around. 'Oh. You don't want us to give the business its best shot and see if it can work?

We've come this far. It'd be a shame to give up now.'

'It's not that.'

'Then what is it?'

Rupert opened his mouth to say something.

Hannah's heart sank. She suddenly had an idea what this was about. 'Look, it's not real, obviously. I'm just going to wear a dress, albeit a very expensive *white* dress, and we're going to take some promotional photos – all right?'

Rupert looked downcast. 'All right.'

'Good. Let's get this done. I just hope the bloody dress fits after all this.'

'I'll wait here.'

'No! You can't see me before the wedding!'

'What?'

Hannah laughed. 'That was a joke. Wait for me here, won't you? I need your opinion on the dress, just to make sure we want promotional photos of me. The last thing I want to do is put people off. I don't think I'm very photogenic.'

Hannah was just legging it up the stairs when she had a thought. She whirled around. Rupert was still at the bottom of stairs, looking miserable. 'What is it now?' he asked.

'Who is going to give your grandmother away?'

'Huh?'

'Your grandmother. The bride's father normally gives her away …'

'Oh, yes. Of course I will do it.'

'Fantastic. That's another thing sorted. Now, let's see what we think of this dress.'

The hair stylist and the makeup artist were still upstairs, drinking tea. They were both now idly scrolling through their phones. They looked quite shocked when Hannah burst into the room and announced, 'I need help getting into that dress!'

Fifteen minutes later, Hannah was standing in the beautiful dress. It was a simple yet elegant design in an off-white with a silk train and a veiled tiara.

The dress fitted perfectly – too perfectly.

The stylist took a few moments to adjust her hair and then handed her the bouquet. He said, 'You look stunning.'

The makeup artist had touched up her makeup too.

Hannah stared at her reflection in the full-length mirror. Even the dainty shoes fitted. 'I don't think I can go through with this.'

The makeup artist heard her. 'But you love him, don't you?'

Hannah swallowed. 'I do.' That was the problem. She didn't think she could go through *pretending* to marry him when she realised in that moment that she desperately wanted to marry him *for real.*

The stylist put a gentle arm around her shoulders. 'Now, there's nothing to worry about. I know you're going to be in front of all those people, but just focus on him.'

'You don't understand …'

'Come on now. Let's go.' They both walked her to the door. 'Deep breaths,' the stylist said, breathing in and out.

Hannah followed his lead, taking a deep breath, and willed herself to think about the wedding business she was trying to get off the ground at Somersby Hall and put her personal feelings to one side. She started down the stairs, taking it slowly lest she trip on the dress.

She saw Rupert standing at the bottom of the stairs. He looked very dapper in his suit. Fortunately, the suit he'd chosen to wear to the wedding would work in the wedding photos.

He turned around when he heard the creak of the stair.

He still hadn't said a word when she reached the hallway. 'What is it? Do you think the dress is too plain for the photos? We could wait for another day to do our pretend marriage, hire a dress, and have the vicar come back and—'

Rupert suddenly took her in his arms and kissed her.

When he drew back, she said, 'You know you're meant to kiss the bride *after* the ceremony – right?'

They both laughed.

Hannah said, 'I take it you like the dress?'

'I think that goes without saying – don't you?'

Hannah touched her lips. 'I think so.' If she could have had one wish granted just then, it would be that they were really getting married. Perhaps Rupert felt the same. She wondered if that was why he'd said he didn't think he could go through with the pretend version.

'The thing is,' said Rupert, 'can we, in all good conscience, put our photos on social media, and on our website, when they're fake?'

'Is that what was bothering you?'

He nodded. 'Of course – what else?'

'Nothing.' Hannah tried not to look downcast at his response. 'Look, other businesses use actors and actresses who play a role or pose for photos for promotional purposes. Why should ours be any different? Just look at it this way – we're playing a role for that reason.'

He sighed. 'I guess.'

Hannah took his arm. 'Come on. You've got to walk your grandmother down the aisle – remember?'

'Oh, yes. Of course.'

'Ah, we must tell the vicar what we're up to, otherwise she'll wonder what's going on when I walk out there in this get-up.'

'I've already spoken to the vicar.'

'When?'

'While you were changing into the dress. I thought you might be some time, so I popped outside and had a word.'

'Was she okay about it?' Hannah hadn't thought to check that the vicar wouldn't mind going along with it.

'Yes, very much so.'

Hannah smiled. 'Oh, okay,' a bit surprised. She said, 'So, we're all set?'

Rupert grinned. 'I think we are.'

They stepped outside in the garden. The other guests didn't know what was going on. There was a hushed silence when Hannah walked over in the dress and handed the wedding bouquet to Lady Jemima. She thought she heard someone comment that they'd never seen a bridesmaid's dress quite like it.

Hannah bent to give Lady Jemima a little hug.

Lady Jemima whispered in her ear, 'You, my dear, look simply stunning.'

Hannah smiled at Rupert, who came to take his grandmother's arm. Together they walked down the centre aisle to the sound of the small band they'd hired playing the wedding march.

Hannah joined Rupert on the raised decking, standing to one side, watching the wedding ceremony. Rupert had the ring that Percy had been carrying around with him for what Rupert and Hannah imagined was a lifetime.

The photographer proceeded to take the wedding photos.

When the ceremony was over, and the wedding photos in different spots in the garden, and around the front of the house, had been taken, Rupert took Hannah's hand. 'Now, let's get our shots, shall we?'

Hannah and Rupert had decided to take a back seat and let Percy and Jemima enjoy their ceremony and the wedding photos that they would cherish.

'Right, can everyone gather round again, please, and take their seats?' Rupert announced.

Hannah whispered, 'What are you doing? We don't need to do our photos in front of everyone, you know. They could be enjoying the buffet, and the band.'

'No, no. I want to do this.'

'Why?'

Rupert said, 'I just do. Let's not argue about this, please.'

Out of the corner of her eye, she saw Percy and Lady Jemima, glasses of bubbly in their hands, each take a seat on the very front row. They were grinning.

Hannah frowned at them. Why did she have the distinct feeling that something was going on?

She joined Rupert in front of the vicar as everyone resumed their seats.

Hannah took a deep breath. She turned to the vicar, feeling, like Rupert, that she didn't want to pose for photos of a fake wedding after all. 'Rupert …'

'Shush,' the vicar said, surprising her. The vicar looked at the crowd. 'We are gathered here today to witness the joining of Hannah and Rupert …'

Hannah was about to whisper a question to Rupert to check that the vicar did know they weren't getting married for real.

Then Rupert suddenly knelt.

'What are you doing?' Hannah asked, looking down at him.

He held up a ring. 'Hannah, will you do me the honour of marrying me?' He added, 'Not today, obviously, because you know, we'll have to plan our own wedding.'

Hannah turned to look at Percy and his grandmother, who were obviously in on it. The vicar was also grinning.

Hannah didn't know what to say. She was speechless. 'I … I … yes! Yes, of course.'

Rupert breathed a sigh of relief. 'You know, you had me going there for a moment.' He stood up and carefully slipped his grandmother's ring onto her finger. 'I hope you like it. It's a real inset sapphire, apparently.'

'I now pronounce you – engaged!' the vicar said. 'You may kiss your fiancée!'

There was a cheer, and clapping, as Hannah kissed her fiancé, before she said, 'Oh, Rupert, is this what you were doing while I was getting into my dress. Planning all this?'

'I told you I didn't think I could go through with it, pretending to get married.'

'I thought it was because the photos would be fake.'

'Yes, exactly. I wanted to marry you for real. When you came downstairs wearing that dress, oh how I wanted to marry you right here, right now.'

Hannah looked at the engagement ring. 'I can't believe we're engaged!' She had a feeling she'd be staring at the ring all night.

Maisie came running up to them both. 'Oh, Mum – you're engaged!'

Hannah stared at her daughter. She hadn't had a chance to ask her first if it was all right. In fact, she hadn't even been thinking of her daughter when Rupert had proposed. She was asking her now.

'Oh, Mum, it's the best thing ever! Does that mean we can go and live in the big house with Lady Jemima and Percy and Lulu when you get married?'

Hannah looked helplessly at Rupert.

'Yes,' said Rupert, Percy and Lady Jemima in unison.

'But we may have to move back into Gatekeeper's Cottage when there are wedding parties,' Rupert said. 'Assuming there are—'

Rupert's phone pinged. So did Hannah's. Then again and again.

'You've got lots of messages,' said Maisie.

Hannah looked up from her phone. Rupert looked up from his. 'It's our social media accounts, Facebook, TikTok, and the new website. There are loads of messages.'

Hannah said, 'But I don't understand. We didn't have any photos taken of us.'

'Come to think of it, no we didn't,' said Rupert. 'Where was the photographer?'

Maisie said, 'He left. I saw him packing up his camera and stuff.'

Hannah frowned. She turned to Rupert. 'Did you remember to ask the photographer to take photos of us, not just the happy couple?'

Rupert stared at her, wide-eyed. 'Ah. I forgot!'

Hannah looked at her phone. 'I don't get it. Why is there all this sudden social media buzz?'

Maisie said, 'Perhaps everyone likes Percy and Lady Jemima's wedding photos.'

Hannah started scrolled through the photos on social media. 'Rupert, the wedding photographer must have shared their wedding photos.'

Rupert stared at his phone. 'And my friend must have uploaded them, like he asked.'

'Oh, dear,' said Percy and Lady Jemima together.

'Oh, my god,' exclaimed Hannah, 'someone's just reserved a date on our website for their wedding. They said the wedding photos have inspired them to remarry. They are a widow and widower, both in their eighth decade!'

Rupert read out loud the caption that his friend in IT had added to their website: *Book a wedding at Somersby Hall – for the young, and young at heart.*

Several more bookings, from both young couples and the young at heart, followed.

Percy chuckled. 'I think it sounds as though people have been rather taken by our story, getting married so late in life.'

'Oh, deary me,' said Lady Jemima. 'The trouble is, they don't know our story.'

Percy was still chuckling. 'You said yourself that nobody is going to find out. So let's enjoy this. Our photos are certainly novel.'

'That's true,' said Rupert. 'When it comes to wedding photos on websites, it's mainly young couples, first time around newlyweds.'

'But there's plenty of people who remarry, or marry later in life,' observed Hannah. She looked at Rupert. 'I think we may have just hit on a niche, rather by accident.'

Percy and Lady Jemima agreed.

Hannah said, 'I need to get out of this dress. I'm worried

something might happen to it.' She walked back into the house with Rupert and Maisie in tow. She said to Rupert, 'I'm not sure how we are going to top that, do you? It was just so lovely with everyone there, and so unexpected. What are people going to expect from our wedding, if that was just our engagement?'

They paused at the bottom of the stairs. Rupert laughed. 'You know what the answer is, don't you?'

She shook her head.

'We elope, then we won't have to worry about planning *our* wedding.'

'You mean like Owen and …' Hannah glanced at her daughter. '… Kitty.'

'Yes.'

'What does elope mean?' asked Maisie.

'Runing away from everybody to get married.'

Maisie's lip quivered.

'Oh, sweetheart, don't worry – we'll take you and Marlowe.'

'What about Lulu, and Lady Jemima and Percy?'

Rupert said, 'Well, of course they'll come too.' He glanced at Hannah, who was smiling. Maisie didn't quite understand.

Maisie said, 'I want Dad to come, and Lili. And my brother.'

Hannah had had another text from Lili. William was out of surgery and doing well. She told Maisie.

Maisie said, 'Good. I'm going back to the garden to get some juice.'

Rupert smiled, watching her. He joked, 'Well, I think if we elope, we'll need a bigger car!'

At that moment an old VW campervan came up the drive. 'Like that,' Rupert laughed, looking through the open front door.

He caught the look on Hannah's face. 'What's the matter?'

She left the stairs and headed towards the front door. 'It's the van.'

'What van?'

'The campervan in the painting.'

'What painting?'

'You know – *Sunrise Over Seashell Bay*.'

Percy and Lady Jemima must have heard the unmistakable sound of the VW engine as it came up the drive. They joined Rupert and Hannah at the front door. Percy said, 'Oh, dear. It looks like we're crossing that bridge sooner that we thought.'

Rupert looked at each one of them in turn. 'What do you mean? What's going on?'

Lady Jemima said, 'I think Owen has returned. And he's brought someone with him.'

They all recognised the young woman driving the campervan – the heir to Somersby Hall.

41

Hetty stepped out of the campervan and rushed over. 'Please don't tell me off for what I did, either of you.' She stole a glance at Rupert.

'Oh, Hetty. I've been worried about you.' Hannah stepped forward and hugged her, forgetting for a moment what her return meant – she might be back to claim what she thought was rightfully hers.

'You got married?' Hetty said when she drew back and registered what Hannah was wearing.

'No, it's a long story. We got engaged.'

'Oh, congratulations.'

Hannah remembered their conversation about relationships the night Hetty had stayed over with her at Gatekeeper's Cottage before she disappeared with the airgraphs and the painting. 'What happened about your flatmate, the guy you liked – Dan, wasn't it?'

'I asked Dan out.'

'You did?'

'We're dating. Actually, we're going to look for a place together. Like my grandfather always says – there's no time like the present. And keep walking!'

'Keep walking?' Hannah looked at her bemused.

An older man emerged from the campervan.

Hannah looked at him wide-eyed. 'Is this … Owen, Owen Hartley?'

'Yes, this is my grandfather.'

Other than Maisie, she'd never met a talented artist before, and someone whose work she adored. 'Oh, I feel quite start-struck,' she admitted. 'I love your paintings,' she gushed.

Her grandfather smiled until his eyes shifted to Lady Jemima and Percy.

'Percy.' He nodded at his brother.

'Owen, I'm glad you are keeping well. It's been quite some time, hasn't it?'

Owen chuckled, surprising Hannah at how alike they sounded. 'It has indeed.'

'We're married, you know,' said Percy, taking his wife's hand.

Hannah wondered if Percy still felt a little threatened by the return of Kitty's first love.

'Well, I'm pleased for you, Percy. I know how much you always loved Kitty. Oh, er … I mean Lady Jemima,' he quickly backtracked, his eyes shifting from Hannah to Rupert.

She stepped forward. 'My grandson, Rupert, and his fiancée,' she said. 'They know, Owen, as I presume does your granddaughter.'

Hetty was looking up at the house.

Hannah stepped back, reaching for Rupert's hand.

He whispered, 'Why were you talking to her and hugging her like she's some kind of friend?'

'Sorry, but she is.'

'She's come back to take my home, my grandmother's home.'

Hannah frowned. 'It was going to be my home too, you know.'

This time, Rupert apologised. He put an arm around her shoulder as they stood together wondering what was going to happen next.

'What are you doing here, Owen?'

Hannah shot Rupert's grandmother a look. Wasn't it obvious? Hetty knew too, and she was there to claim what was rightfully hers.

'I had to tell her, Kitty.'

'But you promised to keep our secret.'

'She found the letters and the painting.'

They all fell silent. Hannah had to ask. 'How did the painting I bought end up in the charity shop in Aldeburgh?'

Hetty affectionately took her grandfather's arm. 'Grandad? Do you know how that painting ended up in a charity shop?'

He sighed. 'I came back, you know.'

Lady Jemima looked confused. 'To Somersby Hall?'

He shook his head. 'No. I came back to Seashell Bay.'

Hannah sucked in a breath. 'Seashell Bay?'

Hetty said. 'There's a real place called Seashell Bay? Wait, I didn't know you'd gone away in your campervan. You never told me.'

Hannah watched Owen turn to his granddaughter. 'I wanted to return to Seashell Bay and spread your grandmother's ashes there. That was always my intention. It took me some time to build up the courage to go.'

Lady Jemima said, 'I'm so sorry, Owen.'

There was a subdued silence until Hetty said, 'But how did

you get here? I thought you didn't drive anymore. That's why I drove here today.'

'Jilly brought me. You know the lady who cleans the cottage and runs the odd errand for me.'

Hetty looked at him in surprise. 'Don't tell me you asked her to drive you all the way here in your campervan? That's a very big errand.'

'Yes, it was. I was surprised she said yes, although I did compensate her rather generously for her time.'

'I wish you'd told me. I would have loved to come with you.'

He took his granddaughter's hand in his. 'I know, but you were busy, and I thought the time had come to let her go. On that trip I'd brought something else along with your grandmother's ashes – the painting I still had in my possession. I was intending to cast the painting into the sea, but something strange happened. The wind suddenly picked up. I'm no stranger to the easterly winds on the Suffolk Coast, but this was a sudden gust so strong it rather stopped me in my tracks, almost propelling me backwards. The painting almost fell out of my hands. That was when I knew it was a sign.'

'A sign?' repeated Hannah.

'That she didn't want me to do that, cast it into the sea. So I left it outside the charity shop in Cobblers Yard. She'd have wanted me to do that, give it away to charity so that at least it would fetch some money for a good cause. Imagine my utter surprise when you returned to visit me, Henrietta, and you showed me a painting you'd found – that very painting – *Sunrise Over Seashell Bay*.'

Hetty squeezed his arm. 'Oh, Grandad. Why didn't you tell me all this?'

'Well, we got quite wrapped up in the other thing you'd brought home to show me, didn't we?'

Hetty looked at the floor. 'Yes. The airgraphs,' she said in a small voice.

'Yes, the airgraphs. And as they say, the truth will out.'

Rupert's grandmother let out an audible sigh.

'Now, Hetty here has come back with me to return the things she … took.'

Hetty looked up sharply. 'But they're your letters, and the painting is yours too.'

'From what you told me, Hannah bought them fair and square from the charity shop where I left the painting.'

'But you didn't know the letters were in that painting.'

'No, I did not. But that doesn't change the fact that they belong to Hannah now.'

'But—'

'No buts, young lady. I won't hear another word about it.'

Hannah stared at them. She watched Hetty return to the campervan. Hannah desperately wanted the airgraphs back, but …

'Wait!' Hannah exclaimed.

Hetty stopped and turned around.

Hannah looked at Rupert.

Rupert squeezed her hand, whispering, 'I think you should do what you think is right.'

Smiling at him, she mouthed a thank you and said, 'I can't take them back. They belong to you, Hetty. They're part of your family history, your heritage, not mine. I always knew I'd face this dilemma if I found the descendants of Owen and the person I thought he'd written to, Kitty.'

Hetty looked at her grandfather.

'I don't want to come between you,' Hannah said. 'But as Owen said, they're mine. I can do with them what I wish. And I wish for you to them.'

'Oh, Hannah, I don't know what to say. I just can't thank you enough.' She paused, and said in a small voice, 'And the painting too?'

Hannah adored the painting, but she knew it wasn't hers to keep either. She had to let it go. She had the other one, *Sunset Over Seashell Bay*, a painting that two people she adored, Percy and Lady Jemima, had given to her because, she realised, they loved her very much. That painting meant much, much more to her than the one she'd found in the charity shop ever would.

She smiled at Hetty. 'The painting too.'

Hetty ran over and hugged her friend. 'Oh, Hannah, you're the best.'

'Well, I guess now that's cleared up,' said Rupert, 'I suppose you're here for what rightfully belongs to you.'

Hetty drew back. 'What do you mean?'

'What do I mean?' Rupert looked at her. 'Somersby Hall – of course.'

Hetty exchanged a glance with her grandfather. 'I didn't come back here to take away your home.'

'But your grandmother was Lady Jemima,' said Rupert. 'You're the true legitimate descendant of—'

'No, I'm not.'

Hannah and Rupert exchanged a glance.

Rupert said, 'What are you talking about? You've got the letters. You've seen the painting of your ancestor that looks just like you hanging in the hall. Your grandfather told you the truth.'

'My grandmother made a decision to give it all up, and she made a promise never to return. She didn't renege on her promise, and on her behalf neither shall I. Although …' she fixed her gaze on the house. 'I'd still get married here, just like I said, Rupert, now I've found the right person.'

'But … but the house. It's your birthright,' said Rupert.

'My grandmother once told me she wanted to leave me a legacy, that she had regrets. I didn't understand at the time, obviously. But I told her I had everything I need. Loving parents, doting grandparents, my job. And now Dan. She loved me very much. That's the legacy she left me. Her love.' She smiled. 'That's what's important to me. That hasn't changed. This house, it's not part of who I am, *my* past – it's my grandparents' past. They chose to leave it all behind and lead a different life.'

She glanced at her grandfather, who was smiling adoringly at her. She continued, 'They say you can never go back. You can never go home. Well, it's true. Life, time, propels you ever forward, doesn't it? Somersby Hall. It's just like any other stately home I've visited. I love it as a house, but I don't feel a connection to it like I do to the cottage in Dartmoor where I spent the summer holidays with my grandparents. It's *your* home, Rupert, you, Hannah, Percy and …' she paused, 'Lady Jemima. I could no more come and take that away from you than you would take away our Dartmoor cottage.'

Nobody knew quite what to say, least of all Rupert and his grandmother. Hannah knew that if Hetty ever chose to sell the rare airgraphs, they might help her and Dan with a deposit for their own home. They might even fetch enough at auction for them to buy their own home outright. That wasn't the reason Hannah had given them to her – to pay her off to stop her from making a claim on Rupert's home – but they were hers now to do with as she wanted.

Owen broke the silence. 'Well, now all that's cleared up, we'll be on our way. Lady Jemima,' he said, walking over to her. 'It's been lovely to meet you again.' He put his arms around her.

She hugged him close, a tear rolling down her cheek.

'She always missed you, you know,' said Owen. 'You were such a good friend to her, such a good … sister.'

Lady Jemima raised her eyebrows. 'She told you?'

'Of course. She told me *everything*.'

Hannah looked at them embracing. When Hannah had found out who had really written the love letters to Owen, she had wanted to ask her whether, if they were to ever meet again, she would tell Owen. But she knew Rupert's grandmother well by now. She knew she'd say, 'Some things are better left unsaid to protect the ones we love.' The real Lady Jemima was gone. It would do no good for Owen to discover he'd fallen in love with the wrong woman.

He kissed her gently on the cheek and turned to Percy. 'You are a *very* lucky man.'

He grinned. 'I know.'

Hannah stared at Owen. What had he just said? *She told me everything*. He already knew who'd really written the letters. She glanced at the campervan. 'Where are you going now?' Hannah asked, stepping forward.

Owen glanced at Hetty. 'We're going together to say a final goodbye to my late wife at the place she loved best.' He looked up at the house. 'It's time.'

Hetty looked at her grandfather. 'We're going to Seashell Bay?'

'Yes, I wanted to show you the seashells she used to love to collect on that very beach.'

Hannah looked at him wide-eyed. 'Wait! Before you go, can you tell me where the beach is? I've wanted to know ever since I saw your beautiful painting in the charity shop.'

He'd just opened the driver's side van door. He turned around and looked at Hannah, then at each one of them in turn. 'I can do one better than that.' He slowly walked to the side of the van and slid open the van door, revealing the seats in the back of the VW campervan.

Hannah stared at him. 'Are you asking me to come with you?'

'I'm asking all of you to come with us. Even you, young lady,' he said to Maisie, who had just run out of the house.

Owen said, 'She left Somersby Hall behind many, many years ago, but this house and its occupants, she took with her,' he held a hand to his chest, 'and always carried you here in her heart. You are all part of her story. I think she'd love you all to come and see her favourite place, don't you? It isn't far.'

'What about the wedding celebrations?' Percy asked. 'Will you come back to Somersby Hall and stay for the reception? We still have the cake to cut, and the first dance.'

'And you must stay with us for one night at least,' Rupert's grandmother added. 'You can't possibly turn around and do the return journey all the way home to Dartmoor.'

Owen looked at Hetty. 'Will you stay for the wedding reception, and leave in the morning?'

She smiled. 'Of course I will. But the sun is starting to go down,' Hetty observed. 'We'd better hurry if we're going there now.'

Owen looked up at the sky 'It's going to be a beautiful sunset,' he observed.

'*Sunset Over Seashell Bay*,' Hannah whispered, thinking of her beautiful painting hanging over the fireplace in Gatekeeper's Cottage. She wanted to step into her painting and see a sunset she knew she would never forget, for real.

Owen closed the van door. 'It's getting late, and it has been a long journey today. I'm tired. I think we will take you up on your offer of staying the night, and I'd love to attend your wedding reception. My dear late wife wouldn't have wanted to keep you from your wedding guests on her account, I'm sure.'

'But what about Seashell Bay?' Hetty and Hannah asked in unison.

'Don't you two worry about that. It's not going anywhere. We, on the other hand, are going to a wedding reception!'

Hannah followed them all into the house, heading for the garden, thinking that perhaps it was for the best to leave it for another time. After all, she really had to change out of Lili's wedding dress.

Thinking of weddings, Hannah took Rupert's hand in hers. Owen had given her the most wonderful idea.

She whispered, 'I know where I want to get married.'

He raised his eyebrows. 'I assumed it would be Somersby Hall.'

'I want the wedding reception here.'

Rupert smiled knowingly. 'Seashell Bay?'

42

'Hannah, there you are!' exclaimed Lili, poking her head around the study door. 'I couldn't find you.'

Hannah was sitting behind the desk, in front of a laptop. 'Sorry, didn't realise you were looking for me.'

'We'll be leaving soon.' Lili cocked her head to one side. 'What are you doing?'

Hannah looked at her sheepishly.

'Oh, don't tell me you're working – today of all days!'

'I just had a spare moment, so rather than hanging around, I thought I'd just check the wedding bookings. You look lovely, by the way.'

Lili smoothed down her dress. 'I think it's gorgeous – such a lovely choice, Hannah.'

Hannah smiled. She'd hoped Lili would like it.

Lili rounded the desk and put an arm around Hannah's shoulders, leaning down and kissing the top of her head. 'You look lovely too, Hannah. You look stunning in that dress.'

Lili shifted and peered over her shoulder, stealing a glance at the laptop screen. 'My wedding photos look good on your website, if I do say so myself.'

Hannah stared at the photos. 'It was a lovely day, wasn't it? I'm so glad that we had the room to put up your relatives at the hall while we reorganised your wedding for a week later.'

'Yes, we were lucky that the vicar was available, and William was out of hospital. He's enjoying all the attention with his cast, and getting everyone to sign it.'

Hannah smiled. She had signed his cast at Lili's wedding.

'All's well that ends well, as Percy said,' commented Lili, whose family had enjoyed an impromptu holiday on the Suffolk Coast while they waited for the wedding to be rearranged.

'I love Lady Jemima and Percy's wedding photos too,' commented Lili. 'I'm glad you didn't take those down after Nate and I got married here.'

'Oh, I wouldn't do that even if they weren't attracting a lot of older couples.'

'I thought not. Although I'd much rather William hadn't fallen off his bike on the morning of our wedding, I like to think it was fate or serendipity – call it what you will – aligning the stars for Lady Jemima and Percy. It felt like it was meant to be.'

Hannah nodded in agreement, her thoughts turning to the VW campervan turning up when it had with Hetty and Owen.

Hannah felt a hand on her shoulder. Lili said, 'Your wedding is going to be amazing too, if a little different.'

'Just a little,' smiled Hannah. She was just closing down the laptop when Hetty appeared at the study door and said, 'There you are! The sun is starting to go down. We'd better hurry.'

They were interrupted by the unmistakable sound of a VW engine outside.

'Oh, that's Percy bringing the van around from the garages,' commented Hetty.

Hannah stood up and looked at her bridesmaids.

'The others are waiting in the hall,' said Lili. 'Come on.'

'Oh, Mum, there you are! We were getting worried.'

'I'd just nipped into the study, sweetheart.' Hannah tried not to shed a tear on seeing Maisie looking even more grown up than at Lili's wedding. Hannah had asked Maisie to be a bridesmaid at her wedding – a junior bridesmaid. She knew her daughter had been so happy to be included in the bridal party, especially as she could wear a bridesmaid's dress made especially for her – a floor-length, simple, pale cream dress with a little matching bolero jacket, matching sandals, and a little clutch bag.

'Are there more wedding bookings?' Maisie asked, guessing what her mum had been up to in the study.

'Oh, yes.'

'Does that mean you will be turning the art and craft shop into a bridal shop?'

Hannah said, 'I think I might be. If that's all right with you, sweetheart.'

'Oh, yes. It will be fun seeing all the ladies trying on their wedding dresses.'

Hannah smiled. She thought so too. Hannah took her hand and looked at her other bridesmaids. 'I hope we all fit into the van!'

Hannah's mum walked over and hugged her. She said, 'I must admit I was a little sceptical at first, wondering what the weather would be like this time of year, but late autumn has proved to have unexpectedly mild, beautiful weather.'

Percy appeared at the door. 'The bridal car … van … awaits!'

Percy had insisted on being their chauffeur and driving the bridal party to the wedding venue.

Percy stood by the van as everyone clambered inside, one bride, three bridesmaids, and the bride's mother and father in the back.

Percy waited by the van door until they were all seated and had made themselves comfortable. He looked up at the night sky as he closed the sliding door and said, 'It's going to be a beautiful sunset.'

Everyone in the bridal party agreed, including Lady Jemima, who was already sitting up front in the passenger seat. Hannah's parents, who'd flown in from Spain for her wedding, had been quite in awe of Somersby Hall *and* Lady Jemima. 'I've never met a *real* lady before,' Hannah's mum had said, offering an awkward curtsy when she first met her as though she was in front of royalty.

Lili turned to Hannah, smiling. 'The stars have aligned for your sunset wedding. Now I can't wait for you to show me Seashell Bay. You and Hetty have been keeping it a secret.'

Not anymore, thought Hannah. The guests had all been given directions to the beach where her sunset wedding would take place. Then everyone would return for the evening reception at the hall.

All the others had left ahead of them, including the groom and his wedding party in Percy's vintage car, driven by Rupert's best man – Percy's nephew, Olly. In the car with them were Owen and Rupert's father, who was no longer estranged.

Rupert had phoned his father after much persuasion from Hannah, and they had talked at length about the recent events at Somersby Hall – especially the secret Rupert now knew about his grandmother. When his father discovered that nobody would be turning up to take away Somersby Hall from his son, he had left

France for good, deciding to return, and surprising everyone by asking to help Hannah and Rupert work on the wedding business. He didn't enjoy working on computers to taking bookings online, and updating their database wasn't for him. But answering phone enquiries about weddings and chatting about Somersby Hall and what the house had to offer was very, very much him. He was a very sociable guy.

Hannah hoped that when her shop was up and running, he would consider helping her out, seeing to the groom, best man, and male wedding guests with their outfits. He'd be perfect.

'I'm so excited,' gushed Lili, and I'm not even getting married. I wish I'd thought of a sunset wedding. Where did you come up with the idea?'

Hannah smiled, thinking of Owen and Hetty turning up a few weeks earlier in his VW campervan. She whispered, 'Maybe one day, when we're old and grey, I'll share with you the secrets of Somersby Hall.'

Lili whispered in Hannah's ear, 'Has it got something to do with Hetty?'

'Why do you say that?' Hannah whispered back.

'I'm just surprised she's your bridesmaid. You've only met her a couple of times.'

Hetty was busy chatting to Maisie, so fortunately she hadn't overheard, and Hannah's mum was talking to her dad, saying she hoped the other guests had arrived at the beach okay, and everything was ready for Hannah's arrival. It was Lady Jemima who turned her head, almost imperceptibly, Hannah noticed. Hannah silently scolded herself for forgetting Lady Jemima's acute hearing.

Hannah changed the subject, announcing, 'I've got a little

surprise – something I hope we will all enjoy doing on the beach after my wedding ceremony.' She winked at Maisie, who'd promised to keep her lips sealed.

There was excited chatter in the VW campervan as Percy drove down a lane towards the beach, passing a row of red brick cottages and quite a number of parked cars snaking down the lane leading to Seashell Bay. Hannah now knew the real name of the bay, but it would always be Seashell Bay to her – it was what she'd written on the wedding invitations.

The lane, aptly named Sandy Lane, ended abruptly at some sand dunes. Percy drove the campervan a little further forward, parking on the sand between the dunes. They couldn't see the bay yet. Everyone clambered out apart from Hannah. She could see Lili and Maisie helping Rupert's grandmother and Percy up the small sandy dune.

Hetty was about to join them when she noticed the bride was still in the van. 'Hannah? Do you need a hand getting out?'

Hannah shook her head.

'Then what is it?'

She'd wanted this moment, the first time she saw Seashell Bay, to be special, and she couldn't think of a more significant occasion than her marriage to Rupert. But now she was finally there she was afraid the bay wouldn't be anything like Owen's gorgeous paintings. She told Hetty.

Hetty held out her hand, smiling. 'It's a hidden gem. That's why it was their favourite place, and now it's my favourite place on the Suffolk Coast too. You should have come with us that morning when my grandfather and I stayed over the night of Lady Jemima and Percy's wedding.'

'I know. But you'd never been to Seashell Bay before, and I

thought you should go with your grandfather, just the two of you.'

'We stayed there overnight, you know, in the campervan so we could watch the sun rise in the morning, just as my grandparents did years ago.'

'Oh, Hetty, that must have been lovely.'

'It was the most beautiful sunrise I've ever seen. And now you are going to see the most beautiful sunset – if you get a move on, that is!'

'Mum!' Maisie called out. 'Come and see the amazing beach!'

'Come on,' said Hetty, holding out her hand. 'You won't be disappointed, I promise you.'

Hannah took her hand, hitched up her dress and stepped out of the van, taking off her strappy sandals to walk barefoot on the sand.

Maisie had returned to fetch her. Hannah held her hand as she walked the short distance up the dune, joining Percy, Lady Jemima and Lili, who had all paused to take a breath and take in the sweeping bay enveloped in a beautiful red-gold hue from the sun, which was setting over the land behind them. Hannah almost cried. It was her dream come true – she felt like she'd stepped into Owen's sunset painting.

Near the water's edge was the wedding party. Rupert was standing with the best man and the vicar. Two lines of jar lamp candles, spaced apart, were positioned along the sand to create an aisle, with the wedding guests standing either side behind the rows of jar candles. They didn't know it yet, but there was one jar for each guest.

William, Maisie, and Maisie's best friend Charlie had been sworn to secrecy about their special wedding project – helping

Hannah decorate the glass jars in a beach theme by sticking little shells, pebbles, starfish and fish shapes, and all sorts of little odds and ends she'd bought from another craft shop online. The decorated jars were all unique, but each came with a string handle attached to a piece of wire running around the perimeter of the jar so they could be carried.

The jar lamp candles were keepsakes from her beach wedding for her guests, but they were also meant for something rather special to conclude her beach wedding.

Hannah couldn't quite believe her dream had come true – getting married at sunset, on Seashell Bay. And she couldn't wait for what she had planned for after the wedding.

A short time later, after the simple wedding ceremony when she'd walked down the candlelit sandy aisle, and she and Rupert exchanged vows, wedding rings, and kissed as the sun set, it was time for Hannah's surprise for her guests. Instead of fireworks back at Somersby Hall, she'd chosen to do something rather special at Seashell Bay instead.

Everyone waited as Maisie and William handed each person their own jar lamp candle in anticipation of the wedding finale. Hannah was so thankful it was a calm evening with just the gentlest of coastal breezes, and a full moon so the beach wasn't pitch dark. There was also light coming from the campervan headlights, left on to light up the sand dunes behind them in a soft glow to guide them back.

Maisie held up her jar lamp, followed closely by William. They both looked at Hannah standing with Rupert for the go-ahead before shouting out, 'Follow me!'

Hannah and Rupert watched as the wedding guests exchanged bemused glances and then held their lamps aloft, the soft glow of the candles lighting the way as the wedding party formed a snaking line, following Maisie along the shoreline.

Hannah hugged Rupert's arm as they each took the last two lamps and fell in line with the trail of people behind Maisie and William.

Up ahead they heard oohing and aahing as they arrived one by one to see what had been prepared further up the beach.

Hannah joined them, all gathered around the large heart Hetty had made out of seashells on the beach beforehand. Nobody knew about this but Hetty, her grandfather, the bride and groom, and the children.

Hannah wasn't sure how long it would have taken to collect enough seashells from the beach, and she did want a good variety, so she had bought these too, large and small seashells with lots of different colours and hues.

Hannah walked over to Hetty, thanking her for making such a stunning heart-shaped shell arrangement before announcing, 'These are for the shell blessing ceremony. Traditionally you all would make a wish or a blessing for the bride and groom, but I've chosen something a little different. I want you all to pick a shell and think of a message you'd like to send to a loved one, or a hope, wish or prayer you hold in your hearts for those dearest to you, near or far.'

She watched as the guests walked around the seashells in the heart shape on the sand, each holding their lamps over the shells and picking one.

Once they all had their shells, and had a little time to reflect, everyone gathered at the shoreline.

There was a hushed silence as everyone held their seashells in silent contemplation.

Then it was time.

Instinctively they all knew what to do next. One by one they stepped forward in silence, holding up their jar lamps as they tossed their shells into the sea. It was such a special moment to share, and a beautiful sight to behold, everyone holding up their jar lamps and illuminating the shoreline.

Hannah put her jar down and stood with Rupert on one side, and Maisie on the other, holding hands and reflecting on their hopes and dreams for the future as everyone stood looking out to sea, the cosy candle lights flickering in the cool coastal breeze.

Maisie said, 'My wish is for another brother or sister.'

Hannah turned to her daughter, wide-eyed.

Rupert said, 'I like your wish, Maisie, very much.'

Hannah wasn't surprised that Rupert had said that. She had always known he'd be a wonderful dad.

'What did you think about when you chose your seashell, sweetheart?' Rupert asked Hannah.

'I was saying a silent thank you – all my hopes and dreams have come true.'

Epilogue

'Are you sure you want to send it?' Hannah asked as Maisie finished covering it in brown paper and tied it with string. It was the following weekend, early on Saturday morning. Hannah and Maisie were in the lounge, Maisie kneeling in front of the coffee table. Maisie, her brow furrowed in concentration, was putting lots of stickers reading *Fragile* on the brown paper. Fortunately, Marlowe was out of harm's way, otherwise he would have been trying to play tug-of-war with the string and getting into all sorts of mischief with the brown paper and stickers.

Hannah raised her eyes to the ceiling. It hadn't taken long for all her good intentions regarding Marlowe not sleeping upstairs, on the beds, to go out of the window. She blamed it on Rupert. He was the biggest softie.

The previous weekend, after the wedding, when Maisie had gone home with Lili, Nate and William for her usual weekend with them, the newlyweds had had their first night together as a married couple in Gatekeeper's Cottage, where they were spending their honeymoon. Hannah knew they couldn't go away for their honeymoon; there was too much to do with their wedding business.

Although Maisie would have been welcome to stay on with Lili and Nate the following week so that Hannah and Rupert could have a proper honeymoon, Hannah had declined their thoughtful invitation. Rupert knew he was marrying into an existing little family unit of herself, Maisie and Marlowe. Hannah was not excluding Maisie, even though she was newly married. They intended to plan a family holiday instead.

Hannah thought that perhaps she should have sent Marlowe to stay with Lili and Nate on the wedding night too. They'd forgotten to shut the door downstairs in the kitchen where Marlowe slept in his dog bed. Sometime in the early hours, they'd been woken by the sound of Marlowe whining outside their bedroom door.

Hannah had accepted that Marlowe was really Rupert's dog now. Wherever he was, Marlowe would follow – right up to bed with them if he could. Rupert had let him in and scooped him up, getting lots of doggy kisses. Despite Hannah's best intentions, after that night, whenever Hannah had attempted to leave him shut in the kitchen, he'd howled, and Rupert had given in to his cries. Hannah shook her head, rolling her eyes. Rupert and his pup were still having a lie-in upstairs.

'Is that enough stickers do you think, Mum?'

Hannah dropped her gaze. The brown paper was covered in them. 'I think so.'

Hannah had paid the money for the package to be sent by special courier that morning. She'd just heard the courier van turn up outside Gatekeeper's Cottage but wanted to check that Maisie was sure about it because once it was gone, it was gone.

Maisie nodded. 'I want to send it.'

'But it's your best one yet.' If Hannah was honest, she rather wanted to keep it for herself, but then her eyes drifted to *Sunset Over Seashell Bay*, still hanging above the fireplace in her lounge. She already had the painting that meant something special to her, and it meant even more since she'd got married at sunset on Seashell Bay. But there was something about Maisie's new painting, apart from how stunning it was, that still intrigued her. 'The lady in the painting …'

'I told you before,' Maisie said crossly. 'I *saw* her.'

'All right,' Hannah said tightly. She didn't want to get into another argument about who Maisie thought she'd seen on the beach on the day of the wedding.

Hannah asked one last time. 'Are you really sure about this? You know what this means, don't you?' Hannah didn't want to tell Maisie she couldn't make such a kind gesture, but then again, they both knew it meant letting someone else in on Maisie's secret.

Maisie didn't answer. Hannah knew her mind was made up.

'Shall we hand it over to the courier?' Hannah asked, giving Maisie one final chance to back out before she opened the front door.

❖

Owen answered the front door to a courier standing on his doorstep holding a package wrapped in brown paper that was covered in stickers marked *Fragile*. He looked at the package, then the courier. 'I'm not expecting a delivery. You must have the wrong house.'

'You are Owen Hartley, aren't you?'

Owen nodded. 'Yes.'

The courier glanced at the parcel in his hands. 'Well, it's got your name and address on it. I picked it up this morning, same-day delivery. It's definitely for you.'

Owen frowned, signed for it, and took it in. He had an inkling what might be inside. The size and shape rather gave it away. He sincerely hoped that his granddaughter hadn't sent him back *Sunrise Over Seashell Bay*.

As he put the package carefully down on the coffee table and sat down on the sofa with a pair of scissors, ready to cut the string and reveal what was inside, he remembered the last time he'd spoken to Henrietta on the phone. She'd told him she'd hung her painting above the fireplace in her and Dan's new home. He would be visiting soon enough, once they were settled in. They had moved into a rented cottage in a village not far from him in Dartmoor.

Owen wasn't surprised that his grandchild and her partner had chosen to move down there, where she had many happy childhood summer memories. Their plan was to eventually buy their own home and hopefully raise children there. Owen stared wistfully into space. It made sense. Her parents would retire there one day. He hoped to live long enough to meet his great-grandchildren.

Thinking of that phone call, he realised Henrietta wouldn't have parted with her painting. It had a new home now.

His gaze settled on the empty space over his own fireplace where the painting used to hang. Owen knew his late wife had loved that painting, but all Owen had felt was sadness whenever he looked at it – it was a reminder that she was no longer there with him.

Owen dropped his gaze to the package and carefully cut the string. As well as the *Fragile* stickers, there were several more with the words, *This side up*. Owen carefully peeled away the brown paper to reveal a painting he had not expected.

'Oh! Oh, my!' It was the most exquisite painting he'd ever set eyes on. The first thing he recognised was Seashell Bay. The painting was similar to his other painting, *Sunset Over Seashell Bay*. Although he knew he had talent, and some might say his paintings were very good – excellent, even, for an amateur artist – this painting was in a league of its own. The red, orange and gold hues of the sunset behind the painter reflecting in the ripples of the water took his breath away. The expert brush strokes bringing the sunset to life were mesmerising, a full moon luminous in the night sky. But it was the figures standing on the shoreline, holding candlelit jar lamps, looking out to sea, that brought a lump to his throat and a tear to his eye.

Two figures had their arms outstretched, as though they'd just tossed their seashells into the sea. Although the figures were facing the water, it was definitely himself and his granddaughter that the painter had captured on canvas – he recognised his walking stick and his granddaughter's beautiful long wavy hair. But they weren't alone. *He* wasn't alone. Standing by his side on Seashell Bay was an ethereal figure of a woman, her outstretched hand holding aloft a seashell.

Owen wiped a tear from his eyes. 'Who painted this?' he asked the empty room. The painting told a truth he hadn't expected. As he hung the framed painting above the fireplace, he knew that whenever he looked at it, he would be reminded that he was wrong; he wasn't alone. She was there with him. She always had been and always would be. Owen smiled as he put a hand to his heart. He knew that one day they would meet again on Seashell Bay.

As he smiled fondly at the painting, he thought he saw a faint scribble of writing, almost hidden. Owen returned with his magnifying glass and read the name of the painting – *Memories on Seashell Bay*. Then he saw the signature of the painter.

Owen drew in a surprised breath. Raising his eyebrows, he remembered a conversation with Maisie at the wedding when she'd talked to him at length about his paintings. Her knowledge of art was quite astounding for one so young. And now he knew why.

'Extraordinary!' Owen chuckled, realising he wasn't the only one who'd been keeping secrets. Maisie had let him into hers. He wiped another tear from his eye. 'Just extraordinary.'

The Sunrise Coast Series continues in

The Little Theatre by the Sea

Paperback and Kindle eBook coming soon

I hope you enjoyed *The Secrets of Somersby Hall*, and would be grateful if you would leave a review on Amazon.

For further details about the author and her novels, visit the author's website.

www.elisedarcy.com

Also by Elise Darcy

The Scottish Highlands Series

Winter in the Scottish Highlands

The Secrets of the Glen

Return to the Lake House

The Boathouse by the Loch

Summer in the Scottish Highlands

Coming Home to Aviemore

The Living Apart Together series

Living Apart Together

It Takes 2 to Tango

Dear John

Love on the Rooftop

Standalone books

Lola & The Man

A Mallorcan Affair

The Villa in Sicily

We'll Meet Again

Printed in Dunstable, United Kingdom

73067833R00206